"Dripping with period detail but fundamentally a modern story, *The Austen Escape* is a clever, warmhearted homage to Austen and her fans."

—SHELF AWARENESS

"Reay's sensually evocative descriptions of Italian food and scenery make this a delight for fans of Frances Mayes's *Under the Tuscan Sun*."

—LIBRARY JOURNAL, STARRED REVIEW, FOR
*A PORTRAIT OF EMILY PRICE*

"Katherine Reay is a remarkable author who has created her own subgenre, wrapping classic fiction around contemporary stories. Her writing is flawless and smooth, her storytelling meaningful and poignant. You're going to love *The Brontë Plot*."

—DEBBIE MACOMBER, #1 *NEW YORK TIMES* BESTSELLING AUTHOR

"Book lovers will savor the literary references as well as the story's lessons on choices, friendship, and redemption."

—BOOKLIST FOR *THE BRONTË PLOT*

"Reay treats readers to a banquet of flavors, aromas, and textures that foodies will appreciate, and clever references to literature add nuances sure to delight bibliophiles. The relatable, very real characters, however, are what will keep readers clamoring for more from this talented author."

—PUBLISHERS WEEKLY, STARRED REVIEW, FOR *LIZZY & JANE*

"Book nerds, rejoice! *Dear Mr. Knightley* is a stunning debut—a first-water gem with humor and heart. I can hardly wait to get my hands on the next novel by this gifted new author!"

—SERENA CHASE, *USA TODAY'S HAPPY EVER AFTER* BLOG

# Praise for Katherine Reay

"Rich with fascinating historical detail and unforgettable characters, *A Shadow in Moscow* deftly explores two female spies who will risk everything to change the world. Katherine Reay eloquently portrays the incredible contributions of women in history, the extraordinary depths of love, and, perhaps most important of all, the true cost of freedom in her latest stunning page-turner. A story that will leave readers examining what they hold most dear and positively brimming with hope, this is an important, timely tour de force—and a must-read for anyone who has ever wondered if just one person can make a difference."

—KRISTY WOODSON HARVEY, *NEW YORK TIMES* BESTSELLING AUTHOR OF *THE WEDDING VEIL*

"Katherine Reay's latest has it all—intrigue, twists and turns, acts of bravery and sacrificial love, and an unforgettable Cold War setting with clever, daring women at the helm. An expertly delivered page-turner by a true master of the craft!"

—SUSAN MEISSNER, *USA TODAY* BESTSELLING AUTHOR OF *THE NATURE OF FRAGILE THINGS*

"This riveting story of two female spies operating in Moscow during different eras has everything you could ever want in a novel—suspense, intrigue, compelling characters, exotic settings, deep insight, and gasp-inducing plot twists. A word of advice: clear your calendar before opening *A Shadow in Moscow*. Once you start, you won't be able to stop until you regretfully reach the last page of Katherine Reay's masterfully written novel."

—MARIE BOSTWICK, *NEW YORK TIMES* BESTSELLING AUTHOR OF *ESME CAHILL FAILS SPECTACULARLY*

"Spellbinding. Reay's fast-paced foray into the past cleverly reveals a family's secrets and how a pivotal moment shaped future generations. Readers who enjoy engrossing family mystery should take note."

—*PUBLISHERS WEEKLY* FOR *THE LONDON HOUSE*

"*The London House* is a tantalizing tale of deeply held secrets, heart-break, redemption, and the enduring way that family can both hurt and heal us."

—KRISTIN HARMEL, *NEW YORK TIMES* BESTSELLING
AUTHOR OF *THE FOREST OF VANISHING STARS*

"*The London House* is a thrilling excavation of long-held family secrets that proves sometimes the darkest corners of our pasts are balanced with slivers of light. Arresting historical fiction destined to thrill fans of Erica Roebuck and Pam Jenoff."

—RACHEL MCMILLAN, AUTHOR OF *THE LONDON RESTORATION*

"Expertly researched and perfectly paced, *The London House* is a remarkable novel about love and loss and the way history—and secrets—can impact a family and ultimately change its future."

—SYRIE JAMES, BESTSELLING AUTHOR OF *THE
LOST MEMOIRS OF JANE AUSTEN*

"The town of Winsome reminds me of Jan Karon's Mitford, with its endearing characters, complex lives, and surprises where you don't expect them. You'll root for these characters and will be sad to leave this charming town."

—LAUREN K. DENTON, BESTSELLING AUTHOR OF *THE
HIDEAWAY*, FOR *OF LITERATURE AND LATTES*

"In her ode to small towns and second chances, Katherine Reay writes with affection and insight about the finer things in life."

—KAREN DUKESS, AUTHOR OF *THE LAST BOOK
PARTY*, FOR *OF LITERATURE AND LATTES*

"Reay understands the heartbeat of a bookstore."

—BAKER BOOK HOUSE, FOR *THE PRINTED LETTER BOOKSHOP*

"*The Printed Letter Bookshop* is both a powerful story and a dazzling experience. I want to give this book to every woman I know—I adored falling into Reay's world, words, and bookstore."

—PATTI CALLAHAN HENRY, BESTSELLING AUTHOR

# A
# SHADOW
# IN
# MOSCOW

## Also by Katherine Reay

*The London House*

*Of Literature and Lattes*

*The Printed Letter Bookshop*

*The Austen Escape*

*A Portrait of Emily Price*

*The Brontë Plot*

*Lizzy & Jane*

*Dear Mr. Knightley*

### NONFICTION

*Awful Beautiful Life*, with Becky Powell

# A SHADOW IN MOSCOW

A COLD WAR NOVEL

## KATHERINE REAY

HARPER MUSE

*A Shadow in Moscow*

Copyright © 2023 Katherine Reay

Published by Harper Muse, an imprint of HarperCollins Focus LLC.

This book is a work of fiction. The characters, incidents, and dialogue are drawn from the author's imagination and are not to be construed as real. Any resemblance to actual events or persons, living or dead, is entirely coincidental.

### Library of Congress Cataloging-in-Publication Data

Names: Reay, Katherine, 1970- author.
Title: A shadow in Moscow / Katherine Reay.
Description: Nashville : Harper Muse, [2023] | Series: A Cold War Novel | Summary: "Two courageous female spies, one with MI6 and the other with CIA during the Cold War in Moscow, must work together before the KGB closes in and destroys them both"-- Provided by publisher.
Identifiers: LCCN 2022053271 (print) | LCCN 2022053272 (ebook) | ISBN 9781400243037 (softcover) | ISBN 9781400243044 (epub) | ISBN 9781400243051 (audio download)
Classification: LCC PS3618.E23 S53 2023 (print) | LCC PS3618.E23 (ebook) | DDC 813/.6--dc23
LC record available at https://lccn.loc.gov/2022053271
LC ebook record available at https://lccn.loc.gov/2022053272

*Printed in the United States of America*

23 24 25 26 27 LBC 5 4 3 2 1

To my Tuesday Morning Crew.
I am so thankful to be counted among
you and love you all dearly.

*I have been meditating on the very great pleasure which a pair of fine eyes in the face of a pretty woman can bestow.*

—MR. DARCY PONDERING MISS ELIZABETH BENNET

JANE AUSTEN, *PRIDE AND PREJUDICE*


*But Levin was in love, and so it seemed to him that Kitty was so perfect in every respect that she was a creature far above everything earthly; and that he was a creature so low and so earthly that it could not even be conceived that other people and she herself could regard him as worthy of her.*

—KONSTANTIN LEVIN CONSIDERING

PRINCESS KITTY SHCHERBATSKY

LEO TOLSTOY, *ANNA KARENINA*

# PROLOGUE

# Anya

AGAIN I ASK MYSELF, *DOES THE END DRAW EVERYONE BACK TO the beginning?*

The golden glow of memory fades. My parents, my friends Dmitri, Scott, Sonya, Tracy. Their faces float past along with my musings on Lizzy Bennet and Kitty Shcherbatsky. Friends can't help me now. Books can't help me now.

I'm at an end of my own making.

There is so much I need to do—and fast. Should I go see my parents? Try to offer an oblique goodbye? Will that put them in danger? Or are they already in danger? What about all those things I said to Sonya? When I die, they'll question her again and she'll be more frightened. How much more will she say, and will that implicate her too?

What a fool I've been. Olivers warned me day one that there can be no cracks in the facade, no truth among my lies. He told me to play a part and to be careful to make sure no one questioned my loyalty, dedication, and commitment to the Soviet State.

My breath shudders within me. I stop walking. Sometime in the past hour, the biting ice and wind have stopped. It's quiet

1

now, almost beautiful. The temperature has dropped and I can no longer feel my fingers, my face, or my feet.

I'm not brave and I have not been careful.

These truths come as a soft whisper. They settle within my soul like softly falling snowflakes. I don't shake them off. I let them melt into me. Standing in the middle of an empty sidewalk, I let myself mourn everyone and everything I love. At the most basic level, the best stories are love stories. And despite my myriad mistakes, mine has been one too—a love story I only recognize now in its final pages.

I pray Peter gets me the cyanide pill. He must. If anyone knows the truth about me, he does. He knows I am not brave. He also knows everyone breaks and everyone talks.

The best scenario in this love story for me—for all of us—is that when the KGB comes, I'm already dead.

# ONE

# Anya

WASHINGTON, DC
*March 14, 1980*

"Noooooo." I repeat my answer. This time I draw out the one-syllable word for several beats so that every note gets recorded. "I have not been contacted by nor been in conversation with any agent or representative of the US government."

"Anya." Sasha clicks off the machine. "You can drop your truculence. This isn't a game."

I almost laugh—Sasha's been reading the English dictionary again—but I don't because it'll anger him. I can't risk teasing him about his English because today this *is* a game and I've already mismanaged too many moves. I walked into the Soviet embassy with such confidence an hour ago, and nothing has turned out like I thought.

I tap the table in a two-fingered fast syncopation. Sasha's eyes drop to my fingers. Only then do I realize how nervous this strumming sounds. I slide my hand back into my lap.

My focus flickers to the recorder centered between us. I switch from English to Russian. "You've asked that same question every month for almost two years. Why are you asking it twice today? Have I caused a problem? Led you to distrust me? Have I ever even been late for a meeting? I brought you bourbon."

3

I hold my breath and wait.

Sasha smiles. "I did like the bourbon."

"See?" I sit on my hands to stop their flailing. "Can I go now? I've got midterms this week."

I stare at Sasha. He glares back. I can't hold his gaze. I'm pushing too hard, but I can't help myself. I had over a week to prepare for this moment and I still wasn't ready.

Comrade Lieutenant Aleksandr Stanovich Galdin has been my "case officer" for the past two years. Only a few years older than me—maybe twenty-four?—he's sturdy, with short black hair, close-set eyes, and an intensity that shatters in rare bouts of deep chuckles. And we've had a few of those together. I like him. Much better than my previous case officer.

That one, an indomitable fellow named Igor, viewed me and everything American as ugly, soft, tainted, and corrupt. Sasha, on the other hand, is as enthralled with some aspects of American culture as I've become—and with the bourbon even more so. I think we come "up to par" on baseball, hot dogs, and music. I have an affinity for colored mascara and leggings he'll never understand.

Our monthly meetings are usually short, light, and end with us swapping our latest and greatest discoveries within our host country—all in English as Sasha is trying to improve his skills and secure that next KGB promotion.

Not today.

Upon my arrival, he walked me straight past his desk in the open office area, where we usually sit, pulled me into a windowless conference room, and set a tape recorder on the table between us.

"What's this about, Sasha?" I airily waved a hand at the four walls, which seemed to close in tighter with each step.

"That was quite a 'senior spring break' trip, Comrade

Kadinova." He toggled his fingers in air quotes to make sure I understood he didn't approve of the American spring break construct. Waiting for me to digest his comment, he sat back and frowned. He also clicked the big red button on his device.

"It's what college students do here." I watched the cassette whirl in the machine for a few beats before continuing. "And that's my job. To be a normal college student here and learn all I can."

"Your job is to represent the Union of Soviet Socialist Republics."

"And I do that by being exemplary in every way. Besides, I told you I was going. I gave you the hotel address— Wait! What?"

Sasha had the decency to look sheepish. That's one reason I like him. Igor never would have seen any lines, much less recognized when he'd crossed one. And to be fair, back home such lines don't exist. Nothing is out of bounds for the KGB. But in my four years studying at Georgetown, those lines and the freedoms they represent have become very real to me.

"You were spying on me and my friends? I told you where we were going so you wouldn't have to. They're Americans, Sasha. They have constitutional rights against that kind of stuff."

"You don't have those rights. And we weren't watching them. We were watching you. They happened to be with you."

"That was your excuse last summer." I kept darting my gaze to the recorder as I worked to keep my voice calm and level. But it wasn't fear rising within me; it was anger. "I didn't balk then and I apologized for not keeping you informed."

I leaned forward and rested both hands on the table, palms up. "What more could I have done? And what was I going to do from Fort Lauderdale anyway? Swim to Cuba?"

"Not funny, Anya."

"Nor is spying on me and my friends when I've been a model citizen."

"A model comrade?" Sasha chastised.

That's when I closed my eyes. I needed to be more careful. Sasha acts like a friend, and perhaps to some degree he is one, but he is first and foremost a KGB officer. One who is hand-over-hand climbing the service's promotional ladder, and one who is recording my every breath.

"Yes . . . comrade," I said, correcting myself.

After a few more questions and a few more of the same answers, I push my chair back and start to rise, only to drop again. "I was accepted into the Foreign Studies Initiative because my scores were exceptional, and because I am loyal. I've never made you or anyone else question me."

I throw the test score comment at him as a reminder that it's a great honor to be chosen for the Foreign Studies Initiative, maybe one higher than being chosen for the KGB. But it doesn't matter. I may hold the honor, but Sasha holds the power.

He shuffles his stack of papers. "You're right. You haven't. But I follow orders." He pauses and lifts his head. "We are moving our monthly meetings to weekly. Mondays at 4:00 p.m. It's standard procedure for your final term. You have three months, Anya—remember that."

My mouth drops open as arguments rise within me, not about my time left at Georgetown but about the meetings. I press my lips tight before any escape. Not quickly enough. He sees and his eyes narrow in challenge.

I don't dare. As he made clear, I have no rights here. Instead I rise and stand still for a minute. It's something I learned from my father. When making a point, he stretches to his full height, which is about six foot four, and stands until he gains the complete attention of the person he's addressing before he speaks. The effect of slowing a moment down rather than speeding it up is remarkable.

I'm about five eight. It's not overly tall, but I find it still makes an impact. I stare at Sasha, dark eyes to dark eyes—also a gift from my father, eyes so dark you can't find my pupils—and wait until he focuses on me.

"очень хорошо, товарищ." *Very well, Comrade.* I say it in clear Muscovite Russian. I then switch back to English as I know, ever striving for that promotion, Sasha prefers it. "I will be here on time and I'll see you next Monday."

It's a weak power play on my part—my Russian carries those elite notes Sasha dreams of commanding and my English is light-years better than his. Sasha's eyes widen the tiniest amount and, with that, I reach for the door, open it, and cross the open office area toward the elevator.

The Soviet Union's *rezidentura*—the KGB's main Washington, DC, office—is on our embassy's fifth floor, and it has the slowest elevator I've ever ridden. I tap the button a few times, all the while feeling Sasha's gaze boring into my back.

Unable to contain myself any longer, I push open the door to the stairwell and take out my nerves regarding Sasha, the interview, and midterms by racing down five flights of stairs, skipping two at a time as I descend the bottom three floors.

Outside the doors and the gate's security checkpoint, a spectacular spring afternoon hits me. The cherry blossoms have just started to bud and every shade of pink bursts all around me. I stop on the sidewalk to take it in and to let Sasha go. It's my favorite time of year in DC. Bright green grass, blue skies, sunshine-dappled parks, pink flowers, and a sense of irrepressible hope. I want this spring—my last one here—to be perfect. I refuse to let Sasha or anything else tarnish a moment of these fleeting idyllic days. I'll need their warmth come winter.

I race across Wisconsin Avenue, round the corner, and find Scott still waiting at the bus stop bench on Davis Street. He's one of the idyllic memories I hope to hold as well, always making me feel brighter, sunnier, and more hopeful than I believed possible.

He stands, grabs me tight, and kisses me hard. "That took longer than usual. I was beginning to worry."

I slip my hand within his and rise on my toes to kiss him one more time. Lowering to my heels, I lie. "Same as usual."

Hand in hand we head back toward campus.

Within a block Scott tugs at me. "What's wrong?"

I shake my head as if it's too insignificant to matter. And it is. After all, unless Sasha catches something on his tape, I played the game well enough. I'm not in danger. As for the rest—these last three months he mentioned—it's only my heart at risk. I'm the only one caught in the abyss between what I want and what will be.

"Anya." Scott stops. "Talk to me."

I reach for my nearest thought and, though it's a lie, I give it to Scott anyway. "They spied on me—on all of us—in Fort Lauderdale."

His eyes flicker, and I sense he's retracing our week. Six of Scott's friends and five of mine crammed into two hotel rooms at the Sea Beach Plaza in Fort Lauderdale and had the time of our lives. Typical seniors, sunburned and still hungover, we just returned last night, to midterms beginning today.

"When?" he asks.

"I have no idea. Maybe the 3:00 a.m. snack at The Floridian?" I try to laugh away my discomfort. It's embarrassing to have someone spying on him because they have to keep tabs on me.

"Or maybe the beach?" Scott lifts a brow. He's not laughing, but he's not furious either. I take it as a good sign as a movie reel of us goofing around and kissing in the waves plays before me. Heat spreads up my neck.

"It's not right, Anya." Scott resumes walking. "We should report this. You're in America, not the USSR."

I pull at his arm. "Don't, please. They weren't tracking you, only me, and I'm sorry your privacy was invaded, but if you report this, it becomes an Incident. A capital *I* incident involving the KGB on US soil."

"That's my point. Maybe it should be one."

"They'll ship me home. No questions asked. No degree. No last months with you . . . And I'll be ruined." Panic rises within me, for myself and for my parents. "And if the embarrassment is great enough, they'll ruin my parents too. You know that."

Scott stares down at me. Blue eyes to dark eyes, we stand at a stalemate until his eyes round and soften. I've shared enough over the years that he understands the truth in what I'm saying.

I lift on my toes to kiss him. "Thank you."

"Only because I don't want to make things worse for you, but it's not right, Anya. You deserve better as a human. You—" He stops with a wry grin. "Do you think they tasked that girl from Ole Miss? I'd like to believe she just found me cute."

I kiss him again in thanks for shifting the tone and we continue our walk, laughing at all the absurd things the KGB's "spy" might have seen. Some boring? Definitely. We spent most of our time asleep on the beach. Some shocking? Perhaps. There was one episode of bar-top dancing we collectively bemoaned the next day. Some illegal? Not at all.

"Why'd Sasha care about spring break?" Scott pulls at my hand again.

"We Foreign Studies kids are the elite of the elite, and all our information is submitted to the US before we arrive. So as much as Sasha watches me, so does the CIA. If one of us embarrasses them or gets lost, there's hell to pay back home."

"The CIA watches you?"

"Maybe not them. Maybe it's the FBI? I don't know. I just know we're watched all the time. In many ways I think it's an excuse for both sides to keep track of each other over our heads. Sasha asks me at every meeting if I've been 'contacted by or am in conversation with an agent or representative of the US government.'"

I mimic Igor's stern recitation perfectly, right down to his heavy Lithuanian accent. Sasha's worked too hard to scrub his outer-Muscovite tones to make imitating him funny.

"Lost?" Scott's voice arcs up, as if only now processing my words. He stops so quickly I stumble into him. "How do people like you get 'lost'?"

"They defect." I offer the word. It's one I seldom allow into my thoughts, much less out of my mouth. "It's rare for Foreign Studies kids to attempt it as we're pretty prized assets back home, being goodwill diplomats and all, but a few have tried . . . There's a lot to love about America." I lift on my toes again and kiss his cheek.

Scott resumes our walk in silence. It drags on long, and just as I'm about to break it, he beats me to it. "What about you? . . . Would you try? Do you want to stay?"

# TWO

# Ingrid

WHEN DID THIS HAPPEN? INGRID MUSED AS SHE WALKED DOWN the steps of Austria's Parliament Building, not breaking eye contact with the man across the street. She watched as a smile spread across Adam's face, and almost involuntarily, he leaned forward before his foot moved in a step toward her.

For two years she'd longed for such a smile and for him to feel that electric pull she discovered the first day they'd met. Sure his affection was never to be hers, two weeks ago she discovered it was suddenly there. Adam lingered one evening at their home after meeting with her father. The next afternoon he passed by on the Rathausplatz as she exited work, and last week he asked to walk her home. He hadn't held her hand or kissed her yet, but Ingrid was sure both would happen soon.

Adam captured her hand as she reached the street's curb, still not breaking eye contact. He threaded his long fingers through hers and squeezed gently. She glowed as he turned them in the direction of her home.

"You're back!" He'd been out of town for three days, and while she knew he would not tell her where he'd been or what he'd been doing, it was a favorite game to hazard guesses. "Let's

11

see . . . You've been putting oranges in Nazi car tailpipes from Berlin to Bangkok, haven't you?" She felt so light she thought she might float away.

"Bangkok?" He grinned down at her, replying in German. "That's a little far-flung. Besides, if I found an orange, I'd eat it, Ingrid. Not waste it on some Nazi car."

"Bananas then?"

"Bananas in Berlin and Bangkok. Someone should write a song about that." Adam winked, his light brown eyes warming to cinnamon.

"You've been blowing up munitions trains."

Adam's lips curled and he tossed her a sideways glance. This time, he did not reply. He simply squeezed her hand and walked on.

The fact that she might have gotten close, or near to close, felt like victory, and the rest of their walk flew by with light laughter and irrepressible grins. Adam was truly the best part of her day, and she hoped she was becoming his.

Once home, they'd fall into the routine they did most nights when Adam came for dinner. Ingrid would help Mutti with the meal as she always did, while Adam—when not abroad doing who knows what—would sit in her father's study and talk lesson plans and books for the classes Adam taught at the University. At least that's what Papa claimed they discussed.

But she'd known from the moment her father ushered Adam Weber into the von Alton home two years ago—a young professor placed within the University by the Third Reich to "teach the next generation"—that this handsome man, with his German lineage and lifelong heart condition, was more than he appeared.

The effervescence filling Ingrid stilled as they rounded the final corner from Liebiggasse onto Grillparzerstrasse. She felt tension crackle the air even before she noted the crowd filling her usually quiet street. Nazi soldiers stood on her parents' front steps. They weren't relaxed and congenial as they usually were when coming to dinner, and they weren't officers.

They were young soldiers, barely out of schoolroom shorts or off their fathers' farms. Their brown uniforms stood in stark contrast to the white-painted brick and stone building; their strident tones and clipped accents ricocheted like bullets off the hard surfaces. The whole tableau felt angry, discordant, and—Ingrid absorbed the jeering faces—terrifying. She followed the crowd's focus and found her father lying at the street's curb. He lay bleeding as if he'd tumbled or been struck.

Ingrid rushed forward as yelling and a commotion drew her attention, along with everyone else's, back to her building's open doorway. Two stocky soldiers hauled Mutti onto the stoop.

"Stop! Stop pulling her," Ingrid's father yelled. "She's not resisting."

Still at a distance, Ingrid watched in horror as her father pushed up from the ground only to be shoved down by a jackboot centered on his back. His wooden leg broke off beneath him. He had lost the limb below the knee in the Great War. It was why the Nazis let him continue teaching at the University rather than conscript him into their army.

*"I am flawed, weak, not an ideal specimen, according to the Reich. But it seems I'm good enough to teach their ideology and their literature."* Ever the true Austrian, he'd sounded cynical, defeated, yet oddly determined the day he'd announced his assignment to his wife and daughter.

"Papa." Ingrid pushed through the crowd. "Pa—"

Nothing more escaped as she felt strong arms bind her from behind. An unseen hand clamped over her mouth as she met her father's gaze through the parted crowd. His pale eyes widened in recognition before his focus drifted above and beyond her. His expression softened with an odd note of acquiescence. Ingrid's brow furrowed in confusion.

Then, with a mighty roar, Christoph von Alton grabbed the full attention of everyone around them. He thrust up and, standing on his one good leg, seized the soldier above him by the collar. His fist flew and a ghost of a smile lit his face as his blow swept across the soldier's jaw. The force sent them both tumbling into the street.

That was all Ingrid saw as the hands lifted and carried her away.

The hands, of course, were Adam's.

A block away, tucked within the safety of a deep door well, Adam spun her to face him. Fear and fury warred like living beasts inside her and she clawed at him, punched him, then tried to push past him. "Let me go! We have to help!"

Adam stood still, a wall of granite and flesh, holding her tight as she raged. Then, after what felt like an eternity, she quieted and he pulled her close. He held her tighter yet as she sobbed into his shirt.

Ingrid remembered little after that, only shadows and shapes until this morning, when the bright light pouring through Adam's apartment windows jarred her awake from turbulent dreams.

"You need to get up and go to work."

Those were the first words she heard, and they felt as harsh and glaring as the sunlight hitting her face. Pulling her hand from across her eyes, she found that, as upsetting and offensive as they were, the words were matched by the equally unwelcome sight of both Adam and his friend Martin Thomas standing cross-armed over her bed.

"Leave me alone." Ingrid wished for quiet, for darkness. To roll over and never wake again.

"Not on your life, and that's what this comes down to. Your life." Adam laid a heavy hand on her shoulder. "Get up and meet us in the kitchen. Martin saved a little real coffee for you."

In the end she obeyed. Not for the coffee but for the promise of a noon meeting. If she went to work, Adam said he'd be waiting on her favorite bench in the Rathauspark at noon—with answers. Only that pledge kept her moving and sane. In fact, her mind was so fixated on that moment all morning, she misdictated memos, misfiled papers, and tripped twice weaving her way through the desks at the Third Reich's Economic and Administrative Office.

"What's with you today?" a coworker asked. At Ingrid's simple reply that she hadn't slept well, her friend shook her head. "Shape up. Obergruppenführer Pohl is here and on a warpath. You'll get written up if he notices you stumbling around making mistakes."

Ingrid nodded, sat at her desk, pretended to work, and watched the clock.

At noon she raced down the steps and across the Rathausplatz to the park beyond. As promised, Adam sat waiting. "What did you learn?"

After a fleeting glance, he shifted his focus back across the green expanse of the park. "I don't want to tell you."

"You have to, please, and don't lie. Papa and Mutti always lied to me. They were so sure I wasn't big enough, strong enough, to handle anything. I'm petite," Ingrid protested, "but not weak like you all think."

Dubbed "my little poppet" by her English mother, Ingrid had been sheltered by her parents for every one of her twenty-one years like a porcelain figurine. A classic Dresden with her blonde hair, blue eyes, and pale skin. Too precious to let venture far. Too delicate to pull close. And when the Nazis absorbed Austria in 1938, their protective tendencies only grew. Ingrid knew her parents worked against the Germans, but she didn't know how—for while they kept her at a distance, they held their secrets tight.

"After your father struck that soldier, your mother was shoved down the stairs. Her head hit the steps . . . She didn't survive."

Ingrid pressed both palms against her eyes. Red sparks shot behind her lids. She spoke through the darkness. "And Papa?"

"Mauthausen. He was put on a train this morning."

Ingrid lowered her hands. The red sparks shot gold in the sunlight, blinding her. She blinked and tears filled her eyes. "They laugh about him at work. Franz Ziereis. The commandant. He's the cruelest there is. Papa won't survive that camp."

Adam nodded. "I know."

She nodded too, appreciating his honesty. The last thing she wanted was the lie of false hope.

"I'm sorry . . ." He turned to face her. "Ingrid, we need to get you out. They will connect you to your parents as soon as the paperwork goes through. You won't be safe here. If anyone is anymore."

"I am." Ingrid reached into her pocket and pulled out her identification papers. She handed them to Adam.

"They're . . . They're fake?" Adam studied them. "Who is 'Ingrid Bauer'?"

"I am." Ingrid pressed her lips shut. Humiliation seeped into her sorrow. "They had no faith in me." She raised a hand to stay Adam's huff of denial. "They hid families in our attic. I heard them, but when I asked, they denied it. 'Mice,' they said. But I know. I lived there. And Papa worked all hours of the night. What professor of literature needs to grade papers all night? Every week? And Mutti . . . All those parties, walks, secrets . . . They lied. Every day. To me, their own daughter. Then that." She pointed to her identification card. "Papa destroyed my papers and handed me those. Bauer is a Russian last name, you know. He chose it because it has 'pre-Volga origins,' he said, to explain my German accent."

Adam studied the papers for a long, silent moment. "Why Russian?"

Ingrid slumped against the bench. "Stalin and Hitler were allies when Papa made those. He thought if it came to it, Stalin was the stronger and he'd subdue Hitler. Then Papa sent me to work here, to cower in plain sight."

Ingrid lifted her eyes to the impressive building towering to their right. The Austrian Parliament Building was now draped in the red-and-black flags of the Third Reich and had been for six interminable years.

"You can't blame him, either of them, for wanting to keep you safe." Adam handed her papers back to her. "Those are perfect, by the way. Your father was good. Really good. He was the best forger we had and he saved thousands of lives."

"Forger?" Ingrid straightened. "That's what he did? It makes sense. He was brilliant with art, languages, even science . . . Who exactly is *we*?" At Adam's closed expression, she shifted to face him. "No more hiding. You tell me right now."

"Your father was a loyal Austrian trying to save his country. What he believed could still be his country . . ." Adam stalled. Ingrid forced herself to remain upright and not tip forward in anticipation. "Great Britain. We both do, did, sorry . . . I work for British Foreign Services."

"Both of you? How?"

"For me it started in school." Adam shrugged. "I was in school outside London while my dad taught maths at Oxford. Friends reached out after I returned to Germany and recruited me. Like your father's leg, my heart was deemed unfit for the Reich's army and they let me teach. And your father? Well, that was your mother. While she's lived here since she married him, she was still well-connected back in London. She was my initial contact after I got assigned to the University. She helped me create my first network."

Ingrid closed her eyes. How little she knew her parents. Outside that vital role they played as parents, did she know them at all? "She said she met Papa right after the Great War. Her family was vacationing on Lake Neusiedl and he was there with friends for the weekend. Was that true?"

"Don't, Ingrid. Don't question everything. I'm sure it was. And they loved you. That was true too. More than anything." He chuffed a sad, derisive sound. "They weren't pleased with me lately, I'll tell you that."

"Why?"

"You." Adam regarded her with such openness and vulnerability that, for an instant, she felt she could see into the very heart of him. His every emotion mirrored her own—loss, pain, fear, and love. She blinked at the last, unsure if it was real or her imagination. She tipped forward and noted the second Adam's brain told his body to do the same.

He pulled her close as his lips covered hers. Their first kiss wasn't hasty, forceful, or demanding. It felt like sorrow touching springtime, a slow unfolding toward hope. It teased all her senses and she felt herself falling into it and into him. It was gentle. It was full of yearning and love. It was—

It was over.

The sudden loss of Adam's counterweight surprised Ingrid, and she caught herself with one hand on the iron back of the bench. Studying his shuttered expression, she realized that whatever she'd seen in the heartbeat before their kiss had vanished and that whatever he'd felt for her in the past weeks of heightened glances, fleeting touches, meeting her after work, and walking her home was over. Her world tipped from that glimpse of spring and all its inherent promises back to the last days of fall with an endless winter ahead.

"I shouldn't have done that." Adam scrubbed his hand over his face. "When your father looked to you yesterday, he looked to me as well. Like it or not, Ingrid, you are my responsibility now."

There it was. She wasn't to be loved; she was to be protected. She was once again to be managed at a distance in order to keep her safe. She closed her eyes. "Why does no one think I can take care of myself?"

"Oh, Ingrid . . ." Adam sighed. "This isn't about that. It's about a promise. You're the strongest woman I know. Let me get you to England."

"*Nein.*"

"Do you want to stay?" He widened his eyes as if he couldn't imagine such a thing. "Why would you try? This isn't your home anymore."

Ingrid gazed out into the Rathauspark. Despite the destruction around her, this one corner of the park remained lush and green. Focusing only on that, she could almost believe the world might right itself and all would turn out well. "Then call it my battleground."

"You don't understand what you're saying." Adam twisted to face her. "Your father wouldn't want this for you. Your mother would be furious."

Ingrid glared at him. His expression appeared tired and worn. He'd aged in a day. They both had. He had also seen more than she had in that last devastating moment, and she'd seen enough. "Papa lost that right yesterday, didn't he? He lost his life, threw it away. Mutti did too. And for what? A few papers, a few whispered secrets? No, they lost the right to tell me what to do because they aren't here. And you don't get to step into their shoes, Adam."

He shifted away rather than toward her. The silence grew long and uncomfortable, but Ingrid refused to break it.

"It was far more than a few papers and a few secrets, Ingrid. And you need to know that what your parents did, what I do, requires you to play a game with no end in sight. It's exhausting and it divides your soul. They were spies. True spies." Adam sighed with a long, deflated breath.

He paused, as if giving her time to absorb his statement, before he continued. "I'm still working as one and it's hard. Harder than you can possibly imagine. You saw what these years did to them. They didn't want that for you. But if you insist on staying, if you won't be reasonable and go, then you must understand what's coming."

Ingrid had seen, perhaps, more than Adam understood. Because alongside her parents' weary expressions and greying hair, the thinning features and worn, slumped shoulders, she sensed a strength and purpose—a peace, solidity, and focus—she had never witnessed before. It came out in whispers, gestures, inflections, and glimmers of light in the dark that were so fleeting she almost thought she'd imagined them. But deep down, she knew she hadn't. Her parents had grown stronger in the crucible of war. They had glowed—but had never trusted her enough to share their purpose, even their joy, with her.

"I'm staying," Ingrid stated again, and contrary to everything Adam said was to come, a calm rather than a tumult settled within her. "Tell me what I'm to do."

Adam studied her and whatever he saw seemed to please him. The corner of his mouth lifted the tiniest bit before he banked it. "Pretend it's a game so the reality of life doesn't terrify you every moment of every day. Then learn to play and live within that game better than anyone around you."

"How?"

Adam's lips flattened into a straight line. "I'll show you."

# THREE

# Anya

WOULD I STAY, IF I COULD?

I never answered Scott's questions last month, and he had the grace not to ask them again. We both know there are no good answers. Besides, the sentence that preceded them still has me reeling.

*"There's a lot to love about America."*

I said that. I said that out loud. Do I think that?

In moments, yes, maybe, fleetingly. But deep down, is that how I really feel? All month that question has danced in the back of my mind. Teasing me. Plaguing me.

I can't say yes. I can't say I love America or I'd ever try to stay. It's too painful to admit—or worse, to secretly desire— something that can never be. And I don't. That would be foolish. I mean, I think I don't. I've worked hard to keep one corner of my heart safely tucked in my immutable reality, trusting it's enough to keep me from shattering when my four years here end. And I've done it. I'll be fine.

But I also can't lie and say no.

I dream about it—a job, a life, a marriage, even kids. I thought these years would be like summer camp. I'd take the classes, learn all the right words to say and things to do so as not to get beat up, and I'd be done. But it's been different. I've expanded; I've grown. And from the day we met, Scott saw more in me than I ever thought existed. I've stretched above and beyond myself. Not unlike that silly fern Tracy placed in our windowsill. A little warmth and sunshine and that darn thing is about to take over our dorm room.

I should've lied to Scott right then and there and said no. It would have at least saved me this month of torment. But I couldn't. I already lied once that day, and I didn't think I had another in me.

The truth is, the day before our spring break adventure, I had in fact "been contacted by and been in conversation with an agent or representative of the US government."

Scott doesn't know. Sasha can never find out.

It all started with a summons to Professor Jamison's office. While unexpected, as we meet to discuss my senior thesis on Thursdays and had just met the day before, I was delighted to drop by.

Jamison's cramped and stuffy book-lined office is my favorite spot on campus. Something about its dusty, ink-and-paper smell takes me right back to my bedroom and my all-night read-a-thons—because at home you get the best books in secret and only for one night.

As usual Jamison was dressed in a rumpled, plaid button-down shirt with his readers perched upon his head. He looked as disheveled as his office, with the remains of a tuna sandwich near his elbow.

"Shut the door, why don't you?" He absently patted his desk. I gestured to his head. He reached up and rolled his eyes. "Oh yes, there they are. Thank you."

I turned to catch the door and froze. Another man stood

in the room, not one meter—three feet, my mind converted—
from me.

"I'm sorry." I faced the professor. "I thought you wanted to
discuss my paper. I can come back later."

"It's in fine shape." Jamison waved long fingers to the man
next to me, who calmly returned a book to the shelf before he
stepped toward me, hand outstretched.

I estimated he topped me by at least six inches, making him
just shy of my father's height. But the similarities stopped there.
I could tell this man was wired for action rather than stillness.
I found that far less disconcerting. He was younger, too, maybe
early to midforties. Light brown hair cut short. Grey-blue eyes.
Cool and impassive.

Jamison continued. "I want you to meet someone. Please. Go
ahead and shut the door."

I slid the door shut with one hand and reached out to shake
hands with the other.

His hand was as cool as his eyes. He still had not spoken.
Perhaps because Professor Jamison, in his normal scattered way,
was still talking.

"Anna, this is Trent Olivers. Trent, Anna. The best and brightest of the year. He was once that, Anna, longer ago than either of
us will admit. Bright as you, but he never pushed his thinking deep
enough. Now he's something different altogether. Now . . ."

The man's eyes had widened minutely at the mispronuncia-
tion of my name. I didn't react. It's never bothered me that, either
on purpose or by accident, Jamison—after teaching me in two
classes and mentoring my honors thesis—still hasn't gotten it
right. I take it as a testament to my ability to fit in.

Jamison, still chattering, lifted his head to capture us both
within the lenses of his readers. "He's the man behind that test
you and the others took last month."

*The test.*

In February Jamison called ten of us in to take a newly designed test, structured to assess the "evolving twentieth-century sociopolitical paradigm," whatever that meant.

In form, the two-hour examination was a mix of multiple choice, short answer, and essay, covering an eclectic array of topics such as math, ethics, problem-solving, science, literature, history, philosophy, ideology, sociology, and religious attitudes. Our reward was unlimited pizza and beer at The Tombs afterward. He never said anything about follow-up meetings or results. In fact, as I cast my memory back to that day, we hadn't signed our names to the forms.

"It wasn't graded, was it? Did I fail?" I sank into Jamison's only visitor's chair. It was scratched, worn, and the leather slippery enough to make me slide deep. A grade hadn't seemed likely and failure never occurred to me. I thought we were simply and anonymously putting a new test through its paces.

Coming from a school system in which you only advance depending on how well you master each step, I've always been terrified by failure. I've always been terrified of scrutiny. There are real consequences at home for poor marks and missteps.

I forced myself upright and addressed both Jamison and Mr. Olivers. "Do I need to retake it or something?"

My professor laughed and returned to grading papers.

Mr. Olivers did not laugh. Instead he perched in front of me on the edge of Jamison's desk. "Nothing like that. In fact, you did remarkably well."

He stared at me, then continued—in pitch-perfect Muscovite Russian. "Anya Kadinova, I read your entrance file when you arrived here. Very impressive. I had not expected to find your answers on the test, especially your long answers, so . . . original." He let the last word float between us.

Jamison's head popped up like a Whac-a-Mole and I knew his mispronunciations were a mistake. "Anna, do you speak—?" He cut himself off. "My TA told me you moved to Illinois from West Germany in middle school."

"Yes, sir, I did tell him that."

It was a lie I made up in my first days on campus. I've always been good—exceptionally good—at languages, accents, and imitations. So good I got written up in Class Six for mimicking my teacher's German. I got written up—she disappeared from school. In my defense I hadn't known she hadn't reported she knew German. That whole incident still bothers me.

Anyway, my first roommate at Georgetown, a silly, spoiled girl named Sandy, refused to bunk with a "Pinko." When Tracy took her place, I came up with my story about being from the German Federation Republic—what Americans call West Germany. Tracy didn't question it. No one did—Americans are generally horrible about accents and languages, by the way.

For the most part it was a good choice. It gave me the chance to become someone new and different in America and feel what freedom of choice, thought, expression, and intention meant in every aspect of my life. I wouldn't have been allowed to do that if people truly understood I hail from Moscow rather than Bonn. Sure, there have been a few crass comments about Germans and Nazism, but nothing compared to what I've heard dished out regarding Soviets and Communism.

It's been exhausting, though. It's an odd form of schizophrenia, knowing myself to be one thing while actively pursuing another identity every waking moment. I've only "come clean" with Tracy and Scott. With everyone else, I'm perpetually playing a game, maneuvering my pieces—actions, reactions, inflections, opinions, and ideas—around a board. It's shredding, and without that hard stop at graduation, I'm not sure I could keep it up.

I considered all this, and my options, as silence hung heavy in Jamison's office. Both men watched me. Neither spoke. I vacillated between pretending I didn't understand Mr. Olivers, as I hadn't answered Jamison's question yet, and diving in to see where Mr. Olivers was headed.

I shifted my focus to Mr. Olivers alone. "You seem to know a lot about me. Why did you have me take the test if you knew I wasn't a real American? Or even a real German?" I replied in Russian. "Why did you not simply talk to me? Why trick me into this office like you did today?" I asked in German. "And what were you trying to learn anyway with that test? What were you after?" I finished in French.

Mr. Olivers's mouth twisted into the smooth-lipped grin of the smug and knowing. Jamison's eyes were so wide behind his readers he resembled a tarsier, that little squirrel-like animal from the rain forest I saw on a *National Geographic* special last summer.

Rather than answer my questions, Mr. Olivers—unaware Jamison was now riveted by our conversation—asked a couple of his own. "Why did you double major in engineering and literature? You've taken several philosophy courses too. What are *you* after?" He returned to English and his tone was no longer overtly challenging but curious with an edge.

Part of me wondered if Sasha sent him. Sasha doesn't have Olivers's cool confidence, but I've seen it in seasoned KGB officers. Either Olivers was one of them, or something terribly close. I had to be careful.

"Knowledge. Understanding . . . Because I could. I asked for permission and it was granted." I caught the defensive uplift of my voice and corrected my tone. "Engineering was required. I'll work in that sector once I return home. In fact, I was on my way to MIFI, the Moscow Engineering and Physics Institute, before

I was offered a spot in the Foreign Studies Initiative. But when I got here and discovered I could take classes outside my major, I did."

"Engineering?" Mr. Olivers lifted one brow high. "You weren't headed for the Moscow State Institute of International Relations?"

*MGIMO.*

I tried not to let my jaw drop. He was really asking very different and dangerous questions. Was I going to be groomed for the Committee for State Security, the KGB? Had I been groomed?

But those were questions that, if he was KGB, he'd know the answers to. Foreign Studies Initiative students are *never* groomed for the KGB. We're too high profile. We're the Soviet poster kids: diplomatic fodder. We are commanded to excel at all our classes, behave as model comrades, and uphold the ideals of the State. At all times we are to demonstrate the superiority of our homeland. And if US Intelligence Services tie themselves up keeping track of us every minute of every day, all the better. That just means the real KGB "assets" have an easier go on American soil.

Still unsure if it was a trap, I tried to form a bland but truthful answer. "Before I accepted the Foreign Studies assignment, MGIMO was offered alongside MIFI. I was lucky. My scores allowed me a choice. That is rare but appreciated."

"I expect a member of the Party's *nomenklatura*, specifically one in the Office of the Counsel to the Presidium and General Secretary Brezhnev, would be afforded some say in his daughter's placement."

That's when my jaw did drop. This man seemed to know more about my father than I did. The best description I can give for my father's job is "high-level Party bureaucrat," and it's accurate—it's the job description most of my friends give for their parents as well.

With that statement I knew Mr. Olivers was definitely not KGB. It wasn't in what he said but in how he said it. There is something unique about the way each country's people express themselves, and it can be revealed in something as tiny as a gesture or an inflection—the way we walk, talk, carry ourselves, or even tilt our heads. Things only an outsider could notice.

But if he wasn't KGB, who was he?

Mr. Olivers grimaced.

I got the sense he felt he'd misstepped and made us adversaries instead of comrades.

"Tell me more about your love of ideas."

He was trying to put me at ease, but his approach missed by a mile. Four years here and I'm still shocked at how easily everyone shares their thoughts. Back home, that's sacred ground. I wanted to run out of the room, but Jamison's encouraging smile compelled me to stay.

"It's what my friends and I did—do. We read and we argue at home—in private, of course. Most of our opinions are crap, but . . ." I took a deep breath, only then realizing I'd been holding it.

I glanced around the office again, allowing the books, the smells of paper, ink, and dust to settle within me.

"Every culture tells a story through its literature and philosophy. I've grown up on a Marxist-Leninist worldview and stories of Russia and the Slavic countries. The Soviet Union isn't a hundred years old, but our history—our people's history—goes back centuries. Books about our past aren't too hard to get, at least some of them. You register on a list and get them after a few months or so, or you can collect recycling. That's what we did. Paper and metal for books, and there were some really great ones."

I thought back to how, sometimes tucked within those books, we found gems. That's where I met all the best Russian storytellers and my favorite science fiction authors from around the world. Asimov, Bradbury, Orwell, Huxley, Clarke, and Le Guin—their stories prepared me for Georgetown by introducing me to worlds so bizarre and experiences so alien I simply had to hold on until I figured out the rules and the culture.

"But the best," I continued, "were the secret books. The one-nighters that got you reported and kicked out of the Komsomol if you got caught reading them. Those books took you to whole new galaxies."

"Pushkin, Dostoyevsky, Tolstoy?"

"Those you could get. Pasternak, Solzhenitsyn, Zamyatin, Pilnyak were tougher. Those were the stories tucked in the recycling pamphlets. But Tolkien. Steinbeck. Salinger. Faulkner. Lee. Those were the one-nighters."

I surveyed Professor Jamison's bookshelves. "Here they're lined up, free for anyone to grab and read. Most of the books I've read while in America will never come my way again."

"What's your favorite?"

"That was a secret book, actually. *To Kill a Mockingbird.* I got a copy for a night when I was sixteen. Scout was the first character I met that I could relate to. She was young, but she had humanity, goodness, and spirit, despite the evil around her. I wanted to be Scout."

"And who is your favorite philosopher?"

I stared blankly.

"I pose no danger to you."

I decided to answer, because that's part of what I learned from my favorite philosopher—that I'd never have big courage if I didn't practice small acts along the way.

"Thomas More. He's not one of the biggest guns in the Western canon, but he was relatable and he taught me something I needed to know. My end point."

"What's that?"

"He showed me there's a line my conscience won't allow me to cross. It's out there, even if I'm not sure what it is yet." I swallowed, noting small acts of courage aren't easy.

"He wasn't what I thought," I continued. "More seems super closed and rigid, but he was a very urbane and brilliant politician. Until he reached his end point. The line in the sand that would separate him from his very soul if he crossed it. I'd never thought about that line before."

"I doubt many have."

"At home, it's a collective line rather than an individual one. It's determined by the State for all society. The idea of such individuality was brand new for me."

I surprised Mr. Olivers. I silenced him. I could tell because his face softened. He was curious. He pulled over a footstool and sat next to me. His knees hit his chest.

"What are your plans after graduation, Anya?"

"I'll fly home the night of graduation and work in a laboratory, serving as a liaison between scientists and the government."

"Reporting to Minister of Defense Nikolai Ivanovich Petrov? That's a very high-profile job."

I licked my lips. I could not answer that question, yet unbidden I gave a single small nod.

Mr. Olivers did not react; he merely asked his next question. "Are you pleased with that path?"

I took a steadying breath. This past year, I've listened as my Georgetown friends pondered what jobs to accept and what might make them happy. Their ability to choose sifts through my hands like sand, lingering only long enough to tease me with the hope it can be mine.

It can't.

At home I, as an individual, exist to serve the State. Anything and everything else is subservient to that primary relationship. And I have been assigned my job.

"A lot is expected from the Foreign Studies Initiative students. I'm pleased to be given such an opportunity."

Mr. Olivers shifted closer. "Would you like a different opportunity?"

"I don't understand."

He turned his head to catch Jamison's eye before answering me. "I work in a business that strives to change reality. We protect American national security and interests abroad, and we also work to promote democracy and freedom. You're right, I could have approached you directly, but that test gave me insights you might hide. Your answers and reading interests reveal you believe in voice, in certain amounts of individual autonomy, and you crave internal freedom. You can't like Thomas More otherwise."

Without studying Jane Austen last year, I'm not sure I could have parsed through his speech. But "it is a truth universally acknowledged" that people often try to make a point while saying nothing at all. It's also a universal truth that we instinctively understand each other. Meaning conveys when words cannot—I knew exactly what he was talking about and what he was about to propose.

"The exam you took was created for the US Intelligence Services, and if working for us, with us, is of interest to you, I am here to discuss that possibility. But I must warn you, it's a double life, a division of soul perhaps, and after More, that will either resonate with you or not appeal at all. It depends on what drives your soul."

I thought about the energy required to play that game and the energy I'd already expended simply pretending to be a West German. "No one can live like that. Not indefinitely."

"You'd be surprised." Mr. Olivers tilted his head as if savoring a delicious secret only he knew. "The best can and do. You could be that."

I sat for a moment chewing and digesting his offer. I was flattered and it was tantalizing. How could it not be? Yes, I've fallen in love with Western literature and philosophy, but I've gotten pretty hooked on Hollywood too. The movies here are amazing. *The Day of the Jackal, The Eagle Has Landed*—I've seen every James Bond movie put out on Betamax. That last one in the theaters, *Moonraker*, had me on the edge of my seat. To be a spy. Wasn't that what every kid dreamed about?

My best friend, Dmitri, and I sure did. We played KGB all the time, with our wooden swords and tin can walkie-talkies. Of course, he was always the KGB agent and I was any other service he assigned to me—and I always lost. After all, if you're going to be the best, you work within the most powerful and elite squad in history. The KGB.

At least that's what I've always been taught. But here everything's different. So different I can't even say what's right, what's wrong, what's true, and what's illusion. I've loved every moment and yet I miss my home. I crave all the freedoms here, but I feel safe within the strictures there. I'm enamored by all the colors and yet I miss grey. How this can all be true I have no idea. It simply is.

I couldn't tell Mr. Olivers any of this. It hardly made sense to me. But I didn't need to. As he sat watching me, his expression changed. Whatever he saw bothered him and a furrow wrinkled his brow right above his nose. All the lines on his forehead moved horizontally, formed over time by surprise or skepticism. This was a new vertical line, a deep trench created by me.

"Don't answer." He held out a hand. "Perhaps we can talk about this another time. You head home, work, and we might reconnect in the future."

"Why?" A surprising sense of desperation washed over me.

Mr. Olivers sighed, as if I'd missed something and he felt disappointed at having to explain it to me.

"That's just it," he finally answered. "The why. It matters most in my business. Everything stands on that foundation. I'll turn away a top scorer, the most perfect-on-paper candidate imaginable, if the *why*, their intangible motivation and driving force, doesn't settle well in my gut. With you I'm intrigued. Your answers reveal far more than I think you realize. But your *why* isn't defined. Your emotions haven't caught up with your intellect . . . You're homesick."

"Of course I miss my family."

He pushed to stand and extended his hand to shake our goodbye. "It's not about your family. You cling to the belief that you can find what you need in the Soviet Union. I want to talk when you finally realize you can't."

# FOUR

# Ingrid

INGRID MASTERED THE "GAME." SHE BECAME A MODEL PUPIL and, for the next two months, continued working at the Third Reich's Economic and Administrative Office with such diligence and dedication, her boss promoted her. No longer given notes to summarize after the meetings, she sat in the meetings. Silently stationed by the door, her pen flying to keep up with the cacophony of raised voices and frayed nerves, Ingrid witnessed the Nazi machine break down.

While requisitions for munitions and troops were written, filed, and executed at the usual pace, a heaviness pervaded the office and a tense desperation gripped her boss, Bereichsleiter Albrecht. He no longer spoke; he barked. He no longer walked; he strode. His clothes were growing increasingly wrinkled, rumpled, and voluminous—he was losing weight. And no one could miss the proliferation of anti-Nazi propaganda and increasing defiance in the streets.

Soon, under Adam's tutelage, she stretched her skills further, recognizing that these hasty redeployments of troops and supplies to one front held consequences for other sectors. She connected the dots, made calculated guesses, and advised Adam and Martin on the best distribution of British resources.

She also came to accept her new living situation. Because she was unable to return home even for a few pieces of clothing, as Obersturmbannführer Skorzeny moved his family into her home within hours of her parents' arrests, Adam and Martin gathered clothes and necessities from their networks of contacts and friends. Within a day, she became a member of their little family, and no one in their building questioned it.

*My two brothers*, Ingrid mused as she watched them lean over a map in their small living room marking coordinates. Adam worked for British intelligence and ran sabotage networks across the country at night. And his work wasn't going well. Sustained and organized resistance, she gathered from his fits of pique, spread like fire throughout France but had not caught even the smallest spark in Austria. Martin, an American, parachute-dropped into the city the year before. On loan to the British, he worked a wireless transmitter and was a master at fading into the background and winding his way undetected through the city morass like a shadow. Generous with his knowledge, he taught Ingrid not only how to clean and fix his transmitter but how to fade away when necessary.

*"Don't reach out to friends. Let them assume you were arrested with your parents."*

*"If someone you recognize does notice you, cough and duck away. Into a doorway. A shop. People shy away from sickness."*

*"Become the quiet mouse of a woman everyone believes you to be."*

After playing on that particular insecurity, he would pull her close, muss her hair, poke her in the ribs, and do anything else he could to make her laugh and forget her pain and worries, as only a brother could.

Adam assumed the role of a more distant brother. He taught her to make notes with symbols rather than words, to remember small details with great accuracy, and to decipher a handful of codes from memory. He coached her in "situational awareness"—the ability to assess how a room felt and note who was in charge, who was nervous, and what was being said beneath the words spoken. He taught her how to trust her instincts and take her thinking and observations beyond what was said into the realm of how it might be employed and even accurately guess what might happen next. But gone were the glint in his eye and the half smile that had once danced at the edge of his mouth, along with any and all affection.

For a while the memory of their kiss was enough for Ingrid. She pulled it out each night in the quiet, safe minutes before sleep and relived what might have been. But after two months, its memory was fading, and she was afraid she would soon lose it—and Adam—completely. Earlier tonight she feared she might have accomplished just that. She had pushed him too far.

As she cleared the table, he had commented, "I remember my first dinner at your house. Your mother made that soup . . . Is it wrong to say I enjoyed yours more?"

"Never." Ingrid turned from the sink. "But Mutti was an excellent cook."

Adam stretched his hand toward her. But rather than take his offered hand and draw him close and try to look to the future rather than to the past, she dragged Adam's attention back to what he believed to be his greatest failure.

"You said you'd tell me . . . I haven't forgotten. What exactly did Mutti do for you?"

Adam's hand dropped into his lap. "She met with me every morning after one of her dinner parties. She was so gifted, Ingrid, at not only learning and remembering details but interpreting what they meant as well."

*Mutti's dinner parties.* Ingrid closed her eyes. Shame wrapped its mantle around her, covering her ubiquitous sorrow.

From the day of the Anschluss, Marie von Alton said that a good table and a generous hand with the wine might save them. She encouraged her husband, the head of the University's liberal arts curriculum, to reach out to the Nazi officers and invite them to dinner. She wanted their home to be a haven in which society could discuss culture, art, literature, and the superiority of the Führer's ideas.

Ingrid had seethed at her mother's betrayal and turned her face away as Marie welcomed Reichsführer-SS Himmler into their home for her first dinner party in 1938, as well as when she hosted Obersturmbannführer Skorzeny for her last, a beautiful four-course affair just nights before her death.

"How can you bring them here? How can you laugh with them and cook for them?" Ingrid had raged at her mother one night over two years ago.

*"Duc in altum,"* Mutti obliquely replied. "The rewards more than compensate for my pain."

Ingrid knew the phrase—her mother had said it before. It was Latin for "push into the deep." But it was a nonanswer and Ingrid continued to rage. "You have to want more than for our home to be safe. You take their gifts. Think what this makes you. Makes us."

Rather than capitulate or make excuses, Marie's face mottled. A petite woman, barely taller than her daughter, Marie rushed forward, and with one hand clamped around Ingrid's arm, she ground out words with slow precision. "Never question me. You know nothing of this."

After that, Ingrid didn't question her mother, but she watched. And she discovered things she had not noticed before. Marie didn't drink at her parties but offered her guests wine with a heavy hand. Ingrid also noticed her mother's subtle, soft, and probing questions, and that her laughter tripped across octaves but never reached her eyes. She also noted how quickly her mother banked any flashes of fear that shot across her eyes. It was a skill Ingrid herself had not mastered.

Now Ingrid understood. It was precisely because she had not mastered that skill, and so many others, that she was held at arm's length. Perhaps that was one reason among many, she thought, for while her father faithfully taught Nazi ideology at the University by day, he worked most diligently at night, creating exit visas and managing safe houses. And her mother worked equally as hard, wielding her hospitality like a weapon within their home, threading through the delicious courses of foods rarely available—*"Personally sought out and requested just for your pleasure"*—and wines—*"The last of our private cellar, saved for this occasion."* She fed and charmed the wolves. She lulled them into loquacity.

"She was good, really good." Adam shook his head in wonder. "By the end of a dinner, your mother understood how her guests thought, what they did, and most important, what they were likely to do next. She often learned of plans or made the most extraordinarily accurate predictions of orders, raids, and troop movements before they happened."

"Did you get them caught?" Ingrid's question carried no accusation.

Adam scrubbed at his eyes and Ingrid's heart sank. It was the second time she'd noticed that gesture. She saw in it the burden he carried.

"I pray not, but I can't guarantee it. Any network can have leaks spring up, and I'm not so arrogant anymore to think ours is immune." He dropped his head, no longer able to sustain eye contact. "I'm sorry, Ingrid. Maybe."

"It's almost over." Martin raised his head from the map, drawing Ingrid back from memory to their living room.

"Then I can quit? I hate working for those monsters. I hate pretending. I hate being something I'm not. It's splitting my head." Ingrid gripped her book so tightly the binding bent. She placed it in her lap, aware her tension and innermost thoughts were on display and they were not to her credit.

After all, she didn't hate working for the Nazis, as it gave her access to work against the Nazis. What she hated was that only two men in the whole world knew that—only two. Her pride bristled within her, and she wanted to bridge the gulf between the shame of what she appeared and the truth of what she was.

Adam and Martin stared at her.

"I just want this over." She ended her sentence on a sigh.

"Not long now . . . Don't lose hope." Martin's flat-voweled American accent made her smile. Even speaking German, he couldn't hide it, and his sentence embodied everything she loved about him—his endless optimism and his belief in both absolute right and a good man's ability to get it done.

Adam scoffed. "Not so fast. Three years of work and we've only managed passive grumbling within the resistance. We don't have mass, we don't have military support . . . The Nazis are still firmly in charge, you two, and wounded animals fight more viciously than healthy or angry ones. We have to be more careful now than ever."

Martin smirked with what Adam called "Yankee arrogance," but he shot Ingrid a warning nonetheless. He might posture, his raised brow said, but he agreed with Adam and she'd better as well.

So the next day, Ingrid went to work early and stayed late. She then searched the markets for meat on her way home, as she did each evening, and found little to buy. She finally returned to the apartment building with a few worn root vegetables and trudged up the stairs. Only to stop on the third-floor landing.

Someone had called her name.

Glancing around, Ingrid found herself face-to-face with Frau Möller. Ingrid knew who she was—Adam had made her memorize everyone's name and apartment number. He said people were less likely to turn on you if you greeted them with a personal salutation. But Ingrid had never met this woman. In fact, she'd been told to avoid the occupant of apartment 3H, as her son was a committed and newly minted soldier within the Wehrmacht.

"May I help you, Frau Möller?" Ingrid fashioned a bland expression as her mind raced through her fictional cover, trying to recall each detail to satisfy the woman's curiosity if questions arose.

Frau Möller moved closer. "The Allies are moving in."

"Where did you hear that?" Ingrid blanched, reminding herself that *Ingrid Bauer*, widow of a Wehrmacht officer herself, would not like this news. She added an impatient barb to her voice. "Why would you tell me this?"

The older woman stumbled back into her apartment.

A still, small voice told Ingrid to let her go. She silenced it. "Please, wait." Ingrid stepped forward and pressed her hand against the door just as it clicked shut. She whispered against the wood. "Please . . . Are you sure?"

Frau Möller cracked the door again. "My son is in the Wehrmacht, like your husband was, Frau Bauer." She nodded to Ingrid in mutual understanding before adding, "He is a good boy."

The older woman paused for the briefest moment, and Ingrid got the impression she was either to bristle at an unspoken comparison or to accept that Frau Möller knew more than she was saying.

Ingrid's neighbor continued. "They have been warned and

are making preparations. He wants me to leave as the bombings will start and come nightly now."

"Thank you," Ingrid whispered as the door shut again.

She raced up the stairs. "Adam . . . Martin . . . ," she called through their apartment, expecting to find either or both. No one was home. She packed a bag and started to prepare dinner.

It was over an hour before Martin arrived. Harried and pale, he darted his eyes first to her small bag standing sentinel by the central table, then to her. "You're packed?"

Ingrid grinned. "*Almost* is closer than we thought. Frau Möller said the Allies are coming tonight."

"Hurry." Martin picked up her bag with one hand and shooed Ingrid out the door with the other. "We need to get you to safety."

"You can't go outside. You—"

Martin shook his head and continued to maneuver her down the stairs at an ever-faster pace. The building felt empty and quiet, and they saw no one as they descended the five flights.

At the front door he stepped into her. "You need to go quickly. They won't sound the sirens tonight because they can be used as beacons. Red Army planes have already been spotted to the east." He looked up. "It's the Soviets and it'll start anytime now."

"What about you and Adam?" As Ingrid spoke she realized word had gotten out. People flooded from nearby buildings. She tipped toward the street before Martin's hand steadied her.

"Soon . . . There's still work to do." Martin tilted his head across the street to the Kirche St. Elisabeth, the basement of which formed their neighborhood's shelter. "Go."

His steadying hand gave a quick shove. Ingrid stumbled and the crowd swept her into its current toward the church. She was almost a full block away when she heard it. A high-pitched whistling, like air shooting from a balloon.

The next moment she felt the world shatter and go dark.

Ingrid blinked. The bright light seared and split her head. She moaned and turned away.

"Can you hear me?" A woman's voice, gentle and soothing, spoke through the glare. "She's waking up." Her voice shifted from conciliatory to directive. "Call the doctor."

A moment later, a firm, cold hand pressed against Ingrid's forehead. "Slowly now. You've had quite a time of it."

"A what?" Ingrid's tongue stuck to the roof of her mouth. She tried to raise her hand to touch her temple and ease the pain in her head, but she couldn't. She couldn't make the connection from thought to action, so she let herself drift toward darkness again.

"They say you flew over forty feet when the blast hit. You are lucky to be alive."

Ingrid heard the words. They poured over her like water, nothing sticking, nothing congealing. As darkness closed in, she felt the evening, the street, the stones flying, a woman's scream, and Martin . . .

Clarity came with a gasp.

"Nurse." The man's voice cut above her. "Get her brother."

The chaos calmed. It was going to be okay. Martin was here. He was alive. She felt his hand touch her shoulder. Her other shoulder, she noted, was encased in something rigid. She opened her eyes.

Adam leaned down and kissed her forehead. He spoke with lips pressed against her skin. "Lie still while the doctor finishes. Then we'll talk."

Cold hands poked at her a moment longer, then vanished, along with everyone except Adam, whose firm grip on her shoulder was the only thing that kept her from crying out. As the door shut, Ingrid tried to push herself up and Adam away.

His hand spread to her collarbone. She could feel his warmth above the edge of the hospital gown. "Don't. You've been badly hurt. The nurse said your left shoulder separated and your collarbone broke. You also have a fractured pelvis, broken ribs, and a serious concussion. Ingrid, I'm so sor—"

"He's gone, isn't he?" Ingrid turned her head side to side despite the pain. Her brain crashed about within her skull untethered. She was untethered.

Adam held firm. "He was right there. He didn't suffer, Ingrid, and to say he knew the risks doesn't help, but he did. He always knew. Your father, your mother, Martin, me . . . We've all known from the very beginning."

"Stop. Don't say that to me. You risk your lives and you die. For what? It's all still coming apart. You've accomplished nothing. Nothing but the pointless deaths of good people. People I loved." Ingrid closed her eyes and shifted onto her side, away from Adam. The world felt kinder and safer behind dark lids.

"I shouldn't have said that about your parents. I—"

"Don't talk about them. Don't talk about *any* of them."

"Ingrid . . . I want to stay, but I can't. I have orders . . ." Adam's hand dropped from her shoulder. "Don't do this, Ingrid. Don't shut me out. Please don't turn away. I don't want to leave you. Not like this. I'm sorry . . . I'm sorry for everything that's happened. I would take it all back if I could. I would—"

"Stop," she whispered. "Stop saying you're sorry, because it's meaningless. Nothing was worth their sacrifices, your sacrifice . . . This game of yours . . . I can't do it anymore." Her ribs hurt. Her head hurt. Her shoulder hurt. Her heart hurt.

"I'll come back. I promise. I'll come back and we can leave together."

Ingrid closed her eyes again. In the darkness she saw loved ones gone—countless friends, her mother, her father, Martin. "Don't make me promises. I'm not your charge anymore. It's not your job to keep me safe."

"I wasn't saying that. I meant—"

"Go, Adam." She cut him off. "You have orders. Just go."

Ingrid heard a scratching noise, then felt gentle pressure as he laid a kiss on her head and pushed a note between her fingers.

"Keep that number, Ingrid. It connects to London and it's always monitored. Do you hear me? Always. No matter when you call or where I go, they'll find me. If you ever need me, they'll find me and I'll be here for you. Do you understand?"

Ingrid did not open her eyes, nor did she answer him. Adam left the hospital room without another word.

But he did come back.

Returning to Vienna a month later, he found Ingrid a shell of her former self and unwilling to listen or leave.

Three months later, Adam returned again and found Ingrid still working at the Third Reich's Economic and Administrative Office. She no longer arrived early nor did she stay late. She did just enough not to get reported or arrested as the Nazis scrambled and fled around her.

Adam tried one last time, arriving in Vienna on April 4, 1945, the day the Soviets liberated the city.

He couldn't find Ingrid at all.

# FIVE

# Anya

*"WHAT ABOUT YOU? WOULD YOU TRY? DO YOU WANT TO STAY?"*
Three months and Scott's questions still plague me. Every waking moment I scrape at them, keeping the wound and the desire fresh and painful.

Some days my heart screams *DA*—an all-caps declarative YES. I want to stay in America. I want to dance to disco music, wear clothes more colorful than the brightest rainbow, be a schoolteacher, and drive my own green VW Bug. I want to grow in America's sunny optimism, can-do spirit, and innate generosity. I want to marry Scott—maybe ask him if he doesn't ask me again—and live in a place that veers to heat nine months of the year rather than frost. Scott promises Georgia—the US state, not the Soviet republic—boasts such a climate.

Does that mean I think America is better or that I'd betray my country? *Nyet.* And if I'm honest, I'm a little terrified Mr. Olivers floated the idea. To show anything but absolute loyalty is dangerous. Beyond dangerous. Is that what Sasha sees in me? Have I grown too comfortable, too familiar, and, as he would say, too soft? Have I truly forgotten my roots and my family? *no.*

It may be a sad and lowercase whisper, but a whisper can be as firm, real, and devastating as a shout.

Mr. Olivers was right. I miss home.

Besides, this was never to be more than it has been. A gift. An honor. A test. One that came with so many strings, it scared both my parents. Mother had tempted me by coming to my room late one night to share with me all the art I might see—but she had only been dreaming, musing aloud. She never expected me to act upon it, and her tight expression signaled she was chastising herself for talking to me at all. My father's expression vacillated between pride and terror. After all, the Foreign Studies Initiative was an honor, one of the highest bestowed, but it was a risk. At a base level we Soviets distrust those who soar too high, and such an honor was sure to get our family noticed, by everyone.

A groan from my roommate, Tracy, returns me to the present and brings my head up and out of the book I have not been studying.

"What is it?" I ask. Her guttural moan means she wants to talk.

"Since you asked." She bounces up from her chair and topples onto my bed. I scoot over to give her more room. "Do you think I'm doing the right thing?"

I laugh, as she's asked this question a hundred different ways. I give her the same answer I always do. "It's the right call. You've got free rent, the job is exactly what you want, and it's a reputable newspaper. Pay some dues, live for free at home, then make your next move."

Tracy wants to be a journalist. A good one. The kind that changes the world. Satisfied, she hugs me and moves back to her desk to study for whatever final she's got next.

I do not return to my engineering.

Instead I sit stunned in another of those weightless moments that lifts me up, shakes me about, and drops me again. It happens more frequently now, and its force takes my breath away. I came to the US ready to assimilate. I wanted to conduct my own social experiment simply because I could. I was curious, despite being raised to hate Americans, how much of America a Soviet could absorb in four short years.

The answer rocks me to my core: a lot.

But now, with two days to graduation, I feel a fissure opening inside me. I carry both cultures within me and I understand both. And to be frank—not that I can truly admit it to myself, nor would I to anyone else—some aspects of America feel more comfortable to me now.

My advice to Tracy illustrates this beautifully.

*"It's the right call."* I agree, deep in my heart, that Tracy should choose her career. Because if she loves it, she'll bring her best to it and that will benefit everyone. I was assigned my job a couple months ago.

*"Live for free at home, then make your next move."* Tracy gets to choose where to live by what she can afford. Someday she also might buy a house, and it'll have a red front door and reasonable home-mortgage loan. She loves both red and math. I haven't been allocated housing yet, but I will be soon.

*"It's a reputable newspaper."* Until I landed in America, I had no idea that papers could publish differing opinions—and so many of them. At home *Pravda* gets delivered daily, and within it, the Party tells us the facts and what our opinion regarding those facts should be. Sure, we have the samizdats—the "self-published"—but, well, they're underground newspapers.

A shout from outside our open window draws me from my mental gymnastics. Someone has probably just finished his last exam because he's yelling for the entire campus to come out to play. How I want to. It's a gorgeous day and I'm going to miss these. The cherry blossoms, fully bloomed and gone, have been replaced by bright green leaves, blue skies, and chirping birds. Flowers cover the campus in neat, colorful rows.

The sunshine and warmth last so deliciously long here. The world awakes in early March, according to my thinking, and returns to rest sometime in November. About as long as Moscow's cold darkness, starting in October and lifting in June. The light and colors are hopeful and bright. They remind me of my mother's work at the State Museum in Moscow. She tries hard to bring the hope and color of the world's art within our borders. Most of the time the minister of culture denies her requests. Here, she would love to openly discuss art, music, and culture and reach new conclusions and even disagree over interpretations. Back home, she hangs State-approved paintings alongside the State-approved copy explaining them.

Yet it's still home, and I miss our traditions and the familiar things that signal comfort and belonging. I miss the smell of Comrade Rudinov's peppermint ointment that wafts through the air vent into our apartment. I miss kozuli, the cookies my mother always keeps in the ceramic jar on our kitchen counter for all my friends. I miss the fall colors along the Moskva River that make the bright red of St. Basil's and the Kremlin pop, exuding a history and a power the White House and the Washington Monument can never touch. I miss the smell of burning leaves in the parks during the first days of September and the scent of snow come the last.

Sure, life is hard and confined in many ways, but there is also freedom within the strictures. We know who we are and what we are about—it's a straight-line mentality, a tough mentality, with very few distractions to veer us off course. Our conformity gives an illusion of power and peace as we are raised to believe our way of life is superior and virtuous. Illusions are powerful things. If you believe them hard enough, they can become one's reality.

It's reality that we are raised to believe Americans are weak.

They don't have the stamina, the gumption, the drive, or the fortitude for the long fight. Their shiny capitalism lulls them into complacency. They won't or can't truly sacrifice for the common good.

That is an illusion too.

I've learned that Americans are hard in ways I couldn't have imagined and find absolutely exhausting. To have all these constitutionally protected freedoms is enviable, but it also means you have to respect them, uphold them, and fight for them. Americans have to watch out for the weak, the marginalized, and the disenfranchised—it's an average citizen's responsibility and vocation. Sacrifice and commitment and the common good are woven into their democracy, their ideology, and their DNA. And within all that, there is a whole world to manage moment by moment on a multidimensional level—with visible consequences and, if you believe in any religion, as most Americans do, eternal consequences too.

The whole thing takes strength—the illusory peace that conformity brings has no place here. Here peace and freedom rest on Americans' ability to live in tension and to discuss, debate, and refine. To live like that takes constant commitment and energy— every opinion, every decision, every day.

Mr. Olivers was right. I miss home.

∞

"Dinner." I launch from the bed. "I forgot. I'm supposed to be at Scott's apartment in ten minutes."

"That poor boy." Tracy twists in her chair again. Her auburn ponytail swirls across her face.

I try to ignore her and search for my new sundress. She is about to give me an opinion I don't want to hear. I find the dress and focus on that. It's so lovely it makes me almost believe in hope. When I saw the dress on discount at a local boutique, I spent the last of my money on it. I may never wear it again—but it was still worth it. A cotton sundress with a sweetheart neckline and thick shoulder straps, it's the happiest yellow sunburst of a color I've ever seen, with little red roses scattered across the fabric and puddling along the hemline.

I slip off my Nike shorts and Georgetown T-shirt. Tracy hasn't continued. She's waiting for me to bite. I give in. "Say it. Why is he a 'poor boy'?"

She smirks, knowing I'd give in and ask. "You could marry him and stay. He wants that and so do you. You're just too stubborn or stupid to admit it."

"You think this is all on me?"

"If you appeal to them, you might convince them. What about that man you meet with every—?"

"Stop." I glare at her through my mirror as I apply lip gloss. "We're not going over this again."

For a year Scott harangued me, even throwing out the *M* word occasionally. Each and every time, our conversation started sweet and ended in a fight. Though logically he got it, he couldn't emotionally understand that none of his ideas or dreams were possible.

Oddly, when he finally stopped pestering me a few months ago—around the time he started his job and got super busy—I began to miss those fights. If nothing else, I felt wanted. How warped is that?

Then Tracy picked up the baton. But fights with her aren't any fun. We don't kiss and make up. And despite endless rounds, she refuses to accept that the Iron Curtain isn't mere metaphor or that it keeps people in as much if not more than it keeps people out.

"That boy has loved you from the day he met you, and even

when the night's long, we Americans believe grit and determination can get us what we want . . . For Scott, that's you. He'll pine over you forever."

Tracy is clearly on Scott's side and, again, this is somehow my fault.

"Cut him a little slack," she continues. "Marry him or set him free. Maybe a little more *Casablanca* than *Romeo and Juliet*, if you don't mind."

That's new. I part my lips to reply but can't. I have always been clear about the plan—I would leave and that would be that. I'd be devastated, but wouldn't Scott move on?

Without another word I gather my hair into a scrunchie and dash out of our room, down the corridor and stairs, and into the first golds of a beautiful early-summer evening. Upon hitting the sidewalk, I slow and take a deep breath. The DC heat and humidity wilt me instantly—as does Tracy's admonition. She's right. On all levels.

Scott O'Neill sat next to me in Introduction to Comparative Politics our first quarter on campus. He forgot a pen and I had two. I got lost exiting the building and he pulled out a map. I could barely grasp a word he said, and my accent made his jaw drop. Try putting a Muscovite accent with a Georgian one (again, the US state, not the Soviet one), and trust me, you couldn't tell the two of us were speaking the same language.

As he not only didn't run away upon learning my true nationality but actually was interested in my home and stories, our first walk turned into lunch, and I started to maneuver through his southern twang. Right away he agreed to keep my secret and help spread my West German origin story to all his friends. He also introduced me to all those friends, including me in anything exciting he was doing around campus. It was like he saw something radiant and fascinating within me, and that alone called it into existence. I felt radiant and fascinating, and now I always want to be that person.

With regard to him, well, I was lost handing over that first pen. My attraction to him defied logic, science, or any other metric by which I tried to understand it. It was simply there and I knew I'd never be the same again. So, yes, he has creeped into that corner of my heart I've tried to keep locked safe, but if asked, I'll deny it.

For almost two years, I thought the depth of my feelings was mine alone. And I was good with that. Better than good. Igor and now Sasha have drilled the cautionary tales into my brain. Stories of Soviet girls and boys who slept around during their Foreign Studies assignments and forgot the rules. No pregnancies. No marriages. No exceptions.

It was only after a drunken night early last year I discovered my love wasn't so unrequited after all.

"Why not? It's not impossible." Scott threw the words at me as fast as he was tossing back shots at an off-campus party.

I matched him shot for shot, but fantasy didn't eclipse reality. I wasn't that drunk.

"It is." I leaned close in an effort to be heard and believed. "After next year I go home. It's not a quick commute, Scott. It's a whole world from you and I can't come back."

"If you married me you could stay."

"Marry—" I barked the word so loudly heads turned despite Pink Floyd adding another brick in the wall at a deafening volume. I pressed my lips together in both embarrassment and confusion. Scott's face told me, thick consonants and flippant delivery aside, he was serious.

"What are you thinking?" I hovered my lips near his ear. I meant it rhetorically, more along the lines of "Have you lost your mind?" but he didn't hear it that way. He heard what he wanted to hear.

He held his hand to the back of my head. "I'm thinking we marry and you stay because I love you. You have to feel that."

"I do—" My words shocked me and I pulled away. I was too close to the flame and was about to get burned beyond my ability to heal. I did that once when I was a kid. I touched the hot plate on which my mother was making tea, and I still have the scar across my palm.

Pain has a memory all its own.

Scott stared at me for a few heartbeats before chaos broke out and a brawl pulled our attention away. We lost each other as the police cleared the party. And after searching for him for fifteen minutes, I gave up and headed back to my dorm. It wasn't kind, but I couldn't reason with him like that. He was drunk, irrational, and dreaming clearly silly things, and the agony of trying to make him understand and talk him out of the very thing I imagined in those cocoon-like moments before sleep was beyond my strength.

So I left him.

He didn't call the next day or the day after that. I figured he was angry and maybe that was best. But then he showed up at my study carrel in the library a few days later, dragged a chair next to mine, and shut the book I was reading.

Pressing his hand down on the front cover, he began. "No commitment. Certainly no marriage. Though I might mention it occasionally." He cracked his adorable half smile. "But we've got over a year and a half, and I say let's not waste a minute. You with me, Kadinova?" He turned his hand over, palm up, eyes wide with expectation.

I placed my hand within his and, beaming like an idiot, believed I had found home. There's no other way to describe it. We've been together every possible moment since. Then this spring things started to change, and are changing still.

After an incredible spring break with his friends and mine,

he began his job with a DC consulting firm working as an analyst in international emerging markets. The company insisted his training begin before graduation so he could get up to speed for some conference later this month on Middle East development funds. Between school and work, he's swamped. He's too busy to hang out most evenings, and he's stopped peppering me to stay. I'm struggling with that. Even if staying is impossible, I want him to yearn for it as much as I do.

I bite my lip and tuck my disappointment and the memories of our last year and a half away. I can't tarnish them with what-ifs. They need to stay safe for the Someday Soon when I've nothing but their warmth left.

Every bit of these halcyon days is slipping away and I need to grab them, hold them tight, and savor them. I'll miss them desperately. But I'll miss him more.

Noting the time, I pick up my pace. The sidewalk feels hot through my thin espadrilles. They've stretched and are beginning to slip off my heels, but they match the roses in the dress perfectly. There's no way I'm not getting one more evening out of them. I turn the corner and find Scott sitting on his building's front stoop. He doesn't notice me, so I take a moment to study him. He's dressed in his usual khakis, a wrinkled blue oxford that sets off his light eyes, and his ubiquitous brown loafers. His blond hair hasn't lightened in the sun as much as it did last year. He's been working indoors too much.

Scott pops up the instant he sees me. "Well, if it isn't the lovely Miss Kadinova." He lopes down the stairs.

"Good evening, sir." I try not to grin. I really do. I grin anyway.

He closes the distance between us and kisses me longer and better than I expect. I wonder if I'll ever stop being surprised and delighted with his love.

He tucks a strand of dark hair behind my ear. "Hey, beautiful."

I melt a little more. Despite working in an office all day, he smells like grass, lemons, and something woodsy. I have no idea what soap or cologne he uses, but it is the best clean, honest smell in the world. I love it. Nothing at home ever smelled so good.

Trying to hide my reaction, as I'm not sure he feels quite the same anymore—why did he stop trying to convince me to stay?—I weave the strand into my scrunchie.

"It's not good form to have you walk here, but I suspected they'd keep me late. And they did." Scott frowns, trying to sound disappointed. He fails. Each syllable drips with satisfaction.

"You love it," I tease. "Tell me about your day."

"No way." He grabs my fingers and swings our intertwined hands like a pendulum between us as we walk toward Wisconsin Avenue. "I am not spending one of our last evenings together boring you with work."

"But I want to hear." I pitch my voice to sound light, but it hurts. Ever since Scott started this job, that's his constant refrain. He doesn't want to bore me in our last months, weeks, and now days with "international debt margins and capital differentiation."

Scotts turns the corner and stops. It takes me a second to guess where we're headed.

"Martin's Tavern?"

"It seems fitting."

I don't ask what he means. Fitting because Jackie and John Kennedy became engaged here? Fitting because he wants to find our own Camelot? Fitting because it's my favorite restaurant but way beyond my budget? Fitting because it's our last dinner together? I try to silence the questions and let the restaurant work its charm. To me, it is Camelot—cozy, colorful, loud, full of magic and history, good food and great music. I didn't even know about Jackie and John Kennedy until that first Comparative Politics course.

Scott leads me to one of the booths tucked right against the window. While the tables, with their white linen tablecloths pressed under glass, look more refined, the wood-benched booths feel more intimate. Tucked within one—Booth 3, no less, the actual one in which the famed engagement occurred—we're in our own world and the warm yellow glow of the Tiffany lamp suspended above is our sun.

I order a tavern favorite, fish and chips, because I'm already feeling nostalgic. It's a delicate dish I won't find at home. We have fried fish, of course, but not fresh halibut battered so light it melts in your mouth. My mother makes an amazing fried sprat with eggplant, but when the salty sprats come from a can and get deep-fried in their packing oil, it's not quite the same.

Dinner is quiet. Not the restaurant but us. We barely speak and it feels like I'm already gone. It feels like he's already gone. I want to rage and cry: "We're wasting our last days! We have to be real! We can't end like this!" But I say nothing because maybe this is exactly how our last days need to go—and maybe Scott has been preparing himself, and me, since March. After all, isn't that what Rick did? He always knew Ilsa needed to get on that plane in *Casablanca*, no matter what either wanted.

Scott finally addresses the elephant in our booth. "You leave right after graduation?"

I nod. "My flight's at eight o'clock that night. A driver from the embassy will pick me up at four."

He says nothing more as we pay the check and leave the restaurant. In the gloaming Georgetown is waking up.

"I won't ask you to meet my parents again, but—if I leave them at their hotel—can I take you to the airport?"

My stomach drops. Throughout the past two years Scott has asked to introduce me to his parents no less than ten times—and I've refused every one. I thought he understood, but when he asked again last month, I tried to explain more clearly. I don't want to meet them because I don't want to lie to them. I don't want to *be* West German, but I can't be Soviet either. To see even a flash of fear, distrust, or pure hatred in their eyes would devastate me. They might forever envision me as the Communist who ruined their son, left their son, didn't love their son—despite how much they'd want me gone.

"No." I reach for his hand but withdraw at first touch. "It's better this way, Scott. Truly it is."

I also don't want to reveal that postgraduation, post my last exam, I will report for a final meeting with Sasha and then be under constant surveillance. The prevailing thought is that earning a degree is sufficient inducement for students to stick around and behave. We have to check in, of course—the monthly-turned-weekly meetings—but we aren't tracked twenty-four seven. But once that degree is earned, the temptation to defect might lead to "foolish behavior." It's happened before. Sasha has my course schedule, and as of 10:00 a.m. tomorrow, I will have earned my degree even if it hasn't been awarded yet. Hence our quick "reminder" meeting at 2:00 p.m. and the watchful eye.

We weave our way toward campus, and rather than turn left to my dorm, Scott tugs at my elbow and leads me to a bench on Healy Lawn. We sit in silence, listening to the sounds of the evening: traffic, crickets, distant laughter, and Journey's "Any Way You Want It" blasting from an unknown and faraway location.

"Do you remember that question I asked you last year?"

I keep my eyes trained ahead, seeing nothing. "As if I could forget. But we agreed—"

That's all I get out before he's kissing me. Really kissing me.

And to be fair, I'm kissing him right back. It's like a champagne cork blew and passion is spilling over and out of us. For a second I let myself get swept away with the fantasy that our long-ago conversation ended differently and that our lives could go differently, and that he can be mine forever.

Moments or minutes later, he pulls away and rests his forehead against mine. "What are we going to do?"

The dream dissolves and we sit surrounded by night once more. Night and that same speaker now blasting Queen's "Another One Bites the Dust." The irony brings tears to my eyes.

"Nothing." I touch his lips with mine. "You must understand." I kiss him again. "This is goodbye. A true goodbye." One more kiss. "Now you'll forget me and someday, maybe soon, you'll marry and raise 1.81 beautiful children."

I feel rather than see his smile as I kiss him once more. It's my best party trick. Everyone in the Foreign Studies program has to memorize pertinent data for their host country. I can name every US state, along with its population, number of House representatives, capital, bird, flower, and unofficial nickname— along with the US birth rate.

"I can't do that."

Just as I tilt forward for another kiss, Scott pulls back to look me in the eyes.

"You must," I counter. Something quickens within me. Our romantic goodbye feels like it crossed the line into something dangerous. And it's a danger he could never expect, anticipate, or understand. Here our world experiences divide us more decisively than the ocean will after Saturday.

"You make it sound like a prison, Anya. It's not. It's a country. I get what you say. But they can't keep you there. Not if we're married."

I want to laugh, but this isn't funny. Scott studied international

59

economics, and while a few of his classes compared and contrasted political systems, he's clearly only been following the money.

I put a hand to his cheek to soften the blow, but I must make myself heard—for his sake. I feel the slight scratch of stubble and the line of his jaw under my fingers. Two more details I tuck away for Someday Soon.

"It is a prison. A 280-million-person prison with a million KGB guards on patrol. The only thing Professor Wilton got wrong is that the KGB is far more ruthless and draconian at home than abroad. There are no rules for them. No limits. Who do you think will drive me to the airport Saturday?"

"A KGB officer?"

"Sasha most likely. The one who set an informant on us in Fort Lauderdale. The one who now records my weekly interrogations. The one who may even be watching us right now and will certainly be watching me after my final exam tomorrow."

Scott leans back. I'm pretty sure Sasha is not out there with binoculars and a Big Mac, but I made my point.

He blows out a sigh. I do the same. Scott's comes out in a frustrated burst, mine in a long pursed-lipped breath, like air escaping a balloon. He's letting go. I'm keeping control.

After a minute of silence, a voice deep inside, sounding suspiciously like Tracy, tells me to end it. *More* Casablanca *than* Romeo and Juliet. There's no point in talking further, and kissing will only make the inevitable more excruciating. It's simply time.

I stand and the skirt of my dress swishes in the breeze. The red roses dance around me and, sadly, a funeral comes to mind rather than a wedding. "Goodbye, Scott."

He stares at me. "You're kidding, right? Goodbye?"

I shrug.

That gets him up and off the bench so fast I stumble back in surprise.

"Don't you dare do that. We don't shrug at each other, remember? You don't get to brush me off and make me wonder how you feel."

He's right. He—we—deserve more than the rote shoulder lift I pull out for almost every ambiguous conversational occasion. I use it to make the person I'm talking to feel like I agree with them or I don't care. Either works for me when I have no clue what's truly going on. But to use it on him or against him is a cheap play. We've always been honest with each other.

Then I feel it. A tear slides down my cheek. So much for that safe corner in my heart. What I didn't want to happen is happening—loss of control, broken hearts, tears, and pain.

*"Weakness,"* Dmitri used to say, *"is for the Americans, not for us. We Soviets are fighters."* He'd thump his chest. *"We're born to battle."*

Dmitri's right. We are a fighting people at heart. Probably because we've been fighting some war or another since Russia's founding over twelve hundred years ago. Our society is completely structured around the military, with a fixed hierarchy in every sector, and we even bring the guns—metaphorically speaking, of course—to the kitchen table where, in an honest argument among friends, far from prying ears and watching eyes, we rapid-fire opinions with such vehemence you'd think it was war. And while it sounds like an aggressive, odd, and cynical way to live, we pride ourselves on that too. Hard cynicism grounds our identity.

Scott likes that about me. I "think things," he says. I defend my thoughts. But he hates the Shoulder Shrug. He claims it's me abdicating my voice to fit in, trying to be among the 999,999 in a million when I'm the one. He's sweet and I love him more than he'll ever fully grasp, but being counted within the 999,999 at home is the safest place to be, and here it can feel really great.

Not now. Now it's time to wake up and remember I come from fighters. Soviet fighters.

"Goodbye, Scott." I shroud the word with steel and, in my father's move, stretch tall and stare at him until he blinks. Only then do I continue. "There. I am saying it loud and clear so there are no misunderstandings between us. I will not ask you to write to me and I will never write to you."

His eyes flicker with hurt and confusion, and I take that moment to summon the courage, even the cruelty, to do what must be done. "I will forget you, Scott O'Neill. Do you hear me? I will get on that plane in two days and everything here, including you, will become a distant memory." I bite the inside of my cheek. The pain focuses me.

He steps back as if struck. "Is it that easy? Can you really do that?"

"It's already done." I stare, unblinking, a moment longer, then I turn and walk away, willing my shoulders not to shake, not to give any visible indication that I can't breathe.

While part of me hopes against hope he'll stop me, spin me around, and kiss away reality, he won't. Scott always gives me the respect of believing what I say.

My heart feels like it's back on that bench bleeding out on its own, but I keep walking. I need Scott to believe me. I need him to hate me if that's what it takes to let me go. He can't comprehend the precarious situation I've put him in. Because there are the other stories—stories of Soviet and American students doing stupid things, even getting caught talking about stupid things, when the Foreign Studies Initiative years end.

Conversations that end in torture. Pregnancies that end in abortions. And elopements that end with a single gunshot to the back of the head.

# SIX

# Anya

IT'S DONE.

I flop onto my bed and take in my sterile dorm room. Only my bags remain. Tracy's dad pulled his station wagon away ten minutes ago, and not even that darn fern is here to keep me company. It's been the loneliest day of my life. There was no question of my parents attending graduation, but everyone else's did. Yearning for any familial connection, I even spent an hour after the ceremony searching for Scott, hoping to see him with his parents, but I never spotted him. Not once. I tried to console myself that this was how today was supposed to go, and that I'm flying home tonight, and that I'll soon be with my family. Soon I can rest.

But not yet.

Yesterday's meeting with Sasha is still cycling through my head, and I'll only be able to rest once I feel my mother's hug and see my father's eyes. Only then will I draw a real breath.

"Tell me more about your boyfriend, Scott O'Neill?"

That was Sasha's opening question—once the door in that small room at the rezidentura clicked shut and he'd pushed the red Record button on his machine.

63

"What? I-I've told you about him. What more do you need?" I stammered, racing through what he might have heard or seen on Healy Lawn the night before.

"You never told me you loved him."

"I never said—" I stopped. Sasha's eyes glinted cold. "You read my letter to Dmitri—"

"Don't act surprised, Comrade Kadinova."

I was no longer Anya, no longer a friend. I was a problem.

"Comrade First Lieutenant Dmitri Dimitrivich Shubin is a loyal young officer. Naturally, he'd let us read anything we asked."

"But you didn't ask."

"Comrade . . . ," Sasha warned.

I closed my eyes. What a fool I was. I had written to my best friend the one thing I couldn't tell anyone else—that I desperately loved a boy, an American boy. It meant nothing. I wasn't going to try to defect. I simply wanted to share one true feeling with the one person I trusted most and who knew me best. And Sasha was wrong. Dmitri would never let them read my letter. He would protect my confidence to the death. Sasha only knew its contents because the censors opened it before Dmitri did—if Dmitri ever got it at all.

"Scott O'Neill was a silly infatuation, and I wanted to share it with Dmitri. It meant nothing. We say 'love' all the time. You *loved* Katya who transferred back to Leningrad last year, remember? And you *loved* Nikita before that. And what about—?"

Sasha cut me off with a raised hand. I let him because I was running out of air and of silly girls to mention. He glanced to the recorder and I realized how lucky I'd gotten. While I was just trying to be light, Sasha would never want anyone to hear of his flirtations. He would, most likely, destroy our recording.

I didn't sigh. Not because I didn't feel relief, but because I was still too scared.

"That's what I thought, and I've said as much when asked about this." Sasha smirked, knowing he held all the cards. "Don't make me look bad, Comrade. Don't make a liar of me. Every one of my reports has praised your dedication and your loyalty. I want to hear only glowing things upon your return to Moscow. Our futures are tied together for now, and everything you say or do reflects upon me."

"Yes. Of course." I tried to swallow. It lodged in my throat.

"As you like to remind me, you Foreign Initiative Studies students are the best of the best. I'd hate to see such a luminary fall." His voice dropped low but not menacing—he didn't need those theatrics. "Do we need to concern ourselves with Scott O'Neill any longer?"

"Not at all. I said goodbye to him last night and never expect to see him again."

"Very well." Sasha tilted his head to the door. "Then we have nothing more to discuss. You've done well here, Comrade Kadinova. I will pick you up at 4:00 p.m. tomorrow afternoon."

"I'll be ready."

There was no bravado in me after that meeting. I ran from the room.

∽∞∾

A firm three-rap knock at the door ends my musings and signals the end of my time at Georgetown. I open it and face a wiry young man, perhaps a year or two younger than I, standing in the hallway.

"Good afternoon, Comrade Kadinova." He nods. "Comrade First Lieutenant Sergei Vasin. You are ready?" He points into the room behind me. "Let me help you with your bags."

His English and intonation are perfect. Dzerzhinsky Higher

School perfect. Moscow State Institute of International Relations perfect. KGB perfect.

He carries the bulk of my luggage, and once settled within the car, I speak. "Are you new? Where's Sasha?"

I can't decide if I'm relieved or hurt Sasha hasn't come to drive me. On one hand, if he still felt I was a risk or a threat, he'd personally fasten my seat belt here and on the plane. On the other hand, I'm a little sad because, for two years, we got along well. On some level I thought we became friends—and I did buy him bourbon.

"I arrived in April. Sasha is busy tonight." Sergei peers at me. "You are sad to leave? It is very different here."

"It is." I answer the last comment, not his question. There's no way I'm going to let anyone, especially some newly-sworn-in agent, report how I feel about anything. I was reminded of that lesson yesterday.

I turn toward the window as the car winds through campus toward the George Washington Memorial Parkway and Dulles International Airport. I cast back to my beginnings in the US.

The agent who picked me up from the airport that first morning had been a woman, already two years in the United States, and "Watch out for the money" was her first bit of advice.

"What's wrong with the money?" Panic seized me as I'd been given an exorbitant amount to get settled. Having "hard currency" at home is a serious offense and a valued commodity. It's dangerous either way.

"Nothing, but you won't know how to spend it. I blew my first paychecks like a kid at the Gorky Park fairground. Everything here is yours for the asking, and you get sick. I can't explain it any better. At home, you take the required coupon, stand in line, and buy shoes when yours grow holes or food when your pantry is bare. We have no concept of buying. Not like here. Here you have *wants*, and those can get warped in your head."

"What do I do?"

She gestured to the bag I sat clutching in my lap. "How much did they give you? One hundred dollars now and twenty each month?"

I nodded.

"Okay then. Don't spend more than fifteen dollars your first month. Take your time. And keep your mouth shut. Listen and learn. Once you open your mouth, you're on everyone's radar. Don't stand out . . . You'll be okay."

She was right. Getting on "everyone's radar" proved disastrous immediately. One awkward hello to a blonde girl from the south and I learned fast that Americans feared and hated us as much as we feared them. I have a hard time even thinking I could "hate" them anymore.

I shift toward the man next to me. "What'd you spend your first paycheck on?"

Sergei's eyes grow wide in wonder. He hasn't learned. "I bought a motorbike. A Honda Hawk. It is black with red markings, five gears, and it travels from a full stop to sixty miles per hour in nine seconds. I drove it down the state of Virginia and into the state of North Carolina last weekend. You can do that here. You can go anywhere. And there is plenty of petrol."

"Yes. I've learned that." Clearly he missed the recent gas crisis.

"Next I will buy leather pants and a jacket. Boots too. All black. I found a store that sells the high-quality leather." Sergei prattles on, helps me check in, then gallantly offers to accompany me to my gate.

Once we're settled in two attached seats, I shift to face him. "You don't need to wait with me."

"I do."

So we sit side by side in blue not-high-quality-leather chairs waiting for my flight to board. Mr. Olivers's words, almost an indictment, cycle through my mind on an endless repeat warring against my fears over yesterday's meeting with Sasha.

*"You cling to the belief that you can find what you need in the Soviet Union. I want to talk when you finally realize you can't."*

Will he reach out again? Do I want him to? After all, what I said was true; the KGB guards Moscow well.

Yet I've been asking myself these questions since the moment I scurried from Jamison's office, growing increasingly terrified with my imaginary answers. And each time, I find myself rubbing the scar across my palm without even directing my fingers to its ridges. Deep down, I am still curious enough to want to meet Mr. Olivers again and frustrated enough with Sasha to creep closer to that flame.

*Nyet.* I'd back away. I'll aways back away. I'm the child my parents raised me to be. And for all that's wrong at home, there is much that is right too.

My mother's listening ear and firm hugs. She may not understand me sometimes, but she loves me unconditionally. I feel it in the way she gives me her full attention whenever we talk and the way she strokes my hair when I can't sleep.

My father's smile on the rare evenings he pulls out a pipe rather than his ubiquitous Primas. A pipe signals a good mood, and our conversations sometimes turn philosophical and, if I'm lucky, I get to hear how he feels about things rather than how he thinks about them.

My friends Sonya, Ulyana, Kaden, and Lev. I trust them with my life and, more importantly, with my true thoughts. Then there's Dmitri, more brother than best friend. I miss him so much I ache. I need to unpack my years away with him. I need him to confirm every truth and help me parse through every lie like he's done since we were six years old.

*Scott.* My mind drifts back to this side of the world, and the reality of him threatens to break me. I never told him I loved him. I couldn't risk it. But I couldn't stuff it down any longer either. It burst out. It had to. Dmitri once told me that's what love does. He was right—so I told the truth, to Dmitri alone. And look what happened. But what if I'd chosen another path? What if saying yes to Mr. Olivers meant I could stay here? Someday return here? I might have agreed or done any number of crazy things for Scott alone.

"Anya."

My head spins as I search, certain my musings have conjured his voice. But there he is, racing down the concourse.

Sergei stiffens and makes to rise with me. I stay him with a hand, now thankful it's not Sasha by my side. "He's a friend from school. I'm only saying goodbye." I'm careful not to say Scott's name and hope Sergei has never seen a picture.

I cross the gate area and meet Scott at the edge of the terminal's main thoroughfare. I position myself to block Sergei's line of sight.

Scott nods past me. "Is he KGB? Is that Sasha?" His voice holds that bit of wonder every American's does when mentioning the KGB. Awe, terror, and fascination grip them in equal measures.

The intense young man bores holes in us with grey eyes. "That's Sergei. He said Sasha is too busy for goodbyes."

Scott pulls me a few feet farther away into an alcove. Sergei starts to stand again. I hold out a palm. He calms and drops back into his seat.

Scott steps close. He takes both my hands within his own. "I'm sorry. I shouldn't have said what I did the other night. I shouldn't have pushed."

"It was me. I'm sorry. It got hard so I fought. I didn't mean to, but . . . I shouldn't have walked away."

"Can I write to you?"

"No." A panic seizes me. I can't live divided like that. Letters will only keep some false hope blinking through the shadows. But Scott's expression clouds with pain and I can't hurt him. "Yes . . . Of course you can. They'll read your letters, but yes."

The clouds clear with his laughter. "Nothing too steamy then?"

"Steamy is fine." I laugh with him. It's wimpy and flat, but it feels better than the alternative. "Nothing political. Nothing real. Don't share true facts with them. And never make assumptions that I'd agree with you on any aspect of American life. And no quoting me. No 'remember when you said' kinda stuff."

"That's pretty specific, Anya."

"No, it's that broad. It covers everything because this isn't a joke. I told you. They have no rules. Maybe it's best if you—"

"Don't tell me not to write. Please." Scott steps closer. "I can do this. Good sterile letters full of nothing. Just as if we're married."

"I said not to joke." I try to pull my hands away.

"I'm sorry." Scott holds them tight. "I have to or I'll go mad."

"Don't go mad. Move on." I step into him, so close I can almost taste his lips. I force myself to keep eye contact. To waver now will only hurt us both. Me, I don't care about. But Scott, I desperately want to keep safe, remember always, and envision him with a family all his own. Six kids. A loving wife. A house outside DC or in Georgia with a white picket fence. 1.81 kids is never going to satisfy Scott.

"I can't." Scott drops a light kiss on my lips. "You're my Rose Beuret. I'll always wait for you."

"Who?"

A corner of his mouth lifts. "Look her up."

"Scott," I moan. "We don't have libraries like here."

For three years, he's given me these little teasing clues. When we first met, he called me "Juliet." It took another quarter and a Shakespeare class before I figured out that our countries represented the Montagues and Capulets, and though I didn't like the play's ending, my heart definitely quickened at the passion his moniker implied.

Then sophomore year he called me "Terry McKay." Tracy translated that one for me.

*"He's been watching movies with his mom . . . She's the woman Cary Grant loves in* An Affair to Remember. *She pushes him away, trying to save him pain, but he doesn't give up and finds her in the end. It's all very old-folks romantic, but it'll still leave you sobbing."*

Now this.

"Scott, don't—"

"Let's write." He cuts me off with a flash of a kiss. "Let's just write with no expectations for the future." He lets go of my hands and holds my head close to his own, his hands cupping my cheeks. "If you meet someone else, fine, I'll understand, but I'm not ready to let you go."

I concede, kissing him again. "Neither am I."

"Good." He searches for Sergei over my shoulder. I glance back as well. Sergei is standing and pointing to the line forming. My flight is boarding.

"I need to go."

"I love you, Anya Kadinova." Scott keeps my gaze locked within his, and I wonder if I've truly appreciated just how blue and intense his eyes are. They are bluer than Lake Baikal and just as deep.

*What does it matter now?* I take a breath and fall. "I love you too. I always have. Since that first pen."

He kisses me again. It's no flashing light peck. It's desperate, firm, and conveys every ounce of his love. "Don't give up on me. Promise?"

"It's no good." Tears fill my eyes.

"Give me time. Give us time. Just promise, okay?"

I nod, I promise, and I kiss him one last time. It's my good-bye, but there's no point telling him that.

He still carries hope.

# SEVEN

# Ingrid

"INGRID . . . OPEN YOUR EYES."

"No, Comrade Second Lieutenant Leonid Igorevich. I will not." Ingrid smiled. The fact that she always used his full first name and patronymic bothered Leonid Igorevich. *"It's too formal for us,"* he'd said. *"You* are *formal,"* she'd replied. In her heart, however, Ingrid had started calling him "Leo" months ago.

She tilted her head back farther, letting the sun warm her face. Leo was back. She sensed him drop onto the bench beside her and partially opened one eye to peek over. She expected to see her own excitement mirrored in his dark eyes, to see them crinkled in laughter and his mustache tipped up, hiding a grin of his own. After all, he'd been gone for over a month.

Instead the light caught the side of his face and the tiny lines around his eyes, along with the vertical creases in his brow. *Always formal, always concerned, and always careful,* Ingrid thought. She longed to reach up and smooth those lines. They had no place on such a gentle man. He should laugh more.

Leo wasn't paying attention to her. His focus had shifted over her head to the building behind her, Austria's Parliament Building. *That was long ago,* she mused. It wasn't even that when

73

she began working there in 1941 at the age of eighteen. It was the Third Reich's Economic and Administrative Office back then. Now it had transformed once again and housed a bevy of offices for the Union of Soviet Socialist Republics, including the one in which she worked: the People's Civil and Administrative Bureau.

Ingrid closed her one eye again.

A firm kiss landed on her lips.

Startled, she shot upright and twisted toward the building, then back to the tall, lanky, dark-haired man next to her—who now sat fully focused on her.

"There's no one around." Leo widened his eyes. Although his Russian still carried a formal lilt, his expression was filled with that little-boy mirth she'd only witnessed a few times in their year-long relationship.

"I should think not," she teased. "Shocking behavior."

Leo shifted on the wrought iron bench to face her. "I am back."

"I noticed."

"I got a promotion. A very good one. Excellent, in fact. Third lieutenant with a promise for captain soon."

"I sensed good news." Ingrid reached for his hand and squeezed. His fingers were long and his nails clipped blunt and short. "You were so anxious, but no one works harder or is more dedicated than you. You deserve it."

Although they didn't work in the same office, Ingrid had long heard of Leo's reputation. No one was more prompt, exact, or punctilious, and he was ever vigilant to uphold every rule, regulation, expectation, and propriety. If Leo hadn't also coupled those qualities with a mild manner, gentleness, and consideration, his colleagues rightfully would have hated him. Instead they treated his fastidiousness with good-natured ribbing and left it at that.

Nevertheless, his summons to Moscow a month earlier had unnerved him. And in the three days postsummons and predeparture, his hair, usually pomaded to sleek perfection, curled at the tips; his uniform, never wrinkled and with straight-line creases down each trouser leg, sagged at the knees; and his shoes, perpetually polished to a black-mirrored shine, showed scuff marks across one toe. He missed calls, misdictated memos, and even skipped a meeting with his superior, Chief Administrative Officer Anatoli Lebedev. He had also chewed three fingernails to the quick.

Wrinkled and wrung out, Leo delivered a final dictum to Ingrid the night before his train north. *"Don't waste energy missing me. A summons is either good or bad. It's never neutral and I may not return. I . . ."* Whatever he was going to say next never came. His words simply drifted away.

Now all was well.

"Welcome home." Ingrid sighed as a cozy blanket of peace drifted over her. She had quit worrying months ago as to how this man had crept past her defenses and simply accepted he had. "We should celebrate with dinner and dancing. Café Dommayer has live music tonight."

The light in Leo's eyes dimmed rather than brightened, and the air sharpened around Ingrid. "What is it?"

"We must talk." He fidgeted, drawing his fingers in and out through her own. "This promotion means a transfer. Home to Moscow."

"I see . . ." She shifted her gaze out into the Rathauspark, taking in her home. Once the grand seat of an empire, Ingrid's beloved Vienna now resembled a doll torn between quarreling sisters. Over 30 percent had been bombed in the last year of the war, and rather than receiving the funds and attention she needed, the city remained beleaguered, wounded, and wanting, divided between four Allies whose turf war was more important than her care.

*Ten years,* Ingrid thought, suddenly feeling as old and worn as the doll herself. Ten years since that first Soviet bombing. Almost ten years of a living death and a half existence, until this gentle man—surprisingly a Soviet himself—joined her on this very bench one day last spring.

He had simply asked, "Can you smell them?"

Not understanding, Ingrid tilted her face up to follow his gaze across the park's canopy. "The trees?" He nodded and she pulled in a deep breath, expecting nothing, and struck upon something she believed lost forever. Life.

Spring carried a smell, she discovered that day, borne on a delicate breeze and magnified by sunlight. It was fresh, green, alive, and warm. She marveled at how she had missed it for so long—pine, maple, fir, and ash, all growing bright new shoots with leaves turning to catch the light. The crab apple trees were in full bloom, sending pink flowers dancing as they dropped. Birds flitted between branches. And the trees in her corner of the park had somehow escaped the bombs and spread their branches, dappling the light over the walkways, the grasses, and even her own bench.

Ingrid felt her breath catch in wonder. "I hadn't noticed."

Leo began a story. "My papa was a carpenter in Krasnoarmeysk, a village outside Moscow, before the October Revolution. He could create anything from wood, beautiful things, and our house smelled of it all year long." Leo gestured into the park. "Trees carry different smells. Some woods are sharp, hard, and green, while others are sweet, soft, and floral." He peeked at her with a glint in his eye. "My babushka's tongue compared to your sweet smile."

Before Ingrid could reply, either to accept or dismiss his compliment, he continued. "I could always tell what he was building even before I entered his work shed. He used maple for tables, pine for shelves . . ." Leo quieted and a silence drifted over them.

Filled with a curiosity she hadn't felt in years, Ingrid asked, "What happened to him?"

Leo stared at her, and with the straight-lined expression of one who understood loss and pain, he exhaled one word. "War."

In that moment Ingrid was no longer alone.

Now he was leaving.

She drew her eyes from the park and back to Comrade Second Lieutenant Leonid Igorevich. She corrected herself, Comrade "Third Lieutenant with an eye to Captain" Leonid Igorevich, and tried not to begrudge him the honor bestowed and the clear joy he felt. He was dedicated to his country and its cause, and this was good for him. It was what he wanted, what he'd worked so diligently each day to achieve—satisfaction in a job well done and a chance to bask in the attendant recognition.

"I hoped you might come with me."

"What?" Ingrid pulled her neck back sharply. "Come with you? To Moscow?"

Leo laughed. "It's not frightening, and why does it shock you?"

Despite the cool day, Ingrid felt Leo's hands, wrapped around her own, grow sticky.

"This is not how I wanted t-to ask." His voice caught on his nerves and broke between them. "I wanted to give you more time . . . I want to care for you, protect you, but I leave next week."

Heat climbed a red streak from his neck to his cheeks. "I'm trying to ask you to marry me. Not well . . . Poorly in fact, but . . . Will you marry me, Ingrid Bauer?"

*Ingrid Bauer.*

Ingrid felt the lie open within her. She still carried the false papers, and after so many years, she had made them her own. Her father had been right from the very beginning—Stalin had been more powerful than Hitler. When the war ended, the Soviets (after switching sides and joining the Allies) controlled most of Vienna. So Ingrid, finding herself without work and without a family, had put her true surname, von Alton, away forever and reinvented herself once again.

With her landlady's help she mastered the Russian language until her fluency matched her German, her English, and her French. Then she marched into the People's Civil and Administrative Bureau to apply for a job, for no other reason than the familiarity that, as the Third Reich's Economic and Administrative Office, she had worked within its walls.

She sat poised on the edge of sharing secrets she didn't dare touch anymore, when a memory carried her to Adam Weber. She felt anew the electric surge she had experienced whenever near him. How differently she reacted to Leo. With Adam, despite the distance he put between them, she couldn't bear to lose him—so she had sent him away, hiding from him the last time he came to Vienna to search for her. Everyone she loved, she lost. Could she let go of Leo now? Would she—?

"Ingrid?"

Could she have more courage now than she had ten years ago? Could she go with Leo rather than send him away? He was gentle, kind, and caring. He loved her and would surely understand when she told him everything. They could have a good life together. It could be enough.

Perhaps, she thought, letting her mind drift further, that was the difference in finding love at twenty-one versus thirty-one; the difference in loving in the midst of war versus finding it in war's prolonged aftermath; the difference in a love crashing over you versus one found in mutual pain, loss, and the reality that life was and always would be a struggle.

*Yes, it will be enough.* "I will," she said simply.

"You will?" Leo blinked.

"You didn't expect that?" Ingrid leaned away, but Leo gripped her hand tighter.

"No. Yes. I wanted you to say yes, but I anticipated needing a more convincing argument. I prepared a speech."

Ingrid laughed. Four years her senior, Leo looked young and eager, almost vulnerable. "You can give it now."

"No," he demurred. "It wasn't eloquent. I'll stop now since you think this is a good idea." He bent his head toward her but shifted before contact and dropped a brief kiss high on her cheek rather than her lips.

Ingrid twisted to see behind her again. Two men in full Soviet military uniform had just stepped from the building's front door and stood at the top of the stone steps. As they surveyed the park, one raised his hand to Leo.

She didn't recognize them, but by the straightening of Leo's spine, one hand absently smoothing a wayward clump of hair as the other waved in reply, she knew he did.

"It's probably okay now that we're engaged," Ingrid whispered.

Red once again crawled up his neck. This time it spread all the way to the tips of his ears. Leo shook his head. "But you should definitely call me Leo now."

With that he shifted to face out into the park once more, and still holding tight to her hand, he closed his eyes and tilted his face to the sun.

⚮

*"He has aspirations and this will not sit well."*

Ingrid's coworker Svetlana's words returned to her once more. Ingrid had denied her friend at first, laughing off her warning. But now she wondered.

She rounded a pillar and, hidden from view, regarded her fiancé more closely. He stood near the altar of one of the Votivkirche's gilded and resplendent side chapels and looked the epitome of calm control in his uniform. Then he swiped a hand at his hair, marring its sleek perfection. Moments later he pulled at his collar. Watching the cracks in his armor expand before her eyes, Ingrid regretted her insistence on a church wedding.

Days earlier Leo hadn't chafed at her request, at least not that Ingrid could tell. He had merely replied, *"A church service? Religion is something we've moved beyond at home."* He then let her plan what she wanted and said nothing more.

Yet he cut the service to its bare bones.

He also cut the guest list.

While colleagues and friends had been invited to the hastily organized dinner the night before, only the most essential had been told about the morning service. Two friends to serve as witnesses.

It hadn't bothered Ingrid until now. Watching his discomfiture, she wondered why Leo hadn't been forthright about his feelings. She lifted a swath of her white dress and wondered the same about herself.

After last night's boisterous dinner, full of toasts and speeches, she had walked Leo to her childhood home on Grillparzerstrasse. The white stone-and-brick building stood fully restored in Vienna's American quarter. Window boxes overflowed with fresh blooms and sidewalks were scrubbed and swept clean.

She hadn't returned to that block in years, and it brought back memories of more desolate days, with empty window boxes, shuttered windows, and suspicious neighbors. Then came images from the last day with a tidal wave of despair that still threatened to pull her under.

Standing across the street, facing the building rather than her fiancé, Ingrid had shared the story of her parents and their lives together, ending with, "That's when Adam clamped his hand over my mouth and pulled me away."

"Adam? You have never mentioned him."

Turning to walk back toward the Soviet district, Ingrid kept her eyes trained on the sidewalk and missed the reactions of the man next to her.

"He was German but grew up mostly in England. He worked as a junior instructor at the University, but really he served in Britain's Foreign Services. I suppose we'd call him a spy."

She continued as they crossed the street. "There were two of them. Adam created and ran resistance networks, and Martin, a demolitions expert who ran the wireless, was on loan to Britain from America. He didn't have a cover, so he had to hide more. It was like he was invisible. A shadow. No one could vanish like Martin. He died in the bombing that hurt my shoulder, and Adam . . . I suppose Adam returned to England after everything ended. I can't imagine he'd ever go back to Germany."

"You loved him." Leo didn't define "him," nor did his quietly spoken words lilt in question. They dropped like stones onto the pavement.

"Martin, like a brother. And Adam . . . I was a girl, a foolish girl." Ingrid had walked on, missing the change in the moment. "It was a long time ago." She finally noted the chill resting between them. "You can't be jealous."

Leo shook his head. "Not jealous . . . How close were you to the British during the war?"

His tone caught her. It wasn't curious; it was considering.

"They were your Allies, you know?" She smiled. Leo did not. "And my mother was British." The defensive words spilled out of Ingrid even as a quickening deep inside told her to keep silent. She rushed on, striving to make whatever felt wrong grow warm and right again. "She was on holiday near Vienna after the Great War. She met and married my father here and never returned home."

"Bauer is a Russian name. I always assumed your mother, like your father, was of Russian heritage."

Although he hadn't phrased it as such, Ingrid knew he was asking a question. He wanted further clarity. Clarity that a soft second instinct told her not to provide. She merely shrugged, tucking the next story she had intended to share—that of her false identity card and her true name—safely away.

They walked in silence through the checkpoint and returned to the Soviet quarter. Ingrid glanced back as the barricade dropped between the two quarters. It was goodbye, and she didn't move, couldn't move, until Leo put a gentle hand to her back and led her away.

They walked another block before he spoke again. "In your security interviews, did you lie?"

He was referring to her annual NKVD interviews, which had recently been reformatted by the KGB, the newest iteration of the Soviet Union's Committee of State Security.

"Lie about what?" Ingrid stopped walking.

"In Moscow . . . there are few foreigners."

"I'm Austrian. People may assume my family migrated from Russia, but I've never lied like that, and I never mentioned my mother was British because no one ever asked. What does it matter?" She tugged at his arm. "What are you not saying?"

Leo tilted his head, considering. "I accept my promotion on Monday."

Ingrid blinked.

His gaze drifted up and over her as if he were making a pact with something unknown and beyond her. His chest rose and fell with several breaths before he spoke again. "You need not share that information now. Or ever. I'm sure no one will ask and your interviews must always remain consistent."

"Why wouldn't they? I've never lied in them."

Leo's mustache tipped up, but his eyes did not crinkle with the expression. "But you've never mentioned this before tonight either. German, Austrian . . . we can accept. But tensions are growing with the West. It's best not to show interest and never any affiliation." He drew her close and rested his chin atop her head. "You understand, yes?"

His question sounded so innocent, yet his arms, so strong and sure, felt like iron wrapped in velvet. Ingrid left his query unanswered.

Now, peeking from behind the pillar once more, she wondered how to answer. *If* she should answer. Was she ready to give up her past? It might be one of pain, but it was her past, her story, and it was filled with everyone she'd ever loved. Could she deny them, pretend they didn't exist? Or had she surrendered the right to hold on to her past long ago when her father forged her papers and she took them?

Leo's gaze shifted from the depth of the church and collided with her own. His eyes softened as he stared at her with loving steadiness. His calm command soothed her nerves and her misgivings and made her feel as though the night before never happened. Certain she'd imagined the strain between them, she smiled back as the quartet, seated to the right of the chapel's altar, began the first notes of Pachelbel's Canon in D.

"Stop being oversensitive," she whispered to herself. It was absurd to expect Leo to be more or less than he was. He was simply Leo—and he'd been gone to Moscow for so long, she'd simply forgotten his quirks. He loathed surprises and never stepped out of line. He found safety in protocol and flourished with clear directives. Total commitment along his chosen path—perfect integration of action, motivation, body, and soul. His discomfiture wasn't an aberration. It aligned with all she knew and loved about him. He was her safe, calm harbor after a decade of tumult.

Alone, Ingrid took her first steps.

Twenty minutes later, her hand clasped within Leo's, she took her last—out of the chapel and into a waiting Soviet Volga sedan. It zoomed through light Saturday traffic to the small reception her new husband had planned.

Within moments the car turned onto the Kärntner Ring and pulled to a stop at the Hotel Imperial. Leo beamed with pride as he helped her from the car.

Ingrid faltered once again, caught between the past and the present, but she kept her face still. The Hotel Imperial. Though it was once a place she'd cherished, she hadn't stepped foot within the building in almost twenty years. During her childhood, her mother had taken her there for tea the first Saturday of every month. Then they'd go shopping. But all that changed on March 14, 1938, the day Hitler rolled into the city, claiming Austria for his own. He had arrived two days after his troops, to assure himself a warm and victorious welcome, but he needn't have waited, Ingrid's mother relayed with derision. Vienna had welcomed him with crowds ten deep—that was before they knew the terror he'd rain down upon them. The arrests, the deportations, the restrictive laws, and the killings began only days later.

Swallowing down the memories, Ingrid let Leo lead her across the red-carpeted entrance and through the hotel's opulent lobby to a small ballroom facing the hotel's inner courtyard. The walls were covered in gold brocade from ceiling to chair railing. The curtains, royal blue with gold trim, made her feel like she was moving through stars burnishing a midnight sky. Crystal chandeliers completed the fantasy, sending a summer shower of diamond shards of light dancing across the high-polished, deep-toned wood flooring.

A group of their coworkers stood with champagne glasses in hand. Another quartet played music Ingrid didn't recognize in the ballroom's far corner.

She found her closest friend, Svetlana, in the gathering. The taller woman raised her glass before enveloping Ingrid in a quick hug. "This is a happy day."

Ingrid felt tears brimming in her eyes. "It is, but . . ."

Svetlana hugged her again. "It's goodbye too."

Ingrid let her friend misunderstand. A waiter with a silver tray full of small glasses pressed near. Ingrid grabbed one and drank deep. She choked as the liquid burned down her throat.

Svetlana laughed. "Careful, little one. That's not water. Vodka." With a raised brow Svetlana took a glass for herself and gestured for Ingrid to take another.

Ingrid noted other servers holding high similar trays. Once everyone was served, Leo's boss, Comrade Lebedev, raised his glass high and bellowed, *"Górko!"*

"Bitter?" Ingrid hesitated, interpreting the word to a more common Russian synonym.

Leo stepped beside her and slipped an arm around her waist. "It's a custom. Vodka is bitter. It needs a kiss to sweeten it." He laid a gentle kiss on her lips.

The room yelled, *"Górko!"* again and drank.

Three toasts and three kisses later, guests began to make their way to the linen-draped tables laden with food at the far end of the room. Comrade Lebedev drew beside the bride and groom.

"Now to Moscow." He pounded Leo on the back. "Good luck to you, Comrade." He turned to Ingrid. "Will you be happy to go home, Inga?"

Ingrid smiled. "I'll be happy to make it my home, but I have never been to Moscow, Comrade Lebedev."

"Your accent . . . You are so proficient I often forget you are Austrian." Comrade Lebedev, absorbing this remembered revelation, nodded to himself and continued his walk toward the food.

Leo stalled and drew Ingrid's hand to his chest. "Let's dance."

Turning back, Lebedev waved them on. "This is your day. Spin about the floor."

Leo led Ingrid to the center of the room, near the musicians and away from the guests.

She laughed. "In all the time I've worked in that office, he has never once gotten my name right."

Leo drew her close. "Your Austrian heritage will obviously come up in your annual reviews, but it is wise not to share it in the everyday world. Perhaps his nickname for you is best. It's Russian and only a syllable from your own."

"'Inga'? Why would I do that? You said being Austrian wasn't a problem. 'We can accept.' Those were your words last night."

"I remember what I said." Leo pulled back. "Comrade General Secretary Khrushchev is implementing important reforms, but there is still prejudice. I tried to say it last night, but . . ." He glanced around. "Outsiders are not well received. One comment. One pointed finger could ruin you, and me. No one can find out. We must give no one a reason to wonder or examine us closely."

"You always knew I was Austrian."

"But there's more to it now, isn't there?" Leo kissed her forehead. "You'll find it's not so hard. No one will ask . . . We are a private people."

Ingrid followed his steps across the dance floor as she parsed through the layers within his statement. She thought she'd find fear or paranoia in his expression, as his request brimmed with both, but she had not. Ingrid had seen only a firm resolve within her husband's dark eyes.

She peered across the room to their guests. Everyone was laughing and drinking. Her gaze collided with Svetlana, whose admonition returned, once again, with force and encompassed far more than a church wedding.

*"He has aspirations and this will not sit well."*

∞

"To Moscow. To home."

Leo's voice rang with pride as Ingrid surveyed their train compartment. It was wood paneled and, though aged, still held the elegance of the interwar years when people traveled for pleasure and business rather than to move men and munitions. Memories of similar compartments and childhood trips faded away as Leo nuzzled her neck.

The train jerked into motion and Ingrid tried to balance herself by pressing both hands against Leo's chest but failed as he dipped her low in a kiss. Pulling her upright again, Leo guided her toward their sleeper compartment's bench and the narrow ladder to its side.

He smiled down at her. "It was a beautiful day, wasn't it?"

With that, he lifted her into his arms and, after gently peeling back each layer of clothing, guided her up the ladder to their narrow bed, which she found—when tucked close in love—fit two people perfectly.

As the train rolled north into the night, Ingrid, wrapped within Leo's embrace, drifted in and out of sleep. Questions resurfaced in the form of images within her dreams. A workroom. Cut wood. Winter. A quiet man. A carpenter. Tales told. Voices raised.

"Leo? Leo, are you awake?"

"No. You've exhausted me." Leo's voice was tender and he squeezed her tight.

"No. Really."

"I'm awake . . . Is something wrong?"

"I've been wondering . . ." Ingrid twisted to face him and noted, in the faint starlight peeking through the crack in the window's drapes, how his eyes, rounded and relaxed, narrowed with his habitual alertness. Did her new husband feel safe with her, and could he be unguarded and vulnerable with her? She was about to find out.

"When I asked about your father, you said war took him, but you never told me more. What happened to him?"

Leo stiffened. The muscles in his arms pressed against her ribs rather than provide the soft covering they had an instant before. "When did I say that?"

"When you first met me in the park."

His voice dropped to the softest whisper. "What made you think of this now?"

"Vienna . . . I've left my home and you said I need to leave it all behind. But my parents will always be there, my childhood, my . . ." She stopped herself, afraid to feel too much and consequently reveal too much.

"You shouldn't be awake with such thoughts, *dorogaya*. Not on our wedding night. I'm sorry . . . I handled it poorly." He slid his arm from around her and brushed her hair from her face. He kissed her eyes, her cheeks, her mouth.

*Dorogaya. Darling.* She pressed closer, savoring the warmth of the endearment and his passion. When he broke his last kiss, she whispered into the curve of his neck. "Please tell me."

Leo sighed and rolled onto his back, pulling her closer with the motion. A quarter atop him, she snuggled within his embrace.

He spoke into the inch between their lips. "He was denounced and executed when I was seventeen."

"Leo." Ingrid gasped and pushed up and off his chest. Her head tapped the train car's ceiling.

He pulled her down and nestled her securely once again. "We never learned what happened or why. He came home from the Revolution a hero, a medal recipient, but he was different. Quiet. He didn't talk much, but he wasn't a dissenter. He simply wanted to return to his woodworking. Maybe quiet wasn't enough. Maybe it was simple jealousy. A neighbor denounced him in '33 and he was shipped to a gulag. There was no trial. Then we received a letter in '36 stating that he was 'sentenced to ten years without the right to correspondence.'"

"You couldn't write to him?"

"No . . . That particular sentence was used to convey that your family member had been executed." Leo nudged Ingrid closer. "That is why I asked it of you. I'm sorry, but so many were taken then, and it's hard to forget. Everyone regarded their neighbor with suspicion, and thousands, maybe millions, died . . . Lives were destroyed."

"You poor thing. I understand."

"You don't. You can't . . . My brother and I were pulled from school. We lost everything. He died in a work camp, but I was lucky. The factory foreman saw I was smart and snuck me books." Leo shifted his focus back to the low ceiling, as if talking to his past rather than to her. "There was no recovery from denunciation until now. Comrade General Secretary Khrushchev issued a proclamation of rehabilitation last year. It was one of his first acts and I applied."

"'Rehabilitation'? What does that mean?" Ingrid pushed up on her elbows.

Leo's voice grew bright and focused like a sunbeam. "He

wiped my slate clean. I was let back into society. I could join the Party. And because I kept up with my studies, I could test into the officer class. I could receive promotions."

He grinned at her. "It's how I received my post in Vienna and met you. It's how I got my new promotion and am now called back to Moscow. It's how we will be assigned our own apartment in one of the newest sections of Moscow. We are on the brink of great things . . . Stalin was father and I must respect the hard choices he made to put us on the right path and honor the Revolution. But Comrade General Secretary Khrushchev will take us higher. He is building housing, offices, theaters, shops, and factories all over the city. He is funding advancements no one has ever dreamed before. Moscow is now powered by the world's first nuclear power plant at Obninsk. Do you see? Our city, Moscow, is the first in the world to do this."

His arms tightened more. In the moonlight Ingrid couldn't see where she ended and her husband began.

"You will be so happy there. Khrushchev and his reforms give us everything—our own apartment, good food, and good work, and we will help achieve the ideals Marx and Lenin set before us, the great new tomorrow. I can be part of that now. We are part of it."

"But the cost . . ."

"Shh . . . You don't understand." Leo ran a hand down her arm. "This is a good story. A happy story."

Ingrid rested her cheek against his chest as puzzle pieces clicked into place. "That's why my mother's nationality upset you. You think someone will doubt your commitment because of me, that I'll put you at risk again."

"I wish it wasn't so, but yes, I do fear that. I considered not marrying you—" He halted as she pulled away. "Not for me, for you. To protect you. But Comrade Lebedev is right. Your accent is flawless and no one needs to know more. I'm sorry to cause you pain. I couldn't walk away . . . It's not too much to ask, is it?"

Ingrid's gaze followed a beam of light to the crack in the train car's curtains and out to the night sky. She could see moonlight striking out between passing clouds as the train charged toward Moscow. While part of her wanted to balk and declare it was too much to ask, she recognized she had made the same calculation that very morning. Peeking from behind the pillar, she had asked herself what Leo's love meant to her and what she was willing to sacrifice to keep it. Her past? Her memories? Then, as the notes of the music reached her, she took her first step toward him on her own. No one had forced her to do it. And in that step, she had chosen Leo and all that came with him. She had chosen to love and to believe in him. She would not withdraw her love and support now.

"No. It's not too much to ask."

# EIGHT

# Anya

IN A SOCIETY WHERE ALL IS REGULATED AND PROVIDED FOR, I was homeless for a month.

In reality, my housing assignment got lost within the vast bureaucracy that makes up everything here and I was not assigned a place to live. Dmitri offered to let me crash with him, but he didn't get an apartment of his own and cramming into a one-bedroom place with three other guys sounded less than appealing. Sonya also offered, but she was assigned communal housing as well. So I asked my parents if I could move back into my old bedroom.

My job, however, started the day after I landed at Sheremetyevo International Airport. I reported, with all the appropriate paperwork, at 8:00 a.m. that morning to research lab NIIR3 in the Kapotnya District.

My facility specializes in radar and electronic technology— it's all very hush-hush, cutting edge, and well-funded. There are about thirty scientists and another fifteen of us who support them. My job, at its most basic level, is to translate science-speak into Kremlin-speak so the lab gets more funding and the Politburo gets technological advances. It's "the best of the best," my father declared, puffing his cigar, as we discussed it my first night back, while my mother served up my favorite dish of oven-braised veal stew with sour cherries and parsley-roasted potatoes. It was a fantastic supper, and most days I really enjoy my job too.

For that first month, however, I complained about it and everything else each night out with my friends. I droned on about the boring work, the confinement of living with my parents, and my beastly long commute. It shocked me how quickly I fell back into the habit. But that's what we do. We pride ourselves on our discontent and cynicism—we complain, we grumble, we rail.

Only Dmitri saw through me. His amber eyes had danced with challenge. *"You're such a liar. Your work excites you, I can tell. You're having fun."*

I smiled at him. It was small and still filled with longing for all I'd left at Georgetown, but it was real.

Several inches taller than me, he swung an arm around my shoulders, ruffled my hair, and led me to a back booth at Drey Bar. *"Spill it all. Tell me about everything. About him. What you saw. What you did. And you'd better stop teasing me about Pavlina."*

I laughed. Pavlina was the strawberry-haired girl in Class Ten who stole Dmitri's heart. He wrote her some horrible poetry and fed me the line that he couldn't help it, the "love spilled out" of him. I've never let him forget that embarrassment. But I understand it now too. So, with our voices drowned out by the club's pulsating beat, I told him everything, starting that night and continuing each night for about a week. Dmitri let me pour out every detail, every day, and every drama. Every laugh, longing, and loss, too, and I began to feel better.

Living at home also soothed my soul. Mom cooked my favorite dishes, and I didn't need to speak, think, pretend, or project. While I had loved America, I was always "on," always hiding to a degree, and didn't realize how it drained every aspect of my being until I closed my bedroom door my first night back and I was suddenly "off."

I cried like a baby. I cried because Mr. Olivers was right—I found what I needed in the Soviet Union. I reveled in the comfort and safety. I was home. I could be nothing more nor less than me, and that was enough. It both surprised me and disheartened me how quickly and instinctively I felt it, as if I hadn't grown at all in my four years away.

That was my first night.

After a couple weeks I discovered something startling and unexpected, even unwelcome. Once I was no longer exhausted, I became restless. I *had* changed. I felt like I did when I was a kid and had stayed up all night reading an amazing story. My mind would expand and grow within the pages. I'd see things in new ways. I'd become new. Then I'd peek out of the book as the sun rose outside my window and discover nothing in my reality had changed with me.

All those philosophies, books, readings, discussions, trips, friendships—every minute of every day at Georgetown had seared an indelible mark deep within me. And looking around my small room, I began to wonder if I could tuck back within my reality tight enough to survive.

My commute became the only time I felt truly free. In my "beastly long" combination of bus rides and stretches of walking to the Kapotnya District, I was outside the system. I was anonymous. I wasn't where I was supposed to be—making me nowhere at all.

I left my parents' apartment early each morning and caught the bus right outside the building. I then hopped off at a bakery in the Arbat District if I saw a line stretching outside the shop's door, because that meant they still had fresh vatrushki. Those buns are the best, filled with cheese in the winter and often with fresh berries during the summer. I would then jump on another bus and savor my treat for the next stretch of the journey. Book in one hand, warm bun in the other, I was in heaven.

Even deep in a story, I would lift my head with uncanny accuracy at just the right moment to relish the bright reds of St. Basil's Cathedral, the Kremlin, and the Lenin Library, all facing off across Krasnaya Ploshchad. Then on to Gorky Park, the famed park of the Revolution, before the bus crossed over to Pirogovskaya Street and traveled onward past the embassies across the Moskva River.

So while I complained to my friends, there was much I truly enjoyed and savored that first month. The only hiccup was when my mother found my smuggled copy of *To Kill a Mockingbird* under my mattress. She probably found it changing my sheets. She never said a word and neither did I. It simply disappeared— and she was silent and stiff for two days.

That's wrong. We had two hiccups. My first morning home, I couldn't keep my mouth shut about *Pravda*.

"Mother, why do you bother to read that?" I used the Russian word for *Mother* rather than *Mama*. It surprised her.

"'Mother'?" She wrapped her tongue around the word.

"Yes . . . I've grown up." I sounded so smug, so sure of myself. I expected her to chide me and remind me of my roots and my place within our family.

Instead, she tucked a strand of dark hair behind my ear and pulled me into a tight hug. "Yes, I suppose you have."

Once she let go, I pushed the paper across our kitchen table. "You can't swallow all this. You can't believe—"

I stopped as a flash of panic filled her eyes. They darted to the light fixture above us, then back to me. I followed her eyes' path to the white ceramic bowl and bulb that hung above our kitchen table as a flood of discussions returned to me, along with the realization of what was missing for this one.

Mother shook her head and crossed to the radio sitting on the shelf right below the window. She flipped it on and turned up the volume. Shostakovich filled the kitchen.

She then perched on the chair across from me and spread her hands across the table, wiggling her fingers to invite me to place mine within hers. I obeyed. That's how she communicates and passes on wisdom and discipline. We have to be connected.

I watched her lips, as any words I didn't catch, I could read. It's a skill I perfected long ago—we all have to some degree. Conversations drowning in Shostakovich happen all the time.

"Your father hasn't swept in years . . ."

I blinked. When I was a teenager, he "swept" for listening devices all the time. He never talked about it, but Mother said he did it to keep us safe. A friend, she said, lent him the device, then moved away, forgetting my father still had it. It's one of his prized possessions.

I always suspected he was overreacting and that no one cared about my teenage rebellion and snide comments. All my friends ranted and no one else's parents took us seriously. Only my father. My poking and pestering used to really anger him. But rather than argue with me or even tell me to stop, he'd grow still and stern—and "sweep" for bugs.

"Anya, you have changed, but here has not." Mother held my hands tightly. "Tensions are high and you must be careful. You will be watched closely for some time. We all will." She bit her lip. "They need to make sure you are still loyal."

"Mother." I groaned, not because she was overreacting or wrong but because she was right.

I expected her usual soft sigh of resignation as she got up to circle the table and hug me again, with a consoling *"This can be hard."*

It didn't come.

Instead her eyes hardened to ice and her grip tightened. "I see you. I see your eyes narrow in annoyance. You walk differently. You talk differently. You think differently. They will see too . . . We have been lucky. No one has turned on us, but people can think we reach too high, that you reach too high, and that you are now *autsayder*. Anyone can talk."

She used an antiquated term for *outsider*, employed more commonly during the purges of the 1930s than today. It made her point. I nodded. "I'll be careful."

She stood to make her morning coffee. I watched in silence. For all my mother's calm conformity—the woman never makes a ripple much less a wave—she has this one tiny cultural rebellion. She adores coffee.

We are a tea nation. Not only was coffee rare until several years ago, it wasn't even coffee at first. She tried to introduce it to Sonya, Dmitri, and me when we were fourteen. We had just joined the Komsomol, that next step in Party membership from the Young Pioneers, and she wanted to celebrate our great honor. She glowed with pride as she marveled at our new pins, ironed our neckerchiefs, and set the mugs before us. She thought the honor was worthy of her extravagance, but we didn't find it much of a celebration at all, considering her "coffee" was a dreadful drink of chicory, oats, and spices that we choked down with grimaces.

It wasn't until a couple years after that, when my father surprised her with real beans, a grinder, and a coffeepot, that I learned what the drink was supposed to be. Mother cried happy tears that day, and it became my first lesson in "reaching too high."

Every neighbor took note of our new luxury and stopped in for a cup. Mother served each and every one with grace, even opening our door at 5:00 a.m. for Comrade Chernov who had just gotten off working a night shift. She was afraid to disappoint, fearing someone might get envious and talk out of turn. She used a whole month's ration of beans that first day, caffeinating anyone who knocked on our door.

I moved out ten months ago and I still miss her coffee. I miss her hugs, meals, and daily care too. I also miss my commute. I now live in my assigned building filled with engineers and administrators, all working here in Kapotnya. We flood the sidewalks and streets at the same time each and every day as we walk the same direction to and from the several labs and facilities situated on the district's south border. I am exactly where I am expected to be now, at the times I am expected to be there.

I also miss my parents' larger allotment of ration cards and their access to the State's better shops and services.

Coming home, that was a shock for me. During my time at Georgetown, the ration-card system grew far beyond ancillary items, like a television, dress shoes, or a new appliance. Coupons now extend deeply into foods and personal products—things I call daily necessities like sausages, grains, butter, deodorant, and soap. Far more of our daily meals come from canned goods, and oftentimes that's all I can find on the store shelves.

While it's true we've always run lean on consumer goods, the West's economic sanctions, protesting Brezhnev's ongoing war in Afghanistan, have cut deep. I miss America's full grocery store shelves. I miss fresh produce—green lettuces, bunches of celery and carrots, broccoli, yellow squash, spinach. Yes, I miss my vegetables. I miss the *snap* when biting into them and the color they gave to my plate. I'm so tired of opening cans.

A knock on the edge of my desk startles me from my

daydreams. "Anya. I have the final circuitry requirements and component list for the RP-23 radar."

I sit straight. It's the new lightweight radar my lab is developing to fit within the MiG-23 fighter jets—a pulse radar that can "look down and shoot down" any target. And considering America's President Reagan's increasingly vitriolic and anti-Soviet rhetoric, many are eager to get their hands on it. The gossip among the scientists is that some Politburo members are so terrified of the US and its nuclear capabilities, they relish the idea of employing this technology in a first-strike capacity.

My stomach drops and I set to work. This is the system Minister of Defense Nikolai Ivanovich Petrov has been waiting for. His office has sent daily update requests for the past two weeks, making everyone on this project twitchy for today's hard deadline. Because finished or not, I fly to Vienna tomorrow for my first face-to-face meeting with Petrov. Everyone is terrified something will go wrong.

Rumor is the minister of defense doesn't care how the radar is wired or about the intricacies of the circuitry, technology, or aviation, though I still need those answers. He wants the details as to how high and low it captures enemy aircraft, its coverage and range capabilities, who has the technology to detect it or stop it, and—if all those answers please him—how much it will cost and how quickly it can be produced.

And lest I forget—as his last request outlined in detail—I need to report on how many lives it can save and, most important, how many enemies it can kill.

Petrov sees a new weapon to use against the United States of America.

I see Scott.

⌬

"Nyet." I spread my feet shoulder-width apart as if preparing to withstand a blow. The leather soles of my loafers slip on the linoleum. I shift, center myself, and repeat my one word. "No."

"No?" Comrade First Lieutenant Wadim Rogov stares at me. He didn't misunderstand either word; he's simply shocked.

I'm shocked, too, but for entirely different reasons. "You can have no reason to ask this of me."

This afternoon I handed my drawings and notes for the RP-23 radar to our lab's KGB officer. He's the one who will arrange their secure transport to tomorrow's meeting. Yet Rogov seems convinced I'm spiriting State secrets away to Vienna on my person. In front of everyone lining up to go home, he has basically ordered me to submit to a strip search.

"You are carrying confidential material out of the Union of Soviet Socialist Republics. This is standard procedure." He waves his hand at me as if I am no more than a bug to him. A pesky one. "You will comply."

"But I'm not. I'm simply getting on a plane, as ordered, and walking Minister Petrov through the work your superior, Comrade Captain Stanslych, took from me earlier today. There is nothing on me." I pat my arms, my hips, my thighs. I hold my palms out. Nothing here.

"Remove your coat. Untuck your blouse. Take off your shoes." He narrows his eyes. "I will not ask again."

He didn't ask the first time, but I keep my mouth shut. His tone tells me I'm not going to win this one. It's a direct order and you obey direct orders. I remove my coat, untuck my blouse, slip off my loafers, and stand stock-still. The line behind me has silenced. Every eye and ear are focused on the two of us.

Rogov takes his time. He starts at my neck, right behind my ears, and pats me down from head to toe. Thoroughly. No floppy disk, piece of paper, scrap of tissue, or errant strand of hair could evade his hands.

Halfway down my body, my mind drifts back to a meeting with Sasha and I hear my words, as if spoken in this moment rather than a year and a half ago. *"They're Americans, Sasha. They have constitutional rights against that kind of stuff."*

The memory is bright and convicting, blinding me with truth. *That's the difference,* I think. Forget the bedazzled clothes, the neon colors, the malls, the plentiful vegetables. Forget it all. It's window dressing hiding the truth. None of that matters because only one thing counts.

Rights.

And I have none.

I glance behind me. Now each person in line is staring at the floor, the wall, the back of someone else's head—anywhere and everywhere but at me. They are all scared they could be next. And they might be.

When Rogov reaches my feet, he gestures to my waist and waits for me to tuck my blouse back into my skirt. He then waves his hand to my shoes. I slip on my second shoe and he tosses me my coat, after running it through his hands like wringing water from a dishrag.

Beyond humiliated but unwilling to let him see a glimmer of it in my eyes, I snatch my coat and march out of the building. A gust of wind hits and fills my eyes with tears. That's what I tell myself.

I dash them away with a single swipe of my hand. Wind or no wind, no one is going to see me cry. Ever.

I march straight home. I'd planned to meet friends out, but I call Dmitri and tell him I can't make it. I lie and say I don't feel well. "It was something I ate at lunch today."

"You can eat anything."

"I'm not coming out," I whine. "I'll see you when I get back from Vienna."

I can tell he doesn't believe me, but I throw down my lie once more with conviction and hang up. I can't tell him the truth, not on an open phone line. Besides I'm not sure he wouldn't side with Rogov. His education at MGIMO was very different from mine at Georgetown.

I crawl into bed until a pounding at my door drags me out. "Stop that banging!"

Dmitri fills the doorway. He says nothing as he steps past me into my apartment. "You're coming out for dinner. Something comforting and easy on that delicate stomach of yours. Get dressed."

I don't argue. I don't want to. I leave him in my tiny anteroom and go pull on a pair of jeans and a sweater. He's holding out my coat for me when I return.

"Bully," I whisper, but there's no bite to it.

"Wimp."

Within minutes we're seated at a little place down my street that serves dishes that remind you of an ideal home—a home in the country where your babushka has fresh produce from her garden and all the time in the world to cook it to slow perfection. An imaginary home.

I try to tell him about Rogov, but I can't. Halfway through my *kundiumy*—dumplings made with mushrooms, greens, eggs, and buckwheat—my anger morphs to shame. Because I should have known better.

"You go to Vienna tomorrow?"

"Yes. But unfortunately, I'll be back tomorrow night. I was hoping to stay and see the city. Have you been?"

"If I have I can't tell you." He winks, but his voice feels forced rather than light.

When I first got home over a year ago, Dmitri brought his MGIMO buddies out with us all the time. They were shiny and bright—newly minted from the State's top school—and they "owned" the atmosphere. They exuded secrets, power, and a slick arrogance that drew everyone to them. Dmitri was the shiniest of them all, calling for shots and wooing a handful of girls each night.

He wasn't interested in any of them. He was simply trying to have fun—frantic fun, yes, but still fun. It was contagious. We'd laugh, dance, and drink, and he made me feel shiny too. I could put away my day and my dreams and, sitting or dancing with him, believe that everything we imagined as kids was coming true for both of us.

Recently, though, he's been wanting to hang out, just the two of us, rather than join our friends at the clubs. He's been wanting to talk. It's in these moments we break through our cynical and glossy veneers and I realize what liars we both are.

I finally open my mouth to tell him about Rogov. I need him to chastise me, to commiserate with me, or to simply hug me. I'm not sure which will make me feel better. He cuts me off, however, before I can begin.

"You and me, Anya? I need to tell you something."

I pause, spoon midway to my mouth. He's invoked our phrase we started the day we met at age six. In one day I saved him from disciplinary action by helping him memorize our Little Octobrist oath, and he saved me from a couple of bullies. After I got knocked down and he'd chased them away, Dmitri reached down to lift me from the dirt and asked, *"You and me?"* I nodded and we've been best friends ever since. We still invoke it to remind each other of our first loyalty: our friendship. I nod.

"Have you heard of the new movement in Poland?"

"What movement?"

He leans forward. "It's called Solidarity . . ."

I feel more hopeful today.

Maybe it's the cool, clear sunshine. Maybe it's the distance from last evening's humiliation. Maybe it's because I spent all night trying to justify Rogov's actions, reminding myself he had authority to do what he did. Maybe it's Dmitri. That he came for me last night. That he didn't accept the lie that I was sick. Maybe it's that hopeful movement he told me about that's growing in Poland, Solidarity. Maybe it's because I'm heading to Vienna.

The feeling only grows as the plane descends. I watch as buildings and open green spaces come into view. Vienna is not like Moscow—grey, industrial, cement, and imposing. And it's nothing like America, all shiny and new. It's old. Empire old. I can see the layout from above as streets circle palaces, parks, and churches. There are so many steeples I lose count.

After my meeting this morning, I have nothing planned until my flight home tonight. I'm going to spend the whole day exploring the city: cafés, museums, and maybe I'll even find a church and listen to music. I loved doing that at Georgetown. The organist at one of the campus chapels practiced every Thursday afternoon, and Scott and I rarely missed one. He played Bach, Beethoven, Haydn, Schubert, and other composers, along with hymns I can't even name. The music wove tonal tapestries that lifted my soul to places it had never soared.

I step off the plane and immediately see a man in a dark suit waiting at the end of the Jetway. Even without a placard, I sense he's here for me. He's short, muscular, and focused. KGB. I sigh, then feel my breath catch in hope as his focus shifts beyond me. My heartbeat of relief vanishes when he nods to someone behind me and includes me in the gesture. I turn my head. His counterpart—equally stocky but tall—stands at my left shoulder.

"You were on my flight? You're following me?" I pull back, bumping into a man trying to walk around us.

"I'm your escort."

I turn to the dark suit facing us both. "And you are?"

"Your guide."

Without another word, even to each other, the two men flank me and we proceed out of the terminal to a black ZiL sedan waiting curbside.

Within a half hour, I'm at our embassy spreading out the packets of materials I find waiting for me on a large mahogany meeting table.

Within two hours, I have walked Comrade Minister of Defense Petrov, who is in Vienna for preliminary Warsaw Pact–NATO discussions, through the costs and capabilities of the RP-23 radar.

Within three hours, he has signed off on all forms, in triplicate, authorizing further development and funding, culminating in a live test scheduled for next January.

Within an hour of organizing, then handing all the papers back to a KGB officer for secure transport to Moscow, I'm given a sandwich-to-go and find myself sitting in a hard plastic chair back at the airport. My still unnamed "escort" sits silent and obdurate by my side. He says we will remain here the full seven hours until our flight boards.

So much for exploring and sightseeing, so much for enjoying a walk, sitting in a café, stepping into a church, or listening to a little music. So much for posting the letter to Scott I've been carrying around, wishing to mail it *outside* the Soviet Union. So much for that feeling of hope that fizzled away a good four hours ago.

I'm so mad I could cry. But I won't.

Ever.

# NINE

# Ingrid

INGRID PULLED THE PIE PAN FROM THE OVEN AND CRINGED. Again.

In ten months of marriage she had tried to learn to cook. Her mother had been an excellent cook and an outstanding host, but the ingredients were strange in Ingrid's new country, the traditions different, and each night she felt lost in her own small kitchen.

Her thoughts drifted to the dishes of her childhood. Wiener schnitzel so light the breading elevated the veal encased therein; *Paprikahendl*, her favorite paprika-roasted chicken; *Martinigansl*, her mother's signature dish, a goose cooked to perfection and sauced with a heady mixture of wine, orange juice, lingonberries, and juniper berries.

In those last years she recalled that Mutti only made that expensive delicacy for the top echelon of the Nazi leadership. Now she understood why—how else was one going to loosen their tongues?

At first Ingrid thought the more soup-based dishes of the Russian countryside would be easier to master. But there were so many variations, she seemed to miss them all rather than land on one that struck the right note.

Borscht could be a cold, smooth, bright pink soup or a hot stew filled with vegetables and meat. It should not, as she commented to Leo after her first attempt, land somewhere between lukewarm and oddly thick, as if all the ingredients simply dissolved.

Her *Ukha* was no better. Certain she could master the fish soup, she stood in line for hours and garnered angry stares as she bought three different types of fish—cod, halibut, and salmon, along with cod liver—at the shop last February.

"How did the broth get cloudy?" Leo pushed at the chunks within his opaque bowl.

"I have no idea. Vada, next door, said it was a clear soup."

"Usually it is."

If it weren't for her early discovery that *smetana*—sour cream—covered a variety of culinary sins, she wasn't sure Leo would not have divorced her already.

Ingrid was so focused on pulling dinner from the oven, she didn't hear her husband enter the apartment.

"Is something burning? It smells like piroshkis."

Ingrid startled, dropped the pie onto the stovetop, and poked at it. "Yes."

"Piroshkis are puff pastries rather than a dished pie."

"I didn't make enough dough. I thought if I put it all together in a pie and cooked it longer, it might work out." Ingrid wiped her hands down her apron and noted the beet stain she left behind. She would have to let it soak in the sink, then take it to the building's laundry room in the morning.

"Stop laughing." She dabbed at the stain with a dish towel. "It's ruined. I can smell that the bottom's burned . . . And I wanted to surprise you tonight. I wanted to celebrate."

"Celebrate what?" Leo leaned against the counter. "Are you?" His voice lifted, as it had with the same anticipation each month of their marriage.

Ingrid shook her head, both in answer to his question and to dispel her growing fears. Her hand reflexively reached to soothe her perpetually sore shoulder. She had begun to wonder over the past few months if the bomb had shaken her more than she'd thought all those years ago.

Ingrid rushed on with her news. "Austria. Vienna. Didn't you hear? We were granted independence yesterday. There will be a treaty signed and all the troops will leave. No more dividing the city."

Unable to share her excitement with anyone else, Ingrid allowed the words to pour out of her in a torrent. "Can we go visit? Can we go see? The barricades will be torn down. They will rebuild now and—"

"Where did you hear this?" Leo's voice emerged tight and low.

"At the butcher. Two women stood whispering in line behind me . . . Isn't it common knowledge?" Ingrid laid down the dish towel.

"Did you talk to them? Did you share that it was your home?"

"No. Of course not. I didn't say a word. I thought—"

Leo pushed off the counter and raised a hand to stop her words. "It won't be in the papers until tomorrow."

"But they talked about it today?" As soon as Ingrid asked the question, she stumbled upon the answer. The samizdats. The illegal papers passed from friend to friend and printed at any hour of the day. She had never seen one, but she had heard of them. From Leo. He repeatedly warned her not to accept one, read one, and certainly never get caught with one.

"Did they notice your interest?"

At her soft "no" he wrapped his arms around her. "Good.

While someone from Vienna might welcome this news, it comes at a high price for the Soviet Union."

Ingrid nodded her promise of silence. She knew he was right. Ten months had proved him right.

Within days of moving into their apartment, Ingrid had found that even the slightest comment could raise an eyebrow, generate a probing question, and leave one doubting. Even worse, any comment might get reported and a knock on the door could come at night, with a "request" for an interview. It happened to Vada.

Ingrid met her next-door neighbor the week they moved into their apartment. Young and effulgent, Vada invited her into her home for tea and welcomed Ingrid with genuine warmth. For months, Ingrid would have named Vada as her only true friend.

Then a few weeks ago, sitting in her apartment folding laundry, Vada congratulated Ingrid on Leo's most recent promotion.

"He hasn't told me this. How—?" Ingrid blinked. "Do you work with him at the Administrative Office?"

"Yes . . . No . . . I merely handle travel for government officials, but I have heard his name mentioned."

"Does he travel?" Ingrid thought back to the nights Leo worked late, even into the next day. "Where does he go?"

Vada's face reddened and her hands fluttered over the socks, underwear, and towels still unfolded between them. Within moments she shooed Ingrid out her door. Two days later she disappeared—for an entire day.

Now she avoided Ingrid. Vada was no longer curious and kind. She was quiet and contained, keeping to herself. She only left her apartment for work or for necessary shopping. And of that day, no one said a word. It was as if it never happened.

"Let's open a bottle of wine to drink with your pie." Leo's suggestion drew Ingrid back to the present. She followed him with plates and the pie to the round table in the corner of their living room.

As she set the table, he opened a large corner cabinet and retrieved the special bottle of wine his boss had given him to celebrate the very promotion, to captain, that Vada had referenced.

Halfway through the pie and the wine, Leo laid down his fork. "It's truly a night to celebrate. I have a surprise for you . . . I have hired help for you here at home."

Ingrid felt her eyes prick with tears. "Is my housekeeping that bad or my cooking that horrible?"

"Not at all." Leo laughed. "Since you began your job last month, you haven't had as much time, and I was given permission for this. It's a rare honor."

*Her job.* That was another of Leo's surprises for which he'd received "permission." He returned home one day with papers outlining her job assignment and instructions to report to an office building just off Krasnaya Ploshchad the following morning. *"The Bureau of Historical Archives needs people with language skills to file old documents. See? You use those skills, which some might frown upon, to benefit the State and no one complains."* Now she worked in a dark, windowless room, filing papers, wondering if warmth or spring could ever reach that dank space.

Stunned, Ingrid sat silent. Leo didn't notice and continued talking. "It's not that I don't enjoy my piroshkis crisp, even burned and served like pie, but this . . ." He reached over and pressed a finger between her brows. "This frown I cannot have. I promised to take care of you. Part of that is helping you as best I can."

He continued. "Her name is Dolores Galecki. Originally from Poland, she worked for Comrade Bortsov before his transfer to London last week, and she has passed all the security clearances to work with people in our office. Bortsov highly recommends her."

An incongruence focused Ingrid's attention. "You worked with Comrade Bortsov?"

She had met the man a couple months earlier. He was watchful, secretive, and sharp, and she had heard rumors as to his occupation.

"We crossed paths." Leo reached for her hand. "Are you not pleased?"

"I am." Ingrid slid her hand back across the table, cut into her pie, and lied. "I was thinking how nice it will be to have someone around."

Leo smiled and returned to his dinner. After a few bites, in what he may have felt to be congenial silence but Ingrid found cool and prickling, he spoke again. His voice was full of its initial jubilance. "She will arrive at eight tomorrow morning and work six days a week. You may choose her day off."

"Tomorrow? So soon?" Ingrid noted Leo's lips turn downward. She waved her fork airily. "I need time to prepare for her."

"Not at all. She is coming to relieve you from that."

"Sundays." Ingrid forced a tone of light enthusiasm. "That will be her day off. It's the only afternoon you are home from work. I don't want someone in our apartment then."

Leo brightened again. "Very wise. I agree. No Sundays."

As the evening progressed Ingrid found her attention captured by small inconsistencies revealed over the months. She parsed through each of her husband's comments, wondering what was true, what was false, and what she was imagining.

She thought of Leo's intelligence, intensity, eagerness to please, and love for rules and structure. She thought of how he had taken her books off their shelves days after she'd arranged them, with a *"No one has these books,"* and tucked them away in their bedroom closet. She thought of how many of his friends, including Bortsov, worked within the KGB, and how he pulled the sheets over their heads at night when they whispered their most intimate secrets or made love. She thought of his slow, thoughtful answers and slight pauses only to be followed by over-bright smiles and conversational changes. She wondered what he was hiding.

And now, with someone in the house to keep watch over her, she wondered if she'd ever find out.

∽

The woman hired was not at all what Ingrid expected. She determined Dolores would be old, thin, sour, and grumpy—a wizened Russian babushka-type woman, with sharp eyes and a critical tongue.

Instead, Dolores was not much older than Ingrid herself, perhaps in her late thirties, heavyset in a healthy way, with light brown hair twisted and pinned carefully at the nape of her neck. Her grey-blue eyes, though wary and assessing, were not cruel.

She stood inside the front door that first morning and examined the apartment in silent consternation. Finally, she turned to Ingrid. "I am Dolores." She said her three words in slow, clear Russian and offered nothing more.

"Hello, I am Inga," Ingrid replied in Polish. While "Inga" rather than "Ingrid" rolled off her tongue smoothly after almost a year, it still scraped within her. "It's nice to meet you."

The woman blinked. "You speak Polish."

"Not well." Ingrid gestured into the living room. Dolores followed her. "Would German work better?"

"I speak German," Dolores replied in Russian. "Comrade Bortsov insisted on Russian, but—" Dolores stopped herself. She stared at Ingrid, then blinked at something she found within her. "I do not enjoy it."

Ingrid felt something shift between them but was unsure if she had stepped closer or farther from danger. After all, Leo had chosen this woman for reasons of his own. She pressed her lips together, nodded, and made a decision. "When we are alone, we will speak German then."

"Danke dir." *Thank you.*

Ingrid sat and motioned for Dolores to do the same. Dolores took the room's only other chair, leaving the love seat empty between them.

Unsure what to say, Ingrid scanned the apartment. Almost its entirety was visible from her vantage point. Identical to every other unit within the building, the front door opened into the living room with the door to the galley kitchen off the back. One bedroom flanked this central room on the right, with their bathroom next to it. Next to the kitchen was one last door—a thimble-sized coat closet that held Leo's coat, Ingrid's two coats, and a pair of boots for each. While it was a luxury to live alone rather than in a communal apartment, it was still only a few hundred square feet in total. Dolores would soon uncover everything within it and everything about her. When not at work, Ingrid conceded there would be no escaping Leo's latest "gift."

Ingrid stopped her racing thoughts and focused on Dolores once more. "Where are you from?"

"Kraków."

"Do you like it here in Moscow?"

"What I like is irrelevant. I have been here since I was fourteen." Dolores stood. "I will see your kitchen now."

Ingrid stood as well and gestured to the door only a few feet away. As Dolores stepped into her kitchen, Ingrid reached into the hall closet for her light coat. Staying was futile. There was nothing Dolores could not see or find within seconds.

Ingrid had asked permission to be late to work, but she wanted out. Her one place of sanctuary no longer existed. "I will be home from work at six tonight."

"That is fine."

Standing just outside the kitchen's open doorway, Ingrid could hear their few cupboards opening and closing.

"I will have dinner ready."

"Wha—? What will you make?" Ingrid swallowed, embarrassed her voice cracked within her own home.

"I haven't taken stock of your pantry yet." Ingrid stepped forward to assist, but Dolores shooed her away. "I will handle it."

With that Ingrid left.

She paused outside her neighbor's door. Vada had once been the one she could talk to. She raised her hand to knock, then lowered it just as fast. Vada was no longer her friend. She no longer spoke to Ingrid. She never even glimpsed at her.

Ingrid continued down the hallway to the stairwell. Two flights below, she knocked on another apartment door. Helka had just given birth and would be home. She was forthright and bold, and Ingrid believed they might be friends. And Ingrid would not make the mistake she and Vada had possibly made weeks before.

She gave the door a soft double tap and Helka answered immediately. "Inga? . . . You're lucky I was passing to the kitchen. I might not have heard you."

Ingrid almost laughed. Helka's apartment was the same size as her own, and she could hear everything, even noises from the apartment two units away. "I didn't want to wake you if you were sleeping."

Helka gestured to the bassinet standing in the center of their living room only feet away. "He's the one who sleeps all the time. Not me."

"Is Boris home?"

Helka nodded toward the bedroom. "He's on the hospital's night shift this month. He's sleeping too."

Ingrid gestured into the hallway. The questions she wanted to ask could not be posed in Helka's apartment.

"I had planned to be late for work today, but . . ." Ingrid swallowed. "Leo's new maid doesn't need my interference. Would you like to take a walk?"

"Yes. Please." The younger woman grinned. "He just ate, so he'll sleep for a while now."

Within moments Helka grabbed her shoes and her sweater and they were down several flights of stairs, out the building's front door, and headed to Vorontsovsky Park.

While they chatted nonsense for the few blocks along Bolshaya Gruzinskaya, Helka turned to Ingrid as they reached the park's green expanse. "What's this about?"

Ingrid opened her mouth to dissimulate, wanting to approach her friend with subtlety and not commit herself to the embarrassment of not knowing or to the risk of probing. But one look at her friend's perceptive eyes told her she could not.

"Leo hired a maid for me, as I said . . . ," she began. "She previously worked for Comrade Bortsov."

"Who was promoted to rezident in London." Helka's statement lifted in wonder. Ingrid had caught those tones before. In a society that proclaimed all equal, she found this particular note of awe, for those rising in power and influence, fascinating.

They walked a few steps before Helka said, "Is there a question there?"

"Perhaps . . . You work for the KGB."

"I manage meeting logistics, Inga. I have no idea about the

115

First Directorate. But they are a tight group, aren't they? Speaking of Bortsov, he was there last weekend."

"Your brother's wedding. I completely forgot to ask. How was it?"

"It was fine." Helka sighed. "Pretty good. They both got what they wanted." She sniggered at Ingrid's blank expression. "Promotions."

"I don't understand."

"The KGB doesn't promote single men beyond the first levels. They must marry." Helka's mouth twisted in a sardonic smile. "Leverage is a powerful motivator, and there's very little with a single man. So Anton married to secure his promotion, and Nikita got one too . . . Let's just hope they don't mess it up. No divorces in the KGB either."

Helka stopped. "I should get back. Stop by later this week. I want to hear all about this new maid." She gave Ingrid a quick hug and dashed off to her newborn son.

Ingrid dropped onto the nearest bench. While she had learned little about her maid, she had learned much about her marriage. Snippets long floating free fell into place.

Questions churned all day, and by dinnertime there was no holding them back. "Do you work for the KGB?"

Leo glanced to the radio, then back to his wife, as if now understanding why she had turned it on the moment he entered the apartment. "What would make you ask that?"

"Dolores. You mentioned she worked for Comrade Bortsov, who is now rezident in London. That's a top KGB title, right? And . . ." She clasped her courage tight. "You asked me to marry you right after your trip here, right before you took your promotion. Was it a requirement? Did you have to marry to accept?"

"Who have you been talking to?"

It wasn't a denial.

"No one." Ingrid's courage, built all day in the silence of her mind, faltered.

"Vada?"

"No. Please." Ingrid reached for her husband's arm, but he stepped away. "She is so frightened she talks to no one." She shook her head. "I've simply paid attention."

"I see." Leo stared at her, and Ingrid felt she was absorbing someone new, a stranger. Gone was his vulnerability, his mild gentleness. There was no trace of any softness in the plane of his cheeks, the cut of his jaw, and especially none in his dark eyes. Had she imagined it all along?

Leo stepped toward her and Ingrid forced herself to stand still and not step back. "Stop paying attention. Do you understand? We will not talk about my work. Ever." He gestured to the stove. "Now, please, let's get Dolores's dinner on the table."

# TEN

# Anya

I BURROW DEEPER INTO MY COAT. SPRING HASN'T COME TO Moscow yet, and a vicious wind kicks up off the river. I pause to stare at the brightly lit Krasnaya Ploshchad, Red Square, standing in stark contrast to the black sky above. Without a single cloud a curtain of stars drapes over the buildings like a canopy of glittering jewels. I miss this in summertime. Somehow the stars aren't quite so bright. They need a chill to bring out their glory.

The power and majesty of St. Basil's and Spasskaya Tower take my breath away, and I'm reminded of my first Victory Day parade. I was about four years old and that May morning was unusually warm. I remember that I wore my new red sweater. My father stood right where I'm standing now, lifted me on his shoulders high above the crowd, and explained each of the glories passing by. He was so proud of our country and so excited to share in my first parade. His excitement made me proud too.

Like tonight's stars, the day was mesmerizing. Red was draped everywhere—symbolizing the blood of the workers, of the Red Army, of the Revolution, and of the Union's new dawn. The bands, the marching, the music—I can still feel it pounding through me, my blood surging in syncopated beat with its tempo. The missiles.

A guffaw escapes.

A couple walking by stops and stares at me. I raise a hand in apology. *The missiles.* Every time I think I've let him go, something draws me back.

Scott was shocked when I let that detail slip. I think I was describing a parade for the Great Patriotic War, but it hardly matters. We pull out our missiles for both. Why is that odd?

"You have missiles in your parades?" His eyes rounded to nearly twice their normal size. "Arms? Real missiles? The kind countries shoot at each other?"

"They're stunning. Huge trailers carry them between the military divisions. They're as big as grain silos. You can't help but gasp in awe at the size and power of them." I blinked. Scott wasn't nodding or smiling. His lips had parted in an odd slack-jawed gape. "Don't you like them?"

When he didn't reply, a new thought occurred to me. "Wait . . . Haven't you seen yours? Don't you have missiles in your parades?"

"No, Anya!" Scott exclaimed. "We have never, I promise you, had a single missile rolling down any American street to celebrate the Fourth of July or any other holiday." Then he winked at me and lowered his voice. "And I doubt the West Germans do either."

Scott privately teased me for weeks after that. And I accepted it—until he started picking on Krasnaya Ploshchad. "Everything about you people is aimed at war and destruction," he claimed one day after a particularly offensive Government Relations lecture.

"*You people*? Have you serious? You speak that about me?" I was so upset and furious I failed to construct my English verbs correctly, which added humiliation to the mix.

He shoulder-bumped me. "I didn't mean it like that."

I sidestepped him and picked up my pace.

"Anya! Anya, wait." He caught up with me within a few strides and slid an arm around me. I wanted to push him away, but I couldn't. Even in those few seconds of walking away, I understood why he said it. It was what he'd been taught to believe—what all Americans believed. They don't know us—the real people living, working, and trying to survive day by day in my country. And until coming to Georgetown, I didn't know them. When I was growing up, America represented everything base and wrong. Americans were "you people" to me as well.

Tucked under Scott's arm, I tried to explain Red Square to him, because, unlike the missiles, Krasnaya Ploshchad is defining for us in all the best ways.

"Yes, we are a fighting culture, but not like Professor Michaels said today. He was right about the military structure behind our government, which came about after the October Revolution. But he's wrong about Red Square. It wasn't named for the Revolution, blood, or the Red Army. St. Basil's is six hundred years old. Most of the towers within the Kremlin are even older. Red, *krasni* in the past and now *krasivi* in modern Russian, means 'beautiful.' It signifies something lovely and right and good. Red doesn't always mean fighting, war, fear, and anger."

"You're right . . . It's also the color of passion, love, and really good wine." He winked again. "Am I forgiven?"

"Yes." I tried not to laugh. I fell in love with him that afternoon.

"Why didn't you raise your hand and correct Professor Michaels today?"

I bit my lip. That was part of why I was upset, furious, and humiliated too. I didn't speak up. I didn't defend my homeland. If anyone who mattered—Igor, for one—ever found out, it wouldn't be good. We Foreign Studies students are to be poster children for a superior way of life. Yet I didn't rise to the occasion. I sat like a silent coward while an American professor berated my homeland.

"I can't fight all that alone. I only *almost* fit in here because people think I'm from the GFR—" I closed my eyes. I'd messed up again. "West Germany. I can't risk it . . . And just because your Senator McCarthy's Red Scare ended, doesn't mean Americans trust us. This ongoing Cold War shows you don't. And we don't trust you. If I've learned anything, it's that we trust you less and fear you more."

"I trust you." Scott slid his hand down my arm and captured my hand within his. "And I'm sorry about all that."

I reached up and kissed his cheek.

Even tonight, I can feel the slight scratchiness of his cheek, the warmth of his skin against my lips. I shake my head to banish the moment and the memory. It does no good remembering that gleam in his eyes, the smell of him, or the electricity that raced through me at his touch. The memories still crash into me each and every night as I try to sleep—I can't let them devastate any more daytime moments as well.

Scott was true to his word. He started a letter campaign within weeks of my departure. Boring letters that brought me to laughing tears at the banality of his days. But through the laughter, there were real tears as well because I felt him in every word.

I went to the grocery store today missing you. They had a new kind of mac 'n' cheese, but I couldn't buy it. It cost $1.17! But I think the inflation that's plagued us is coming to an end. Which is a good thing, as I now pay my own bills and I have seven bills every month. Electricity, rent, telephone—it's a big number for a simple guy like me.

I got so worked up about all those bills, I walked right out of the grocery store with nothing but apples, Doritos, and Cheez Whiz. So that was dinner.

Afterward, I tried to go running. It ended as badly as you'd expect, and I thought of you then, too, because I had to stop. I almost threw up. I could hear you laughing.

I sat down on the steps of the Jefferson Memorial to let my stomach settle, and as the sun set, I thought about life and love. It was all very poetic.

*Life and love.* To the KGB readers, it was a throwaway comment. But it meant the world to me—and Scott knew it would.

We once stayed awake all night, sitting on the brightly lit steps of the Jefferson Memorial, debating life, thought, love, and eternity. And in the early hours of the morning, our debate turned confessional and I shared with him dreams I'd never shared with another soul, not even Dmitri. There was never any freedom at home to dream. But sitting on those marble steps facing the Potomac River, I let myself imagine desires rather than duty. Scott did the same.

I fell a little more in love with him that night too.

I dig my hands into my pockets. I wish summer would come. I'm so tired of this cold. My fingers feather the edges of Scott's last letter. I've been carrying it with me for a week now, and its once-crisp edges are soft and fraying. He again mentioned his Rose Beuret with no hints as to her identity.

He thinks it's endearing, but it's been almost two years. His letters arrive less frequently now, but they still arrive, and the searing pain and loss they bring haven't diminished one bit. I feel most saddened for the hope Scott still carries. He needs to let me go. When he does that, maybe I can let him go too. But this open question—this silly Rose Beuret—somehow keeps us together.

I release the letter, pull my hand out of my pocket, and pound the night club's door.

Cat Club is located just around the north side of Red Square in the basement of an old office building. If you aren't aware of it, you'll never find it.

It's our new spot. We've got one each week, as such clubs are popping up all over Moscow. Crowded basement scenes filled with our generation—dancing, drinking, laughing, yelling, and doing who knows what to whom in dank and dark back corners.

The bouncer lets me in with a grunt, and I work my way through the crowd searching for my friends. Instead I land upon Dmitri, alone and slumped over at the bar. While disappointing, it's not surprising. Finding him this way, too drunk for this early in the night, happens more frequently these days. I search the dance floor and locate all the others. My heart breaks for Dmitri—he loves to dance.

"Hey." I drop onto the stool next to him and shoulder-bump him. We were great when I first got back, but Dmitri has put distance between us lately. I sense he's hiding things, and I'm not sure if it's that he won't share or that he can't. I can't blame him; I'm hiding things from him too.

He has no clue how deeply I still love Scott. He'd deem such senseless dreams perilous and a weakness. I'm not ready to lift them or myself up to such judgment.

I have no clue as to what Dmitri does at work. I do know, however, that he travels often, and each time he comes back, he's a little more hollowed out, a darker shadow of himself. He was always thin, but he's approaching gaunt. And the gold flecks in his eyes have darkened. They don't gleam any longer.

I also suspect he drinks to forget his present, while I choose sobriety to remember my past.

Although Dmitri told me to meet him at nine o'clock and it's only three minutes past, the fact that he's propped on his elbows with an empty shot glass in front of him is a bad sign. I inwardly groan, anticipating his glassy eyes and lips drooped in the telltale lazy smile of lots of drink and little food. It's worrisome. The stakes are high for him, because if I've noticed his drinking, someone else will too—if they haven't already. His superiors don't frown on it. Heck, I think it's a KGB survival tactic. But they do a lot more than frown if drinking compromises an officer.

I lean close and yell into Dmitri's ear. The music is so loud I can barely hear my own words. "I'm sorry I'm late. Have you been here long?"

"Nah. Just a few minutes."

I shift to look him straight in the eyes and pull back at what I find. They are clear, focused, and there's something moving within them that puts me on full alert. "What's up?"

"I saw your mama." He uses the affectionate name we used as kids. I melt a little, regretting that moment upon returning when I, so grown up, insisted on calling her Mother.

"You did?" I wave my hand to the barman, needing a distraction, as a quick flash of loss and jealousy surprises me. Working until six each night, six days a week, I haven't made the bus trip home in months. I haven't been a good daughter. Mother has called a few times with enticing dinner invitations, but I haven't been able to accept.

That's not true. She's perceptive and she loves me. She'll see right through me; I'm not sure I want to be so closely examined right now. I'm struggling too much. Dmitri, on the other hand, has always welcomed her insights and care, her guidance and wisdom. He's more vulnerable with my mother than with anyone in his life, including his own mother and me.

My mother, unlike his, took the dispensation to not work when we were young. So, starting at age six after that knockdown at our Little Octobrist meeting, Dmitri and a few others came to my apartment after school each day. Everyone fell in love with my mother and love her still. Unlike other parents, she laughed with us, played games with us, devised scavenger hunts for us throughout the parks, and designed obstacle courses in our building's courtyard. She created codes and treasure maps and teased that she was training us to be good comrades and soldiers. She made us feel like we were clever, invincible, and good. We ate it up—Dmitri most of all.

"Did you go to the museum?"

He shakes his head. "I dropped by their apartment on Sunday. We sat in the kitchen while her kozuli baked and talked for a while. Your dad was at his desk, working as usual."

Now I'm really jealous. My mother baked Dmitri my favorite cookies—and he was with her on a Sunday. For most, that day is like any other. But my mother loves Sunday. She goes to church—even though it's the State Church where the "sermons" are propaganda and her name gets recorded.

She then spends hours humming in our kitchen, making a multicourse meal. She often invites other families to join us as well. Neighbors crowd into our apartment, spill out of the kitchen and into the living room, and we all stuff ourselves silly. Friends vied for dinner invitations each week when I was growing up. In fact, Dmitri and Sonya kept going even after I left for Georgetown.

I don't ask, but I wonder if Dmitri accompanied her to church as well. When I was a kid, neither my father nor I went with her, but Dmitri did.

*"Guess who I found lurking on the stairs?"* she'd say with a laugh upon entering our apartment. It took me a couple years to realize she didn't find Dmitri on our apartment stairs but on the church stairs an hour earlier.

"What's she up to these days?" I miss her so much I can almost smell the hint of jasmine her hair holds, and I can definitely feel the tight hug she gives whenever I'm home.

"She's opening a new show. She says we should go see it. She got permission to display some French artist, Marc Chagall. He's actually Russian, born in Belarus, but he left long ago. His light, his colors . . . She showed me pictures of some of the works she couldn't get for the show." Dmitri scrubs his eyes with both hands. I can't tell if he's trying to recall the art or forget it. "They were beautiful. Almost painfully so."

"Dmitri?"

He shudders, brushing away my concern. "We went for a walk."

"A walk outside?" My voice arcs in question. My mother only goes for walks when there are things to say she wants no one to overhear—it was usually me doing all the talking. Shostakovich can only cover so much.

I thought she, like my father, was completely paranoid with all her walks, until the year I left for the United States. One night that summer our upstairs neighbor Comrade Sokolov got arrested. His wife screamed so loudly the whole building was up and standing in the hallways, watching as KGB officers pushed Sokolov down the hallway with stiff arms and pistols.

When I asked what he'd done, my father merely replied, *"He said things he shouldn't have. In the Federovs' apartment."*

A Federov turned him in or the Federovs' apartment was bugged. I never asked which because it doesn't matter. The end result is the same. Sweet Comrade Sokolov, who used to tell us stories and give us homemade candies, was arrested; his kids got pulled from school; and his family lost their apartment. I never heard about any of them again. Now a hard-eyed little man, his grumpy wife, and their shifty teenage son live there.

"My work has unexpected challenges." Dmitri's comment jolts me back to the present. "I wanted her advice."

I say nothing. Of course his work has challenges. Nothing feels right here. Some people believe we are closer than ever to the utopian and global Marxist-Leninist world dream, but we aren't. It's slipping away because it was never attainable—the Afghans are still raging an all-out guerrilla war, a harsh winter decimated Army 40, and the entire world is lining up behind NATO against us. And that's *outside* our borders.

Inside it's worse. Our grain supply can't feed us, embargoes are crippling our already-stagnated economy, our infrastructure is crumbling—my 1950s Khrushchyovka apartment is a good indicator of that—and people churn with anxiety and hunger.

Despite a good supply of ration coupons and an ample salary by all standards, I can't find goods in the stores that were available when I got home two years ago. Three or four days a week, lines stretch down the block for the most basic things. And you can only get in those lines fast enough if a friend "inside" tips you off that something decent might be available. With no friend, there's no chance.

No one understands where all the funds go, but I do.

A lot goes to the KGB. Comrade Captain Mikael Stanslych, the KGB officer who oversees my lab, told me they inducted over one thousand new officers in this year's class alone. He also told me that Brezhnev had given them "a little more license in and outside our borders." That's how he put it. *License.* I try not to wonder how far that privilege stretches.

Then there's defense and armaments. My lab is part of a network of five military-development facilities, and there are at least seven networks—that's potentially thirty-five facilities at or below my security clearance alone. If those other labs get anywhere close to the funding my one lab gets annually, we collectively just about match the country's GNP. That's if Georgetown's Professor Michaels is right about the Soviet Union's GNP. It isn't a number readily publicized here or abroad.

Yes, Dmitri's right. Unexpected challenges are all around us. I lean toward him again. "Did you share your challenges with my mother?" I ask very calmly, but I'm nervous.

It isn't that my mother can't keep a secret. I expect she can. But secrets put people in danger. She's a museum curator, loyal and fearful of misstepping. She believes that by getting along, we can go along. She does her job, takes care of her family, and lets the rest swirl around her. I've never seen my mother with a samizdat, a black-market book, or anything else not permitted. She keeps her head down and her mouth shut. That's one reason I sometimes feel Dmitri understands her better than I do. He has an innate desire to shelter and protect her. Whereas I keep poking her to wake her up.

"A little." He shrugs to allay my concerns.

"Be careful, Dmitri." I sigh. We've traveled this road a hundred times. "You took that oath. She didn't. You can't—"

"Заткнись." He stares at me, his face inches from mine. *Shut up.*

I do. Something in his tone tells me to back off, and fast.

I stare at him and notice he's again missed shaving deep into the cleft in his chin. The stubble there is more pronounced. Then I realize how well I can see it across his jaw. He's pale, more so than usual. His hair, once long enough to crash into his eyebrows, is cut short, a brush cut that lies close to his scalp. He's thinner, more severe, even forlorn. We're together several nights a week when he's in town, and yet it feels like I'm sensing new and disturbing changes at this very moment.

"I would never bring harm to your mama. She just let me talk. Okay? Give me some credit. You have no idea what it's like."

His hand rests on the bar near his drink. I lay mine on top of it. He's right. I don't have any idea at all.

Growing up, we knew Dmitri's father was in the KGB. I'm not sure what he did, but we all thought he was the most dashing and daring of the fathers. Mine, working a boring office job in the CPSU, the Communist Party of the Soviet Union, could never compete. But debonair turned to despair by our twelfth birthdays as Dmitri's dad drank more, grew taciturn, and became super jumpy. The littlest noises made him twitch. It got so bad his mother, always stoic and strict, forbade us to go to their apartment at all if she wasn't home. We were sixteen when he killed himself. No note. No explanation. Just a bullet beneath his chin in their building's communal bathroom.

Dmitri squeezes my hand so tight the bones roll over each other. I don't cry out and I don't pull away. He's in more pain than I am.

"I can't take much more of this, Anya. I can't."

I press closer. The music has shifted and, if possible, it's louder. Part of me hates it, but the better part is thankful for the cover it provides. "What's going on, Dmitri? Tell me . . . I'm right here."

He shakes his head. "You don't see it. It's all around you and none of you see it."

"See what?"

He straightens and twists to stare into the club and across the dance floor. I follow his gaze and realize it has grown crowded while we've been talking and, lit only by harsh strobe lights, it feels surreal and chaotic. Dystopian. I pull in a breath and, rather than feel better, I shrink back, struck by the pungent smell of alcohol, sweat, and something sour and stale.

Dmitri watches me. "That's it." He bumps my shoulder to recapture my attention. "We chase it away at night, but it catches us every morning. Desperation. Hopelessness."

He didn't need to explain it to me. I feel it myself. A mania grips the dance floor, everyone gyrating with every ounce of their beings to keep up with the music and the endless race to nowhere and nothing. My energy, maybe my hope, too, oozes away.

Dmitri toggles two fingers toward the barman and a couple shots slide our direction. He picks his up and throws it back in a fluid motion.

I stare at mine, remembering the letter in my pocket and what hope once felt like. Cherry blossoms. Warm sunshine. Blue eyes. Lemons and sandalwood. And while I've been carrying this letter around for a week, it's already two months old. I toss back the shot.

"Thank you," I say to him. "Now I'm just as depressed as you."

"I'm sorry." Dmitri drapes an arm around my shoulder and pulls me close. He kisses my temple in a punctuated motion. It feels like the quick rap he used to give my arm when we were kids. "What's that phrase you keep telling me?"

"Misery loves company?"

"That's the one." He waves to the barman again.

"You're not sorry," I grumble as two glasses slide our direction. "Maybe you should slow down a little."

"Being sober makes this better?" He taps his full glass against mine. "Either keep up or go home."

"Don't tempt me," I tease.

He doesn't reply and he doesn't slow down. Instead he downs his shot and mine, then lifts his hand again. Another glass, this time only one, lands in front of him. He tosses that back too.

The barman throws me a challenging glare and turns away. I get the impression he sees something in Dmitri I don't.

"What's really going on, Dmitri?"

"You were smart." He sweeps a hand across his eyes and his nail beds whiten with the pressure. When he drags his hand away, his eyes glisten. The skin around them is red and swollen.

"About what?"

"If you hadn't gone to America, you wouldn't have taken that spot at MGIMO. You would've sided with your mama and gone to MIFI . . . It's killing me."

I peer around us. No one can hear our conversation, but his words are charged. Others must feel their impact. "What's killing you?" I speak into his ear.

"I got transferred to Directorate K, Anya. Illegals. And to Poland . . . To bring him down." I straighten. Dmitri slumps. "It's what we train for."

I scan the bar once more. No one is near, but that hardly matters. He can't say these things. I can't hear these things. I shoot to standing and haul Dmitri to his feet. He stumbles as I drag him through the dancing throng toward the club's back door, but I don't stop and he doesn't resist. He keeps shuffling after me almost as if pleased to be led. I pull him up the short set of stairs to the back alley. My hope is that the bracing cold will shock sense into him.

The metal door slams behind us, and I push Dmitri against the club's brick wall. He slides to the ground. Forget the drinking. This is far worse.

I kick away a few broken bottles and crouch beside him, noting we are alone in the alley. No one but a single mewing cat is present.

"You can't talk like that. What are you thinking?"

He grips his chest, wadding his shirt in his fist. "What am I to do? That hope we had? It'll be gone, Anya. Wałęsa and Solidarity will end like the Hungarian Revolution, the Prague Spring—plowed into submission . . . Dozens of us are being sent this month, with one goal."

"No." I can hardly breathe. Until this moment I had no idea how much the tiniest bits I've gleaned from Dmitri and the samizdats mean to me. Solidarity started as a trade union in Poland about a year and a half ago over wages in Gdańsk, but it's so much more now. It's social change and political reform, working through civil resistance, not destruction. It's about citizenship, rights, voice, and a respect for the human dignity of all Poles. It's about freedom.

It is happening—even if it's not happening here—and that has been a lifeline for me. Only now do I see the hope it gives me every day as I walk by that smug guard Rogov at work, every month when his boss, Stanslych, searches our desks, and every time I hear the delayed *click* on my office telephone line. And while I wasn't alive for the Hungarian Revolution and wasn't aware of the Prague Spring when I was ten, I've been tracking this and—even despite serious setbacks—Solidarity continues to gain steam. It's *the* light that, given the chance to grow, might shine bright enough to free us all.

I press my hands against Dmitri's, pushing both down into his chest. I want to compress him, stop him, put all the loose parts of him back in place, and lock them down tight. I want to keep him from traveling to Poland. I want to go back to that night months ago in another bar and another booth, where we sat whispering in wonder about this movement and what it meant.

"*They posted a list of '21 postulates' on the shipyard door, Anya. Rights. Freedoms. And they're not backing down. What started with seventeen thousand people is now nine million. A quarter of Poland's population. Even Brezhnev and his Supreme Soviet can't shut this down.*"

I want to go back to minutes before, when I believed something good could survive. I want to stop the KGB from destroying it. But there is only one thing to do. One thing that won't get Dmitri killed and, perhaps, me along with him.

I close the distance between us until only an inch remains.

I lock my eyes on his and pray I can hide the horror I feel—for everything he'll soon do in Poland and for what I'm about to do in this moment.

"Never speak of this again, Dmitri. Don't even think about it. Go to Poland and do your job. That's the oath you made."

# ELEVEN

# Anya

MOSCOW
*January 22, 1983*

DMITRI VANISHED. HE MOVED TO POLAND AND THERE WAS NO
communicating with him for over nine months. The job description of a KGB "illegal" is to enter a country as a worker—builder,
banker, taxi driver, mailman—but to act as a spy, doing everything possible to destroy your assignment: group, country, or
cause.

According to the samizdats, Dmitri and his brethren did
exemplary work. To a degree. A couple months ago, the new
Polish prime minister, Wojciech Jaruzelski, put all Poland under
martial law and arrested every Solidarity leader he could get his
hands on. But the movement didn't die. It went underground
and, by last estimate, has five hundred underground newspapers
reporting its gains. And if what I'm reading is true, President
Reagan of the US, Prime Minister Thatcher of the UK, Pope
John Paul II, Spain's General Secretary of the Communist Party
Santiago Carrillo, and lots of other leaders globally—on both
sides of the ideological spectrum—support it. Heck, I bet some
of them are funding it.

It's definitely not the KGB win that *Pravda* would like us to
believe. Of course, the paper reports the win to be the legitimate

Polish government's victory, as it regains control over a violent and illegal protest. Never once does it mention that the protest isn't violent and that Jaruzelski is Soviet-backed, or that he's wielding the KGB sledgehammer.

But as of tonight, Dmitri is home.

I rush out of work right on time. A glance down reminds me how awful I look in my plain and stiff work clothes, but I don't have time to go home and change. I catch the bus into the central city and find Dmitri already at the restaurant waiting. He is thinner, almost skeletal. As I cross the room I watch him roll his cigarette through his fingers and use its stub to light the next.

He finally sees me and stands, pulling me into a hug the moment I'm within reach. I grip him tight and stifle a gasp. I can feel all the bones within his shoulders and neck. They're so sharp they frighten me.

"You got back today?" I drop into the chair across from him. "I've missed you so much." I babble on, probably because I find his weight and the circles under his eyes disconcerting. I feel like if I keep talking in bright and happy tones, he'll catch them and color will suffuse his cheeks again.

"Come for Sunday dinner. Sonya's coming too. I'll ask my mother to make that stew with boar and beets you love."

He doesn't answer me, but he's smiling. I get the impression he wants me to keep talking, so I do. Until there's nothing left to say.

"Tell me about you. What have you been up to?" I press my lips shut. That's not what I intended to ask.

I pick up my menu before returning my focus to Dmitri. When I do, I stop. It's like a curtain has been lifted. The actor, the man, the spy, the—who has he been this past year?—is gone and I see the face of the boy I've known for nineteen years. My best friend. He blinks with the understanding that I've seen him and with the soft sigh of one with nothing left to hide.

"At least you're safe and home now."

For some reason that bothers him. His attention drifts over my head toward the restaurant's front door.

"What is it?" I scan the dining room. It's only half full and no one sits particularly close. "Is something wrong?"

"Nothing you need to worry about." With a long exhale he returns his focus to me. "That's not true. When I got back today, I heard Renet committed suicide a couple months ago."

My heart drops down or my stomach pushes up, I can't tell which. I can only tell that I feel sick.

When receiving our VUZ options all those years ago—our version of university assignments—Renet was awarded a place at the Science Academy to study geology. Ever cynical about the propaganda and daily dose of deceits, we all envied that Renet got to study the hard sciences. Especially Dmitri. He really wanted that assignment—maybe for those very reasons. But with his high scores and a father formerly in KGB service, Dmitri only ever had one path.

I finally find my voice. "I'm sorry . . . He was a good guy."

"What hope is there for the rest of us?" Dmitri turns his fresh cigarette in tiny half rolls between his fingers.

I snag Dmitri's free hand from the table and hold it. "What happened to Renet has nothing to do with you or me."

"Do you think if I got that assignment and learned about rocks, earthquakes, and tsunamis, all this would feel okay? On some level I could study a thing and know what it was." Dmitri watches his cigarette burn low. "Why wasn't it enough for him?"

I keep hold of his one hand and tug it across the table. "You have to stop. You have to eat, laugh, drink, something . . . You're scaring me."

"Good." His voice comes loud and strong. "Maybe you'll wake up. There's a word for this, Anya, this living two truths—one deep in your heart and one you act on every day. *Ketman.* It comes from Persia. It translates to doublethink. You divide your soul as you deceive others in order to stay safe, but you deceive yourself in the end."

"Don't tell me about ketman." I grind the word out slowly. "I learned about it at Georgetown and I live it every day, too, Dmitri. But I have you. And you have me. We can be honest with each other." I wave my free hand back and forth between us. "That's all we need, right? One place to be real and we're going to be fine."

"We'll never be fine. No one survives a divided soul." He hangs his head and swings it from side to side as if trying to shake away reality. "'One word of truth outweighs the whole world.' Do you remember when your mama told us that proverb? Back when she told us about the Hungarian Uprising?"

I stare at him. Nothing comes to mind. "My mother?"

Dmitri blows out a long, heavy sigh. "You can be so smart, Anya, and so blind."

"What? Hey—"

He lifts a hand, cutting me off. "Stop. It's not about that. It's about what's happening now . . . I joined a group. An underground church. You need to come with me sometime."

"Dmitri." This time my heart *and* my stomach bottom out. "Tell me you're joking . . . You can't risk involvement with those groups."

He lifts his chin. I turn and see Lev and Sonya make their way through the tables toward us. Dmitri leans forward. His voice is soft and hurried. Whatever he's going to say is for me alone. "Have you ever heard the first words of John Paul II's papacy? He's Polish."

137

"No."

"'Do not be afraid.'" Dmitri, again, lifts his chin past me toward our approaching friends. "I'm not afraid anymore, Anya, and I don't want you to be either. If you only knew what has started in Poland, you'd understand . . . It's all going to come crashing down. No one can stop it now."

He pushes his chair back. I reach out. "Dmitri . . . dinner? Where are you going?"

He shakes his head. "I gotta go."

Lev and Sonya finally reach the table. Dmitri is gone. Both look to me for answers. I shrug. I have none.

The ringing wakes me.

At first I think it's my imagination. So many sounds are still there, pounding into my brain. After dinner we trolled Cat Club, Drey Bar, and a couple others in search of Dmitri. We never found him. I finally left Lev and Sonya dancing at Metropol Disco and took my headache home.

I pull my clock over. Ten o'clock. Six hours of sleep. I push up but then, recognizing it's Sunday, drop back into the covers. The phone rings again.

I climb out of bed and shuffle around the corner to the kitchen. I can practically reach the telephone from my bed, but it still takes until about the tenth ring for me to get the receiver off the base. The cord is in a tight twist that won't stretch to my ear, much less the two feet to the kitchen sink. My glass of water will have to wait.

"Hello." I arch my back. Who is awake and why are they calling me? My fingers work to loosen the twists within the cord.

"Anya?" Sonya's voice is tense. "Dmitri is—"

"Nyet," I bark. "I'm not taking three buses to come clean your couch again. If he got sick, it's your mess this time."

"He's dead, Anya." I hear Sonya's voice before I can process her words. It's tight and clogged, like she's speaking through a wet cloth.

"What?"

"He's dead. His mother just called. She said you didn't answer your phone so she thought you might be here. He was mugged walking on the paths near the river last night. He—"

"Noooo." I sink to the floor. The cord barely reaches.

"He got beat pretty bad and then . . . they shot him. They shot him for a few rubles." Sonya starts to cry.

I feel boneless. The world closes around me and fades to black. My head hits the floor and the bump brings the colors back, but it doesn't stop the tight feeling compressing my chest. "No. No." I can only repeat the one word, certain that it can make all this go away.

"Anya. Do you want me to come over?"

"Did you say by the river? But we never go—" That fact sucker punches me. "Who said he was there? Who found him?"

"What? Anya . . ." Sonya sounds confused, like I'm crazy or missing the point. "His mother told me. Some man out walking this morning, I guess. What does it matter?"

"Where is he, Sonya?" Silence meets me. "Where's Dmitri's body? I need to see him."

"I'm not lying. It's real, Anya. He's dead."

"Sonya, stop. Just tell me where he is!" I'm yelling now. "I need to see him."

"The Tverskoy Morgue. His mother is trying to get permission to bury him Wednesday, but—"

I push myself to standing. "I gotta go."

"Anya—"

I hang up on her. My kitchen wavers around me as if I'm seeing it through water. I lean against the wall to let the feeling and the past wash over me.

Dmitri and I found a dead body by the river when we were nine years old. The man's dark eyes were wide open, staring at us, and we could tell he had been scared. I can't say how we knew; we just knew. He had died terribly afraid. His mouth was wide open, as if in a scream, and an orange scarf was wrapped tight around his neck. I've never liked the color orange since.

At first we drew close. I'm not sure if we wanted to prove ourselves brave or if we thought we could save him. But we got close enough to touch him, and that's when we felt it. We never talked about it, but Dmitri's eyes mirrored my own. It wasn't fear that gripped us; it was far worse. It was desolation, aloneness, futility. I can't describe it other than to say it was Death. Capital *D*.

Only now do I even have words to convey that feeling. Back then we simply knew it as cold. Cold like we could never be warm. Cold like we'd always be alone. Cold like no matter what we did, we would always face the ground rather than savor the sky.

We ran. We ran until I threw up. We never talked about it, not to each other and certainly not to anyone else. And neither of us *ever* got anywhere near those paths along the river again.

I throw on a pair of corduroys and my boots and head to the Tverskoy Morgue. It's not that I don't believe Sonya. I do. But I need to see Dmitri. Confirm for myself that this is real, that my best friend—my true brother—is gone and that he'll never laugh again, never pull my hair, call me out, or hug me tight. My mind grows paralyzed with all the "nevers" ahead of me.

It takes a half hour of bus rides and walking to reach the morgue, and the numb feeling deep within pulses ever outward in cadence with the bus, my stride, my breathing, and my exhaustion. It dulls reality from a sharp pain to one I suspect

I'll carry forever, along with the recriminations I'll carry forever too. Everything I didn't say and didn't do last night, everything I didn't say and do a year ago before he left for Poland.

I push through the single steel door at Tverskoy Morgue and walk a few steps into the beige-painted cement-block hallway. I stop to let my eyes adjust to the dark, windowless corridor. It smells sharp and pungent, like iron and antiseptic.

"May I see Dmitri Dimitrivich Shubin?" I ask the attendant behind the desk. A choked sob escapes. It wasn't planned, but his wide-eyed surprise gives me an idea. "I'm his sister."

The boy, because he can't be over seventeen, straightens. He worries I'm about to start sobbing and points through the double doors to his left.

I walk down another hall and repeat my lie to the next attendant.

This one doesn't let me pass like the boy did. Instead he studies me, and a prickling heat climbs up the back of my cotton blouse. My coat feels heavy and hot. I shift, about to shed it, then stop. Something tells me I'm becoming too memorable. I stand still, hoping sweat doesn't break out across my brow.

"Only family." The man, dressed in a blue jumpsuit, steps closer. "They've already come and identified him."

"I was at work and couldn't get here. Mama said . . . I came all this way. May I see him?" Again the tears start falling. "Only for a moment?"

"Papers?"

I pat my empty pockets. I have forgotten them. Yet an odd realization strikes me that I didn't forget at all. The lie comes so easily. "I ran out from work. I can go back. They're on my desk. If you'll wait . . ." I let the words trail away in tears.

"No. My shift ends—" He doesn't finish his sentence. He backs against the door, opening it for me, and points to a gurney in the far corner. "Last on the right. Be quick." He steps away and the door falls shut between us.

Five draped gurneys fill the room. I hold my breath and walk to the last on the right. I lift my hand to draw back the sheet and my courage fails. I can't move. I'm not sure how long I stand there listening to my own heartbeat thudding in my ears, but when a sound draws me back to the room, to the smells, and to Dmitri, I realize I need to hurry.

I pull back the sheet. It's him. Somehow that surprises me. I mean, I hoped it was a mistake. Not a lie. Sonya wasn't lying. She'd just made a mistake. Because this is Dmitri she was talking about. Dmitri is alive. He has to be. He's always been there for me. He'll always—

*Peaceful.* It's the first word that comes to mind. His eyes are closed and his face isn't clenched tight. I can almost imagine he's sleeping. I trace the scar along his hairline, the one I gave him with my wooden sword when we were seven. It stands stark yellow against his pale skin. I pull back the side of the sheet just enough to see and touch his hand, to say goodbye.

His hands are not peaceful. A few fingers are broken. The knuckles enlarged and red, the tips of each veering off at odd angles. He fought back. I close my eyes, imagining what he must have done when confronted. I lift his hand, drawing it close, and see his nails are clean and clipped. But that's impossible. Did they surprise him and he couldn't fight back? But—

Then I see it. His father's ring.

The solid-gold wedding ring circles Dmitri's finger. It's heavy and thick, and it's been in his family for generations—like days-of-the-tsars generations—when his father's family was well-to-do. No mugger would take rubles and leave behind pure gold.

I step around Dmitri to block anyone's line of sight from the door and bend over. With my hands working in front of me, I slide off the ring, wrestling it over the knuckle, trying to convince myself I'm not hurting him. It can't go with him. It can't go into the ground and disappear like nothing happened, like they didn't murder him.

Clarity and truth strike me with the force of a blow and steal my breath. Cold now, and more scared than I've ever been, I remember Dmitri's words, *"Do not be afraid,"* and other words, *"It's all crashing down,"* and more words, *"I've joined an underground church."* I slip the ring onto my middle finger and back my way out of the room.

"Wait!" the attendant calls as I rush past him. "You need to sign the ledger."

"I told you. I'm his sister."

"You must register in the log."

I keep walking, pretending I don't hear.

"Stop," he calls again.

I break into a run, slam my way out of the morgue's metal door, and race down the street to the first corner. I turn and press myself against the building.

No one has chased me. I almost laugh. What trick is my imagination pulling on me? Then I lift my hand and stare at the ring. No trick. Dmitri didn't fight because he knew he wasn't being mugged. He was being tortured. Before being executed.

Although I'm certain the morgue attendant isn't after me and has no idea who I am, and probably doesn't care, I take a long, circuitous route back to my apartment. It feels right, almost as if Dmitri is with me, guiding each twist and turn. As kids we used to play spies and pretend that someone was after us and we needed to "lose our tail."

Back in my apartment, I drop into a chair and pull off the ring. It slides off easily and I notice my nail beds have turned blue. At first I think it's a strange reaction to shock. Do I need to eat? Drink? Lie down? Then I note my breath is making a cloud of white with each exhale.

I push myself up. The thermostat reads zero degrees Celsius. The heat is out again. I bang my broom on the ceiling. My building's maintenance man, who lives above me, bangs back.

*I'm working on it.*

I tap once more. *Thank you.*

I heat a pot of water on the stove, pour the scalding liquid into a mug, and drop in a tea bag. Then I retreat to my chair by the window and stare out toward the park and the zoo beyond.

I see nothing. I can't imagine life without Dmitri. I can't imagine tomorrow without him. I think about the day I pushed him against that alley wall and told him to do his job. I think about Renet. I think about Dmitri's years at MGIMO. I think about mine at Georgetown. I think about the day I got my Foreign Studies Initiative invitation. I stop there.

How have I missed it for so long? Because for all Dmitri's talk about ketman and a divided soul, he wasn't divided. He had no false persona, no fake bravado, bold talk, cool cynicism, or rebellion. Dmitri was consistent through and through—he hated life here and his bosses knew it.

We were sitting in an empty part of Gorky Park, just beyond the skating rink, all those years ago. Dmitri's VUZ assignment hadn't come yet.

"You'll get MGIMO and then the KGB."

"Da." He stared out across the park in that calm, focused way he had. "And you'll go to America . . . They're nervous, but your mama's eyes brightened at the honor."

"You should hear how many of her requests for paintings get

turned down. Nothing from museums in France, the GFR, or the US gets approved. If I go, I'd get to see some of them. I almost feel guilty."

"You have to go. Then you can share it all with her someday."

"You should have been her son." I sniggered. "You'd go to America and all those museums for her alone." I said it, but we both knew the Foreign Studies Initiative would never be an option for Dmitri. He had other skills, along with family and test scores, that funneled him straight into the KGB.

"I'd go in a heartbeat." He stared across the park. "I found a bug in my room."

"A bug? What kind?" I hated bugs.

"The listening kind, dummy." He rolled his eyes. "I thought it was a spider, but it didn't move. They do that before they offer MGIMO. They have to be sure. We've also been searched at least two times this spring."

"How can you tell?"

Dmitri only lifted a corner of his mouth. He didn't answer; he didn't need to. He knew because he placed traps. Always had. A strand of hair between two drawers. A paper exactly a pencil-width from the edge of his desk. He started this compulsion after his dad died.

We sat in silence for a few minutes.

"I hate it here," he whispered to the breeze.

"Don't say that." I nudged him. Although we were far from prying eyes and ears, such talk made me nervous. Still does. It's one thing to complain and "dissent"; it's another to truly hate.

He turned to me. "When you go, don't come back."

I laughed at what I thought was a joke. I stopped with the realization it wasn't. "I can't do that. They'd kill me. It's the Foreign Studies Initiative, Dmitri. You can't be serious."

"I am, and they can't kill you if they can't find you."

We left that conversation there that day, but it always stayed with me. It toyed with me at Georgetown and has filled me with recriminations since the day I kissed Scott goodbye in the airport. I remember his eyes, his lips, his smile. His questions. *"What about you? Would you try? Do you want to stay?"*

*Yes* finally wells up within my heart and nothing shouts it down. I wanted to stay. I should have tried. Dmitri would have tried. Now it's too late. Exactly three years too late. I sip my tea, surprised to find it now ice-cold. I stand up and stretch, unsure of how long I've been following these trails into memory and loss.

The phone rings.

I answer and just hearing my mother's voice opens a floodgate and drops me to the floor.

"Come home." Her voice cuts through my tears. "Pack a bag and come home."

I obey.

Within forty-five minutes I'm hugging my mother tight, not sure if I'll ever let go. Dressed in her favorite tweed skirt—she only has two—a brown sweater, and her red-and-blue-checked apron covering it all, she embodies the perfect working wife and the most comforting mother.

She's been making my favorite dish. I can smell the sour cherries cooking along with the veal, and it brings me back to my childhood when all was well because I didn't know any better.

When I tuck closer, the smell of stew drifts away and I catch summer orange, jasmine, and orchid. Her perfume. I inhale as if hope lingers in that scent just out of reach, and if I press into her hard enough, I might find it. But just as I sink deeper, she pushes me back, holding me by the shoulders. She studies my eyes as if trying to unearth all my secrets. I can't hold her gaze and dart mine away.

"You need to be careful."

"Me? Why?" I step back, and without even thinking I've pulled my hands behind my back to hide Dmitri's ring.

"You will be angry about Dmitri; you already are, I can see, but he was a reckless boy who became a reckless young man. He never should have been in that area late at night."

"You can't believe that." I step back again. "It's a lie."

My mother moves so fast I have to break down her actions in my mind to grasp them all. She flips off the stove, grabs me by my ear, and drags me to the bathroom. She twists on the shower and the sink, while still wrenching my ear, its top curled over the bottom. My father is not home, clearly, because we would have passed him during our awkward trek.

She presses so close to me I feel her breath as well as her pinch. I'm too shocked to cry out, resist, or even react. Her hand is wet with my tears against my cheek. She shuts the door behind us. We are bound body-to-body in our tiny bathroom. Her fingers still mangle my ear.

"I am going to let you go, but you will listen, Anya, and you will not speak. Am I clear?" Her words are clipped and precise. Her eyes dart between mine as if trying to see deeper into me than I think exists.

I nod and she lets go.

"You may be right, but you have to be more careful. You have to be smarter. You keep your thoughts to yourself. Always. Better yet, stop thinking them at all."

She sounds like I did with Dmitri that night in the alley. But it's not then and I can't go back there. "No. I won't—"

"Open your eyes." She cuts me off with a finger to my lips. "Who do you think Yuri Andropov is? The KGB chairman now runs the State, which means the KGB and the Party and the Politburo are one. Total control. Do you understand? That's not just words; that's thoughts and ideas. Andropov will enforce monitoring and arrests. He will force submission and engender paranoia. Don't think that because you meet with Comrade Minister Petrov, you're safe. That kind of visibility only puts you in more danger because your job is important. You will be watched, if you aren't already. Knowledge makes you a threat. Ideas can get you killed. People talk . . . Dmitri was like a son—"

Her voice breaks and she pulls me into another hug. She continues, crying into my shoulder. "But you are my daughter. I love you and I can't lose you. Everyone knows . . . Everyone knows how close you two were."

"Shh, yes, Mama. Yes . . . I'm sorry."

My mother is usually calm about everything. She rarely gets angry and she never raises her voice. And despite the heated delivery, one look into her eyes reveals she's not angry now.

She's terrified.

# TWELVE

# Ingrid

MOSCOW
*April 14, 1958*

LEO WAS SINGING. AGAIN.

After four years of marriage, Leo had begun to despair. He never said anything, but Ingrid could tell. At her time each month, he'd clean the dishes after dinner, ask her to rest, wonder about her health, or do something else equally leading but appropriately oblique. But each month, she felt unchanged—physically. Emotionally, she began to despair long before Leo did.

Though she'd come to accept it, Ingrid's life wasn't what she'd anticipated, nor did she enjoy the marital love she'd witnessed growing up. While her parents kept secrets from her, and probably from each other, she always knew they loved one another, relied upon each other, and considered the other their greatest gift, their greatest asset, and an integral part of their very being.

Ingrid could not say the same. She was lonely—yet never alone. She was quiet—unsure of what to say and to whom she could say it. She was careful—in every part of her life, even the most private aspects. Ruefully, she finally admitted to herself that with Leo's admonition to "stop paying attention," she had truly diminished into the small, weak woman her parents and others had always assumed her to be.

Only Adam, once upon a time, had seen something different, something more. She remembered those few weeks before her parents' deaths. How his gaze had lingered on her more, a spark lit his expression, an interest his aspect. He found strength in her. *"You're the strongest woman I know."* She savored that compliment. Even all these years later, it sustained her with the fleeting light that it might once have been true.

Now the only times she felt free and truly herself was on her daily walks to and from work at the Bureau of Historical Archives. Yet even then, when drawn outside an inner world of what-ifs and dreams, she noticed things around her actively working to strip away her fleeting freedom and delight—cameras atop light poles, patriotic music blaring from speakers mounted on traffic lights, and ever-present black KGB Volga surveillance cars. Once Leo pointed them out, Ingrid realized that one was never more than a few minutes or a few hundred meters away— from anyone.

Home was no better.

Even in her most intimate moments with Leo, Ingrid found herself playing a role in reaction to his own charade. Gone was the vulnerable man who had once loved her. He'd received yet another promotion in the last year and it pulled him further away. He worked longer hours and was more secretive and distant. He confided in her less and chastised her more. Lately, she began to wonder if she couldn't find the man she fell in love with because he was no longer there or because he had never existed in the first place.

Ingrid also felt certain, if asked the question again, Leo would change his answer. He would not have chosen to marry her, despite his time limitations. He would have called off their wedding and quickly found a more suitable bride to secure that first promotion. She even wondered why he stayed married to her now. Certainly another arrangement would please him more. And she could return—

She stopped herself there, as she always did. Helka had shared that tidbit during their first talk and elaborated on it over the years, making such musings impossible. *"The KGB is rigid in its ideology and rules. Officers stayed married. No matter what . . . Infidelity gets you sidelined and divorce is a permanent demotion."* So this was her marriage and her life. For while she had no direct confirmation Leo worked within the KGB, she knew he did.

Unable to sleep one night a few months ago, Ingrid lay silent as tears slipped from the corners of her eyes. Leo reached for her and she startled at his touch.

"I thought you were asleep." She dabbed her eyes with two fingers before she turned to her husband.

"I was watching you. You're so beautiful." Leo laid a gentle hand across her stomach.

"I wasn't sure you noticed anymore."

"Are you angry with me?"

"Angry? Why?" She rolled toward him.

"I'm too old to give you children." He threaded a finger through her hair, pulling it forward. Although she couldn't see the strands in the dark, she knew a few grey ones wove through her blonde. "I'm a disappointment."

"Never." She pulled him close, hoping to find warmth. Maybe love. "What about me? That bomb in Vienna? My age? I'm thirty-five years old." She scrunched her nose.

"I'm forty." He chuckled.

She nestled herself within his arms and he kissed her. At first soft, his kisses became more demanding, more urgent, and Ingrid felt herself respond. Yet even in the midst of making love, it wasn't the same. The urgency wasn't for each other. It was for something lost yet unfound, or perhaps something that never was nor ever would be. And once the moment was over, the room felt cool and quiet again. Ingrid wrapped herself tighter within the blanket.

A month later she missed her cycle.

By the second month she felt the first queasiness of morning sickness.

By the third month she shared her news with her husband. That's when Leo started singing.

"Your husband is happy about the baby," Dolores commented one morning.

"Yes." Ingrid looked away, as if fascinated with drying her hands on a kitchen towel. After three years, she still felt wary of Dolores.

Dolores watched Ingrid fold the dish towel, then gestured to the kitchen table. "May we speak?"

"Of course." Ingrid lowered herself into one of the two chairs tucked under the table. She drew herself straight as Dolores sat across from her.

Without breaking eye contact, Dolores reached to where the table met the wall and turned on the radio that sat there.

Ingrid's eyes widened. Her ears filled with both the music and the sound of her own heartbeat.

Dolores pulled her chair around the table's small circumference, closer to Ingrid's. "I lied to you," she whispered in German.

Ingrid closed her eyes. She didn't want to hear that Leo had hired Dolores to spy on her. She didn't want confirmation of the sham her life had become.

"I am not from Kraków. I was given doctored papers long ago. I am from Smolensk, a small village at the edge of the Katyn Forest in Poland."

Ingrid opened her eyes, a quick gasp escaping before she could stifle it. Instantly she was back in her father's study in Vienna, on a spring afternoon in 1940. Although there was a small vase of flowers on his desk, there was a fire in the grate. That was a detail she couldn't forget—she had needed the fire's warmth that day, as what he told her chilled her straight through.

She'd come home and found her father in a rare candid moment, sitting in an armchair in front of the fire with his head in his hands. He told her how the British army had planned to move into Norway and, from there, cross into the Soviet Union to fight Stalin along his poorly supported northwest flank. It was a brilliant strategic move, he'd said, as Stalin, allied with Hitler at the time, had moved his army south.

*"It went horribly wrong."* Her father sighed.

Stalin, he continued to tell her, quickly recognized his mistake and became paranoid—paranoid that a British victor would not only free his prisoners along the border regions but liberate his millions of dissidents and "traitors" enslaved in his Siberian gulags.

So on February 2, 1940, Soviet troops, under orders from Stalin's state security, the NKVD, raided Poland's border villages for men. They rounded up anyone capable of leading a military or intellectual revolt—and they found thousands. Stalin didn't want their expertise; he wanted no one else to have it.

He then shipped this "intellectual capital" to camps—Ostashkov, Kozelsk, and Starbielsk—and over the following weeks, he emptied those camps, moving about three hundred men each day in trains and buses to the Katyn Forest.

Ingrid could envision, as if watching it anew, her father's tears that day as he described what had happened next. In a small hut, deep within the forest, a soldier put a pistol to the nape of each man's neck and shot him. Another soldier then efficiently pushed every father, brother, son, friend, and neighbor into a pit. The murders went on for weeks. Thousands of men. An entire generation.

Tears filled Ingrid's eyes. "My father told me. He didn't mean to . . . I am so sorry." Ingrid paused. Later, her father revisited that afternoon and told her another element of the story with the caution never to repeat it.

When switching sides from Hitler's ally to his enemy, Stalin claimed the Germans were responsible for the Katyn massacres—and that deception lived on. Even now, eighteen years later, the world's accusatory finger still pointed at the Germans.

"You must hate the Germans." Ingrid stopped there. The lie tasted bitter in her mouth.

"I was there." Dolores stared at her. "I heard the screams. I saw the uniforms."

Ingrid swallowed. An electric charge, not a shock but a sustained surge, passed between the women. "Why are you telling me this?"

"You will now keep my secret." Dolores leaned forward. "As I will keep yours."

"Leo hired you to spy on me." It wasn't a question. Ingrid found it easier to simply state the fact.

Dolores nodded. "He hired me to assist you, to train you, and, yes, to keep an eye on you. He wanted to keep you safe, perhaps quiet. There are many who would like to see him fail. It is not uncommon."

"I am a liability." Ingrid closed her eyes as the truth, finally stated, washed over her.

Leo's need to conform, excel, deliver, direct, and his hunger for acclaim didn't come from a place of confidence or peace as she'd once imagined. Yes, he had been "rehabilitated," and he was thankful for that. But more important, he was keenly aware that as one arbitrary act made him whole, another could easily rip it all away. And that act needn't be large or even real. Something insignificant, such as a petty jealousy, a misstep, or the fact that his wife was Austrian—or worse, that she carried British blood in her veins—could ruin him.

Ingrid sank against the kitchen chair. The metal shifted under her weight. The sound reminded her that she needed to tighten the screws where the plastic seat met the framing.

Dolores shifted her chair closer. It, too, groaned in protest. "English, not German, is your first language."

Of its own accord, Ingrid's hand moved over her belly. She only noted the gesture once complete.

Dolores's gaze dropped, settling on Ingrid's hand. "You coo to your growing baby. In English."

All the blood that had drained from Ingrid moments before flooded back with red heat and anger. She shot forward and seized Dolores's hand and squeezed. Although her hand could barely wrap around the larger woman's, Ingrid felt she could break her bones if necessary. "I told Leo my mother was British, but I was born in Vienna. I speak fluent German. He never questioned further and I—" Ingrid cut herself off, afraid to venture too close to the truth. If she told one truth, where would she stop? Where would it end? And what might Dolores do with such power?

"But your first language, as a baby, was English. You think in English." Dolores's words dropped between them with all that "thinking" in a language implied.

Ingrid opened her mouth to deny it, but searching Dolores's wide pale eyes, she found no condemnation—and she was so tired of hiding.

She nodded so minutely she wasn't sure Dolores, or anyone, could see the gesture. But Dolores was right. English, not

German, had been the language spoken in the von Alton home. Her mother had only learned German after her marriage and, in private, never felt it conveyed her true feelings.

"I understand. I think in Polish. I am Polish." Dolores clapped her free hand over their bound ones. "I will never tell your secret."

Ingrid's fight drained away. Her hand felt boneless now trapped between Dolores's, who tightened her grip in companionship.

"Leo didn't, doesn't, speak English." Ingrid shook her head. "I never meant to hide it, but the lies started long before Leo, and when I tried to tell him the truth about my family, he didn't react like I'd hoped. Nothing was what I thought. And we married so fast and . . ." Ingrid paused. "Everything changed."

"You must be more careful," Dolores countered.

"I am. Everywhere. All the time." Ingrid felt the emptiness of her loneliness wash over her.

"You aren't . . ." Dolores shook her head. "Not when you think you are alone. Not when you are scared or when you are sad. You forget and you go back to your roots. I sing in Polish. You sing in English. It's soft. I don't think a recording device could even capture it, but perhaps . . . You must never forget, even here in your home."

Dolores scanned the kitchen, pausing on the cream corded telephone hanging from the wall, the light fixture above the table, the vent in the ceiling.

"You are never alone in this city."

∽∾

The life inside Ingrid changed her.

All her hesitancy about her marriage vanished at the baby's first kick. She was besotted and determined. She would be better;

they would be better; the world would be better. Because she was needed. She was wanted. She would be seen. She would love and be loved. Ingrid laughed at herself. She, the mother, was to give everything to her baby, but already the baby was giving Ingrid's greatest desire to her—a place to belong.

Flooded with second-trimester energy, Ingrid tried to find ways to let this growing love spill over to Leo. She settled upon meeting him in the one thing he truly cared about—his work. Whatever love they once had shared might have grown cool, but she could step into his world where she could, try to want what he wanted, and perhaps bridge the chasm between them.

After all, they were a family.

One evening, Ingrid suggested hosting a series of dinner parties. Her offer pleased him and Leo sent out invitations the very next day. His bosses came. Another night, neighbors came. Soon he asked his wife to host a series of small parties within a single week. Diplomats from various embassies came.

At every party Ingrid listened and learned. She memorized her guests' tastes, habits, and quirks. She paid attention as to when to insert herself into a conversation and when to become invisible. Over a couple of months, she became the consummate hostess. She became her mother.

Through these parties, she found a way to connect with her husband. She had a purpose, one valuable to him, and, once again, he began to regard her with something nearing love. He was delighted. And with Dolores helping her, Ingrid no longer felt small and alone.

She set herself to the task of hosting a few dinner parties each month, and within four months, Leo was awarded another promotion. And they were assigned a new apartment. They moved within a week. Two weeks before Ingrid was expected to give birth.

It was a stunning new building and Leo stood, shoulders back, chest out, staring up at its twenty floors rising in stone and cement above them.

"Twenty-eight Ulitsa Novatorova." He sighed. "This is one of the finest apartment buildings in the Obruchevsky District. That's where we are." He gestured to the streets surrounding him as if, after four years, they were new to Ingrid. "This is Moscow's top administrative district . . . Come."

He pulled at her hand with one of his own and waved to the young men from the moving company with the other. "We are on the fifteenth floor and our apartment has a direct view of Vorontsovsky Park. It's beautiful. The best."

Leo was right. The building was grand on a scale beyond her imagining. It was not one of the hundreds of Khrushchyovka, the low-cost cement apartment buildings that now dotted the city, but a brand-new design with a central tower, twenty stories tall, flanked by four corner towers, rising ten stories each. Shops and cafés filled the first floor with tiled floors and glass chandeliers. Stores she'd never had access to before now became the places she was expected to shop. The lines were few and far between at such select and exclusive stores.

After several days of unpacking and cleaning, Ingrid and Dolores put the final touches to their preparations for Leo's open house. He had invited a small group from work, but an important one. Ingrid could tell by the way he fussed with his clothes and gave a last polish to his shoes moments before he answered the door.

That night his guests were louder than usual, as men often were with wives not in attendance and with food and drink in endless supply.

Additionally, from the kitchen Ingrid heard Leo make an unusual announcement before dinner began. "I scanned today and we are completely clear." He offered a boisterous, arrogant laugh. "I can't promise about tomorrow, but I can vouch for tonight."

"Good for you." Another man chuckled. "This morning I scheduled phone taps for a new diplomat and got my ear chewed off by some youth in the Twelfth Department for sidestepping the approved processes. They've got us coming and going now."

Ingrid didn't hear what came next, as she was preparing a platter of meats and cheeses in the kitchen, but she noted a change in tone with whatever had been said. Something about the stillness pricked at her senses and her memories. Something deep within her shifted. She set the platter down on the counter. But rather than retreat, she stepped closer to their living room's entrance.

"Yuri Vladimirovich is furious." She heard Leo cut into the silence. "He wants immediate military reprisals, and if we aren't shrewd, he'll get his way soon."

"Yuri?" a deeper voice questioned. "What does he have to do with this?"

"Everything," another man scoffed. "He was our ambassador to Hungary in '56 for that debacle, and he certainly did nothing to end that affair quietly. He had the whole world watching and condemning our private business. He now claims that without immediate action, the Grozny riots will escalate to the same scale."

"Hungary? That was nothing," another man commented with condescension.

"Don't be foolish. We lost seven hundred of our soldiers with only twenty-five hundred Hungarians killed. It was an uprising that carries repercussions to this day."

"You're talking nonsense. It was rabble we dealt with."

"Rabble that made international headlines." Leo's calm voice inserted itself. "Boris is right. The Hungarian Uprising was poorly handled and was made worse as over two hundred thousand fled West . . . No, if we aren't careful, Yuri Vladimirovich makes a strong case for military intervention. The numbers leaving the German Democratic Republic grow alarming."

"The Grozny riots are over. That was two months ago," a firm voice chimed in.

"Risk still remains." Leo's tone was gentle, consoling. Ingrid knew those notes. He was drawing his listeners to his side. "Bricks were thrown. Mobs swarmed government buildings. It sets a bad precedent to let things go so far. We must be more vigilant."

Ingrid felt the hairs on the back of her neck rise. Leo's soft delivery grew menacing.

She flinched as someone barked a derisive, bitter laugh, and the mesmerizing effect was broken. "*Vigilant?* Who do you think Yuri Vladimirovich is? He will squash this. He's rabid, and now that he's been promoted to lead Directorate K, expect our counterintelligence division to grow and squash this, with more funds of course. That's how he'll destroy this uprising. He'll send illegals and kill it from the inside."

"And he'll bug our homes to learn how we feel about it." Another laughed. "There's no quarter with Andropov. He sees dissent everywhere and he's on the rise. He's chasing promotions so fast he's got the Politburo paying attention now."

Ingrid froze as the man's name became complete. *Yuri Vladimirovich Andropov.* She noted that each man in the living room said Andropov's name differently, signaling how well he knew him. Some used only Andropov's last name. Others his first and his patronymic—they knew him better. Others still, just his first—those men knew him very well indeed.

She only knew what little Leo had let slip, but—listening to how he talked rather than what he said—she knew Leo feared him. Yuri Andropov was climbing the KGB and Party ladder quickly. He was the type with whom "rehabilitation" would not be possible, dissent not tolerated, and British blood a deadly liability.

Leo spoke again. She could tell by the lilt of his voice that he was bringing the conversation to safer ground. "To tomorrow. To a new dawn."

The men chimed in accord and Ingrid heard the clink of their crystal glasses in toast. The successive *tings* made a hopeful sound, clear and beautiful. One completely discordant with the dark thoughts pressing against her temples, her heart, and her baby. Ingrid turned back into the kitchen and sank onto one of the chairs tucked close to the table. Her baby kicked inside her, and the platter of meats and cheeses rested forgotten on the counter.

⟡

Three days later, Ingrid gave birth to a baby girl.

"You are finally here." Leo gently lifted his daughter from her hands. "My beautiful little Liybimaya." *My darling. My love.*

Ingrid smiled at her husband's gentle tone and his endearment. Every note that had once been hers, now long dead, rose anew to be lavished upon their daughter. Yet rather than feel any jealousy, she felt hope at his tenderness toward this beautiful little baby.

Leo glowed, unable to tear his eyes from his daughter's small, perfectly featured face with rosebud lips and tiny button nose. "We will make a better world for her. A new tomorrow. A new dawn."

He repeated his toast of a few nights earlier, making it a promise between them.

"Yes." Ingrid tucked the hospital's thin blanket more tightly around herself and reached for the baby. She, too, had felt something change within her during that dinner party. She'd still host parties, but not to support Leo's career any longer. She had an entirely new purpose in mind for her efforts.

Ingrid looked down at her daughter's dark eyes and the shock of dark hair sticking up from the crown of her head. She kissed her forehead, pressing her lips firmly against her daughter's soft skin.

"I love you, Anya Leonidovna Kadinova, and I *will* make this a better world for you. I promise."

# THIRTEEN

# Anya

MOSCOW
*April 16, 1983*

EVERYONE WONDERS WHAT'S HAPPENED TO ME. I WONDER, TOO, when I let myself think about it. But I don't think about it. Stepping close to it all proves too painful, so I tuck and roll like that American animal, the possum, hoping that if I deny I'm still alive, living won't hurt so much.

I've become the most diligent worker ever, and it's angering my coworkers. They say I'm purposefully making them look bad as I arrive early, leave late, and, other than a quick lunch, don't take cigarette or tea breaks anymore.

I also haven't answered my apartment phone much in the past four months—my door either. When Sonya pounded on it a few weeks after Dmitri died, I let it go on so long my neighbor came out and shooed her away. But there's no one I want to see or talk to. I tried to write Scott a few times, hoping that pouring out my heart to him eight thousand kilometers away might help, but I destroyed each attempt. I couldn't lie about what happened to Dmitri, and I certainly couldn't write about it.

Then, one night at the bar a couple weeks ago, Sonya poked me. Pointer finger right beneath the shoulder bone where you get your immunization shots. It hurt.

"Hey—"

She drove her finger into the nerve again. It took me a second to remember. Her brother learned this, and he said it was an easy way to "break a friend." Gentle, he claimed, no permanent damage.

I swiped at her hand. "Stop it."

"Make me."

"I will. I swear to you."

"Really?" She pressed again. And again. "Come on, show me. What are you going to do about it?"

Instantly she reminded me of a secret book that same brother got us years ago. Salinger's *The Catcher in the Rye*. I have no idea how he got it. We never share that information in case someone gets caught. But I've never forgotten the protagonist, Holden Caulfield. He was so lost and in pain. He needed a Sonya.

However, if he'd had one, we never would have had *The Catcher in the Rye* because he'd have dealt with all that pain and "phony" stuff, not ended up in a mental hospital. He would have recognized he had a true friend—not in a hug but in a fight. Because that's what he was searching for. He didn't need someone to pat his back and whisper platitudes; he needed someone to challenge him to live, to rage, to mourn his brother, and to grab on to his life again.

He may have needed a Sonya, but I guarantee he didn't want one. To get pushed like that is almost more painful than the slough through which you're treading. I slapped her hand. At least, I tried to. Sonya always was a better fighter than me. She even won a ribbon in Class Ten. Dmitri was first in our class; Sonya was second.

Sonya raised her arm to deflect mine, sliced down, and in a single swipe, captured my hand and twisted it between us. "That's how you try to stop me?"

With her free hand, she had the nerve to poke me again. I pushed her back and found myself stumbling instead. People started to stare, but we weren't making a ruckus. Only a few inches apart, our "fight" was tight and compressed.

"I can't do this," I whispered, no longer struggling as she gripped my arm to hold me steady.

"You can and you will." She twisted my hand until I yelped. It broke the dam between us and she pulled me close. "I loved him too, Anya, and I still love you. Stay with me."

I hugged her with all my strength. "I'm trying, but . . ."

"I understand." She smoothed my hair with one hand. "I really do."

Things got better after that night, but I'm still struggling. I'm struggling because something has happened over these past three months. I reached my line. My Thomas More line that I cannot cross. I knew it that day in the morgue, and I feel it with blazing certainty now. I cannot and will not accept the lie about Dmitri's death, and that means I cannot and will not accept the entire foundation upon which it stands.

"Jacket." Comrade First Lieutenant Wadim Rogov nods at me. I decided to be good to my coworkers and leave on time today, and this is what I get: Rogov. A far nicer guard goes on duty next. Grigor has waved me by without a second glance almost every night these past months.

I shake my head. I'm not wearing a jacket. It's a light sweater over a thin blouse, and I am not taking it off. Anger burns within me. *Small gestures. Make a stand.* "No."

"Jacket," Rogov repeats. I feel the line of workers behind me stiffen and fall silent. They, too, are wondering what's coming next.

"This is unnecessary and inhumane." I drop my bag onto his table. "Search my bag, but you can clearly see there is nothing on me. You simply want to humiliate me."

Rogov digs through my bag. Then gestures to the side. "You will stand there."

The heat within me cools and I don't push back. While speaking, Rogov lightly touched the pistol at his side. It was reflexive, quick, and I'm not sure he even caught it, but I did. I close my eyes, accepting that I've just crossed the line between bravery and brash insanity.

No one meets my eyes as Rogov checks each bag and the line clears. Soon we are the only two left in the corridor. He turns to me.

"You are no better than me. You will stand here and take off that jacket or I will take you into custody and someone else will handle you."

"Yes." My small word cracks midsyllable. His eyes glint with satisfaction. He was always going to win. I just wanted . . . I don't even know what I wanted.

I remove my sweater and he pats me down. Again, it's humiliating, but it's not sexual. For some reason I note that. And while that would be far worse, his clinical approach is dehumanizing nonetheless. I am being searched not as a person but merely as a conveyor, a thing. Some *thing* with no voice, no rights, no ability to protest at all.

"Sign here." He points to a black book resting on the table.

"What?" He slides it toward me and I ask myself, *Am I ready for this?* "I obeyed." I offer the statement hoping he'll back down and I can ponder my "line" another day. His expression tells me I cannot. It's today.

Rogov slams his palm down. "Sign."

One offense. It's often all it takes, and once my name is recorded in that book, it will be logged, filed, tagged. I could be questioned, fired, arrested. I could lose my livelihood, my apartment, my life. While any or all of this *could* happen to anyone,

I work with too many secrets for a violation to be taken lightly. Something *will* happen to me. Rogov could report me without my signature, of course, but that's his point. It's the ultimate mind game—signing your demise with your own hand.

"I'm sorry." I drop my eyes. I'm not faking submission now.

"Go."

I hear the triumph in his voice. I don't look up. I simply grab my things and flee. I'm humiliated but not scared of being reported. His one word made it very clear: Rogov will not report me. He will make me pay. At the very least, he will relish my humiliation every time our paths cross. I push my way out of the building's heavy metal door, dreading all that is to come.

My mother stands waiting outside.

It's dark. It's late. I'm ashamed. Why is she here? What will she say? Then reason kicks in. She can't find out—ever.

I have a vague memory from long ago. Something happened and my mom was upset and angry, but fear eclipsed all those emotions the second she turned around and saw I was there to witness it. I remember her crying, hugging me, begging me to forget what I must have misunderstood. My mother never shares the dangers that must touch her life, and that means I definitely can't share mine.

I stop in front of her. "How long have you been waiting?"

She steps toward me and brushes a strand of hair back, tucking it behind my ear. It's such a loving gesture I feel myself wilt. I stiffen and step back. I can't tell her what I've just done. I can't upset her. I can't make her afraid for me, and I especially don't want her to sense the toxic brew within me.

"Did you work late?"

I nod. I can't lie, at least not with words.

"You haven't returned my calls."

I shake my head. Words won't come. Words haven't come for

167

four months. In fact, thirty minutes ago was the first time I've felt alive since Sonya poked at me, and that ended horribly.

"You're too thin."

I try to be annoyed but can't rustle up the energy. Besides, she's right. I've lost weight. I see it in my face, my breasts, and my stomach. My skirts used to fit. Now they barely catch on my hips.

"I'll walk you home." She tucks her arm within mine and directs us down the road.

We walk in silence and having her near feels good. But I want her to talk. I want her to distract me. I think up a million starter sentences, and each dies on my tongue before it escapes. I'm angry. I want to fight. But who? I've imagined this line, and yet— Did I back off it because there was no way to win? Is it futile to try to be strong when everything against me is stronger? What is there to think, believe, and hope in? There's no way out. There's no way—

Almost to my building, I can't hold it in any longer. One word, a question, escapes. "Mother?"

She seizes me and holds me tight—so tight all my pieces come back together and so painful I can't bear it. I break apart in sobs. My mother shifts her weight to hold me up as she slowly steps us toward a nearby bench and leads me to sit. Still tucked within her arms, I hear the gentle whispers of my childhood, lullaby tunes and soft notes uniquely hers. She holds me until we are both cold. She starts shaking and I come to my senses.

"I'm sorry. It's freezing out here. You need to go home."

"Don't be sorry. Never be sorry to need your mother. Do you want me to stay with you?"

I swipe at my eyes and my nose. My head is full, it hurts, but nothing like it did. "No. You go home. Father will miss you. I'm okay." She tilts her head, considering me. "I am now. I promise I just miss him, Mother. I miss . . ." I let my words trail away. To list all that I miss would open a gulf within me I'd never bridge.

I hug her again. Maybe she is enough. Maybe she and my father are enough. A tiny bit of strength returns. I can feel it and I squeeze her tight.

She laughs. "I guess you are."

I wait with her for a taxicab, then after waving her away, I cross the street and walk the final blocks home. And for the first time in four months, I sleep.

∞

An outrageous plan forms within my dreams and I wake early, clearheaded, and go for a walk. That's another thing I used to love to do on Sundays and haven't in months. Walk. Breathe deep. Relish the illusory sense of freedom that fresh air and sunshine can bring.

I cross through the Moscow Zoo, then head toward Krasnaya Ploshchad. Something leads me there. I think about the parades, the missiles, and the pageantry. I think about Scott. I think of how his eyes softened as I spoke of home.

*"You don't describe it as I imagined."*

*"Most things aren't. We're so busy with our day-by-day living, we don't have time to be scary."* I throw him a smirk as most Americans truly do find the thought of Soviets quite scary. *"In many ways the first victims of the Revolution were the people."*

*"I never thought of it that way."* He reached for my hand.

I remember leaning into him and closing my eyes, envisioning my mother and my father and my friends. *"No one does, I suspect, until it becomes so obvious it can't be hidden any longer."*

I think about the time Tracy dragged me to hear Pope John Paul II in DC the fall of our senior year. He officiated a mass on

169

the National Mall and implored his audience, the whole world, to respect the dignity of human life as a concrete reality and not an abstraction in service to the State or anyone or anything. He espoused the same ideals Solidarity champions. I never shared that moment with Dmitri. He'd have savored it; I'd forgotten about it.

Yet Dmitri knew. Maybe through his underground church or through the samizdats or maybe even through the Polish people he met working as an illegal. He knew and he tried to impress upon me that Solidarity promulgated the truth that our inherent dignity exists for nothing more or less than the beauty that we are human. That's why the movement was still growing and why it was quickly becoming too big and too deep for the Soviet juggernaut to crush. That old Russian proverb again, the one he said he learned from my mother. *"One word of truth outweighs the whole world."*

My heart hurts. I stop at Krasnaya Ploshchad and soak in the Kremlin towers in all their fierce glory. Dmitri chose sides. He was no longer posturing or pretending at dissent. He really did find his line and his cause. His bosses understood what I failed to see. And for the first time since we were six, he left me behind.

I turn away, almost as if to escape the Kremlin's long-reaching stare, and without noticing where I'm walking, I cover the city over and over. For hours I weave my way down alleys and streets, watching as people walk in and out of restaurants, some laughing, most not. We are not a chatty, smiley people.

*Why not?* I ask myself this question for the first time and wonder at the answer. After all, if we are a superior society, why are we not happier about it?

I think of my parents, my father's focus on work, "pushing the papers uphill" as he likes to say, conforming to life and its demands without question. I think of my mother's quieter loyalty, her work at the museum, and the tiny glimpses into the fear deep within her. Fear I had never truly detected—remembered—until Dmitri died.

I circle back to watch the soldiers, suited in the grey uniforms of the Kremlin Guard, change rotation outside the Great Tower. I walk toward the river, past the park, and find myself a block from the American embassy with the certainty I've been heading here all along. I see the red-white-and-blue flag blowing in the breeze from its rooftop, and I pull the hood of my sweatshirt up.

Large cameras are mounted on the side of the building pointing out. I assume they are American. I twist, using my hand to shield my eyes from the sun. Larger cameras are mounted on the street poles beside me, facing the embassy. I assume they are Soviet.

Hood up and head down, I cross the street for a closer view. A black Mercedes sedan pulls out of the gates and pauses at the street. The woman inside is blonde with sunglasses on. She's got that uniquely American bearing—something about the way she holds her head—and her sunglasses are those fashionably large lenses not for sale here. I note the license plate starts with the D04 of diplomatic plates.

In that moment the pieces click into place and a surety covers me. It's not peace—it's too focused and energetic—but it's like peace. I feel firm, resolute, and that's enough.

I will not cross that line. Here I make my stand and I'll bring the whole thing crashing down.

I walk home.

Every day at work, I do my job with care and diligence. I am again arriving early and leaving late, but I no longer work to avoid life. Work becomes life. And every evening I submit to any search Comrade First Lieutenant Wadim Rogov feels is warranted. I even thank him. The glint in his eyes tells me he thinks it's about him and he's won. After three weeks, he grows bored.

Four weeks later, on the day I slide a small scrap of tracing paper into my tights, he barely pays me any attention. There's nothing on the paper. I simply want to get it out. It feels like such a simple and basic thing to do compared to Hollywood movies and novels, but that's what my plan requires and what I suspect true spy work entails—a lot of nothing wrapped around a little dangerous something.

It's the nothing that holds it all together.

So I persist. I work, I smile, I tuck scraps of blank paper within my tights, and—each and every Sunday—I walk and canvass every last detail of my plan.

On my eighth Sunday I see the car again. Walking to beat it around the corner, where I've noted no cameras on any of my walks, I set myself to cross the street in front of the woman's sedan. My note is ready, rolled, and tucked within a Pepsi can to give it substance and make it easier to toss. I'm hoping for an open window and the warm June day is working in my favor.

The car slows at the pedestrian crosswalk. Its windows are shut. I turn to walk away and realize it is now or never as there are virtually no pedestrians about. No witnesses.

I step from the curb and tap the driver's window. The woman—the same blonde I've seen each week—startles, then stares. Today she is not wearing sunglasses. Her hazel eyes widen in surprise.

"Please roll down your window." I speak clearly in English and note the remnants of a certain Georgian boy's accent within my words—again the American state and not the Soviet one. "Please."

She rolls it down a few inches and I slip the Pepsi can in. She reaches for it, and as it tumbles from her fingers into her lap, she stiffens. I reach out, then stop, fearing I will cause her more panic.

"It won't hurt you. It's only a note. Take it to your embassy. Immediately." I turn and walk away. The note will have to do the rest.

I cross in front of the car, trying to keep my steps measured but quick, and head to the next block. If she believes me, she will turn right, circle the block, and return to the embassy. If she does not, I expect she'll do what she does every Sunday and turn left at the next light and head north out of the city.

I race through an alley that ends a block farther from the embassy, but it gives me a clear view of its entrance gate. I watch for the black sedan. Within a minute it turns onto the street and slides through the embassy gates. As the gates close behind it, I tighten my hood and walk away.

Heading home, I mentally recite every word I wrote. I can't turn it off—it's a recording on endless repeat that feels like it will only stop when someone else reads my words and they become theirs.

It took me almost a hundred iterations before I got down exactly what I wanted to say, and it took me at least twenty matches to burn each rough draft to such fine ash that no one could discern a single word within my failed attempts.

And to prove my worth and sincerity, I offered a tiny bit of the "dangerous" up front too. While there was nothing on those scraps of paper I secreted out every few days, there was something tucked within me. Each day I memorized sections of my lab's new defense-shield schematics and added those details to a drawing each night, hiding the paper beneath a loose floor tile in my bathroom.

Please contact Mr. Trent Olivers and tell him Professor Jamison's "best and brightest" realizes she cannot find what she wants or needs at home.

To prove my sincerity I offer him the following hand-drawn schematic of a new defense shield, DFT357, to counter US short-range U45 missiles. If he is willing to meet, I will look for a note under the southernmost bench on the east side of the promenade entrance to the Moscow Zoo.

I will stop every day on my way home from work at six o'clock for the next month. After that time, I will assume he is no longer interested in a discussion.

Thank you.

The idea for the note and the meeting place came from the American spy movie *North by Northwest* that Scott and I watched one night. But as I recite my copy over and over, it feels childish. It was a movie. Maybe no one sets up "meets" like that. And what if my note never gets to Mr. Olivers? Worse yet, what if our meeting in Jamison's office was a KGB ruse?

I try to push all the thoughts away. What's done is done. After all, only one lab in the entire Union of Soviet Socialist Republics is working on that defense shield. If any part of this plan fails, it won't be the USSR that comes crashing down—it'll be me.

# FOURTEEN

# Anya

MOSCOW
*July 22, 1983*

Is a month enough time? As I haven't been arrested or assassinated, I begin to breathe and ask myself this question.

If all went as I hoped, I expected my note to reach Mr. Olivers within hours and a reply to rest beneath the bench within days. I had thought that by the end of a week, perhaps two, I'd be "activated." After all, I had handed him gold. Hadn't I?

The first week after I dropped that Pepsi can, every noise made me jump. I was sure someone knew, everyone knew, and it was only moments before I'd be hauled away. I also questioned what I'd done—too many spy movies and not enough common sense. Who puts a note in a Pepsi can and hands it to a stranger just because she holds her head like an American?

During the second week, I mentally recited my note again and again. Was it clear, right, and enough? I also envisioned my drawing in the minutest detail, suspecting I'd forgotten something that discredited its authenticity.

During the third week I questioned my motivation. Was it pure? What did *pure* mean? What was my *why*? Was it noble? Did it need to be noble? What would my mother say? What would my father do? What would Dmitri say, if he could? How would Scott react? Had I signed my own death warrant and that of my family simply because I wanted . . . I wanted . . . ?

I laid my head on my desk almost daily. *What do I want?*

*I want to sleep*, was one answer. Another was that I wanted to do everything I could to make the world a better place, one that honored the dignity of humans and allowed each and every person to thrive. Yes, it felt grand, but it felt small and deeply personal too. Because no one is thriving.

After the third week passed, I rarely slept, barely ate, and felt certain I was being watched. I saw the same people over and over, and while the rational part of my brain knew they, too, were following their daily routines, the irrational part had them surrounding me. That's when I started smoking again. It's a disgusting habit I gave up in college, but why else would someone stop and sit on the same park bench each night?

"What is going on with you?" Sonya demanded last week. "You barely come out with us anymore. Do I need to start poking your shoulder again? Right now . . . you're not even listening to me."

Then she jabbed me. So hard she left a bruise.

It was in that moment I realized what Mr. Olivers had truly meant. The game had to be complete—no cracks. I hadn't even done anything yet, not really, not formally, but I was already acting jumpy and suspicious. If I was a card player, I was "showing my hand." But that was the problem—I'd never had to hide anything before. Dmitri always carried the weight of our world and secrets for me. "I miss him," I told Sonya. "I'm not sure who I am without—"

Nothing more escaped as she crashed into me, grabbed me close, and squeezed all the air out of me. With three older brothers, Sonya is someone to get used to. I have and I love her.

"You can do this and you're not alone."

She was talking about simply living life, and for the first time I believed she might be right. Just as Mr. Olivers was right. The *why* matters most—maybe both in living and in spying. And, held tight within Sonya's arms, I realized I didn't need Dmitri's help, but I still needed Sonya. I needed all my friends and my parents. I needed to fight for them and I needed to protect them. And that meant, if Mr. Olivers accepted me, complete commitment to the game once it began.

That's when I started sleeping and eating again.

Fairly certain I missed the mark somehow, I also began to strategize what my second attempt might entail. Nevertheless, I still checked the bench each and every day. And yesterday, sitting there smoking my Prima, I realized my note hadn't specified which side of the bench. Perhaps a reply was taped to the other end weeks ago and I missed it.

So I devised a new plan. I twisted from side to side, as if releasing a kink in my back, then dropped my bag to my feet. Bending to reach into it, I searched for my pack of Primas again. Digging around in my bag gave me a few seconds to scan the underside of the bench. Nothing. I sat up, lit my next cigarette, and stewed for a few moments until I burned it down to a nub.

Then tonight—it's here.

A small square of white is taped to the underside of the bench. Out of easy reach. I drag my bag, a worn canvas thing, off the ground and into my lap. I rustle through it, dropping some of its contents onto the pavement. Then, bending down to gather everything, I shift to the side and, reaching for an errant pen, swipe the note free.

I practically whoop with my own brilliance and stop myself just in time. I don't crack a smile and I don't open the note—though I have never wanted to do anything more in my life. I bury it deep within my bag, draw out my cigarette, and calmly go through my routine. But the second I get home, I—very dramatically—climb under the covers of my bed with a flashlight like I used to do as a kid and pull the note from its plastic sleeve.

Zatsepa 89. 3pm. 24 July.

❦

An old maps book shows me Zatsepa is a small street outside the Ring Road in the Danilovsky District. It's not far, but it takes me three hours hopping on and off buses and cutting through alleyways to feel confident no one has followed me or is watching me. Again, I suspect I've seen too many spy movies.

But I'm on time, and exactly at the stroke of three o'clock, I sit across a scuffed table from Mr. Olivers in a one-room apartment on the second floor of a narrow walk-up, situated above a row of dilapidated shops.

"I wondered if our paths would cross again," he muses.

The apartment is no more than a couple hundred square feet. The kitchen and a toilet are situated in the corner, and the only pieces of furniture are our small table and its three chairs as well as a cot. I'm surprised to find a toilet.

Mr. Olivers sits in one metal chair. I'm in another and the third remains empty as its potential occupant stands against the wall.

I say nothing to him. He doesn't introduce himself.

"I didn't expect to meet with you. Not in person." I take a breath to keep my voice from wavering. I've been so confident, even brave in my self-congratulatory righteousness for the past couple days. But now all my bravado is gone and I feel small and unsure faced with the magnitude of what I'm about to do.

"I thought a familiar face might put you at ease and . . ." He stalls, assessing me. "I wanted to hear from you personally what's changed. Tell me your why."

I study my shredded cuticles and catch sight of Dmitri's gold band. His smile comes to me and covers me more comfortably than the jacked-up frenzy that has dogged me the past few weeks. I sit with it for a moment before replying. When I do consider what to say, only one word comes to mind. "Hope."

"Hope?"

"There is none here. We are a culture of 'I can't' rather than one of 'I can.'" I envision Scott's bright eyes and accept he's been a vital part of this journey as well. It was through him that I first began to understand hope and what a life with it might feel like.

"I never realized what a real and vital thing it truly is until—" I press my lips together, keeping Scott to myself. "Georgetown . . . Hope is not desired and certainly not cultivated here, because it puts something above the State. It would divide our loyalty and make us look above and beyond, maybe as far as eternity. It's such a little thing . . . I mean, you don't need much, but you do need it. I miss it."

"Join an underground church." Mr. Olivers's words and face carry no expression.

His statement doesn't surprise me. Everyone knows they aren't actual "churches." They are groups of people from all faiths who secretly gather to look beyond, dissidents who find courage and companionship together, who may even work to fight for freedom together.

"I may . . ." I return my focus to the present. "But one thing I've learned about hope is that you have to carry it, act on it, and take risks to grow it. I have a friend who did that. He took risks because he found hope, maybe even faith, and he showed me that line. The one I told you I feared I'd find and not be able to cross."

Mr. Olivers leans forward, inviting me to expound.

So I do. I tell him about Dmitri, about how he picked me up when a bully knocked me down and we became best friends. I tell him how we made forts when we were young, how we played at spies, and how he stood up for those kids with the bast shoes who were excluded from the Little Octobrists and the good clubs. I told him how Dmitri excelled at MGIMO and how he'd been sent to work as an illegal in Poland to undermine Solidarity. I tell him about Dmitri's growing disillusionment, growing anger, growing drinking, and growing faith. I tell him about his murder.

"*Murder* is a strong word. He could have been mugged as reported."

I hold up my hand. Dmitri's gold ring sits bold and bright on my middle finger. "No mugger would leave behind this gold. Besides, at School number 227 we are trained to fight from Class Six on. He was always good, really, really good. MGIMO only would have made him better. His fingernails were clean."

Mr. Olivers nods as he, too, catches the detail's significance. "And if they hadn't found him in a place he'd never be? Would you be here now?"

"Maybe not," I admit, straining to be as honest as I can. "Maybe I wouldn't have gone to the morgue and seen him. Maybe I'd have convinced myself that it was an accident and forget everything that came before. Maybe I could have gone on. But that's not what happened and here I am."

"What about your parents?" Olivers leans back in his metal chair. It creaks with the shift of his weight. "Do they share your thinking, even your anger?"

His question stops me. I hadn't thought that I'm working from anger. I had placed my motivation on a far superior philosophical plane. But he is right. I am angry, and I need to own that too.

"Is it wrong to be angry?" I ask the question sincerely.

He glances to the man standing, who shakes his head so minutely I almost don't see it. Olivers returns his attention to me. "No. To be angry about something that's wrong is a good thing. Anger fuels us, sharpens our instincts, but it takes energy, too, and it can be destructive. It can deplete us too soon, wear us down, make us sloppy, and get us killed."

I think of Dmitri. I think of my past few months.

"I don't want to be angry. I don't want there to be something to be angry about." I lean forward and lay my hands on the table between us. "My parents work and live by the rules and I don't want to get them hurt, but they don't see what I see. I'm not sure their generation can."

"What do you see?"

"I see we fear you more than you fear us. We're fed lies about you. My years in the States taught me you don't want to destroy us. Sure, Reagan's talk is vitriolic, but you have an innate brashness that eclipses fear. You truly trust that your Constitution, your way of life and your freedoms, are superior. I also see that what one believes becomes reality. We have fear. Real fear. Our leaders are reactive and paranoid, and that makes them dangerous—to the world and to our own people. Fear is worse than anger. If one has to drive you, let it be anger."

I peek at the other man. His face reveals nothing, but I can tell he's listening. Olivers crosses one leg over the other, resting an ankle on his knee. He slides a pack of cigarettes across the table.

I shake my head. I've smoked so much this past month my stomach sours at the thought of another. He lights one for himself, and only when the cloud of smoke hovers above him does he speak again.

"Most students who come to the US in the Foreign Studies Initiative are already KGB activated. Your answers are, after all, exactly what I want to hear."

"That's not true. We are never 'activated.'" I trace a patch at the edge of the table where the laminate has pulled away from the top. "However, if I was planted to trick you, I probably would have given you all these perfect answers three years ago or I would've offered you old military intel now. Something you could confirm, but nothing that could tip the scales in America's favor. In Professor Jamison's office, you said you have good instincts. I can only ask you to trust them."

Olivers again defers to the man still leaning against the wall.

He starts speaking. His voice is deep. He speaks with intention. "It's not easy running an agent in Moscow. Near impossible, and I'm going to be honest with you, we've been ordered to stand down for a number of years now. We've got rust to shake off." He shifts his focus to Olivers. "This is risky."

"But doable." Olivers's eyes take on the glow of reminiscing, and his gaze drifts to the distance, somewhere between the man and me. "With the right approach, she could be better than LUMEN. Military access. Schematics. Her access to Petrov? We haven't had anything like this in years."

"Lumen?" I catch on to the one word I don't understand. *Light.*

The unnamed man speaks. "Code name for a ghost, a shadow, a legend operating somewhere in Europe, and it bugs him that LUMEN isn't ours." He gestures to Olivers. "We lost an agent and got pulled outta Moscow, yet some other service found a way in. LUMEN could be Dutch, British, Swedish, Finnish . . . No one has a clue. But his intelligence is top grade, expertly controlled, and given such random provenance no one can track the source. For twenty-five years now, someone has accomplished the unthinkable in the intelligence community—a true living secret."

The man shakes his head. Now he, too, has a wondering

glow about him. "He's the one who told us last year it was the Soviets feeding troop locations to the Argentines during the Falklands War. The Brits had no clue as to how their every move was countered."

"Falklands?" I rack my brain. "Oh . . . Do you mean the Malvinas? They aren't called the Falklands here. But why would Brezhnev help Argentina?" I think back to my political science courses at Georgetown. "There's no ideological love there."

"That's what we wondered, until LUMEN spelled it out. He realized there was a debt to be paid. Argentina is one of the few countries who defied the call for sanctions against the Soviets for Afghanistan in '79. You eat Argentine meat, produce, and foodstuffs on a daily basis."

"No one eats meat or produce on a daily basis."

The man cracks a faint one-sided smile. I like him.

Olivers cuts between us, waving a hand toward me, but he's talking to the man. "Anya could be that good."

Rather than answer, the man slides the third metal chair from beneath the table. He studies me. "Don't listen to him. Don't believe the grandiose dream he's peddling. He's not taking the risks. You and I are." He stretches his hand toward me. "Peter Crenshaw."

He holds our hands between us, not in a gesture of kindness or chivalry but to maintain my attention. His grip is firm, almost aggressive.

"Actually, only you. I might get a little roughed up and PNG'd, declared persona non grata if caught, but I'll get tossed onto a plane and shipped home to beers and hot dogs. You, on the other hand, *will* be tortured, you *will* break, and then they *will* kill you."

A sense of blue cold washes over me. There's no other way to describe it. It's like all red, all warmth, leaves me. Crenshaw takes note of however that experience shows on my face and nods with satisfaction. He lets go of my hand and leans toward me.

"People enter this game for many reasons—money, revenge, the power of secrets, ideology—and some reasons are qualitatively and quantitatively better than others. One scale is measured by the asset's internal peace and integrity. The other is numbers based, measured by money, output, and the days, months, and years the asset stays alive. It sounds harsh, but it's reality. It's a lonely life wrapped in a dangerous game, and if you come in for the wrong qualitative reasons, the quantitative ones won't matter. You'll get torn up, slip up, and you'll die in a manner far worse than your friend."

I almost remark that his sales pitch needs help, but I don't. The thought, fleeting as it is, doesn't sound funny in my head. It feels empty and naive, just like I feel at this moment.

He continues. "On the other hand, it's also about this." He waves his hand between us. "Connection. Hope. And trust. You trust me and earn my trust, and I expect we'll do good work. Shed a little hope and light on this big, dark world. My goal is not to let one world power drop any more darkness onto another. The world can't sustain this *mad*ness for too long." His emphasis on the first syllable, breaking it from the second, grabs my attention.

*MAD. Mutually Assured Destruction.*

He stares at me, unblinking, for a long moment. "And anger has no place here."

"Pete—" Olivers interjects.

Crenshaw's narrowed eyes silence him. I get the impression they've had this conversation before, and their motivations don't fully align. "Am I running her or are you?"

"You. All you."

Crenshaw turns back to me. "You in? There's no halfway

here. You do what I say and how I say it, and part of the commitment is to leave the emotions behind. Anger. Love. Fear. Pity. None of them play here."

Whatever Mr. Olivers might think, Peter's motivations align with me perfectly, and the order to leave emotions behind, to somehow not feel so much and not hurt so much, is tantalizing. I find myself twisting Dmitri's ring around my finger, remembering his gold-specked eyes and the way his tawny hair flopped over his eyes when we were teenagers, long before he got the standard KGB close clip. I remember his toothy grins and his laughter. I remember those glowing days of childhood in which we thought we could change the world—when "can" was stronger than "can't." I close the door on all those memories and realize I have only one question.

"When do we begin?"

# FIFTEEN

# Ingrid

MOSCOW
*November 22, 1958*

"A NEW TOMORROW. A NEW DAWN."

Leo's words played within Ingrid's imagination all month—
through every nappy change, late-night feeding, and quiet
moment. She wondered what they could mean, for her and for
their daughter.

For Leo, what they meant became immediately apparent.

He worked longer hours and started bringing work home.
Oftentimes, during Anya's midnight feeding, she'd find Leo
shuffling through files, his reading glasses perched on the end
of his nose. He was more dedicated and more secretive. And one
evening, weeks after his *liybimaya*, his little darling, was born, he
brought an odd device home with him. It was the size of a deck
of playing cards, and it made a buzzing sound as he carried it all
through the apartment.

"A friend gave me my own." He waggled the device at Ingrid.
"We will always be clean now."

Ingrid squeezed Anya tight. "Why wouldn't we be?"

"They listen everywhere." Leo waved his hand. "And more
so lately." He kissed the top of his daughter's head. "But not here,
not to you, my little darling."

He locked the new device in his desk's top drawer and never mentioned it again. But he used it almost nightly.

Which was a good thing, Ingrid surmised, as Leo was a doting father who shared his secrets and his world with his *liybimaya* deep in the night as he rocked her to sleep. And things were not going well.

The wellspring of optimism following last year's Sputnik launch had dried up. By insisting that all domestic hardware be kept under government control, the Central Committee now believed they'd lost the space race to the West. The United States was surging ahead and had just passed the 1958 Space Act to create NASA and do exactly what the Soviets forbade—drop all barriers to scientific collaboration between the government and civilian enterprise.

Additionally, defections from East Germany, the German Democratic Republic, continued to increase at an alarming rate, and the discontent in Grozny had not, in fact, faded away. It, too, was growing increasingly precarious.

"It's a complex problem, you see," he softly crooned. "But you are right, my baby girl. We must focus on here and now. The stars can wait. I will see what we can do about the GDR . . ."

Yes, Leo's answer as to how to make the world better for his daughter was immediate. He worked relentlessly to solidify the Soviet Union's supremacy and control at home and abroad.

Ingrid took longer to find her answer, but a month later, she believed she had.

She stood staring at the British embassy. She had never seen it before as she had never sought it out. Her ancestry always felt like a secret too hazardous to approach. But no more. She had watched her parents for years. She had listened and learned from Adam and Martin. And over the past several months, she had mastered fading into the background, a shadow within her own home. During that time, she had learned much of the inner workings of the CPSU, the Central Committee, the Politburo, and even the KGB. Information that could bring about what Leo desired—"*A new tomorrow. A new dawn.*" Just not the one he'd envisioned.

Ingrid shifted her gaze down the river lest her stare garner attention. The embassy's location surprised her. Housed in an opulent mansion from pre-Revolution days, it sat on the embankment of the Moskva River in silent challenge to the building directly opposite. The Kremlin.

She took in the expanse of Krasnaya Ploshchad and, for the first time, was not intimidated by its sheer size and its immeasurable power. Hope was stronger than she'd given it credit for. She thought it had died long ago, yet here it was again, alive and well, possibly stronger and brighter than ever.

With that thought Ingrid straightened her spine, tucked Anya deeper within her blankets, and pushed the pram back home.

⌘

Ingrid trusted her teachers were as good as she always believed them to be.

Martin had taught her that the secret to good espionage was a routine and the color grey. She had laughed at how boring it sounded, but he'd claimed that was the whole point.

"*Fade into the world around you. Lull anyone watching you into believing they can predict your next move. That's when they let down their guard.*"

Adam, while also teaching her to be invisible and read a room, had taught her how to read the world—how to see what was happening around her and how it might affect her at any moment, as well as its consequences.

"*You watch patterns, not people. People make decisions based on a fixed set of expectations. Learn those, listen, and calculate what's coming next. Hone your instincts, then trust them. You absorb far more than you realize."*

Now, three months after Anya's birth, Ingrid steadied her nerves, bundled her daughter into her pram, and walked across their building's marble-floored lobby. The day was frigid and few people would be out. But if the routine was established in the harshest of conditions, no one would question it during the warm days of summer. So every day that week, as she had the one before and the one before that, Ingrid fed Anya her late-morning bottle, bundled her tight, and went for a walk—all so that today no one would notice.

"It's too cold today," a neighbor, Masha, called from across the lobby. "What are you thinking?"

"The air is bracing and it gets us both outside. I'm so tired of being stuck inside our apartment."

The older woman laughed. "I remember those days . . . And who am I to question you? You go out every day and you both are so strong and healthy."

Masha leaned down and touched the baby's cheek before holding the door for them and waving them goodbye. Ingrid could feel her neighbor watching as she pushed the pram toward the neighboring park. She kept her pace controlled, her head turning side to side as if taking in the bustling city street.

It was a low-slung cloud-heavy day and Ingrid walked straight into the park's south entrance as usual. Yet rather than turn right as she did at least three times a week, she turned left.

In one circle of Goncharovsky Park, with the trees barren and the paths empty, she tested herself to recognize the regulars and make note of any newcomers within her space. After two circles, she assessed what she'd seen, noted what was missing, and concluded no one was paying her any attention. Ingrid patted the blanket swaddling her sleeping daughter and felt the surety of peace wrestle a rising bubble of hope. She crossed over to the pay phone at the southeast corner of the park and took a moment to confirm, once again, that all was as it should be.

During one of her earliest dinner parties, with tongues loosened over a fine wine Leo had received from a Politburo member, Ingrid had learned about the *click* of bugged phones. The men had been laughing about how many people incriminated themselves across the telephone lines. *"How can they be so stupid? How can people not notice the delayed click? When will technicians work around that obvious giveaway?"*

No one, thankfully, had an answer for that last question.

The next day, Ingrid had picked up their apartment phone, the phone at work, and three pay phones on her walk home. Their apartment did not have one. Her desk phone at work was clear. But the main line at the Bureau of Historical Archives clicked a second late, as did two of the three pay phones within the park. Ingrid agreed it was an obvious sound.

Yet every couple of days over the past three months she had stopped at this particular pay phone and found it clean each and every time. Today, she lifted it off its receiver, listened, and dialed a number she'd been given long ago and never forgot.

The telephone number Adam Weber promised could always find him.

◦◦◦

*"Pretend it's a game,"* Adam had advised years ago. Now the game had begun.

Ingrid watched the people passing her along the sidewalk. A man tucked deep within his coat, his *ushanka* pulled so low she couldn't see his eyes. A young mother bustling along her lagging children. No one paid any attention to her. *Who would?* she asked herself. She'd spent months establishing a routine that would have lulled anyone interested into complacency.

On Wednesdays she always left Anya with Dolores and walked alone and longer, doing her shopping along the way. On this particular Wednesday, exactly one month after making her telephone call to a receptionist, who then took only thirty minutes to find Adam Weber, it was his voice that filled her head.

She was to be at the south bench in Bolotnaya Ploshchad at 3:00 p.m. *"'Dry cleaning' is what we call it. It's how you come out clean. Now listen . . ."*

Ingrid walked her usual path. Then, just as she was about to turn right for her regular stop at the butcher, she stepped left and hopped on a bus ready to pull away from the curb. She didn't expect her skin to tingle. She didn't expect the rush of adrenaline, but she welcomed it. It felt like a jolt of sunshine running through her veins as she found a seat halfway down the bus and across from its back door.

Two stops later, she stepped off, turned left, and strode, without missing a step, into an alleyway. She kept along the wall of the alley and, emerging on the other side, hailed another bus traveling the opposite direction. Three stops later, and now wearing the brown scarf she carried in her handbag, Ingrid followed a similar circuitous pattern before ending up at Prospect Kandvosk and the entrance to the park.

She sat on a bench and, as instructed, took a roll from her bag. She pulled it apart and dropped a chunk onto the ground beneath her. She picked it up before the pigeons could snatch it and tossed it into a nearby trash can. She returned to her bench.

Within seconds a man in a *petushok*-style hat and great overcoat crossed the grass to her right and sat at the opposite edge of her bench. He pulled a brown paper bag from his deep pocket and started tossing bread crumbs, gathering a flock of pigeons around them.

"Adam sends his regards." The man finally spoke, in Russian.

"I expected him to come in person."

A tiny head shake answered her. After a few moments, the man spoke again. "He's too important now, too well monitored. But he sent me. If you want to . . . continue talking . . . you and I will work together. My name is Reginald Bishop."

"Is that your real name?" She glanced at him again and noted his lips curl.

"Yes. Yes, it is." He sat back. "You've created quite a penumbra, Mrs. Bauer."

*A space of shadow.* Ingrid nodded. *Bauer.* Ingrid smiled. She had insisted on keeping her own last name when she'd married Leo. It wasn't that the name meant a great deal; it was simply one last element of a past she didn't want to let go of. Something of her own when he'd required her to forget so much. And as Bauer was an accepted Russian surname, Leo didn't protest. Reginald also said *Mrs.*, not *Comrade.* Ingrid felt her heart expand.

Reginald pulled a small bottle from another pocket and a scrap of paper from his sock as he shooed away a peckish pigeon. He handed the paper to her, then quickly leaned over and sprayed it. The summer scent of citrus filled the air. "From Adam."

As the ink appeared and she read Adam's note, Reginald talked on. "That's what you need to become, Mrs. Bauer. A shadow. It won't be easy, but if we do this right, those will be the spaces in which you are safe. We tend not to notice the quiet, bland, and grey things in our lives."

Ingrid finished reading the note. Reginald gestured for her to hand back the thin sheet. "The ink will fade in a moment. It reacts to lemon juice. Easy to come by and not tricky to get caught with."

Nevertheless, he shredded the scrap within the protection of his brown paper sack, then chewed and swallowed the strips as he continued. "We've not run an agent in Moscow. Warsaw Pact countries, yes, but this is a different beast altogether. We won't be able to meet often after you get trained up . . . This is new ground."

"For me too."

"Not entirely. Adam said you were very brave in Vienna."

"He is being generous."

"Perhaps, but he's not prone to exaggeration." Reginald chewed the last bit of Adam's note before continuing. "Mrs. Bauer? Before we begin, you need to understand the all-encompassing size and power of the KGB. We won't enter into this lightly, and you certainly shouldn't. You told Adam you have a daughter. You need to consider her before we proceed."

"She is why I'm here."

Reginald absorbed this as he tossed another scattering of bread crumbs across the sidewalk. The birds scrambled around them, and he took those few minutes to canvass their next steps.

If, on the following Wednesday, she found a yellow wax line on the wall across from the bus stop nearest the butcher, they would meet the following afternoon at a safe house the British held on Volkhonk Street. A green wax line meant a meeting two days later at a bakery on Gogolevsky Boulevard. A red line meant she was to stand down until further notice. Reginald would find her and make contact when and if possible. Any which way, Ingrid was to be ready with an answering mark and a plan for how to get to each meeting clean.

"Are you wondering why crayons?"

"No . . . Adam taught me to always use wax. Chalk washes away in the rain."

Reginald offered a ghost of a smile. "Well, then, Mrs. Bauer . . . Welcome to MI6."

# SIXTEEN

# Anya

MOSCOW
*October 15, 1983*

"Don't underestimate your enemy, Anya." Peter frowned at me.

For three months I'd practiced "dead drops," passing nothing to no one, hoping I wouldn't get caught, basically tossing rubbish into a bin while really placing a soda can behind it. I'd also executed "foot-timed drops," which meant I had to make sure I was "clean" at a certain time and place so that whatever I dropped—a secret wrapped within a crumpled cigarette packet, an orange peel, a used yogurt container—could be retrieved within minutes. It all seemed pretty basic.

At our first real meeting he set me straight. "Everyone gets tailed, especially anyone working at the level you do. The KGB isn't as good as its hype—it's better. Even in something so deceptively simple like a dead drop, you must learn to work in the gaps, the tiny breaks in their ever-present surveillance."

I scrunched my face, certain no one had ever "tailed" me.

"We'll see . . ." Peter chuckled. It was short, cynical, ending as quickly as it started. "With well over a hundred thousand KGB in Moscow alone, they've got to do something with their time, and they are more active in this city than anywhere else in the world."

He tapped the table between us. "Let's see what you can do. I'm going to put tails on you next week. You'll never see them, and if the KGB is on you too, they'll drop off. But along with dead drops, you need to learn 'dry cleaning.' That's the process by which you monitor, assess, and lose surveillance while appearing not to notice it at all."

He then spent the next hour basically describing Cat and Mouse—a game my friends and I played on the streets all summer long as kids. We'd have a couple of cats and a few mice and we'd see how close the mice could get to my apartment without getting "eaten." If a mouse got inside, the reward was a cookie. Everyone loved my mother's cookies.

That next week, on Tuesday and Thursday, I spotted his "tails." One was a woman in a grey coat with a brown hat and sturdy shoes. She was very Russian. And she walked with a slight limp. She made the mistake of pausing too many times in concert with me. I lost her by ducking into the grocer, buying a can of beans, exiting out the side door, and catching a bus south rather than north. I never saw her again.

Two days later it was a man. He was harder to spot, as most men wear similarly styled dark coats and fur hats and move like drones along the city sidewalks. And it was unexpectedly frigid that day. Only October and a cold front brought below-zero temperatures. Hats and coats were out, as were gloves. Soviet men wear gloves and this man did not.

I caught his reflection in a shop window as he pulled his hand from his pocket to tighten his scarf. Once I saw that, it only took a couple minutes to confirm he was following me. I lost him a block later by bending to tie my shoelace, then doubling back, which forced him to duck away. Once he was out of sight, I tucked into a doorway until he passed. He doubled back, too, but missed me. I was then tailing him.

But it was the next day that made an impression. That tail was different, more persistent, and it took me two hours to shake him, and even then I wasn't sure. As it was a game, I thought about giving up, walking home, and calling it quits. After all, there was no downside. But I didn't do that, because there *was* a downside—loss of my pride. I didn't want Peter to think I was weak or incapable. And despite Peter telling me to leave the emotions at home, I have this odd mix of anger, fear, faith, and hope that I can do this job. The belief planted itself within me the morning I took Dmitri's ring from his finger, and it has grown every day since. So I kept at it. Another hour and I was sure I was clean.

It isn't until our meeting today that I learn the truth.

Peter grins at me, genuinely pleased. "Impressive. Both my informants lost you and reported they did not sense you spotted them. That's high praise from two of my best."

"Three."

"I didn't tail you three times."

I walk him through all the particulars, and as I recount each detail, his smile morphs to a smirk.

"What else did you see?"

I think back to the afternoon, only days before, and envision what I saw around me, who was there, and how it felt. "There was a Volga. It circled me twice."

"KGB. But they may not have been following you. Volgas are a little high up the food chain for regular tails. They're more for spot surveillance. What you're describing is a specific assignment. What else?"

I couldn't remember anything else odd other than that Volga circling, as they are expensive and not overly common on the streets.

"No Zhigulis with a triangle of dirt on the hood? Stopping near the man tailing you at any time?"

"No, but there's one in our lab's parking lot. I've always wondered about that triangle."

"We suspect the KGB car wash brushes can't reach the center of the hood. All their cars have that triangle. Seems no operative cares enough to clean it himself. Car or no car, you had a KGB tail."

My jaw drops and his smirk widens into a broad know-it-all grin. He reaches to a side counter and lifts a plate I hadn't noticed. "Cookie? They're good."

I feel like a kid who is being rewarded for a good grade. I grab one, and at first crunch Peter starts talking again, walking me through a series of marks and countermarks, each of which signals something different and can be placed discreetly throughout my daily commute. He draws them on white copy paper with crayons. He says they use wax because marker doesn't work on all surfaces and chalk washes away.

"I can't carry around crayons. Someone is definitely going to notice that."

He slides a pack of wax pencils across the table. "You can get these in a few shops here in Moscow. Start marking your schematics with them so people expect to see them in your work and on your person."

He talks me through the logistics of "brush passes" for information that is too sensitive to leave even in a foot-timed drop. I would come off the bus and brush by the agent boarding, passing him something in our fleeting moment of connection. I walk down a flight of stairs, out the door of a hotel—it could be almost any crowded and jostling place—and I always make the pass from my right hand to his right hand, each and every time. No fumbling allowed. I swallow the last of the cookie and notice Peter has stopped talking.

"Are you ready?" He hands me a pen and several pages of copy paper.

I nod. This is why I came today. This is significant enough to schedule another meeting in a safe house.

I pull the paper toward me and write down everything I remember on my lab's new RP-37 radar. It's more sophisticated than the RP-23 with offensive rather than defensive applications. It's the item I will present to Petrov the day after tomorrow in Vienna. It takes me over an hour to record and diagram all its details.

Peter examines the ten sheets, one eyebrow raised as he leafs through them.

"Comrade Defense Minister Petrov is eager for this. The fact packet went by KGB courier yesterday to Vienna," I tell Peter.

"I've been wondering . . . Why Vienna?" Peter leans against the kitchen's one counter. "You've gone before, but it's unusual to let this, and you, leave the country."

"Petrov is there again for meetings. I'm not sure with whom. Personally, I think he likes to take our meetings out of Moscow so he can manage the variables—what people see and hear. I suspect it's about control."

"Everything usually is."

"What do I do?" I shift forward. The flimsy chair wobbles beneath me.

"What do you mean?" Peter waves the pages at me. "You give him everything here. You do your job."

*Everything?* I feel my face warm. "How is that going to bring this crashing down?" I scoff. "That technology has some incredibly aggressive applications."

"Anya, don't mistake what you're doing here." Peter steps to the table and sets the papers between us. "You are not trying to sabotage the Soviet Union and you're certainly not trying to commit suicide."

"But you said we could end the madness. That's how you phrased it. I'm handing you millions of dollars of military data to do just that, to end all this."

Peter drops into the chair across from me. "No." He says the word softly, and he lets it rest between us. Peter understands stillness, but his is not intimidating. It invites me to listen. Although I try to resist, I'm curious as to what he's thinking and why.

He continues, "If that's what you're after, you'll reach too far and you'll end up dead by the end of the week. This information is being checked right, left, sideways, and diagonally. You can't offer Petrov a single lie. But by sharing it with us, we'll better understand how to deploy our resources and how to take this and lessen its impact on a global scale. That's enough for now."

"It doesn't feel like enough." I slump in my chair. Dmitri didn't die for "enough."

"Victory doesn't always *feel* like we expect, and it doesn't always come from destruction, Anya. Sometimes it comes quietly, in peace. Try to remember that. And breathe. You're too tense." Peter gathers the papers into his hands again. "Do your job well the day after tomorrow and try to get a peek at Vienna this time."

∞

Of course I'm tense.

I've been tense for three years, and the four before that, and the eighteen before that. Come to think of it, when have I not been tense?

On the flight to Vienna, I take Peter's advice. It isn't breathing that's the problem. It's the rate at which I'm doing it. I draw in air so fast it's become too shallow. I'm always starving for that next breath. I work to moderate it, and as soon as I see the towers and turrets of Vienna, I feel something within me shift and slow.

I've only been to Vienna that one time and only for a morning, but I instinctively love this city. Even in a car ride, I picked up on a warmth, a smell, and an energy that felt uplifting and grounding at the same time. Somehow I belong here. It's part of my DNA.

Flying to the US to study at Georgetown was my first time outside the Soviet Union, and it was a riot of colors, lights, sounds, and stimuli previously unimaginable. The US feels like a fireworks show on the Fourth of July. It's always changing, reaching, and stretching—almost exploding with innovation and determination.

After the fireworks finale on one Fourth, I turned to Scott and asked, *"Do you all feel like that every day?"*

He laughed at me—and bought me cotton candy. That was a revelation too. So light, pink, sticky, and sweet.

My "escort" and I check into our hotel, and after dropping my bag in my room, I head outside. No one has technically told me I can't.

Within steps along Kärntner Strasse, Vienna settles into my paradigm. She is older, subtler, and carries the elegance and gravitas of living art. Vienna is the art fair, enjoyed hours before the fireworks display.

At St. Stephen's Cathedral, I sense my silent and stern KGB shadow trailing after me. I don't try to lose him. I try to forget him. I walk into the church and, catching notes of a piano deep within, follow the soft music down to the crypt.

It's one of Mozart's concertos. I can't name which one, but I recognize the trill and the cadence of his compositions. It takes me right back to college. Tracy loved R & B, but she also loved classical music. *"It slows you down and clears your head,"* she said. It lifted me up and set me soaring. She'd laugh at how often I absconded with her cassettes and her Walkman.

The music does its job again and I feel light, emboldened, and alive. And suspecting that Minister Petrov will send me home immediately following my presentation tomorrow morning, I stop playing at exploring and get to it.

I head back down Kärntner Strasse and beyond, following Prinz-Eugen-Strasse to the Belvedere Palace. My mother once mentioned she submitted a request to borrow paintings from it for the State Museum, but the Ministry of Culture denied it. I want to see what they deemed unacceptable for Soviet eyes.

Gustav Klimt.

*Farm Garden with Sunflowers* brings me hope with its golds, yellows, and reds in a verdant field. I almost want to cry with the simplicity, beauty, and peace the garden evokes within me. I want it to be real, to sit on a bench and smell its fragrance and watch it grow. It holds me transfixed—until I notice *The Kiss.*

That painting stops me. It undoes me. It is a poignant expression of longing, giving, surrendering, and possessing—in all the best and most human ways. A true gift of love. And it isn't a kiss at all. It's the heartbeat before the kiss. The glorious moment when all dreams can be fulfilled and nothing is out of reach, and when vulnerability and surrender don't feel treacherous but intoxicating.

Maybe it's Mozart or maybe it's Klimt, but I'm oversaturated with memory and a longing that can never be fulfilled, and I fear will never end. It's been three years and five months since I've seen Scott, held his hand, touched his face, or kissed him. The letters still come, but they are less frequent now, and while that hurts, I find myself delaying my replies. I'm trying to give him permission to quit writing. I should simply stop, but I can't. I can't let go.

He's still in DC, but he has switched jobs. He didn't tell me what he's doing now, and I suspect it's because it might violate one of the many rules I gave him. The KGB would be very keen to find a consultant, a government employee, or even someone in academia writing to me. Other than that, he owns a dog, lives with two friends, and has taken up running in earnest, probably to exercise his new Labrador. That's so like him. Getting a dog to give himself companionship, then changing everything in his life to accommodate the dog.

It's those everyday details that hold the greatest power over me. I remember one of them and I'm lost in the past, walking with him hand in hand, laughing at something he's just said. Something for my ears only. I wish I'd comprehended the sway of those ordinary moments each and every second I lived within them.

Now Scott's gone yet forever out there, and someday soon he'll fall in love with someone else—and I know how amazing she'll feel right beside him. It's *The Kiss*. I am trapped in that split second of expectation and anticipation, of excitement, butterflies, and passion. Not passion exercised but the more tantalizing and delectable dream of passion yet to be experienced. And I fear it will never end. Without having seen it before, I realize that painting is exactly what torments me nightly just before sleep saves me.

Upon leaving the final room of the exhibition, I quit the pretense of ignoring my KGB escort and walk straight up to him. I gesture to the exit and invite him to move along.

"Where are you going?" He finally speaks as I pass the taxi queue and walk toward the city's center. I guess he's happy to end the charade too.

"I'm headed back to the hotel. I have work to do before tomorrow's meeting."

"We'll grab a taxi."

I shake my head. The evening remains clear and lovely—and markedly warmer than Moscow. I want to walk.

"It's over three kilometers," he protests.

"Then by all means, take a taxi. I'm walking."

Groaning, he follows me. Rather, he walks, silent and stalking, beside me. But despite his presence, I feel freer walking these three kilometers than I've felt in as long as I can remember. I try to relish every step, every smell, and every inch of Vienna's pavement beneath my feet.

Part of me wonders if it's Peter's breathing advice, but I suspect it's more. Maybe it's that hopeful *Farm Garden with Sunflowers*. A weight is gone and I can finally see and accept the realities of my work and my life. I'm okay with missing Scott. I'm even okay not "ending the madness" with a single sweep of my hand, as if I ever could.

∽

The next morning I am not okay. Nerves clench my stomach tight and the sights and smells of the coffee, tea, and delicate and decadent pastries laid out on the large side table almost send me running for the embassy's ladies' room. I keep telling myself to calm down; I'm not going to lie. I'm to tell every truth, and Petrov is going to salivate over this new weapon. This is my job as usual.

Minister of Defense Comrade Nikolai Ivanovich Petrov walks in surrounded by a cadre of aides. I swallow the lump in my throat and cycle through my speech. I'm here to first give a full report regarding my institute's last quarter's deliverables and budget before I move on to the capabilities, expenditures, and time line for the new RP-37 technology. It's about six hours of information. Minimum.

My allotted time has been compressed to thirty minutes. Another reason I feel sick.

When I arrived, an aid spilled the beans as to why Petrov is in Vienna, and his schedule. She assumed I knew. He and a delegation are here on behalf of General Secretary Brezhnev to discuss our country's purchasing of US grain with a team sent by President Reagan—and the irony isn't lost on anyone within the embassy that we are requesting food from the very country that imposed the embargoes against us in the first place.

I remain standing as the last of Petrov's entourage enters the room, and unlike last time, he does not sit. He stands and rifle-fires questions at me. He has already reviewed everything in great detail.

"Will the RP-37 be operational by end of year?"

"Is its design transferable to older operational systems? Can it be configured with low-altitude radar?"

"Page 47 outlines a modular structure. Is this versatility reflected in the projected costs and time line?"

"There's a 15 percent overexpenditure in electronics, an 8 percent overage in laboratory costs, and 3 percent in liquid coolants."

"Explain to me the outlay of . . ."

I misjudged Petrov. In the few minutes before he arrived, I determined that, considering the importance of his meetings this afternoon, he would be distracted. Instead he is laser-focused and aggressive. He asks tough questions and asks them so quickly I don't have time to think up lies if I wanted to. I silently thank Peter for his wisdom.

Defense Minister Petrov has always been a hard-liner with respect to the US, and from his tense demeanor, I get the impression he finds asking the US for handouts humiliating. I also get the impression he isn't about to give any military concessions to garner them. If he has his way, we'll get our grain and keep our weapons aimed and hot, right on Washington, DC. With the RP-37 constituting our latest addition.

At the half hour mark, I'm shredded and sweating and my back hurts from leaning over the table. I've gone through fifty-three pages of material and answered every question I could and scribbled reminders to myself to find answers for those I couldn't.

"You should come work for me." Petrov gestures to my slew of charts and graphs spread like confetti across the table. "You have good technical understanding and communicate clearly. Far better than some."

"I do work for you, Comrade Minister." I shuffle my papers together. They will now be either shredded or sent by courier to Petrov's Kremlin office.

"Yes," he laughs. "I suppose you do. I was speaking of the Office of Defense, but perhaps you are best where you are. Where did you train?"

"I . . ." I stall and stand straight.

As I said, Comrade Minister Petrov does not like the US. But I can't lie either. "I was part of the Foreign Studies Initiative for my entire university education. I was assigned to the United States."

He nods again and again, as if chewing on this revelation, and I begin to wonder if he hadn't known or, now that he does, how quickly I'll get demoted or transferred. It's not a new feeling and it isn't just Petrov. At the least we are a nation still wary of outsiders, and even a loyal son or daughter can become contaminated through close contact. At the most we fear and loathe the US in equal rabid measure.

My mother's words of warning my first days home proved

prophetic—everyone at work gave me the side-eye for months, and it took even longer for the scientists to stop withholding vital information.

"Da. Georgetown University."

I blink and press my lips together. Everything is a test.

Petrov points to the papers again. "I confirmed every number and projection before today. I'm impressed. Comrade Captain Stanslych also speaks highly of your dedication."

I force enthusiasm into my expression, making sure it reaches my eyes as well. He must believe his praise delights me, when in reality I'm devastated with the reminder of how vast the machine is, that the KGB's Stanslych accesses my office safe at night, that every bit of every day is recorded and examined, that nothing is mine, not my comings and goings, not my work, not even my trips to the bathroom. Nothing.

"Thank you. I am glad my reports are favorable."

"So am I. I don't believe in the Foreign Studies Initiative, but perhaps I am wrong. Perhaps there are advantages to such an education."

I tilt my head. Petrov is leading somewhere, but I'm not sure where. He studies me, as does every other man in the room. Six sets of eyes stare at me and all I want to do is run. I, again, smile and warn myself not to fidget.

"You will come today. Your years in the United States may give you a different perspective on these talks. I'll be interested in your thoughts." Petrov flaps a hand at one of his assistants. "Get her security clearance."

"The Talks?" I gulp. That's what the aid called them. The Talks. Capital *T* for both words.

"I . . ." I stall again as panic rises in my throat. I can't swallow. I must refuse. What if someone on America's side gives me away? What if I mess up? What if—? I stop the chaos swirling within me. Like Rogov's searches, refusing is not an option. "Thank you for the honor, Comrade Minister."

The assistant nods and exits the room.

Petrov straightens, glancing across the men standing beside him before addressing me again. "Krupin will get you a pass. Take a few minutes, collect your things, and leave them at the security desk. Meet downstairs. You will be assigned to one of the cars." With that, he's gone and every man files out of the room after him.

Only my KGB shadow remains. He isn't sneering anymore.

The cars drive in an escorted caravan to a tall, stately white building with a red carpet stretching to the street curb.

The Hotel Imperial.

Stepping through the front door is, again, like stepping into another world. It's light and bright, red, gold, and white, with ornate moldings and a large, marble reception desk. Guards stand watch at the door, and every employee freezes as we walk, silently and in a single-file line, through the lobby toward the back of the hotel. Petrov and several others proceed into a wood-paneled antechamber. I glance into the room as I am escorted past. It's full of men, some in green uniforms, others in dark suits. Everyone is talking softly, as if devising a game plan.

My guide opens another door for me, and I find myself in what must be the final meeting room. It isn't as large as I expect for such an important meeting. It's an almost intimate setting. A small ballroom.

The walls are beautiful. Covered in pale gold silk, they appear ethereal against the midnight-blue curtains. There is a long table in the center, running the length of the room, with ten chairs pulled up to each side. No chairs rest at the table's head or foot.

I'm directed to sit at another long table. This one is tucked against the wall with chairs situated on only one side, facing out into the room. There are fifteen chairs against the wall, and across the room is a second identical arrangement.

Two men join me and we wait, silent and stiff, until the doors on either side of the room open simultaneously. We rise.

Comrade Minister Petrov and a couple of his aides, along with seven other men in full military regalia, enter and proceed to one side of the central table while representatives from the United States do the same on the opposite side. More men come from each open door and fill the chairs along the walls.

Everyone remains standing on our respective sides until a man dressed in a dark suit enters and gestures to the room. The scraping of chairs, wood against wood, drowns out all sound for a moment as every person—every man—sits and slides his heavy wood chair close to the tables.

Now sitting, I survey the room more thoroughly. I truly am the only woman here. My gaze trails down the row of men beside me. I recognize none of them. I let my eyes comb the assistants opposite. Haircuts seem to be a little shorter than when I left DC, and except for three men in military uniform, each man wears a red tie to complement his dark suit. It's a good look. It's . . . My eyes stop.

At the opposite end of the row on the Americans' side—as far from me as possible—sits Scott O'Neill.

He stares right at me. And once I spot him, I'm unable to do anything else. Heat rises from my toes to my face, flushing me with what must be a visible red, and I can't drag my eyes from him, or any other senses, for that matter. From more than a hundred feet across the room, I can smell him, feel him, touch him. Yet at the same time he has never felt more foreign, more distant, or more alien.

Oddly I recall our conversation about the color red. How I

told him red was the color of anger and fear, and he retorted, *"It's also the color of passion, love, and really good wine."*

*Love?* I close my eyes for a brief moment. Was that what we had? I feel awash with it, along with desire, but then come those other "red" emotions—revulsion, anger, betrayal, fear, and disgust. What was real? What was a lie? How is he here now? Questions with no answers pound in my brain as every second of our time together races through me like a VHS tape on fast-forward.

I pull the pad and pen on the table in front of me closer. I must focus. This is my job. My very life—and that is not an exaggeration. Comrade Minister Petrov will scrutinize every insight I give him, through a very particular lens—my loyalty—so I shift my attention back to the center table, and I attend to every statement, gesture, inflection, and translation. I listen for the subtle shifts in languages that the interpreter uses, wondering if I would have made the same word choices. I watch faces. I take notes. I concentrate so hard on the task in front of me I'm surprised when a break is called and the room stands as one to exit to the antechamber for tea.

Scott approaches and panic seizes me. I am not alone. I am never alone. He's an American. And this is not a conversation we can have among witnesses. This is not a conversation we can ever have. His eyes lock on mine and I subtly shake my head. It's so small I almost don't feel the motion, but he catches it. I see it in his eyes, a flash of confusion swiftly followed by awareness and even resignation. His gaze shifts away, and without breaking stride, he proceeds out of the room.

I'm relieved.

I'm devastated.

I'm lost.

# SEVENTEEN

# Ingrid

SIX YEARS WORKING FOR MI6 AND EVERYTHING WAS DIFFERENT, yet nothing had changed. Until today.

After all, Ingrid spent her days listening and learning. She'd always lived that way. Long before Adam and Martin trained her, she had watched her parents. So in love, so vital to each other's lives, yet so full of secrets in those last years. In reality, Adam and Martin merely honed skills born through years of being small, quiet, and often overlooked. Now she stretched those skills further.

At Reginald's suggestion she also applied for a job at the State Museum. After taking the dispensation to stay home with Anya for several years, she and Reginald agreed the museum provided more opportunities for her, and its mass amounts of paperwork and art shipments provided the perfect conduit for passing information to and from Moscow.

At home Ingrid dropped farther into the background. She continued to host parties for her husband and create a loving home for their daughter. She made their home the favorite place to play by making up scavenger hunts, riddles, and a game she devised called Cat and Mouse. Everything was fun, right, and good. Only once had she messed up—well, twice.

When Anya was barely four in 1962, Khrushchev placed missiles off the US Florida coast in nearby Cuba. It undid Ingrid—her greatest fear, nuclear war, was imminent. And what was worse, she knew what the US should say and do to end the conflict, but Reginald couldn't convince the CIA to listen. In despair she'd fallen apart in her living room, until she noticed her young daughter watching. She was still unsure if she'd truly convinced Anya that she'd merely been upset over a trivial matter that afternoon. The US had finally listened. Within days of that panicked moment in the living room when Ingrid stood before Anya's wide and worried eyes, President Kennedy played on Khrushchev's weaknesses and pushed all the right emotional buttons, just as Ingrid had advised. The Soviet leader unequivocally backed down.

Then, only a few months ago, Ingrid faltered again. Anya and her new friend Dmitri came home one afternoon—so young, so certain, and so proud.

"*Mama, Mama,*" Anya called, racing through the door. "*Guess what we learned today? We showed them. Bam!*" Anya threw out her hand as if throwing a bomb, and Dmitri, with wide, adrenaline-filled eyes, explained the day's lesson. The glories of the Soviet answer to the 1956 Hungarian Uprising.

Forgetting herself and all the lectures she'd given herself following that frantic day in their living room, she gathered the children close and whispered the truth. She told them of the horrors of the Soviet military invasion on sovereign soil, of the execution of Hungary's Premier Imre Nagy, of the murders of thousands of civilians and the mass arrests, of the installation of Hungary's puppet government, along with a recitation of the strict and punitive laws, the suppression of freedoms, and the desperate flight of over two hundred thousand Hungarians west—and how no one was allowed to discuss it.

The children's eyes morphed from proud to panicked, and Ingrid finally remembered herself once more and the danger she had now put them in. Interrogations. Arrests. Anya could be taken away from her.

She gripped them both tight. Anya squirmed. Dmitri stood perfectly still. *"Never say a word of this. Never speak of it to anyone. This is our secret, but even we will never talk of it again. Do you understand?"*

The children nodded their assent, and Ingrid quickly gave them a game and cookies in hopes they'd forget. As neither mentioned it again, she believed they had. But she kept both failures before her at all times—along with the promise never to falter again.

Holding all this in mind, Ingrid continued to work. Each day and every night.

Upon leaving the museum, she spent her long walks home making sure she had every detail prepared for Leo's evening parties. And at those soirees and dinner parties, as Leo engaged in late-night drinking over cigars with his friends and colleagues, she listened as the Soviet Union's top leaders talked freely among themselves. She memorized every detail and passed each along, through a series of coded messages among the mass of paperwork that came and went from the museum the following morning.

Her real skills, however, developed beyond these tactical measures. By watching and listening, she grew to understand the Soviet psyche from the outside. Once she understood how they thought, she could accurately predict what they would do. On numerous occasions she properly assessed directional shifts in the mercurial winds of politics—she anticipated increased tensions with China; she foretold how the Soviets would approach the seemingly "impromptu" 1959 Kitchen Debate, the 1960 Gary Powers U-2 spy plane incident, and the 1963 Limited Nuclear Test Ban Treaty, not to mention her insights surrounding countless other meetings, intrigues, plots, and plans.

While all that had been significant, Reginald still gaped at her predictions regarding the Berlin Wall. He called it her coup de grâce. With her intel and insights, both Britain and the US were able to extract their "intellectual capital" from Berlin's east district days before the wall's hasty construction in 1961.

Over the years Reginald parsed each of his champion spy's facts and intuitions into small bites of intelligence and scattered them across Europe. Every bit was used to shape Western policy, form diplomacy, create official positions, and even structure seemingly offhanded and insightful remarks that shot across the Soviet leadership's psyche with chilling accuracy. Ingrid was even able to warn the British earlier this year of Khrushchev's fall from power a full month before he fell. Her insights prepared British Prime Minister Wilson and US President Johnson for the USSR's new troika—First Secretary of the Soviet Communist Party Leonid Brezhnev, ruling alongside Premier Alexei Kosygin and Presidium Chairman Nikolai Podgorny.

But everything changed today. This was something new and different, and for the first time, Ingrid was truly scared.

To deal with the issue, Reginald created a secure line at Safe House #19 on Krymsky Val, a feat Ingrid knew wasn't easy to accomplish outside the British embassy. He also placed watchers throughout the neighborhood to make sure KGB technical surveillance teams, in their unmarked black vans, didn't show up to her conversation unannounced.

Upon her arrival Reginald connected the call and handed her the telephone's receiver.

Adam's surprise at what she said morphed to intrigue and ended with a declarative, "No."

"I'm not asking your permission, Adam. I'm telling you what's about to happen, because if it goes wrong I'll . . ." She let the words drift away.

She couldn't say goodbye. She hadn't said goodbye to her mother, her father, Martin, or even Adam in the last days of the war. She'd run away to avoid that pain, and she couldn't bring herself to do it now—she certainly couldn't imagine saying goodbye to her daughter, Anya. But there was no stopping tonight. That's what Adam needed to understand.

"No," he said again, this time more softly. He paused. The telephone line crackled with static. "I'm rubbish with goodbyes, Ingrid." His voice clogged. He cleared his throat. "You listen to me. Get out of this any way you can. It's suicide."

"Adam, this is what we call a command performance. There's no avoiding it. And you don't want me to. Leo would be furious and believe I had harmed his career."

That silenced Adam—for a few seconds.

"I wish I could tell you what contacts he still has, but I can't, Ingrid. We simply aren't sure . . . He's bloody brilliant. One of our best . . . If any detail tips him off, it's over and this truly is goodbye." He stopped, then added, "You're too important."

"I love you, Adam." Before he could reply, Ingrid handed the phone to Reginald.

If Reginald was surprised by her words, he didn't react. He sat silent, listening to Adam rail into his ear with such force, Ingrid heard every word.

Reginald replied with a simple, "Yes, sir," and laid the receiver back on the telephone's base. "It's my head if you get into trouble."

Ingrid pinched her nose to stop any tears. "I'm sorry for that.

We were close during the war. He was close to my parents too. He's still very protective."

"I can't say I don't feel the same way." Reginald spread his hands across the table between them. "Are you sure about this?"

"I am." Ingrid reached for his hand and squeezed it tight. For over six years they'd been working together, and Reginald understood her better than anyone. He knew, even before the call was made, what her decision would be, and he already had a plan—many plans—in place to give her the best protective cover he could if things went wrong.

Six years and she had already become MI6's longest-running—and still living—agent behind the Iron Curtain. Pyotr Semyonovich Popov had been discovered and executed by the KGB in January 1960. Colonel Oleg Vladimirovich Penkovsky had been arrested and killed just last year.

Part of their success in keeping her identity secret, Ingrid credited to the fact that she trusted Reginald completely and he felt the same. While most handlers worked with an asset for a couple of years, Reginald kept getting promoted but kept handling Ingrid exclusively and distributed her intel across Europe through a variety of channels and in a rotation only he understood.

Furthermore, while Popov's and Penkovsky's identities had been shared across agencies, Ingrid's remained a secret within their circle of three. To the greater intelligence world she remained a ghost, a phantom, a shadow, the impossible—a true secret.

But the KGB had finally cleared Kim Philby for work, and tonight was his coming-out party, a formal dinner to honor him as well as introduce him to a larger audience within the KGB and Party.

An intelligence officer within Britain's Secret Intelligence

Service—Ingrid's same MI6—Harold Adrian Russell "Kim" Philby had been the Soviet's man all along, recruited by the NKVD back in 1933. For thirty years he'd betrayed his homeland countless times and in massive ways. And, although he defected to Moscow the year before, the KGB had kept him sidelined in the relative seclusion of his gifted apartment and dacha. The KGB used the year to debrief him; Philby used the year to prove his loyalty. Now with all questions put to rest, he was starting work with the KGB as both spy-hunter and spy-trainer.

Coming only a year after Colonel Penkovsky's KGB execution and a series of other setbacks, MI6 was reeling. Adam was scrambling. And Reginald was frantic.

Reginald pulled his hand from Ingrid's and stood. He stepped to the nearby counter and slid a cigarette from his pack of Primas. "You need to get back. We don't want anyone asking about your whereabouts today."

Ingrid reached for his cigarette. She pulled a long drag on it and exhaled the smoke even more slowly. She rarely did that, but her nerves were overfiring. When she tried to hand it back, Reginald grabbed her hand rather than the cigarette and held it in front of her face.

"Do you see that? You're shaking like a leaf. How do you think you can walk in there tonight like an innocent housewife, a naive museum curator, a loyal comrade? If that were the case, if you were those things, you'd have nothing to fear, and that's all I see in you right now . . . Philby is no ordinary spy, Ingrid. He's a viper."

"I will manage." She yanked her hand away.

"You are so stubborn." Reginald flared, then backed down. He dropped into the hard metal chair and put his head in his hands.

"Reg, trust me." Ingrid touched the top of his head. His hair had morphed from grey to white over the last six years, thinned too. "I can do this. No one but the three of us know who I am. That's what makes me different from Popov, Penkovsky, and all the others. It's what keeps me safe. No one *ever* looks at me twice."

Reginald spoke without lifting his head. "Philby might. He's not Soviet, Ingrid, as much as he pretends to be. He won't under-estimate women as easily."

Ingrid smirked at both the compliment and the truth it con-veyed. They had long mused upon the fact that despite all the claims for an equal society, the KGB, the Central Committee of the CPSU, the Supreme Soviet, and the Council of Ministers held no women within their top ranks.

She tapped the top of Reginald's head with her finger. "Who do they think I am today?"

He lifted his head and gave her a half smile, unable to keep his lip from curling with pride. "The latest rumor is that LUMEN is a low-level Dutch diplomat. In fact, I'm withholding your thoughts on the troika for a while. No one with such low-level clearance could have your insights into how Brezhnev, Kosygin, and Podgorny will work together . . . So, yes, you're still a shadow with no more substance than an errant thought. You can't be on Philby's radar yet. I'd like to keep it that way."

"We will."

"Then breathe." Reginald reached for the cigarette. "And stop shaking so much."

Ingrid obeyed. She clasped her hands and drew a deep breath.

Reginald shook his head as Ingrid's breath shuddered on her exhale. "You're going to need to do better than that."

Five hours later, she did.

It was to be a small, intimate affair at Comrade General Kamenev's home with only a few members of the nomenklatura—elite Party members—invited, along with all the top officers of the KGB. But it grew and became the most sought-after evening in Moscow, as everyone wanted to meet this new hero and hear what he would do to assure Soviet preeminence.

The Kamenev home, with its high ceilings and intricate moldings stacked a foot deep, was the most opulent and decadent Ingrid had seen in her almost ten years in the city. The domed front foyer was detailed in gold, and the marble stairs were polished to such a shine she could almost see her reflection as she climbed them to the second-floor gallery. There, along deep-green lacquered walls, hung massive landscape paintings and portraits. The grandeur brought her to a halt at the gilded door to the home's ballroom. Leo bumped into her from behind.

"It was once an imperial palace," he whispered in her ear as he pressed a guiding hand to her back, his other arm outstretched to greet their hosts.

While Leo waxed eloquent about the home and the honor of the invitation, Ingrid surveyed the guests already in attendance. A cluster gathered around a corner table where a waiter, dressed in starched white, stood offering drinks. And despite not recognizing several of the men nor any of their wives, Ingrid spotted the guest of honor immediately. He stood shifting from one foot to the other as if unable to stifle his energy. He was lanky and lean, his suit coat a touch large, his eyes darting from person to person. He was sizing up the people, the room, the country, and his status within it all. The great spy: Harold Adrian Russell "Kim" Philby.

Ingrid watched as Philby shifted again. Shrewd and assessing, he didn't gaze across the room; he scanned it, taking in every detail. He didn't meet and greet; he stared into his conversational partner's soul.

Ingrid felt him watch her for an overstretched moment until he leaned close to a young uniformed KGB officer who seemed to be relaying the who's who of the party. With a quick nod, their conversation ended and Philby crossed the parquet floor to where Leo stood in conversation with the evening's hosts.

His left hand still on her back, Leo guided Ingrid the last steps to meet the man of the hour.

The great spy shook Leo's hand first and spoke to him in Russian. Ingrid noted how comfortably he rolled over verbs and contractions. His linguistic agility surprised her, and she was still parsing through his accent when he turned his attention to her with an outstretched hand.

"It's a pleasure to meet you both." He tilted his head to include Leo in his opening comment to her.

"We are delighted to be here. This is the invitation of the year, and you are the most-sought-after guest in Moscow," Ingrid replied. She gestured into the room in an attempt to pull Philby's gaze away from her face, but his focus remained fixed.

"I am deeply honored by my reception in your beautiful city." Philby sneered, small and almost cruel.

Ingrid widened her eyes and glanced, with feigned befuddlement, to her husband. Philby had spoken to her in English.

"Forgive me." Philby returned to Russian. "I thought I detected an accent."

With a light laugh, Ingrid touched his sleeve and stepped close to whisper, "It please me." She offered her English slowly with studied care—as Leo believed she had limited facility with the language—and a misconjugated verb. She then switched to German. "I learned a little of your language in my early childhood, but I have regrettably forgotten most of it. But my roots? One never truly forgets."

Leo's eyebrows furrowed into the all-too-common crease above his nose.

Ingrid leaned closer to Philby, relying on one outsider to understand another. "Thankfully everyone else has." She finished with a wink and spoke in Russian.

Philby grinned and tucked her arm through his own. He turned them a quarter away from everyone's gaze. He, too, returned to speaking Russian. "They are a xenophobic people to be sure. Your secret is safe with me."

"Thank you." She laughed. "While I miss Austria on rare occasions, I confess to loving my new city more. Everything and everyone I love is here." She stepped back toward Leo, who stood stiff and silent, and reached for his hand.

"I couldn't agree more." Philby thumped her husband on the back and Leo visibly relaxed. His features softened and he squeezed his wife's gloved fingers.

"Well done. He adores you," Leo whispered to her as Philby moved on to the next guest. "I sometimes forget myself you aren't a true Muscovite."

"Don't you think I am by now?"

Again, her comment visibly pleased her husband as he peered deeper into the room, determining who to converse with next. Ingrid peeked back and willed the butterflies in her gut to settle. She watched as Philby stood spooning out stories to his admirers. But just as she drew her eyes away, the man inexplicably stopped in the middle of his tale and winked at her. She forced a smile to bloom across her face as butterflies took flight again. She'd gone a step too far—she'd made herself memorable.

Proceeding with Leo to the large table in the dining room, Ingrid noted that her place card situated her far from the guest of honor. She laid her evening bag beside her plate and scanned the table for her husband's card. She eventually found it—directly to Philby's left. Leo, she noted, was staring at the same thing with satisfaction settling in his dark eyes.

Leo never talked about work. He obviously shared whenever he received a promotion, and those had come fast over their decade of marriage, but he never said what those promotions entailed or even within which department of the government's vast bureaucracy they occurred.

In fact, if she followed all his clouded comments and leading remarks, he still worked as a bureaucrat within the CPSU as he had in Vienna. It was only by listening to other remarks made by a variety of people on a vast array of topics over the years, including their awkward silences, pauses, and slipups within those conversations, that she came to learn he was lying—and perhaps always had been.

Perhaps not when they'd first met, but without a doubt from the day he proposed and every day since. *Is anything real? Did he ever love me at all?* She banished the questions as quickly as they rose. They were for the dark hours when sleep eluded her. Not for here. Not for now.

In an unthinking gesture, her hand moved to her belly. That was real. At least it had been. She'd been three months along when she lost the baby, and Leo had been as devastated as she had been. That was real too. He had desperately wanted a son. She had desperately wanted someone more to love.

Ingrid shook away her sadness. The very night it happened, young Anya had climbed into bed with her, sensing her mama was sad. And she'd done that each night for a week until she'd sensed Ingrid was okay. And the wise little girl had been right too—after a week, Ingrid knew she would, in fact, be okay.

She stepped toward her husband and gestured to his place card. "You are positioned well."

Leo's eyes gleamed. "I have no idea how. Come. Let us mingle."

Ingrid knew Leo not only was pleased with the honor but had expected it. His controlled grin gave him away—as had the papers in his desk.

Reginald had given Ingrid her first Minox camera in 1960, and since then she had used it as often as she dared. Perhaps a dozen times in the past four years. The most recent documents, photographed several months ago, consisted of a series of memos detailing background information on new Party and Politburo promotions. The content led her to believe Leo's latest promotion was within the KGB's Seventh Directorate, internal surveillance.

Leo, like Philby, was a spy-hunter among his own.

And that meant Ingrid never had a real moment. Because a real moment, such as her outrage over the Hungarian Revolution, could get her killed or—worse—get Anya killed. That boy's father worked for the KGB! Daily Ingrid chastised herself to stop struggling, to stop trying to bridge the gap between what she appeared and what she truly was, to relinquish her pride and simply accept this was the path she'd chosen. Someone, everyone—including and especially her own daughter—needed to view her as small, weak, and insignificant.

"We have a line of sight to all the top players now," Reg told her after he'd developed that batch of film rolls. "Leo is clearly head of the—"

"Don't." Lost in those same thoughts, she raised a hand just in time to stop Reg from continuing. "Don't tell me. Please. Let me live within the fantasy that because no one has ever told me directly, Leo does not work within the KGB."

Reginald nodded and said nothing more. But even she couldn't deny it now, and looking at Leo, she knew he didn't want to. He was proud of his success and his accomplishments. And if she was right about the rewards within the service for loyalty, and the costs of proving one's loyalty, she suspected her husband had paid dearly for each and every one.

She thought back to her friend Vada all those years ago. She thought back to colleagues, friends who once had frequented his parties, who—one day—simply never came again. "They've been transferred out of the city," he would say when she asked. But the way he said it, just like when his father was "sentenced to ten years without the right to correspondence," Ingrid knew these friends would never return to their homes or to Moscow again.

Ingrid followed Leo back into the foyer where guests began gathering before dinner. He paused at the door and stretched out a hand, waiting for her. She knew he only stopped, reached for her, and even now curled his arm around her back because Philby had complimented her. She was an asset tonight, when almost every other day she was a liability.

He had tried to hide it, of course, but games required energy. And on days when Leo was stressed or tired, he had no energy for his wife. There was a curl of contempt to his lips. He spoke down to her rather than to her, or he ignored her altogether. The KGB was rumored to be puritanical, rigid, and almost pathologically xenophobic. And Leo was, as Reginald quipped one day, a "company man."

After dinner, a quartet played in the ballroom. Guests strolled into the room, drinks in hand, as General Kamenev and his wife started the dancing. Ingrid watched Philby cross the room, only realizing once he was halfway toward her that she was his intended target.

"May I have this dance?" He spoke like a Russian but with the bow and intonation of a Brit.

Ingrid let him lead her to the center of the floor.

"Your husband tells me you have a daughter starting primary school who has just joined the Little Octobrists."

"She was the first to memorize the oath and motto." Ingrid widened her eyes with glowing pride. "In fact, the first to memorize the songs too. Though I wish she would perhaps not sing those all the time." She lifted her hand off Philby's shoulder and touched a light finger to her temple.

"I can imagine." He laughed, leading them in perfect time across the floor. "Little voices. No tone . . . But what an exciting time. I have great hopes for this next generation."

"Yes, I heard you are starting a training school. Every young KGB recruit will benefit from your experience."

Philby studied her but did not answer her. "You intrigue me, Comrade. I hope to spend more time with you."

Ingrid's face warmed, and by the gleam in Philby's eye, she knew he mistook it for a blush. She dipped her head and let him believe what he wanted.

The next morning, as soon as the apartment was empty, Ingrid and Dolores scoured it from top to bottom. There were a few things Leo had packed away long ago, reminders of Ingrid's childhood she thought he no longer remembered. But she knew where they hid—books in the back of their bedroom closet, pictures in her bedside table drawer, jewelry from her mother, and various other items scattered across small private spaces. Memorabilia of a Vienna and a past she needed to purge.

"You're going to throw away your Shakespeare? Your Austen?" Dolores pulled a box from the back of her closet and held up a green leather-bound book in one hand and a red one in the other.

Ingrid reached for both. She ran her hands over the smooth covers with titles embossed in gold. They were her mother's books, and never telling that part of their history, Ingrid had read the plays and stories to Anya when she was younger—far too young to remember and repeat—and she often read them herself at night when Leo worked late.

*You fool*, she scolded herself, feeling the full weight of her indulgence. "It all goes."

Dolores took the pictures and books and proceeded to tear them apart before she dropped them section by section into the trash bin.

"Let's divide them into small bags and take them to bins throughout the city. I don't want any debris left in or near the apartment." Ingrid then, unable to watch as Dolores burned her family pictures in the kitchen sink, walked to the apartment's bathroom and shut the door. Inside she faced the mirror.

*Are you ready for this? You're forty-one years old.* She pressed her hands against her jaw, her cheeks, the soft skin around her eyes. Did she have the energy and the stamina for all that lay ahead?

She ran her fingers through her hair. It was still blonde, but there were more than a few strands of grey near her temples now. Her eyes, still blue, carried new lines at the corners and seemed to have darkened with shades of grey in the irises. She wasn't sure if that was a real change or a perceived one—was there a difference?

Shaking away her fear, she stared straight at herself in the mirror. "No cracks in the facade. Because it's not a facade. This is who you are. Like Mutti used to say, '*Duc in altum.*'"

Dolores knocked on the bathroom door. "Are you okay?"

Ingrid opened it. "I'm just giving myself a pep talk." Dolores stared at her. "What is it?"

"Your husband just called . . . I'm to go to the market. He's bringing Comrade Philby and a few others home for after-dinner drinks tonight."

"It was expected." Ingrid leaned against the doorjamb. "Take my Party card and food voucher to Universam and get caviar and anything else we'll need. I'll take the papers and find bins."

"It's too risky for you. Let me do that."

Ingrid shook her head, feeling oddly comfortable with her new reality. "The risks are just beginning, my friend."

# EIGHTEEN

# Anya

MOSCOW
*October 30, 1983*

I RETURNED HOME UNTETHERED—UNABLE TO THINK, EAT, focus, sleep.

Thankfully, however, Petrov was impressed with my thoughts and insights from the meetings. So impressed I sense a subtle change in my world. Rogov no longer harasses me. Stanslych's tone carries a tiny bit more respect. They are little things, to be sure, but they matter.

A letter arrives.

It is unsigned and carries only a few lines. Although it's stamped *Tennessee*, it's from Scott, and he drove across state lines to further separate himself from the postmark. Who told him to do that? Or has he always known? As if reading my mind, the letter merely says,

I never lied. I would tell you everything if I could. You were the start. You are the journey. It's the color of anger, but also the color of love.

All I see is Scott. I picture him writing this note, debating what to pen that only I could understand. I see that questioning moment when his eyes flashed to mine in Vienna, and I sent him away. I had to do it—to be seen talking, even for an instant, would have ended my career, perhaps my life. But as much as I want to forget that split second of connection and all the questions flooding my brain—because I'll never get any answers—they're consuming me.

After two weeks of this stupor, my office mates stop talking to me. I fumble through work, through lunch, through the security line. Walking home, I see my life stretching before me and it's not bad. It's predictable, comfortable. I have it so much better than most. I could quit all this—what am I doing other than putting myself and my family at risk? Why am I doing it? Was it for Scott all along? I can't be that lovesick, that shallow.

Focus on life here, that's what we're raised to do. Not to question. Not to dream. To work. To live. I could find a nice man. We could marry. We would work our jobs each day, make dinner, make love at night, and start again the next day as families do. We would endure. We could survive. Maybe we'd even have children. That's where my imagining stops. Children require hope. I'm not sure I have that anymore.

Yet whenever I feel I've almost given up, something roars to life inside me. Call it fight, call it dissent, call it anger. Whatever it is, it rebels against capitulation. Those years in the US were mine—not Scott's, not anyone else's. I grew within the Thursday music at the chapel; I grew through learning the philosophies and ideals of dignity and freedom; I grew within the pleasure of open debate and discussion. All these things sound theoretical, but they weren't. They were real and tangible, and I lived in and among them four whole years.

And no matter whether Scott lied to me or not, those were my experiences and they changed me.

I chuckle to myself as I walk the final block to my apartment.

Scott read me well. Red. The color of love. A nice reminder. The color of anger. He knew where I'd go first. We really are a fighting people.

I turn to walk back toward the zoo. After tossing an empty pack of Primas into the bin, I place a red wax mark on the cement wall right behind a trash can.

I want to pick a fight, and I'm just getting started.

⁓⧜⁓

"Is Scott O'Neill CIA?"

Peter shuts the door to Safe House #2 in the Basmanny District behind me. "Hello to you too." He raises a brow.

He's annoyed and I don't blame him. A red mark signals an emergency, and most likely Peter and a whole team worked nonstop today to secure this moment—which, by my attitude, he suspects is not an emergency.

Without saying hello I turn inside the doorway. "Tell me about Scott O'Neill. Does he work with you?"

"Who?" Peter's face contorts with such consternation I can't tell if he's asking or overacting.

I go with my gut. "You're lying . . . I'm not in the mood for games, Peter. You're probably buddy-buddy. He must be CIA." I fill a glass with water and take a few sips, watching him. He seems genuinely perplexed.

"I have no idea. And of course we're not all buddy-buddy. This isn't grade school," Peter says, mimicking my tone. "And I can give you a thousand reasons to Sunday why it'd be stupid if we were. Who's this O'Neill?"

"Playing dumb doesn't suit you."

I glare at him and he glares back. After a minute, he raises a brow and concedes. "Georgetown boyfriend from Atlanta,

Georgia. Second of three kids. Works financial markets and fiscal policy in DC, specializing in emerging markets. You saw him in Vienna."

"You knew he'd be there? And you didn't warn me?" My hand shakes and I set down the glass. I don't want Peter to notice it too.

"After the fact. We got the list of delegates after you'd left for Vienna. It should've come earlier, but it didn't, and it was too late to warn you. I'm sorry."

"So he's CIA? Was he always?" A bit of me has moved on, but most of me still wants answers. Peter drops into one of the metal chairs at the kitchen table. "Not that I've heard. He could be private sector with some special skill set in grain, Russia, widgets, I have no idea. Or, yes, he could be CIA." Peter stares at me. "Did something happen? Is there something you want to tell me?"

I sit across from him. I feel my heart hammering. It makes an audible sound within my ears. How can Peter not hear it too? Working with the CIA was never going to get me Scott, yet deep down, I can't deny a part of me said yes to Olivers for both Dmitri and him. One to vindicate. One to love.

I keep my eyes steady and employ the same strategy of calm I used to use on Sasha. Only it's me I'm trying to subdue into stillness. "Nothing, but . . ."

"Seeing him, you wondered if he used you?" Peter chuckles at my expression. "That's hardly a leap, Anya. Why don't you lay low for a while? Get over him and get your head back in the game."

"Absolutely not, and what you're implying is insulting." My bark surprises us both. So much for calm control, but that is the one thing I can't do. Maybe all this did start in some way for Scott and certainly for Dmitri. But it also has little to do with either of them now.

Without this work, this adrenaline, and this mission, I'll come undone. It may not be a better motivation, but it's real.

While memorizing diagrams and details, I'm outside myself and focused. I don't feel hurt, or lonely, or sad. I'm not questioning anything or anyone and I'm not a hair's width away from losing it. It's the only thing left in my life that feels good and right, a true virtuous fight.

I can't tell Peter any of this. It makes me sound as desperate and crazy as I feel—not good for someone working in a world of secrets. So I say, "I'm ready for more. Give me a camera," instead. "The tiniest you've got. Like in James Bond."

"You can't be serious." Peter's intonation leads me to believe he senses all I've left unsaid.

"Just hear me out." I hold up a hand to keep him from interrupting me. "We can't slow down, and I can't get any drawings out. You see how long it takes me to memorize all that data, and then it takes hours with you in a safe house to recreate them. It takes too long. It increases the danger for everyone. Someone is going to come looking for you, if not for me. With a camera we can speed this whole thing up."

"There you go again, trying to 'speed things up.' What exactly are we speeding up, Anya?"

"The end of all this. War, destruction . . . the Soviet Union."

"That's a little ambitious. Listen, the smallest camera out there, a Topel, has only one purpose. You get caught with one of those and there's no talking your way out of it." He reaches over and taps my knee. "Is this about O'Neill? I'm sorry it was a shock. I get that, but it doesn't change anything."

"I'm not talking about him. I'm talking about every aspect of life here. Don't treat me like some lovesick girl."

Peter straightens.

"I'm sorry." I reach for him to recreate the connection

between us but pull back and press both palms to my eyes instead. Because he's right—I am acting like one. "I'm sorry. I don't know what to do."

Yet somehow Peter does. He pushes up from his rickety chair. I hear him and open my eyes. He flaps a hand at me. "Come here."

"Why?"

"Just come here."

I step toward him and he pulls me into his arms. I find myself laughing, light and low. It's family, brotherhood, and understanding. I'm not alone.

"What would your wife say about this?" There's nothing romantic in his hug, but I still ask.

He chuckles. "She'd chastise me for not recognizing you needed this sooner."

"You've told her about me?" I speak into his shoulder. "You never talk about her."

He chuckles again. "I suppose it's my way of keeping her safe, but the CIA doesn't send a couple to Moscow without training them both. Who do you think runs surveillance? She berated the whole team for not warning you about Scott in Vienna."

"She did? She works with you? I had no idea."

"You're not supposed to. That's my job, Anya. I keep the information on a need-to-know basis so none of us become more of a liability to the others than necessary. But we are a team. All of us." He squeezes my shoulders tight. "You okay now?"

"I want to be."

"I told you to breathe, and you need to figure out how to do that. This was never going to be easy, but even I can't imagine how hard it is. We're asking the impossible and you're delivering, but don't lose sight of your goal."

"And what is that?"

"You told Olivers 'hope,' but I suspect it's peace too. Within you. You wouldn't struggle so much if you didn't want it pretty badly."

My lips part and Peter smiles. It's not quite the smug thing he often gives me, but it's darn close.

With a you-can't-fool-me wink, he continues. "Nations will always jockey for power and they will fight and they will fall, Anya, but you as an individual matter more. Every individual matters more. That's what you've been about since day one, and I believe in you, if for nothing else than that intrinsic motivation alone. Don't get caught up in the peripherals."

I absorb his words and they feel right. They calm me, and yet. "Can you do me a favor?"

"What?"

"Find out if Scott O'Neill is in the CIA for me." At his expression I rush on. "He's not a peripheral for me, Peter. I've been trying to convince myself he is, but he changed how I talk, think, dream, and live. I can't separate him from every ideal that brought me to you."

"What will it change? Say he did trick you?" Peter holds one hand out to the side as if weighing some invisible object. "Or say it was all real?" He holds out his other hand.

Glancing between the two, I understand. I don't want to, but I do. "Nothing . . . But maybe I can stop being in love with him." There, I said it.

Peter sighs and retreats into the apartment's only other room, the living room through which I entered. He perches on the only chair's armrest. I expect it to cave under his weight.

"Fine." He stares at me. "We've got a new guy on the DC Soviet desk, Aldrich Ames. I'll ask him."

"And you'll also ask him about the camera?"

Peter shakes his head. "No. You're being impetuous. I don't

trust this anger I sense in you. Get your head on straight and we'll talk again."

"*Get your head on straight*? What does that even mean? What are we doing here if you can't trust me?"

"I didn't say you; I said this anger and fire inside you." He circles a finger as if drawing a ring around my heart. "Slow down for a few months and we'll see."

"Forget that. I've got a packet heading by KGB courier to Petrov tomorrow afternoon. We will not slow down, so you'd better be ready."

"Anya, wait—"

I hear nothing more as I stomp out, slamming the door behind me. Halfway down the block guilt swamps me. It takes a lot of time for Peter to "dry-clean" and prepare a safe house. He's told me stories of some of what he goes through—identity switches, decoys, a whole team trailing red herrings from the embassy out into the city streets. Huge undertakings to keep me safe. And here I called a meeting just to whine and vent, then stormed out like an impulsive and petulant child.

I almost turn back, but I catch myself. I'm not as naive or as arrogant as I was a year ago. Within these passing minutes, anyone could have caught sight of me, any random KGB tracker could simply be curious about me. I keep walking and anger, fear, sadness, and a chaos of questions bubble within me.

Only one thing is certain. I am not slowing down.

∽

On my way to work the next morning, I mark the wall behind the zoo's southernmost trash can with an inch-long slash of orange.

Brush Pass #5. Tonight. 7pm.

I told Peter to be ready, and I was serious.

I continue my walk to work and find the final schematic outline for the updated low-range "anti-stealth" radar system sitting on my desk. I love working with scientists. They're so exacting. I was told this would be ready today and here it is, on my desk first thing in the morning. After one last perusal to confirm the numbers, my report will be ready to present to Comrade Minister Petrov next week.

I spend the morning sifting through the scientists' changes, making notes with my wax pencils, and updating my report. After that, I head to the copy room to create the duplicates. One batch will remain in our facility's vault and another will be sent via the KGB to Petrov's office. Once the copies are made and handed off to Stanslych, this stage of the project is over. That means there's a protocol to follow.

I open my office safe and gather from it the scrap papers I've created over the past weeks in calculating my reports and tracking this system's new design. Normally this is when I would test my recollection of all the numbers and details and commit any new ones to memory as well.

Not today.

Today I follow protocol without delay. No trace of what I do, what any of us do, ever leaves the building. Once any stage of a project ends, nothing is to remain within our facility other than the single copy that rests in the vault. Everything else gets burned in the building's incinerator, making it a very popular stop for many of us before passing through security and heading home.

Today, however, I can't join the usual evening procession. I need to be alone. And if I move fast, I'm minutes away from the quietest part of the afternoon. It's just after the day's third cigarette break and just before everyone's final trek to the break room for late-afternoon tea.

I grab my papers, including the thin tracing paper duplicates I made of the final data this morning, and head to the incinerator. There are three flights of stairs without cameras until surveillance picks me up again upon entering the basement hallway.

It takes me one flight to make sure I am truly alone before I slide the hand-drawn papers from the middle of my stack and, pressing the entire pile against my chest, maneuver the few folded ones into the waistband of my tights beneath my skirt.

I shift the pile back into one hand as I exit the stairwell. I make sure to walk on the left, in clear view of the security cameras. At the end of the hall, I slowly feed the papers into the incinerator's chute.

On the way back up I pause in the stairwell to shift the papers flat across my abdomen. I then head to my office, greeting colleagues as I pass them heading to the break room for last cups of tea.

I can't contain my elation. It feels great. It seems so little, so silly, so less than anything James Bond would do. And yet it's huge, and I did it. I almost laugh at the simplicity of "spy work" and wonder why Peter gets so uptight. I—

Comrade Stanslych is standing by my desk.

All my bravado falls away and my ebullient smile freezes into a stiff proxy plastered across my face. Panic lodges in my throat.

He turns at the soft *click* my loafers make against the linoleum floor. "You haven't been to see me."

"M-Me? Why?" I croak out the words. I swallow and almost choke on that too. I reach for a glass of water on my desk, waving my hand at him, and take a few sips to calm down. "I'm sorry. I got dust or something in my throat at the incinerator. Why was I to see you?"

"I saw you down there." He points to a camera in the corner of our office.

I follow his gaze, as do my office mates, and stare like it's some foreign object I've never seen before. All I can envision is the thin sheaf of papers tucked into my waist and wonder if there are new cameras in the stairwell I missed. I turn back to him, still wide-eyed and wondering, and careful not to twist at the waist.

He points right at it.

My lips part, but nothing comes out.

"That should have been replaced two weeks ago."

I drop my head and memory strikes like a light beam. New badges. I was in Vienna when they were implemented, and rather than answer the memo upon my return, I'd forgotten about it. Excluding Scott, I'd forgotten about everything.

"I'm sorry. That was my fault." I unclip my badge from my skirt's waistband to pass it to him.

He shakes his head. "We have to take your picture first. Follow me."

My nervous energy turns to chatter. "We got new badges last year. I remember because I'd just gotten a haircut. Why are they being replaced?"

"There was a leak in another lab. It was contained, but we're instituting new pass cards at all Level 3 facilities and above. You'll need it for internal as well as external doors starting next week."

"Ah . . . You'll be able to track *all* our comings and goings." I try to pitch my tone light and airy.

I succeed to some degree because Comrade Stanslych smirks. "Don't worry, Comrade, we already do."

It takes only a few minutes. I sit on a stool as straight as possible, terrified the papers at my waist will crinkle with every shift. Stanslych snaps my picture with a Lubitel camera and, once again, I try to hand him my badge.

He waves it away. "It'll be a few days before your new one arrives. Stop by next Wednesday."

"Yes. I'll remember." I tap my temple and try to keep my expression light—every movement feels stiff and overacted. The papers bite into my abdomen. I flee his office.

By six o'clock I'm ready to throw up and my hands are shaking. I've sat on them for the last hour and I still have another half hour to sit here if this is going to work.

Most of us leave right on the dot of 6:00 p.m., but a crowd at the security checkpoint will hurt me tonight. To prove he's good, our newest security guard likes to be thorough and he likes to make people wait. He can be worse than Rogov, as impossible as that sounds, but at least he's egalitarian about it—everyone is subjected to the same indignities.

I stay at my desk and pretend to be absorbed in the most fascinating work ever.

"You coming?"

I will my gaze not to shift to the camera in the corner. My three office mates are packed and ready to go. A glance to the clock above the door completes the illusion. "How'd it get so late? You all go ahead. I still need to pack up."

I return the papers I've scattered across my desk to the safe and move slowly through my routine, straightening my desk and packing up my personal effects. As I walk to security, I remind myself to stay calm. This part of the plan I simply must trust to unfold as it should.

The shift changes at 6:30 p.m. after the end-of-day crush. So the new guy is gone and Grigor, our usual night guard, has just come on duty. He sits slumped watching a special program on the glories of Victory Day parades and celebrations on CT USSR.

I point to his portable Silelis television. "How'd you get that in here?"

Grigor glowers. "My brother let me use it. Captain Stanslych gave me permission."

I press my lips together, chastising myself. I had meant my question to come out conversational and light, but my nerves tipped it toward accusatory. Grigor is now annoyed with me. I focus on the TV and pretend to be riveted by the massive marching band filling the screen.

Victory Day, commemorating the day Nazi Germany surrendered to us in 1945, is a huge deal, and considering our losses in the Great Patriotic War, it remains one of our country's biggest and most emotionally poignant celebrations. I was describing this day to Scott when he exclaimed, *"What? You have missiles in your parades?"*

Thinking of him makes my stomach churn, so I push him away and point to a shift in the television coverage. A horse brigade marches across the screen right in front of the Politburo dais. "I love those parades. I used to sit on my dad's shoulders, and he'd let me stay all day."

Grigor softens, but I'm not forgiven for challenging him. He pokes an impatient finger to my bag.

I open it wide. While I never carry work from the building, I do carry my planner and a ton of junk and silly scrap paper, like my grocery lists. Tonight everything is stuffed in to distract from my person. It's a ploy I've practiced several times, with about a 75 percent success rate. Grigor pulls the bag open wide and raises a brow.

"You search bags of mad scientists," I quip. "This can't be the messiest you've seen."

That elicits a short chuckle and I feel my breath release. A second more and I was going to start hyperventilating. He gestures to my blazer, which I've buttoned over my blouse and waist.

I roll my eyes as if I'm stupid to have forgotten and start to tug my shoulders out while turning around, as we are also required to do. Grigor isn't one to regularly pat anyone down, but like Rogov and every other guard, he could.

He can't tonight.

Halfway through my turn, I'm hoping I haven't truly ticked him off because this is the moment. Right as I'm about to fully face him again, I planned to feign dizziness. But I strike upon something better. A clip from last year's parade announces that General Secretary and Chairman Andropov, along with his wife, Tatyana Filippovna, is entering the chairman's box.

Twisting my head faster than my body, I gasp and point to the TV, faking great love for our nation's leader. "Oh . . ."

Grigor follows my gesture, spins around, and drops into his chair again.

Yuri Andropov strikes people one of two ways, and there is no middle ground. He is our first national leader, both general secretary of the Central Committee of the Party and chairman of the Presidium, who has also served as chairman of the KGB.

As KGB head he cracked down on dissidents and those guilty of not only illegal acts but "subversive thoughts" too. As head of the Soviet Union, he's cracking down on all of us. Just last month he instituted some pretty stringent punishments for truancy from work and school. Basically, through Andropov, the KGB now runs the country. You either love him, believing he is recapturing the discipline and vigor of the Revolution in the truest vein of our ideology, or you hate him, scared he will come—using his exponentially expanded KGB—after you and your family.

Thankfully, Grigor loves him.

His focus glues onto his small, snowy black-and-white television, and I quickly shrug my blazer back over my shoulders and pull on my winter coat as well. I then speak over the announcer, who is now reciting Andropov's long list of accomplishments.

"He's very impressive in his uniform, don't you—?"

I stop speaking at Grigor's raised hand, not willing to drag his attention from the TV for an instant more. He waves me gone.

I walk away from the desk and down the short hall to the outer doors. It's done. Five more feet and I'm free . . . Two more feet . . . Cold night air. A quick brush pass at the Hotel Metropol and I can go home to plan what comes next. As I said, it's time to speed things up.

I step down the stairs outside my building and walk straight into Sonya. "What are you doing here?"

She pulls back at my tone. "Coming to see you."

"I'm sorry." I reach out to half hug her, making sure my abdomen doesn't crunch with the motion. "You just surprised me. This is far out of your way."

"I wanted to talk."

I start walking but not talking. I get the sense Sonya has something on her mind, and considering all that's on mine, I decide to let her take the lead. Besides, unlike my friends at Georgetown, my friends here aren't afraid of silences. We're most comfortable deep within them.

"What was it like?" Sonya finally asks. "You don't talk about America much."

She's right. I don't. Because I can't. It took me months to get the scientists in my lab to forget I studied in the West and start to trust me. It took me months to catch all the subtle ways my mannerisms had changed so I could start replacing them with what had come before. It took me months to banish that feeling of personal ownership and autonomy over my days, my thoughts, my life.

"Why are you asking?"

She doesn't answer and I realize, just like me, she can't. To even ask what she's already asked is a step too far. Sonya is a teacher at School #265 for Class Five. She teaches the next generation, ideologically trains them. Getting reported for asking her one question could get her fired, or worse.

I stop waiting for her to answer and start talking. "You know GUM?"

She throws me a *duh* look.

"Well, while we have one state universal store, they have streets of stores and even malls with stores packed tightly together within a huge building. Stores within stores. And it's not all brown and grey, cheap attempts at the originals. Jordache jeans, Keds, Benetton sweaters, Walkmans, endless books . . . All that stuff we find on the black market? They've got whole stores packed with them. No empty shelves either."

"That's the allure?" She loops her arm in mine. "You're kidding me."

"Just wait . . ." I roll my eyes. "My point is there are choices. Unbelievable choices every moment of every day. It's not one sweater out of the back of Edik's car; it's a store with a thousand sweaters in any color you can imagine."

She's still got a superior smirk on her face.

"Now take all that external stuff and internalize it—and there you have even more choices."

She blinks as if trying to see through smoke. Her expression isn't smug any longer. "I don't get it."

"I didn't either." I sigh. My thoughts drift back to my first days when all the choices overwhelmed me. I felt like a blind person suddenly getting her sight at eighteen—she might have been told both humans and trees are "tall and thin," but how could she discern at first glance which was which and not wonder if some trees walked and talked?

"There are a million ways to think about almost any subject, and Americans believe almost all can be justified, even if they conflict at the most basic level. And they want to debate them all the time. Openly. In class, with friends, in their government . . . I can't tell you how many books I read and lectures I heard about human dignity, republicanism, governance, social contracts, inalienable rights . . . It's mind-blowing. We have no under-standing of freedom at that level. Even the major newspapers can print headlines that completely contradict each other—and both believe they are right."

"How?"

"They just can. It's all allowed, even encouraged."

And while all that was exciting to share, I couldn't get to the heart of it. I could barely glimpse it myself. All those freedoms, the externals of where to go, what to do and buy, as well as the internals of what to think and believe, didn't get to the nugget Dmitri hinted at, Solidarity pointed to, and Tracy shared with me at Georgetown—the truth that deep inside, even in the most challenging and restrictive places, freedom is possible by the meaning we give to the events of our lives and how we let them seep into our souls.

But as much as I want to, I can't share these thoughts with Sonya because I can't fully wrap my own mind around them yet. They dance out of reach like light dappling through shadow, and she would never begin to understand them. I can barely under-stand them, and for a time I lived them.

Sonya breaks into my meanderings. "There's so much more than we've been told." Her gaze travels along the street and drifts up to the light poles, to the cameras mounted atop them.

I grip her arm, now sorry I got carried away. "Forgive me."

She puts her hand over mine. "For sharing something that sounds pretty great? Nah . . . I asked. I always wondered what it was, what it truly was, that makes them fear the West so much. It's not sweaters."

"No. It's not the sweaters."

Sonya finally realizes we aren't headed toward her apartment or mine, and asks where we're going.

"Didn't I say? I need to stop by the Hotel Metropol. A colleague left something at work he needs."

A few blocks more and we reach the famed hotel's front steps. Sonya stops and gestures to the massive doors. "I'll wait here."

I nod and walk up the few steps. Once inside, I check my watch. I'm early. I go to the ladies' room to reposition the papers, then walk to the waiting area just inside the front door. The lobby has seen better days, but it still feels luxurious. I pause, pretend to dig through my bag, and check my watch again. It's go time.

I push out the lobby door and head to the stairs, slightly left of center. I see Peter himself walking toward me. He's wearing a dark wig and makeup has changed his skin tone. Something in his cheeks must be broadening his face because I barely recognize him. And I was half expecting him.

We are three steps apart and I shift the papers, now rolled into a tube, down the sleeve of my coat.

Two steps. His gaze skitters away.

One step. He bumps into a woman to his left and backs away.

The papers are down my arm and into my hand. I almost stop. I almost turn. I definitely react, then mask that reaction by tipping to the side myself as if I've been surprised. I bump into an older woman and have to reach out to keep her from falling.

The tip of the roll slides past my fingertips and I drop, using the pavement as a leverage to push them back into my sleeve.

Peter is gone.

I grab my elbow as if I've hurt it and push the papers up farther toward my shoulder.

Sonya turns. "There you are. Did she trip you?" She points to the older woman now stepping through the hotel's front door.

"No, I bumped her. He wasn't there . . . I . . . I . . ."

"Come on." She grabs my arm, the one not holding the papers. "Give them to him tomorrow. It's his fault for forgetting them anyway and I'm starving."

I follow her with no understanding of what's going on or what to do next. One thought consumes me—*I've got the schematics for a top-secret radar system shoved up my sleeve.*

# NINETEEN

# Anya

*IN-PERSON MEETING ON SUNDAY. SAFE HOUSE #6.*

My heart sank at the purple mark. I messed up badly, yet purple meant I had to keep the plans hidden for four more days. Even for a night, the loose floor tile in my bathroom wasn't going to cut it, so I'd spent hours searching for a hiding place. Around 1:00 a.m., I discovered that the air vent's metal casing in my kitchen didn't quite meet the wall. I tucked the pages inside. They were undetectable there and could only be retrieved with tweezers. But even with that masterful hiding place, four days? How would I survive?

I was too nervous to eat, I barely slept, and I jumped at every bump in the night. And with my building's thin walls, there were plenty of bumps. I almost cried this morning I was so happy it's Sunday.

I retrieve the papers, slide them down the leg of my tights, and begin my dry cleaning early. I arrive five minutes late.

"What the hell were you thinking?" Peter can't risk yelling, but his whisper-yell is just as devastating.

"I'm only a few minutes late." I suggest an alternate offense.

"Wednesday. You were followed, Anya. How did you not see that? You almost blew us both. You risked your friend's life too."

"Sonya? Who told you about her?"

"It was obvious. To both me and the KGB." He runs his hands through his sandy hair and holds the short strands tight. "They could've been tracking you or her, maybe even me, but you had two agents on you. One following and one crossing into our scene right as you came out the door. If you'd been caught, you and Sonya could be dead right now and over half the embassy declared persona non grata and sent home. Olivers told you this . . . There are lots of lives involved here, Anya. You can't be that selfish or that stupid."

"Maybe it was just a fishing expedition. Why'd you come anyway? Last brush pass you sent that short guy, Paul. He, at least, moves like a Soviet."

Peter morphs from angry to offended. "You didn't give us much time, did you? I wasn't about to risk anyone's life but my own in what was a stupid, impulsive move. There are protocols on brush passes, Anya. Days of planning go into that split-second sleight of hand, but you didn't give us that, did you? You had to prove you knew better. You couldn't listen. You couldn't obey—"

"Please. Stop." I whisper the words. He hears them and he stops. He's right. I didn't think, listen, or obey orders. I thought only of myself. Speeding things up made me feel better, made me feel valuable, worthy, and not such a fool. "I'm sorry. I won't do it again."

The fight falls out of Peter as well. "Do you need a reminder as to what they'd do to you? And don't pretend you could be brave because there is no brave. The KGB breaks everyone, Anya. Everyone talks. Then everyone dies."

Peter clenches his jaw. It's already square, but now it's rigid and there's a muscle flickering beneath his right ear. He might still be a little angry, but he's mostly scared.

I accept his silence for the gift it is and I wait.

After a few seconds, he sits in the small chair at the kitchen table. The chair isn't small, actually. I fit just fine. It's that Peter is large. He's tall, bulky, and built like a college baseball player. Even in his midforties, Peter is an impressive man.

I watch and realize that in these few short months, our relationship has grown deep. It has taken on a life of its own. Technically he works for me. He "handles" me and gets me what I need when I need it. But in reality, I need him more. I need him to keep track of the larger picture I cannot see. I need him not to lose faith in me or give up on me, even if I did come super close to destroying it all. I need him to believe in me. He's like the older brother I always wanted, never want to disappoint, and would hate to see deported.

"We got away with it this time." I lift my voice, offering my olive branch.

"How can you be sure?"

I reach down through my waist into my tights. Peter quirks a brow watching me. "This." I slap the roll of papers into his hands with all the bravado in me. I turn into the tiny living room and collapse into an armchair. Because it isn't much bravado.

"Don't look so cocky. The KGB is like a cargo ship, Anya. Slow to pivot, but it gets there eventually."

He leafs through the thin sheets. "You've had this with you for four days?"

I nod.

"I can't say this isn't big, but it was also crazy."

"I can do more . . . I don't think you believe I can." It sounds like I'm begging for his approval. Maybe I am.

He carries his kitchen chair over and sets it in front of me. "I do believe you can, but you have to trust me. Do. Not. Do. This. Again."

"Get me the Topel and I won't have to."

"Is that a threat?"

I bite my lip. I was so close to saying, *"It's a fact."* But I stopped myself just in time. It's not a threat and it's not a fact. It's simply a compulsion. I can't explain it any other way, and that is not a good explanation or a reason. Yet I still can't stop this ticking bomb inside me, compelling me to chase more, and faster.

Peter lets his question go unanswered and tilts his head back to the kitchen. We position ourselves at the table and sit for the next two hours as I walk him through every detail of the pages and write out everything else I remember on the blank papers he stores at each safe house.

Just as I'm about to leave, he brings up compensation.

"What about 'qualitative motivations and rewards'?" I toggle my fingers because he really did sound a little pompous at our first meeting.

"Don't mock it. That's most important, but Uncle Sam believes in cold, hard cash too." Peter slides a piece of paper across the table. "Here's the amount so far. Do you want it in rubles or US dollars?"

In the end we decided on dollars held in a US bank account for some nebulous future. Although I'm fairly certain I'll never have a chance to access it, dollars far away are better than rubles close. In a world where money doesn't mean much, everyone sure notices when you have more.

I leave the safe house around 2:00 p.m., and with no place to go, I head home. It's odd. I thought I'd feel this great sense of relief or that flush of accomplishment I got when I first slid the papers into my tights, but I don't. I still feel confined and trapped and anxious. I'm not happy like I thought I'd be. I'm not—

Alone.

My apartment door is cracked open. I push at it with two fingers and find myself facing Captain Stanslych.

"I did knock." He gestures to a living room chair. I assume he's inviting me to sit. I do. "I received a report yesterday of an incident at the Hotel Metropol Wednesday evening. It involved another department and, well, these things take time."

"I don't understand."

He scans my apartment with a casual air as if I've invited him for lunch. "It doesn't matter. Tell me what you and Sonya Vitya Anatova were doing at the Hotel Metropol Wednesday evening at 7:00 p.m."

"I . . ." I try to remember what I told Sonya that night and try to guess what she might say. I can't let her get caught in my lie. Heat floods my face and Stanslych's eyes narrow. He doesn't move any other muscles, just the tiny ones around his eyes. I'm taking too long.

"I needed to get a coworker some papers. Sonya met me outside work and walked with me."

"Which coworker needed papers?"

"There wasn't one. I lied. I lied to Sonya because . . ." I run out of lies. I can't name anyone real or he'll be tracked down too. My mind draws a blank. Scott's face rises before me. "There's this guy. I like him, but I think he lied to me and he's seeing someone."

"Luka Evanovich Chaban?"

I blink. Stanslych has just named a man at work who has asked me out a few times. "No. Not him. We've never gone out." I keep my thoughts focused on Scott—a face far away and untouchable. "I've never really spoken to this guy, but we've danced at a club, and I didn't want to believe he was leading me on. I'd heard, by chance, he was going to be at the hotel . . ." I let my voice trail away.

The story is either going to work or not. Spinning it further hardly matters.

"Does this young man have a name?"

Stanslych's question surprises me so much my thoughts skitter to a stop. I can't come up with a name. I can't think of my own name. But I need one. One that doesn't belong to anyone real. One that's common, easy to believe, hard to trace.

After what feels like another ridiculously long stretch, I blurt, "Ivan." I shake my head. "It was stupid. But—"

I stop myself. Again, I'm spinning the tale too far. I then realize, if I'm innocent, I ought to be curious. "Why would someone report that to you?"

"Another department was following a person of interest and you were close by at one point." Stanslych stands. "Your friend said the same thing. About the coworker."

"You—" My voice cracks. "You talked to Sonya?"

"An officer spoke with her yesterday. She said you were delivering work papers. I knew that could not be the case."

"I will tell her I lied."

"That is up to you." He scans my apartment again, absorbing every detail. "I will see you at work tomorrow."

I follow him to the door, and just as I'm about to close it behind him, he turns. "By the way, she also told my colleague about your conversation during your walk. I found all those sweaters most interesting." The corner of his mouth twists up and he turns away, calling behind him, "Have a good afternoon, Comrade Kadinova."

I close the door. My legs can't hold me any longer and I slide to the floor. It strikes me that I'm in the same spot and in the same position I was in when Sonya told me Dmitri was dead. I look around my apartment, just as Stanslych did, and I feel certain he's planted bugs throughout it.

I can't think. I can't go to Peter. I quickly pack a bag and go to the only place truly safe. Home.

$$\infty$$

Have I made a mistake? While home is safe—there are never bugs—it's not a place I can fall apart. Weakness like that isn't allowed. My mother will fret and worry, then try to hug me back together, and my father will caution me never to mess up in the first place. *"We owe everything to the State,"* he always says. Everything. I quit arguing that one with him years ago. Now I must keep silent so neither will ever guess what I've done and continue to do.

"We didn't expect you." My father opens the door with a smile that doesn't reach his eyes. He appears more tired and thinner since I last saw him. I've sensed he's pulled too tight, like a rubber band stretched to reveal the thin sections just before it snaps. I've encouraged him to cut back at work, but he always shakes his head and asks what he would do instead.

I usually retort that at sixty-four he should simply enjoy himself and spend time in Sochi. He loves the sea. He laughs that off, too, saying it is his honor and his duty to serve the nation. But Sochi is the only place I have ever seen him truly relaxed and happy. I often wonder if "honor and duty" should take such a toll.

Tonight, after shutting the door behind me, he leads me down the hall to the living room. I drop my bag on a chair and pause. I want a hug, but my father is not a hugger. "Should I tell Mother I'm here?"

"She'll learn soon enough." He waves his hand over his shoulder. "Join me."

He heads straight for the high chest in which he stores his liquor and pulls out a bottle of Mamont. It's the best vodka he owns. He pours fifty grams. No ice.

"You're enjoying the good stuff tonight," I tease, pretending to be calm in hopes I'll become that way soon.

"*We* are." He lifts the glass to me. "I hear good things about you and you haven't come home in a while."

I try to read his expression. I find nothing hidden within it so I step forward, accept the offered glass, and lift on my toes to kiss his cheek. It's cool and he is definitely thinner. I curl onto the couch, one leg tucked beneath me as he settles into his favorite armchair.

My parents' home is about ten times larger than mine, along with being on the most prominent street in Moscow. It's a beautiful apartment, and it's funny how only in coming back from America do I realize the stark inequalities within my own country. Their home has high ceilings, carved crown moldings, a walk-in kitchen, two bathrooms, and two bedrooms. It's extravagant by any and all standards. And while I concede these are the privileges and gifts for years of hard work and dedicated service, and my father deserves them, I still can't reconcile their existence with the ideology that decries them.

"I'm presenting new technology to the Ministry of Defense again next week. Nothing earth-shattering, but it's got broad applicability."

"Oh?" My non sequitur surprises him. It surprises me, too, but I had to say something. Father absorbs my comment and sighs with little humor. "Are you trying to make my life hard too?"

"Who else is?"

"Who isn't?" He takes a sip of his drink. "You'd be surprised the wrangling required to reappropriate funds. Everyone wants something."

That's as close as my father has ever gotten to telling me what he does. And to be fair, my comment is as close as I've gotten as well. Discussing work or "bringing it home" is not something we do. Not something anyone does.

"It's hard to wrangle through red tape and get things done around here?" I raise a brow, feeling something close to happy for the first time in days. It's rare my father lets me in, and here is a tiny crack. "Yes, that is surprising."

He dips his head, and I can tell he's trying to decide if my comment was made with snide humor or if it cuts too close to criticism. He lands on the former and raises his glass again. We salute and we drink.

Later, long after dinner, dishes, and my parents' retreat to their bedroom, I hear a soft knock on my door. Mother, backlit by the hall light, crosses into my room and sits on the edge of my bed.

She strokes her fingers through my hair, sweeping down the full length of it, spreading it loose and long across my shoulder. She did this when, as a young child, I couldn't sleep. I feel my eyes drift shut in the darkness.

"Anya? What happened today?"

"How do you do that?"

"A mother knows."

I shake my head. I can't tell her the truth and I don't want to lie again. What happened to me is no different from what happens to many people on any given day. We get searched, we get questioned, we go on with life. The only thing that made it terrifying is that I wasn't checking up on some guy at the Hotel Metropol Wednesday night; I was committing treason. I certainly can't tell her that.

"Did you love him terribly?"

"Who? Dmitri?"

"We all loved Dmitri." She threads her fingers through another curl. "I'm asking about Scott O'Neill."

"What made you—? How do you know about him?"

"Darling." She laughs. It's light and warm and wraps me up

within the aura of safety she's always provided. "You wrote about him for four years. Silly stories. Fun stories. Tender stories. Your letters were full of him. Yet you never mentioned him after you came home. Not once. It's been over three years. I've been waiting . . . And something has changed. Something is different now."

Tears flood my eyes. "Oh . . . Mother." I can't tell her our past, three years ago or three weeks ago. Even if I could, where would I begin?

I don't need to. Without words she bends over me and gathers me into her arms.

"It can hurt so much," she whispers. After I quiet, she asks her next question. "Do you keep in touch?"

I tell the most basic truth. The one I would tell anyone who asked. "We did. We do. Sort of. Generic letters that say nothing and mean less. When I left, I warned him everything would be read, so there never was much real either of us could say. A relationship can't live on that." I think of our meeting. His presence in Vienna and the fact that Peter still hasn't told me what Ames said. Is Scott in the CIA?

Feeling safe, I share the one thing I told myself not to. "I saw him in Vienna. He was at that meeting I told you about."

My mother straightens. "Were you seen talking with him?"

"No . . . We didn't speak." I'm disappointed that's the first thing that comes to her mind, but I can't blame her. I really can't. Especially not after my day.

She shifts on the bed. "What about your body language? That meeting will have been recorded. They'll watch for everything."

"Come on . . . I hide what I think and feel every single day, Mother. Don't you think I'm an expert by now?" I push back on the bed to rise to her level. Disappointment transforms to anger. It's such a short, easy step.

"You do?"

"Of course I do. And in a moment of weakness, I almost got Sonya in trouble because she asked about America. I answered a simple question, and the KGB broke into my apartment. Three years of silence and one conversation about sweaters and choices gets me on their radar. But I have all these thoughts in my head all the time. None of them I can talk about. I shouldn't even think them because they make everything around here so much worse. I can't talk about it. There's no one to trust with all this . . . If I'd known it was going to be this hard, that I wouldn't belong in my own country anymore, that'd I'd have to live here knowing all I do now, I never would have gone to the US."

I stop. I've upset her and it's not true. Even if I never say another true word to a living soul, I wouldn't change all I've learned and how I've grown. I just wish I didn't feel so alone and so divided all the time.

"When you came to me that night and talked with me about the art and paintings you'd always wanted to see and the things you'd heard about America, did you know how it would change me?"

"Never. I was selfish. I was curious. There's so much I read at work, so much I'll never see. I wanted that chance for you, and you earned it. It was such an honor, but the rest? No. I never realized the cost could be this high."

"Some days it's too high." I think about Scott and wish my heart wouldn't go there anymore.

My mother shifts closer and holds my hands within my lap. "Anya, listen to me. You must accept what you learned and how you changed. All that is real. But also accept you are here now and you cannot change what is. This is real too. By rejecting it, wanting it to be different, you add anger, rebellion, and resentment to your heart."

"I don't understand."

"You need to accept reality for what it is. And make peace in your heart with that."

"Mom, reality sucks. This country is falling apart."

"True." She shakes her head. "I'm not saying be resigned to it. There is much that's wrong here. I'm saying to willingly allow yourself to accept it as reality, while you strive every moment, if you choose, to change it. There is no visible difference on the outside. You will still get pulled from the line by Rogov and you will still have to report quarterly to Stanslych for your KGB interviews. But inside? That's where the difference lies." She lays a hand on my heart. "You transform the strictures into your free choice; you transform resentment into love and loss into gain. Only then can you survive in here"—she presses down, and I sense she can feel my heart beating as clearly as I myself can—"while trying to change the world out there."

I sit speechless. I can't rage and argue because there is something true in what she says. It feels like my thoughts from a few nights ago, when I struck upon the conviction that even in the most challenging and restrictive places, freedom is possible by the meaning we give to each moment.

I thought I was alone in those musings and wonder how my mother ever got to them first. It's almost as if I don't know her, haven't seen her clearly, like she—rather than those ideas—has been dancing out of reach.

Her head dips, and even without seeing it in the darkness of my room, I sense the soft look she's giving me. She's given it a thousand times before when I resisted, either willingly or not, the wisdom she shared with me.

"*Duc in altum,*" she whispers.

It's Latin and means "put out into the deep." My mother has said this to me only a few times in my life. At turning points. In tough times. I've never truly understood it, but I've always paid attention, knowing it's *for* me in every sense. It calls me to stand when I want to crumble.

"What am I to do?" I ask, sure she holds the answer to everything.

"Live." Without another word, she leans over me and kisses my forehead.

I lie in the dark and let her words dance over me. They remind me of another's. Words I have read and pondered, unable to understand.

Just as I'm drifting to sleep, the words come to me in that final falling moment. Konstantin Dmitrich Levin from *Anna Karenina*. He was the character who always drew me in the most. He reminded me of myself, struggling—always struggling—wishing, debating, wrestling with himself, yearning for greater purpose and meaning. And only when he stopped struggling did he find they had been there all along. He found peace and love, not by chasing them or even focusing directly on them but by seeing all else through their lens and light. The love and peace I just heard in my mother's voice. The love and peace that pervade all her actions and all her care.

But how do I get there? The answer comes as quickly as the question. A line I oddly remember from long ago, but truth does that—it lodges within you.

*"When Levin thought about what he was and what he lived for, he found no answer and fell into despair; but when he stopped asking himself about it, he seemed to know what he was and what he lived for, because he acted and lived firmly and definitely."*

∞

The next morning I'm up early. My commute to work will be longer from here, and I want to leave enough time for my old routine. I want to stop at my favorite bakery, if the line is long and the vatrushkis are hot. I want to hop on the next bus and enjoy the bun while reading my book, glancing up as we pass the Kremlin and the embassies and the Moskva River. I want to go back to the beginning and enjoy my "beastly long" combination of bus rides and stretches of walking to the Kapotnya District. I want to be outside the system again, anonymous again. Because if I'm not where I'm supposed to be—I'm nowhere at all.

I find my mother sitting at the kitchen table, drinking a cup of coffee and reading the paper. I don't comment. I simply reach for a cup, pour the last from the carafe into it, and join her.

"Your father has already left." She watches me a moment. "Do you feel better this morning?"

"I do. Thank you." I don't say anything more, unsure where to begin or where words would lead. It's all still a jumble. Like Tolstoy's Levin, I'm still pondering, wrestling, struggling, and resisting.

She folds up the paper and stretches her hand across the table. It is only then I notice the radio is on. It's not loud, but loud enough.

Once my hand is within hers, she speaks. "You must also remember that while your generation thinks it's 'cool' to be angry and protest for change, my generation remains firmly in charge. I'm not saying things can't or won't change in the future, but at this moment we make the rules. We are the great advancers of the Marxist-Leninist dream, pushing us into space and building a military-industrial complex second to none, and we pride ourselves on forging new and, in many ways, more diabolical ways to fight. We can be ruthless." She nods as if I've answered her and we sit in agreement.

"I'm sorry." She squeezes my hand one last time before standing. "I never wanted this for you."

"What?"

"Any of this." She carries her cup to the sink. "Especially heartbreak." She walks out of the kitchen.

"Mother?" I call her back. "Have you ever heard of Rose Beuret?"

Juliet came from a play. Terry McKay from a movie. Perhaps Rose is from art? It's the one area, the one sector of life, I never considered. And despite all that is now tarnished between Scott and me, I want the final piece of our puzzle firmly in place so I can put it away forever.

"Who?" Mom rounds the corner.

"No one. I just—"

"Where did you learn about Rose Beuret?"

I set down my coffee cup. "Who is she?"

"She was Auguste Rodin's most famous muse, his lover, and finally his wife. But you've never been interested in my work." Mother steps to the table and sits again. "He's not an artist I've been able to bring here. 'Too sensual,' I've been told. But I suspect it's *Le Penseur* the minister of culture worries about. He'd rather us not get any ideas about thinking."

She smiles playfully. My mother always glows when she talks about her work. I chastise myself for never showing interest, for never letting her share that joy with me before. Peter's indictment from yesterday crashes through me. *"You can't be that selfish or that stupid."*

My mother continues. "Rose was the love of Rodin's life. She finally married him or he finally married her—there's debate as to which one kept them from the altar—sixteen days before her death when she was seventy-four years old and he was seventy-six. It's a beautiful story in some ways. Come to the museum. I have a couple books of his work in my office. One is French and the other English. You can help me with some of the translations, and I can show you her picture. Did you take an art class?"

The translations. Working in a museum, my mother is exposed to a variety of languages. It always bothered her that she didn't know them well. She made sure, growing up, I had extra tutors so that I could.

"Sure, I'd love to help. I'll come by after work tonight." I shrug and lie to her. "No class. I simply heard Rose's name and have wondered about her. I couldn't find her in any books."

Her head tilts and I can tell she doesn't believe me. But she doesn't press. I'll give her that—my mother has always respected one's right to keep secrets. She rises and, without words, kisses me on the forehead and leaves the kitchen.

I sit stunned. Of all the people to ask—my mother held the answer.

# TWENTY

# Ingrid

MOSCOW
*June 27, 1973*

"HOW DID IT GO?" INGRID STOOD IN THE DOORWAY. SHE RAISED her hand in acknowledgment that she should have been polite and said hello, but that was all she could give to niceties. She'd been waiting over a month for this meeting. She didn't want a salutation. She wanted an answer.

Reginald drew her within the apartment and shut the door behind her. "It couldn't have gone better."

Ingrid let out a deep sigh and tears filled her eyes. She reached for Reginald's hand and pulled it against her heart.

Titled the Washington Summit, the meetings started on June 18 and had ended only two days earlier. President Richard Nixon and Secretary of State Henry Kissinger had welcomed General Secretary of the Communist Party of the Soviet Union Leonid Brezhnev and Chairman of the Council of Ministers Alexei Kosygin to the White House in Washington, DC.

It was Ingrid who had advised, through Reginald, for the US to broaden the discussions from armaments exclusively and to start them with topics such as oceanography, transportation, agricultural research, and cultural enhancements and exchanges. In no uncertain terms she told Reginald to impress upon the US that by *not* focusing on nuclear disarmament they'd get closer to achieving it.

"*Comrade Brezhnev expects and is prepared for a frontal attack,*" she had explained. "*But he needs the cultural concessions from the US just as badly. So advise your 'cousins' to tell their president to offer generously first on a variety of cultural, social, and scientific fronts. To save face, Brezhnev will need to match his generosity later when the only issues left are weapons and disarmament.*"

Reginald had parsed her advice, sent it around the world, and managed to land it in the CIA's lap in a variety of small bites just as talking points were being devised. Bites that, when put together, made a most satisfying meal.

He gave Ingrid a quick hug. "We did it. You did it. It's just so good. It's a high point for the détente, Ingrid, and it's beyond anything the West could have hoped for. Britain's aglow too. Prime Minister Heath is thrilled."

Ingrid raised a brow.

Reginald shook his head. "Your identity is safe. He's simply grateful we received some of the best bits." He winked. "After all, those American 'cousins' can be awfully arrogant. It's nice for us to have the upper hand occasionally."

"So it's over . . . No nuclear weapons?" Only in asking the question did Ingrid realize how much she hoped for it.

"Oh . . . Ingrid." Reg dropped into a chair. He gestured for her to sit as well. "We still live in the real world, and that's not possible. But it's close, closer than we've been in years. They titled it the Agreement on the Prevention of Nuclear War. It's not an original title, but leaders on both sides signed it, and it outlines emergency measures and diplomatic procedures in case of conflict . . . Smile. It's a true win for all of us." He offered one himself, trying to convince Ingrid to do the same.

"And you were right," Reginald continued. "Brezhnev jumped at the geology programs and your Foreign Studies Initiative idea. He also agreed to increased cultural exchanges."

"Of course he did." Ingrid rolled her eyes. "It means more KGB operatives on US and British soil."

"True, but we can handle that. Besides, it means we can get more of ours here too." Reg leaned forward. "This détente is as close to peace as these countries have been in forty years, longer even. All thanks to you. I can't imagine what will shake it . . . Feel proud, or at least pleased."

Ingrid sank back into the armchair. "I am. Truly. I've just been waiting for so long. I forget how important small steps can be."

"These aren't small steps."

Ingrid conceded his point with her first smile. "Was it as beautiful . . . Were you there?"

He had been. In thanks for the intel received, the US allowed a couple of operatives from Britain and the Netherlands to attend the Summit. They were hoping LUMEN himself might show up, but word soon circulated he hadn't.

As Reginald described the meetings, the dinners, and the ball following the final day of negotiations, Ingrid felt her mind slip away. Nothing he described matched what she'd seen the year before.

In May the year before, the summit meetings had been held in Moscow—and they were far grander than anything Reginald was describing. She couldn't envision it, but the White House sounded like a small and relatively uninteresting place. The Great Kremlin Palace, however, had been spectacular. Leo had been invited to the final dinner and ball for the Moscow Summit, and President Nixon, his wife, Pat, and Secretary of State Henry Kissinger had been the guests of honor. It was the first time a US president had visited Moscow—only President Franklin

Roosevelt had visited the Soviet Union—and Nixon's visit was declared a national cause for celebration.

By hosting the first Summit in 1972, Moscow felt it had the upper hand and pulled out all the stops. Not only that, both countries signed the Anti-Ballistic Missile Treaty and the first Strategic Arms Limitation Treaty, SALT I, during those meetings. It was considered an unqualified success.

But it was the ball that lingered in Ingrid's imagination, a ball as grand as the fairy tales of her childhood. A long, black ZiL limousine had taken Leo and her to the palace. Once there, they followed a line of attendees from the drive to the dinner via a long hallway, lacquered in red and framed by gold-topped jade pillars. The procession was over a hundred meters long.

*"This site has been active since 500 BC,"* Leo whispered with pride. *"A fortress city right in the center of Moscow—a citadel, a church, a town, a palace. It has evolved with us. But the crowning glory is this, the Great Kremlin Palace."*

A single dining room table seated every person present. Over one hundred in all, seated on gold chairs with white silk brocade cushions. The chairs matched the curtains—huge swathes of white silk, puddling to the floor, with red silk edging. And the floor—a mosaic of wood colors and types, intricately cut and fashioned into a tapestry the length and width of the entire room.

Then came the ballroom. That was a sight she would never forget. Gold. Everywhere. Scenes and design work wrought in gold covered the massive doors entering the room. Gold ribbons and detailing lined the arches. Gold and brightly colored mosaic tiles and stone worked intricate patterns into the domed ceilings. Chandeliers as big as cars hung above and sent out a million points of light, burnishing the gold all around. It was like dancing among the stars and the sun, high above the mundane world and all its concerns.

How she had danced. Dressed in a beautiful crimson silk gown that floated around her, Ingrid almost forgot with whom and where she was dancing. She had danced with Chairman of the Presidium of the Supreme Soviet Nikolai Podgorny and with General Secretary Leonid Brezhnev himself. Leo had been so impressed that night. She thought he'd never regarded her with such warmth. Of course, Podgorny wasn't involved in this year's talks in Washington—Brezhnev had deftly removed him from power months ago. But what a fine dancer he was.

And that night, she'd felt truly happy. For a moment she'd let herself believe the fairy tale—that all could be well, that she had made a difference, could make a difference, and that maybe even her husband loved her.

It wasn't until they were in the car heading home that the golden bubble burst.

*"We conceded too much. They think it's a win, but the United States played us for fools. We have our work cut out for us now."* Leo said nothing more and all her illusions died.

"Ingrid?"

She shook her head but didn't apologize for drifting away in thought. Reginald knew that a safe house, no matter which one they secured for any given meeting, was the one place Ingrid felt truly free, truly safe, and let her guard down. She let herself dream and she let herself mourn.

Reg reached across the table and held her hand. "Are you okay?"

"I am. I'm simply tired . . . I let myself believe we could end another war."

"That's the pain of the Cold War, Ingrid. Cold can burn low for a long, long time, never reaching the heat necessary to burn out . . . I'm sorry."

"Me too." Ingrid stood, still clasping Reginald's hand. She

held it within both her own. "Thank you. I needed to hear this today. And you are right, it is good news. But now . . ." She dropped his hand. "It is time for me to return to reality."

❦

Ingrid unlocked the apartment's front door and felt a cold creep up her spine.

It was quiet. Too quiet.

They had only lived in this new apartment for four months, and although she was still getting used to it, she knew when something felt terribly wrong.

She peered down the hall and into the living room, straight to the bookshelves. She focused on the one book that could get her killed.

While packing for the move, Leo had found her previous hiding spot. A cigarette box in the bathroom air vent. He carried it into their bedroom where she was folding shirts and waved it at her.

"*I wonder what the previous tenants were up to,*" had been his only comment. The box was empty. Just a few days before, Ingrid had handed Reginald not only five rolls of film but also her Minox camera, as it had jammed and no longer worked.

Now she hid her film and her new Minox AIII in plain sight—within a hollowed-out copy of Tolstoy's *War & Peace*. It rested on the shelf undisturbed. Exactly one centimeter deeper than the copy of *One Day in the Life of Ivan Denisovich*—a defiance Leo had yet to notice—sitting next to it.

"Dolores?" she called out without expecting any reply. Anya was away at Komsomol camp and Dolores usually hummed or sang while working.

Ingrid hung her coat in the closet, then walked down the

short hall to the living room. She wanted a better look at her books. Her heels made firm strikes against the marble, then a deeper note, but no less firm, against the living room's hardwood floor.

She stopped only a meter within the room, noting a still shadow in the corner. "Leo? Why are you home so early?" She gathered herself within a single step and crossed to where he sat at his desk in the room's far corner. She bent to kiss his cheek. He didn't move and his cheek felt cool to her lips. "Darling, what's wrong?" She stepped back and surveyed the room. "Where is Dolores?"

"Gone." Leo shifted his focus from the desk to her. "Tell me where."

His tone sent chills across her arms. Rather than reach around her body and hug herself tight, she dropped into the velvet upholstered chair next to the desk and reached to its side table. She picked up a pack of cigarettes and held it out to Leo.

"With Anya away, she takes longer with the shopping these days. It's a nuisance but hardly a concern."

Leo waved away the packet. Ingrid pulled one out for herself, willing her hands and voice to stay steady. "I assume she's still at the market."

"I assume she fled, Inga."

Ingrid swallowed. Years ago her husband had taken up the altered name in private as well as in public. It never failed to wound. Especially as she was certain even their own daughter didn't know her true name.

Leo brought her attention back to the present, one fist slamming onto the desk. "This was open. I came home early and found my desk drawer unlocked and open, and when I approached her, she grabbed her coat and ran."

Ingrid pointed her cigarette to the desk. "Is that unusual?"

Leo glared at her.

"I am not trying to be obtuse. I simply don't bother with your desk. Perhaps you opened it last night?"

"No . . . I never would have opened it with Philby in the house."

Ingrid caught the competitive note Leo always had when mentioning his longtime friend, but she hid her interest as she always did. She'd done her job well. Philby, initially intrigued by her, had given up showing her any interest or attention years ago—as she had shown none in him.

"I hardly think . . ." Ingrid's mind raced, trying to find the delicate line between outrage and nonchalance regarding Leo's desk. "You didn't open it before you left this morning? You were running late."

Ingrid took a pull on her cigarette. She had never liked them but found them incredibly useful when one needed a moment and a distraction.

With a slow exhale she continued. "The KGB interviews Dolores annually. You must have friends and colleagues there . . . If they had any concerns, surely they would reach out to you. Ask your friend Philby."

She waited for Leo's reaction on both counts. One, he'd never confirmed he worked for the KGB. Two, suggesting Philby might help would ensure Leo didn't ask him. Whatever this was, Leo would now keep it close. He clearly admired his friend, but true to form, Leo didn't trust him.

"Besides," Ingrid continued. "What of importance do you keep in there? You never bring work home."

"It was unlocked." He dropped his head into his hands.

Ingrid's eyes widened at the vulnerable gesture. It was unexpected and out of character. She said nothing. After a few moments, she stood and stepped to her husband. She lifted her hand and hesitated, unsure. She hadn't touched her husband in a long time. He hadn't touched her in longer. She closed her eyes for a single heartbeat, then dropped her hand into his hair.

It was still dark, though threaded with grey. It felt soft to her touch, and she wondered if he missed her, if she missed him. She wondered what they had become and what would become of them after this moment. She threaded her fingers through his hair and whispered, "What's wrong? What's really concerning you?"

Leo spoke without lifting his head. "There's trouble at work. There was a leak about a new elevation within the Presidium, an appointment only a few of us knew about."

"What can that have to do with Dolores?"

Leo lifted his head as Ingrid crouched to bring them eye to eye. His eyes rounded at the edges, his brow furrowed above his nose. "I keep racking my brain, wondering if it was me somehow. We talked about it here during dinner a few weeks ago. We shouldn't have, but it's generated excitement . . . I also had a letter in my desk."

Ingrid let a little outrage creep into her voice. "Someone took it? It's gone?"

"No." Leo shook his head. "I filed it at the office days ago. But to come home and find the desk open. There are still confidential papers here . . . What if I'm the leak? What if Dolores has been watching us, watching me, all these years, and I've been played for a fool? Or worse, painted as a traitor?"

"Not possible," Ingrid declared as she rocked back onto her heels and stood. "Dolores is loyal to us. You must have scared her . . . When she gets back, we'll sort this out."

"I didn't— I asked her about it and she said she noticed it when clearing last night's glasses. She said she occasionally found it that way but had never touched it."

"There you go. You can talk to her again tomorrow. Maybe she had enough of today and went home."

"Have you ever seen me leave that drawer unlocked?" Leo stood, feet shoulder-width apart. He was challenging her now.

Ingrid dropped into the chair, changing the power dynamic. "I'm sorry. I couldn't tell you. I never check your desk."

"We need to find her." Leo stepped behind his desk again and lifted the phone off its receiver. "This leak . . . I've been called in tomorrow."

Every fiber within Ingrid stilled. Once again, she could feel the small hairs on the back of her neck and her arms rise with the tension, the electric crackle of the room.

"Are you in danger?" This time fear seeped out, as she had, in fact, photographed Leo's papers early that morning, then delivered the film, along with twelve other rolls, to a foot-timed drop on Kaunin Prospekt before continuing on to the safe house. She and Reginald had determined years before never to carry film longer than necessary and never to bring it to a safe house personally.

Leo replaced the receiver and stepped around the desk again. He surprised Ingrid by pulling her up from the chair and into a hug. She sank into his embrace, her head fitting in the soft spot beneath his clavicle.

"No . . ." He sighed. "But questions must be asked, which is why I must to talk to Dolores. Today." He stepped back. "I need to call my office for help. Maybe they can send someone to her apartment."

Ingrid lowered her cigarette to the ashtray and stubbed it out. "I'll let you do that and go see to dinner. Though if Dolores didn't go to the market, I'll need to go out."

At Leo's nod she headed to the kitchen. She hesitated at the phone in the front hallway. She could already hear Leo talking a room away.

She had to work fast.

Within a minute she had her light coat in hand and was back at the edge of the living room. Leo was on the phone. She whisper-called to him, "She didn't go to the market. I'll get us dinner and be back soon."

He waved her gone.

Rather than wait for the building's elevator, Ingrid raced down the back stairs and, upon exiting, walked immediately to the park. Dolores knew Ingrid walked the park three days a week. In fact, she was the only one who knew Ingrid's routines. And while Ingrid suspected Dolores would carry her secrets to the grave, she did not want the KGB to put her theory to the test.

Ingrid spotted her immediately. But rather than walk to her, she crossed away from the park, circled the outer-ring path, and returned by another entrance. The day was bright and clear and pedestrians filled the green expanse, either cutting through it on their way home or lingering on benches to sit and talk.

Dolores remained fixed. She looked just like everyone else. A woman enjoying the afternoon sunshine. Only her purse, clutched tightly on her lap, signaled any tension.

Once Ingrid assessed no one was watching either Dolores or herself, she gestured for Dolores to join her on the sidewalk that bisected the park. Dolores rose from her bench and walked an adjoining path until the two met under a copse of trees.

"How are you?" Ingrid asked, not in German as they usually spoke but in Russian so as not to draw attention to themselves.

Dolores understood immediately. "I'm sorry. Did I mess up by leaving? I got scared."

"Don't apologize. This is my fault." Ingrid resumed walking. Dolores fell into step beside her. "You can't stay in Moscow."

"If I run, he'll think it's me."

"He already does . . . I can give him me, but . . ." Ingrid reached over and squeezed her friend's hand.

"It won't save me." Dolores finished her sentence. She added with vehemence, "Think of Anya. Don't you dare."

Ingrid dropped her friend's hand and continued walking. "Then you must run . . . I can get you out. I'll get papers and money. Where can you go?"

"Home. My papers say Kraków because I was sent to work there first. I've kept Smolensk a secret, and I still have an aunt and two sisters there."

"That's not dangerous?"

"We are women. Who pays attention to us?" Dolores cut a quick glance to Ingrid. "In Poland it is not like here. We more frequently take our husbands' surnames. My sisters and I don't even share a name anymore. Besides, over forty years have passed. There is no one else to remember me."

"I'm sorry."

"Don't be. It's still home."

Facing forward, Ingrid nodded her agreement. "I'll make sure you're cleared, regardless."

"How?" Dolores stopped, then had to double-step to catch up again. "Why? If I'm gone, let him think it was me. What does it matter?"

"It can't be you. Because if you, then me." Ingrid bit her lip. "It shouldn't be too hard. The leak simply won't stop . . . If you and your access disappear and it continues, it can't be you."

Dolores matched Ingrid's earlier tone and question. "That's not dangerous?"

Ingrid cast her closest friend a sideways smirk. Over the

years she had learned that if she didn't find humor in her work, it would destroy her. She had also learned that she needed places to be honest and true—places in which her soul was whole and could rest. Reginald was such a place. Dolores was such a place. Now she was leaving.

"No more so than any other day," Ingrid replied sardonically. "And less than a few." She turned to face Dolores. Part of her wanted to thank her, share with her all she'd meant to her, and cry over how much she'd miss her. But there was no time.

Ingrid shared her love the only way she could—she focused on the job of getting Dolores out of Moscow safely. "Don't go home. Stay with a friend tonight. Not a good one. An acquaintance who won't ask questions or check up on you in a few days. Say your apartment is being fumigated or something. Call no one. See no one."

Ingrid surveyed the park. She had found it a good spot for dead drops and foot-timed drops and prayed it would remain so, if only for one more. "Tomorrow morning, tell your friend you're coming to work and go to that bench."

She pointed to a bench positioned directly in front of a large maple tree. "There is a divot in the tree trunk behind it. Inside you'll find a black bag filled with cash and papers at seven o'clock. Be as close to that time as possible. Pick it up and drop the bag within one of your own and go—no looking back—straight to the train station. There, use one set of papers. When you change trains in Vilnius, destroy them and pull the other set out of the bag's side lining. Do you understand?"

Tears ran down the older woman's face. She nodded. "Yes, but . . . ," she whispered. "You have been my family. I love you and I don't want to leave you. Who will . . . Who will help you?"

Ingrid pulled Dolores into a tight hug, then pushed her away just as quickly. "I love you too. Thank you. Thank you for being beside me all these years." She sensed no one was paying attention to them at present, but how long could that last? "Now go . . . and Godspeed."

As Dolores walked one direction, Ingrid walked the opposite. She headed straight for the nearest pay phone, lifted the receiver, and listened for the delayed click. The line was clear.

She dialed her emergency number.

Within the half hour, after backtracking through a maze of streets, alleys, and shops, she stood inside an MI6 safe house facing Reginald and someone new.

"I didn't expect to see you again today, but . . . here we are." Reginald gestured to the young man and Ingrid's heart sank. She thought she had more time—especially since Reg hadn't mentioned this man earlier that afternoon.

George Milner. Her new handler.

Reginald, upon announcing his retirement the year before, told Ingrid he had personally handpicked his replacement. A new officer, *"young, eager, and even a little in awe of you."*

The young man—twenty-five years old if a day—held up a bag. "The ambassador sends his compliments and his fish for your dinner."

"Thank you." She took the bag. There was no way she would have time to do all that was needed and still make it to the fishmonger without raising Leo's suspicions.

Reginald gestured for George to continue. Ingrid sent him a sharp glance, to which she received a small dip of his chin in reply. This was it. Right here. Right now. The changing of the guard.

George registered none of this. He was busy pulling out a pad of paper and a pen. "We'll get acquainted another time. Tell me what you need."

Ingrid dove in. "You need to get ten thousand US dollars

and two sets of travel documents, one readily available and the second set sewn into a black bag's side lining for extraction. Use the name Dolina Jankowski for the second set. Drop the bag at 6:55 a.m. at Dead Drop Site 8. US dollars, not British pounds, as they are easier to trade."

"For your housekeeper, Dolores?"

"Yes. She's been compromised." Ingrid took a breath. "I've compromised her and the KGB will begin a full-scale hunt by tomorrow midmorning at the latest. It'll take them a few hours to get through the bureaucracy, but Leo is tense and he may be able to set things in motion by tonight."

"It's awfully tight."

Ingrid stared at him.

George's gaze shifted from one of consternation and questioning to eyes wide with excitement, like a kid being let into the game. "Consider it done. I can do this."

Ingrid recounted the details one last time, picked up her fish, and left—praying her new, young handler was right.

∞

Young George got the job done.

How he'd done it and on such short notice, Ingrid never learned. Because she never asked. All she knew was that two weeks later she received a postcard from "Svetlana" saying hello.

Ingrid had told Dolores of Svetlana and their friendship in Vienna all those years before, and how she was the one who had introduced her to Leo. Dolores also knew that for years Svetlana and Ingrid exchanged postcards to keep in touch. But the final detail, the one only Dolores knew, was that Svetlana hadn't sent a postcard in over five years.

Ingrid sat holding the postcard. It was a plain card postmarked in Vilnius. Noticing that, she felt the easing of the tight, hard knot that had twisted her gut for two weeks. With it, she felt the tension in her neck, her shoulders, and her back release as well. She stood to stretch, stepping toward the window, and watched the summer sunshine pour a warm yellow light like soft butter onto the room's wood flooring. For the first time in years she felt herself relax. Truly relax, if only for a moment. Dolores was safe. And for the first time since hearing that Reginald was retiring the year before, Ingrid knew she'd be okay.

She had chided herself for her selfishness many times. After all, Reginald needed to retire. He was almost seventy years old, with a heart condition. It was time, but how she would miss him. Every day. With every breath.

It was a delicate dance, after all, this marriage of sorts between handler and agent. While not amorous, it was a romance—a bond and trust like no other. And she wanted the best for him, as she did for anyone she loved—years ahead with his wife, children, and grandchildren.

Now, for the first time, she knew the best for him could be the best for her as well. Young Milner had gumption and energy, and he had her back—which was a good thing, as they had a problem. Someone had sent her information on too quickly and questions were being posed, and fingers pointed, much too close to home.

By slowly trickling her intel and insights, Reginald and Adam had not only protected her as the source but also been able to hide the truth of how high-grade her intelligence really was. But recently the name of a top-level promotion within the Presidium had been revealed too quickly, and now everything was jeopardized. Only someone in Moscow could have learned that detail so soon, and Leo wondered who that might be.

Ingrid left a red wax mark behind a trash bin in Sokolniki

Park, calling for a face-to-face meeting. She wondered if Reginald had made an error and tried to clear the decks too quickly, wanting to pass a clean slate to Milner. She didn't plan to ask, but she did need to deal with it.

When she met with George, she got straight to the point. "You need to pass something teasing along. A dangle that circles back. Not too close, but it must land here in Moscow."

"It's too dangerous. We should stand down and let all the intel grow cold. We'll start again in the winter."

"That's what's expected. It won't diffuse the light; it'll focus it." Ingrid shook her head. "I need to keep Dolores safe. No one can wonder. I have just the teaser for you from an embassy cocktail party . . ."

Confirmation of George's success, again, came quickly. A week later, Leo arrived home visibly relaxed.

"Good day?" Ingrid busied herself in the kitchen.

"Very good. We haven't found the leak, but it's not me . . . Something recent and completely out of my purview came through the same lines. It was the same kind of political gossip, so this traitor is well informed, but it's not me. I hadn't heard any of it. KGB Counterintelligence confirmed it came from the Dutch embassy. The KGB will certainly have their next party well monitored." Leo laid his bag on the counter and paused until Ingrid gave him her attention. "I'm sorry about Dolores, Inga. You valued her."

Ingrid shrugged, feigning the nonchalance that had become the hallmark of her character. She bent to pull her *kulebyaka* from the oven. "I did. Will you continue to search for her?"

"There's no need. Other than my curiosity, it's of no concern." Leo breathed deep. "She hasn't shown up anywhere between here and Kraków, and without money, there's nowhere else for her to go. I'm beginning to wonder if you were right all along and I was, perhaps, too strident that day. She won't find good work without papers, so she may return yet." He canvassed the kitchen, a gleam of satisfaction in his eyes. "I'm just pleased it's over."

Ingrid pointed toward the kitchen door. It was the first time Leo had smiled in weeks, and the gift was for Anya, not for her. She wanted no part of it. "Go say hello to your beautiful girl . . . Anya's in her room doing homework." As Leo turned away, Ingrid called him back. "Tell her something about Dolores. She loved her and has been asking."

"She went home to Kraków?"

"Without saying goodbye?" Ingrid's tone made it clear their clever daughter was not going to believe that.

"Why not? We weren't friends or even family. There's no reason she'd give us special consideration."

"Of course not. You are perfectly right." Ingrid turned back to the stove.

Leo stepped behind her. "Another special dinner?"

"Not special. I have simply enjoyed cooking this week." She inhaled the scent of one of Russia's greatest culinary creations, a large fish pie made with salmon, sturgeon, buckwheat, mushrooms, hard-boiled eggs, and vegetables.

Yes, George had done it. He leaked tiny whispers, gleaned by eavesdropping on an intoxicated Swede at a Dutch embassy event, and sent them around the globe before landing them in Moscow. With that morsel the KGB's spotlight had quickly shifted from Ingrid's home to foreign Western shores.

Dolores was safe—and that was worth celebrating for an entire week.

## TWENTY-ONE

# Anya

VIENNA
*November 10, 1983*

"Excuse me? Is Comrade Minister Petrov busy? Did he reschedule this meeting?" I stand at the doorway to my now-usual conference room in our Austrian embassy, another huge table of pastries beside me.

The green-uniformed KGB guard's head bounces up. He stares at me like I'm a ghost, an anomaly, a problem. "You're still here?"

"Of course I am." I gesture back into the room. My papers are arranged in neat piles at every seat. "This meeting should have started fifteen minutes ago."

The guard surges from his desk and toward me with such alacrity I stumble back. "Come with me." He follows me into the room and scans the table. It's truly an impressive display of drawings and numbers and terribly official-looking papers. I can tell the young man feels out of his depth.

"You need to leave."

I blink, sensing something has gone horribly wrong. I point to the table. "You need to put all this in the embassy vault." I hastily gather my piles into a single stack and hand it to him. He wears a brass name badge, as do all embassy guards. "Dubow?"

He raises his eyes from the pages to my face. "I am giving these to you. They are in your care now. Do you understand?"

"I will secure them." With his free hand to my elbow, he leads me out into the hallway again and calls to another guard.

Without words, this one hustles me out the embassy's back door and into a car. Minutes after that, the car pulls up to the airport's cargo terminal, and I'm led to a jump seat in the back of a cargo jumbo liner. There are a few others in the plane's cavernous hold with me, and though I have questions, I don't ask them. No one talks. There is no eye contact. Everyone is cold, quiet, and stares straight ahead.

Hours later, after being shuttled off the plane in silence, I arrive at work and find the doors locked. Fear envelops me. There's one place I might find answers—as no one in my world will provide any.

Peter.

I notice the crumpled cigarette packet while still a few meters from the trash bin. I stop and dig through my bag for a scrap of paper, anything I can throw away. I need to make bending down beside the bin seem natural—even today, especially today.

There are a few memos and a pamphlet for some talk at the Ministry of Commerce I crumple and pitch toward the bin. They come so close to dropping inside I almost moan. One bounces off the edge and falls close to the packet.

I bend and scoop both up. I palm the packet, drop the paper into the bin, and continue walking. As I walk I slide the packet into my bag and pull the note from inside. Peter wants to meet. Now.

It takes an hour to be sure I'm not being tailed. But it needn't have. The world feels normal. I canvass the park, the streets, and the stores as I walk, as I hop on and off a bus, as I cross through an alley and come out the other side. I see no one twice. I sense no one following. I don't even catch sight of any spot surveillance. No one appears tense, wary, or dour. At least no more so than any other day.

Peter pulls me inside. "Good work. Checking today."

"I wasn't supposed to be in town. What's going on?"

"The Soviets believe ABLEARCHER is real. NATO was warned about this, but they still went through with the exercises as originally delineated. We are on the brink of nuclear war because NATO wouldn't listen."

"Who is Able Archer?" I shove Peter's shoulder. He's not making any sense. "Listen to what? To whom?"

He waves a hand toward the small kitchen table. It's our meeting spot of choice as the kitchen has no windows. I slide a chair from under the table and drop into it.

Peter sits, arms crossed. It's not an overtly protective or aggressive gesture. It's a little of both. He's angry and he's scared. "Not a who. A what. ABLEARCHER '83 is the code name for a series of nuclear drills NATO is running out of Casteau, Belgium. But the Soviets believe they are real."

"How real?"

"So real all Soviet personnel have been called back to Moscow. So real the Soviet military opened missile silos this morning across the border republics. So real . . . We are, no joke, on the brink of a global nuclear war."

"You said NATO had been warned?"

"We got intel a couple months ago. LUMEN advised that the West needed to stand down—in drills, funding, rhetoric, everything. He reported that Soviet paranoia had reached a frenzied, pathological level. He shared details on Operation RYAN." I widen my eyes as I have no clue what that is. Peter interprets it into Russian. "Raketno-Yadernoe Napadenie."

"Operation Nuclear Missile Attack?"

"The KGB has itself so wrapped around its own paranoia that they're seeing bogeymen in diplomats and nuclear threats in vitriolic talk. Basically it's a KGB operation that rewards operatives for reporting evidence that the West is planning a first-strike offensive. To find anything, even just a rumor, secures promotions, gifts, privileges. Andropov has started a witch hunt, and his operatives are creating the witches."

"What do I do?"

"Pray." Peter stares at me. "And against my better judgment, I'm to give you this." He reaches to the counter and hands me a small box.

I open it. "No," I whisper on a puff of surprise.

"I sent your camera request up the flagpole. I expected it to get shot down, as it's a terrible idea, but here we are." He crosses his arms again. Peter is not pleased with the world, his bosses, or me right now. "Ames got back to me about O'Neill too. He's not CIA, Anya."

I hold the camera in my hands. "He's not?" For all I've just been told, my mind drifts to Scott. I want to hug him, kiss him, apologize for ever doubting him.

"Anya," Peter barks at me. "Focus. What are you going to do if you get searched? No story about following a crush to the Hotel Metropol will get you out of owning that."

I have no reply but assure him I'll figure it out. I leave the safe house with an odd disconnected feeling. It's like informational overload. One, Scott's not CIA. I want to believe him and in him. The surety that what we had was real saturates me. Two, we're on the edge of nuclear war. Can that be true? For all the angry talk, my professors constantly made it clear that the US never anticipated being the aggressor—and most of them worked second jobs as advisors within the administration. Our leadership must see that too. I mean, it's all talk, right? Propaganda. Posturing.

On both sides. The Americans want to flex their brawn and the Politburo wants to ignite our loyalty and scare us into conformity. Or does Operation RYAN reflect what the KGB and, by extension, the Party really believe? Three, Peter just handed me the ultimate tool. How do I use it?

Upon entering my apartment I walk straight to my bathroom and turn on the shower. My search last week revealed two bugs, which I left in place, and I can't assume Stanslych didn't leave more.

The shower covers the noise of me playing with the camera. Within a few minutes, I feel like I've figured out how to get the film loaded, spooled, and unloaded. And using receipts and other random papers in my bag, I discover that about thirty-five centimeters is the best distance between the subject and camera for a perfect shot. I'm ready. I turn off the shower, slip the camera under a floorboard in my bedroom, and make dinner.

While making *solyanka*, and enough of the hearty soup to last me a few nights, I find my mind drifting back to my visit home last week and my mother's statement that I cannot reject what is. That simple truth I can grasp. A fact is a fact, no matter how I feel about it. But then she went further, as Tolstoy goes further with Levin, and there I get lost.

I am not to resign myself to those facts, but I am to consent to their reality? My attitude toward them changes my position within them?

I wrestle with this until another line, this time from a Western novel, comes to me, forcing me to laugh my consternation away and finally enjoy my steaming salty soup.

"*Your defect is to hate everybody.*"

"*And yours,*" he replied with a smile, "*is willfully to misunderstand them.*"

Work is quiet today. Everyone feels something is wrong in the lab and in the world. None of my three office mates even lift a head as I pick up my handbag and head to the bathroom. I take the stairs to the third floor as that's the bathroom we women use at "that time of the month." It's very private, as the lab on that floor lost funding a few months ago.

No one is inside. I quickly check under the counters and run my fingers along the mirror. No bugs that I can tell. No one has reported ever finding any, but you can never be too sure.

I enter the first stall. There is a disgusting floor drain behind the toilet that will be perfect for what I've planned.

Before leaving for work, I sealed the camera in a plastic bag with a thin black thread that I left hanging long. I pull it out of my bag now, and after wedging the cover off the drain, willing my breakfast not to come up after seeing all the grime and slime within it, I tie the black string to the drain cover. I then drop the camera down the drain and replace the cover.

I also wiped my prints from it this morning, so I figure the worst that can happen if it gets found is that everyone will get questioned. There's nothing to link me directly to the camera.

On my way back to my desk, I pause, realizing there's an opportunity before me. A golden opportunity. I hadn't been able to memorize a few of the schematics attached to my proposal for Minister Petrov, and I couldn't risk carrying out the papers. Now I can take pictures of them.

I head to the KGB office, making my plan as I go. My entire presentation sits in our vault. And, as I didn't get a chance to present it yesterday in Vienna, I should probably review it again.

Grigor sits alone at the desk.

"I need a file from the vault. Number six-three-five-two."

"Sign here." He slides the ledger toward me and walks to the back of the office to the vault. He comes back with half the file.

"I also need the schematics." As he turns, I step forward. "Can I?" I gesture around the desk toward the back of the office. "I don't need to bother you, but I do need to review everything before presenting to Defense Minister Petrov."

I hate name-dropping, but sometimes it really helps. Grigor waves me past and sits at the front desk again.

I step into the vault. It's a small room, and I open the filing cabinet that stores all the schematics. They're larger than written reports, about the size of architectural blueprints, so they are stored separately from the standard pages. As I'm pulling out my packet, I can't help myself. I slide the drawer above an inch open. Nothing catches my eye. I slide another drawer, and another, and— I see the word *Nuclear* written in bright red ink across a page. It's stamped from NIIR8, the nuclear and defense lab three buildings away. Rumors abound on what the scientists are working on in there. Even Peter has wondered aloud.

My golden opportunity has gone nuclear. I congratulate myself, thinking how excited Peter will be to see this and how this is the intelligence coup of a lifetime. I slide the papers, a thin stapled stack of only a few pages, in between my own and close both drawers.

"Thank you," I call to Grigor as I sail out of the office.

Twenty steps down the hallway and I realize I've overstepped my abilities. I can't bring these files back to my desk—not with the new pages stuck in the middle. There's no way to study them and find out what's worth photographing. My schematics are drawn in green ink. These pages have red all over them. They are clearly not from this facility. My coworkers will see. The camera in our corner will record.

I walk straight to the bathroom.

One woman is in there washing her hands. I rush to the side of the room, lay the papers on the floor, and with a "This is so embarrassing" I dash toward a stall. As I shut the door, I see her face reflected in the mirror. I hear her dry her hands and open the bathroom's heavy door. As soon as it clicks behind her, I walk over and lock it. It's a risk, but what I'm about to do is far riskier.

I pull the camera out of the drain and, spreading the papers across the floor, take pictures of each. I then pop out the film, wipe down the camera, tie it back into the plastic bag, and drop it down the drain again. I slide the film down my tights and inside my thigh. I have no idea what I'm going to do with it now.

I walk back to the KGB office. The film feels like it's cutting me with every step, but I have to move fast. If Stanslych returns, Grigor will never let me return the papers myself.

Grigor is alone and a few minutes later the files are back and I'm sitting at my desk in a full sweat, wondering what to do next. During my tea break I finally solve the problem of how to get the film out. Of course, I have to stay late and wait for Grigor to come out to the security desk at 6:30 p.m.

"What is this?" He holds up the plastic container of clearly moldy food I grabbed from the back of the break room refrigerator.

"That was *kartoshka* I forgot from last month." I shrug. "But I need the container so I have to take it home and scrub it."

I have no idea if *kartoshka*, a rustic potato dish, is inside the plastic tub or not. It's too black, green, and slimy to tell. But potatoes still sit on most store shelves—stores that workers like Grigor, with more limited options than I've got, frequent. I'm hoping it creates a connection between us.

"That's disgusting." He thrusts it back at me. "Use chloride."

"I hadn't thought of that. Thanks, I will." I shove the container back into my bag and walk out the door.

⁓

It's two months before I meet with Peter again.

And in that time, nothing returns to normal. The morning after taking the pictures and executing a flawless brush pass at the Hotel Ukraina, security tightened at our lab and full pat-downs are the rule rather than the exception.

A month ago, I got so scared by the heightened scrutiny that I pulled my Topel from the bathroom drain and smashed it with the heel of my loafer. It then took me six days to carry the tiny parts to the incinerator with my papers at day's end.

Today I reach the safe house a few minutes early. Peter is ready and waiting. He doesn't greet me in his usual easygoing manner. He merely points toward the kitchen.

"Did the pictures not come out?"

"We'll talk about that in a minute."

Only when seated does he start to talk. "Britain and the US have agreed to back down. On all fronts. No more 'Evil Empire' rhetoric. Prime Minister Thatcher reached out to Andropov last week."

"Isn't that good news? Why aren't you pleased? What about Operation RYAN?"

He holds up a hand to stop my questions. "I am pleased. Everyone is. And we hope this ends RYAN, but there's no word on that yet. ABLEARCHER was a nightmare. The world hasn't come that close to nuclear war since the Cuban Missile Crisis."

"How close was that?"

"Much closer than anyone outside our line of work suspects. Word is LUMEN got the West out of that too. He advised how to get Khrushchev to back down. And now . . ."

I watch Peter. There is something he's not telling me. When I can't stand the silence any longer, I prompt him. "And now?"

"You messed up, Anya." He raises his hand again at my quick inhalation. "The nuclear intel you photographed? The only other copy from NIIR8 has been in a KGB vault at Lubyanka headquarters for six months. It's clear your lab leaked it, as it had the last copy, and the young scientist who developed it is dead."

The world turns blue.

"It was fine, until last week when we shared some of it with another agency. Either we or they have a mole because the whole thing has blown up. The KGB is now on the hunt for another traitor and everyone is scrambling. CIA, MI6, PET, Mossad, DGSE—"

"What are those?"

"Lives, Anya, in the American, British, Danish, Israeli, and Dutch intelligence services. People working within other agencies doing the same job you are. They're getting rounded up because you overreached. I told you from the get-go to stay within your mandate, the data you work on . . . You and that camera." Peter holds his hands out like he'd like to stick my head in between them and squeeze really hard. "You've got to destroy it."

"I did. Is that why security at my lab has been so tight?"

"Everything's tight since ABLEARCHER, but it'll ramp up now. Ames on the Soviet Desk wants to cut you loose and Director Casey agrees. You've put too much at risk, Anya."

I reach out, maybe to touch Peter or to protect myself. I simply see my hand, palm out, in front of me. "I'm sorry. I'm so sorry."

"Sorry doesn't cut it." He peeks at his watch. "You need to go. The KGB is running spot surveillance at three times the pace. The embassy, every embassy, is surrounded. We determined we only had a few minutes for this." He stands and steps to the door. "Go. And when they question you, play dumb. It's the best I can advise."

"The best?" I stumble up and out of the chair to follow him to the door. "They will interrogate me, Peter. It won't be a nice chat. After the Hotel Metropol, Stanslych will call me in first. Can . . . Can you get me a cyanide pill?"

"Don't be such a coward." The bite in his tone surprises me.

I shrink back. "I'm not. I mean, I screwed up. He'll come for me . . ."

"Who?" Peter stares down at me.

"What do you mean who? The KGB. Stanslych."

"So naive." Peter chuffs a short cynical noise that chills me. "Anya, you've made more enemies with this stunt than you can fathom."

"What does that mean?" This time I do reach out and grab his arm. He doesn't pull away, but he does nothing to soften at my touch either.

"You've put every Western agent at risk. The KGB has already 'disappeared' at least two good men, Anya. No bodies. No funerals. No contacting loved ones . . . Those agencies I just mentioned? Any one of them might grab you and leave you on Lefortovo Prison's doorstep to end the manhunt and save their own people. If you weren't ours, we'd do it."

"They want me dead? The CIA wants me dead?"

"Some do. Perhaps. Only LUMEN seems to be keeping everyone quiet." Peter shakes his head as if for once he disagrees with the great spy. "He's advised caution, as division among Western agencies puts us all in greater peril. He's calling for a unilateral intelligence shutdown until things cool. Do you have any idea of the implications of that?" Peter grips his jaw. His fingers are stiff with the pressure. "But you'd better hope people listen to him."

"They always do, don't they?"

"ABLEARCHER proved otherwise."

Tears fill my eyes and spill down my cheeks. I feel my nose leaking. Everything is leaking. And I don't have a tissue, a paper towel, a rag. Peter hands me a handkerchief. I examine it like it's an alien thing. It's so thin and soft.

"Don't stare at it. Use it." The infinitesimal kindness in his voice makes everything drip faster. I blot my face and blow my nose. Peter shakes his head at me. "You're a mess, SCOUT."

He uses my code name and I know he's relented. He may be annoyed, but he's not against me any longer. He doesn't want me dead. Olivers chose my code name at our first meeting and Peter only uses it when I need cheering. It's spunky and brave—the little girl from *To Kill a Mockingbird* who stood up for what was right and never lost herself in the process.

But I did lose myself. No, I never knew myself. Every step of the way, this has been about me. I said it was for Scott, for Dmitri, for right versus wrong, and for freedom and hope, but it was about me. About me needing to rise above everything cramped, wrong, and corrupt around me. About pride. About arrogance.

*Enough.* I grind my thoughts to a stop. "Apologize for me, will you? Send word around to LUMEN, to everyone, that I'm sorry. I'll quit, I'll stand down, I'll do whatever they want."

"It's not a tea party, Anya. We don't send around personal regrets."

I blow my nose again. "I'm serious about the pill."

"Think about what you're asking."

"I'm asking for a chance not to get anyone else killed. You said it yourself—everyone breaks, everyone talks. Please. And send me word if someone else gets caught, and I'll turn myself in. No one else should die when—"

"Everyone accepts the consequences when getting into this game."

"Do they? I didn't."

"That's my fault then. You were too young. I'm sorry too." He scrubs at his face. "I'll ask, Anya, about the pill, but I can't make any promises. You'll need to manage the coming days, weeks, or months as if it's not your way out."

*Does the end draw everyone back to the beginning?*

I leave the safe house and all I can see is my past. Not the snow, not the cars sliding by as an ice storm moves in, not the old man in his dark *ushanka* hat who flings his gloved hand up as I bump into him.

I quickly lift my own in apology. I want to stop and grab him close and say, "I'm sorry," over and over until he believes me, because at least then someone will hear it. But I don't because he'll think I'm insane.

I shove my hand back into my pocket and keep walking. I see my childhood, running the streets with Dmitri, swimming at our Sochi summer camp, snuggling close to my mother as she reads to me far past my bedtime. I hear my father's admonishments to behave, my teachers' endless dronings, my friends' laughter, teasing, and secrets. All these images play before me in a golden glow, and they feel far more real than the ice, snow, cold, and grey that press close.

At Georgetown I thought I'd discovered something new and better. Words and ideas filled with light and truth. Austen, Brontë, Dickens, Shakespeare, Forster, Fitzgerald, Salinger, Rousseau, More—ideas I could accept or reject as I wished. There was no requirement, no compulsion to follow them. I wanted to follow them. They beguiled me with a different story, a different worldview, an alternative meaning and message for life. They danced across the pages into my heart. A minuet rather than a dirge.

But with each step, my memories chastise me for my disloyalty. *Treachery* is another word for it. I forgot what I had, what mattered most, my very roots. And for what—to satisfy my vanity and to play hero, savior, spy? Over the past few years, I've gotten so used to saying that no one fights like a Soviet that I forgot no one loves and endures like one either.

If I were to stack Lizzy Bennet—the undisputed queen of Western literature—against Tolstoy's Kitty Shcherbatsky, Princess Kitty would win every time. Kitty embodies the bright and sparkling Lizzy, but so much more too. She's Marianne, dramatically wasting away from disappointed love; Elinor, growing in equanimity, sense, and purpose; and Jane, the embodiment of loveliness as she matures from beginning to end. Austen took six books to explore the depth Tolstoy captured in one, and Kitty's not even the title character!

Neither are we.

We Soviets have never been the title character of our stories. We toil, suffer, work, hurt, sacrifice, and give everything to the State; we call each other "comrade" in the belief that the moniker makes us equal. It doesn't and it never has. Ours is another's story—the tsars', the Bolsheviks', the Party's, whatever dictator rules our day. The best that can be said of us is that we endure.

We endure everything except this: disloyalty is not endured and it is not forgiven.

The KGB will come for me—because, as Dmitri used to say, they're the best—and they will interrogate me, torture me, and kill me. It's as simple or as complex as that.

I pause in the cold and let that thought settle deep. I expect it to drop me to my knees, but it doesn't. Another truth replaces it. The reality that while I'm not ready for it and never will be, I also wouldn't turn back the clock to avoid it.

In my naïveté, I said yes to the CIA.

In the modicum of wisdom I've gained since, I'd say yes again.

I'd say yes because, like Tolstoy's Princess Kitty, we can do more than endure. We can and should thrive. This false peace of conformity has not saved us, and what I did was in the hope that the gentle discomfort and tension of freedom might.

I went about it all wrong. Selfishly. Impetuously. Arrogantly. But perhaps, in the end, Peter will help me. He has to—he won't let others pay the price.

# TWENTY-TWO

# Ingrid

VIENNA
*February 17, 1980*

JUST LIKE THE KGB'S SEARCH ON "FOREIGN WESTERN SHORES" for the leak six years earlier, Ingrid found herself far from Moscow.

In twenty-six years of marriage, she had not left the Soviet Union once. There had been visits to Yalta, Odessa, Sochi, and other vacation towns along the Black Sea, but no trips abroad. It was uncommon for families to travel abroad, unheard of for KGB families. When Leo traveled, he traveled alone. But not this time. This time she was going home.

Leo's meeting with the Western and Warsaw Pact intelligence delegations had been a surprise. That he had been asked to take his wife along had been a shock.

"Vienna?" Ingrid felt all the blood drain from her face. She could not have heard correctly.

"Yes. Vienna. Western diplomats often bring their wives. We are to do the same. You will attend dinners with me."

"Vienna? Vienna, Austria?" she asked again.

They went through the singsong question and answer three more times before she believed him, and even then, it wasn't until she stepped out of the airport that she was sure.

295

The smell. The hum. The energy. Vienna seeped into every pore with wafts of chocolate, pastry dough, and petrol.

There were no loudspeakers blaring the pounding notes of marching music onto the streets. There were no cameras mounted on light poles. There was silence. No, not silence. There was the memory of Mozart's lilting notes, Haydn's string quartets, Beethoven's symphonies, and Schubert. She closed her eyes and felt herself drift away in the slow, haunting power of Schubert's Piano Sonata No. 21. *We are here*, his notes whispered. *Come find us.*

A lightness enveloped her. She hadn't realized how heavy, grey, and oppressive Moscow had become until its weight was lifted.

"You're lit up." Leo took her suitcase and handed it to the young man springing from a black sedan. "Remember. You have not been here before."

Ingrid nodded. "I won't forget. May I wander while you are in your meetings?"

"You'll need to take an escort."

Ingrid stopped beside the car. "An escort?"

"It's required for the entire delegation. Standard protocol. You won't even notice."

Ingrid dropped into the black ZiL sedan. While they drove into the city, she saw nothing. All her vision and energy were focused on how easy or hard it might be to lose her "escort."

The car pulled up to the Hotel Bristol. She caught sight of the Hotel Imperial only buildings away. She had wondered if they would stay there and was glad they were not. It held too many memories, most wounding.

As soon as they settled their bags and Leo left for the first round of negotiations, Ingrid darted about their hotel room with curious fingers. Sliding them across the wallpaper, floorboards, carpet, lamps, tables, under the bed, and around the bathroom, she found no trace of any bugging device. She untwisted the room's telephone receiver and the bedside lamps' bulbs. Nothing. It gave her a tiny bit of relief. But not enough. Now she needed to discern how good her escort was.

It took only ten minutes. She dropped him easily a few blocks from the hotel, near the State Opera House, but she made sure to pick him up again on the other side. She did this five more times to lull him into complacency. If he only lost her once—when she wanted to be lost—he might find it suspicious. But after losing her nine times in a single afternoon, as she flitted like a child enraptured by each new shop window and curio, she felt certain even disappearing for a couple hours would be doable. She didn't anticipate needing a couple hours. She just wanted to know they could be hers if desired.

The seventh time she dropped the young man, around the corner from her childhood home, she saw him. Instantly thankful she was not under watchful KGB eyes, Ingrid stood still and stared until his eyes captured hers and widened.

*Adam Weber.*

He was older but hadn't aged a day. He was leaner, but it looked good on him. His hair was still the color of straw touched by a warm setting sun. Would he ever turn grey, or perhaps he already had? In the pink afternoon light, she couldn't tell. He looked wonderful.

He didn't step forward and neither did she. In one focused moment, before he turned away, she knew, with a certainty that defied reason, where to meet him and when.

Demel—the following day at three o'clock. The place where he'd taken her the week after her father's arrest and her mother's death and the time he always said was best for an afternoon snack.

Starting at eleven o'clock the next morning, Ingrid blazed a shopping and sightseeing trail throughout Vienna that would exhaust an Olympic athlete. By the time two o'clock approached, she sensed her KGB tracker was wrung out and barely interested in her any longer. Nevertheless, she did an hour of the most thorough "dry cleaning" of her life, her mind drifting to Martin, Adam, and their lessons long ago, now melded with years of training on her own. Dry cleaning had become *proverka* for her. Moscow had left its mark in the very language of her internal thoughts.

Yet it was Adam's English that filled her head as she recalled those first lessons. *"Go with the flow of traffic, whether it's cars, people on the street, anything. You must make your moves appear accidental. You spot something in a window. Check your watch and catch a bus as it's pulling away. Everything seems spontaneous because planned gets you killed."*

As she walked into Demel, she reminded herself to keep from falling apart. No cracks in the facade. Ever.

Yet tears filled her eyes—how she wanted to turn back time, accept his offer in the hospital, not fight with him when he returned, and, on his final trip to Vienna, not wait in the shadows of the building next door until he gave up and finally left her forever. Given another chance all those years ago, she wouldn't let him go. Yes, if given that chance again, she would have told him she loved him and she would have let him love her.

Adam had stood for two hours outside her building that long-ago day and returned every day for three days. She knew because she'd stayed with a friend nearby and had gone each day to the opposite corner to see how long he'd search for her. Back then, she had told herself she was brave. She was letting him go. She was giving him the chance for a good life, the chance for a love not damaged by loss, war, fear, and pain. She told herself it was for the best. Now she knew the truth.

She'd been a coward and had lost her best, and perhaps her only, chance at true love.

She shook her head. That was wrong. If she'd taken that path, she wouldn't have her daughter, and Anya was worth any sacrifice. True, Anya was trapped in a world she'd never imagined before living in it, but hadn't she tried to make it better?

*No*, Ingrid thought. She didn't fall into her life. She chose it. She chose it for Anya and she chose it because true love took many forms.

Ingrid wove through the tightly packed tables. Demel was as crowded as she remembered it from the jubilant years before the war when she and her mother used to come for afternoon tea and cakes. Languages from around the globe turned her head this way and that as she caught snatches of conversations and words she hadn't heard in years. German. English. Dutch. French. But not Russian. She didn't hear a single Russian word.

Then she saw him. Seated in the far back corner, facing the front, he commanded a good view of the room in all directions.

"Darling Ingrid." Adam stood and kissed both her cheeks.

She sat and "I'm sorry" were the first words out of her mouth. Without Reginald between them, she went straight to the heart of their past.

Adam's expression clouded with regret. "Don't think on it. We were hurting. I . . . I hated leaving you. I had a CIA buddy of Martin's search for you too. But he couldn't find you."

"I didn't want to be found. I didn't want to be saved."

He nodded, soaking her in. "You look wonderful."

"I am old." She shook her head. "I blinked and it happened."

"You've done more than passive blinking, my dear."

She dipped her head in acknowledgment.

"Ingrid . . ." Adam reached out and touched her gloved hand. She pulled it away, gently removed her glove finger by finger, then laid her hand on the table again. Her fingers touched his.

She knew he felt it too. Understanding. Not romance any longer. Not passion anymore. The deep, honest connection of old friends and present colleagues with no shadow dimming the space between them.

"I never asked." Adam tilted his head toward her hand and the simple gold band circling her finger. "Why?"

She twirled her wedding ring with her thumb. "I was dead inside." She blinked Adam another apology. "I had been for years. When I first met Leo, he was gentle, kind, eager to please, and persistent." She smiled, remembering those early days. "He is still many of those things. They simply bow to another loyalty."

"You remain safe?"

"I do," she replied instantly.

"Happy?"

"Enough." She laughed. "That's far too complex to answer."

Adam sank back into his chair. "I came because . . . Do you want to defect?"

Ingrid sat back as well. "Is this why you didn't let George and me know you were coming here? Surprises aren't wise for people like us."

"I want this off the table. Just between you and me. I can get you to London today if that's what you want. It's been done before and it's really only possible from here, in Vienna." He took a sip of his coffee. "Svetlana Alliluyeva is happily situated in Connecticut, if you'd rather go there."

Ingrid raised a brow. "Stalin's daughter may be happy, but she has lost her children. They can't or won't talk to her anymore. That's not for me . . . I will not lose my daughter."

"Anya is not an insurmountable obstacle. She's studying in the States right now. One call and she's secure."

"That's too risky. She is trained to fight. She is Leo's daughter and she might feel she needs to protect herself, or her father and me. I've hidden so long I'm not sure what my own daughter would do or what she believes." Ingrid reached over and took Adam's fork. She sliced off a bite of his torte and savored the dark chocolate before replying. It was a tempting offer. An interesting offer. An impossible offer.

"And Leo would never let her go. He'd have the entire force of the KGB searching for her." Ingrid raised her hand before Adam could protest. "He's a good father and Anya may be the only person he truly loves . . . I may not have fully comprehended what I was getting into when I married, but it was my choice."

She felt a small laugh bubble inside her. "I blamed them so much, my parents. I blamed you, too, in a way. I thought you all were reckless with your lives and the cost was too high. I believed there was nothing worth dying for. But maybe there is, if you choose it for yourself?"

Ingrid took another bite of Adam's dessert. "But it's not just ourselves, is it? It never is in our work. Here I am, playing with her life, moving her like a pawn in our game. The one I love best . . . No, I will stay to protect her, but one day I may not be able to. Will she hate me for what I've done?"

Adam didn't answer quickly. Ingrid appreciated that. There were no easy answers to such questions.

Finally, he shifted forward, bringing his face only inches from her own. "If we do it right, she'll never find out."

Ingrid laughed. That was the confident, daring Adam she remembered. "Tell me about your wife and your children. Tell me what I lost all those years ago."

Adam lifted a teasing brow, then shared with her his life—his real life, not the sanitized and shadowed version either of them gave to acquaintances to divert attention from themselves, their jobs, and their reality.

He told her of his wife, Marilyn. A wonderful woman who had worked as a nurse during the war. He told of their three kids, two boys and a girl, who thought he worked for a bank and were bored by his musings on the gold standard and interest rates. He told of his love for gardening—and she laughed and said they were both truly old. And when she stood to leave, he pulled her close and hugged her tight. It was goodbye. Never could they risk such a meeting again.

She inhaled the scent of him—still a wonderful mixture of starched linen and salt, with a note of mint. Reluctantly she let go and wove her way back through the tables toward the bright light of day, shining through the front door of Demel.

Before reaching it, however, she glanced back to the table one last time.

Adam was already gone.

∽

He didn't go far.

Keeping tight control over Ingrid's every insight, Adam assisted George in sprinkling her intelligence across Europe. In early 1983, she cautioned the West regarding their rising vitriol against the Soviet Union and sent a discreet warning in March that year to US President Reagan when he dubbed the Soviet Union the "Evil Empire."

She got a little more forceful as the West aimed its guns at the Soviet Union following the downing of Korean Airlines Flight 007 by a Soviet Su-15 interceptor. What the West deemed an act of war, Ingrid learned—by eavesdropping on one of Leo's late-night drinks gatherings—was a series of unfortunate mistakes and lies, none of which Soviet leadership planned to acknowledge.

And she got positively forceful right before NATO launched its nuclear ABLEARCHER tests in November 1983. In no uncertain terms, she demanded that NATO reconfigure their drills in Casteau, Belgium, and take into account the Soviet Union's pathological paranoia, coupled with its unstable leadership and nuclear capabilities.

She cautioned restraint. She cautioned patience. And one afternoon, she instructed George to relay a vital message to all Western agencies working behind the Iron Curtain. No one was to touch, and certainly not to assassinate, one of their own because the young spy—code named SCOUT—made an impetuous error. Killing him would only shine the KGB spotlight on them all. And that would prove far deadlier.

# TWENTY-THREE

# Anya

MOSCOW
*March 12, 1985*

FOURTEEN MONTHS.

I "stand down" for fourteen months, and in that time, the KGB did a thorough sweep of every lab in Kapotnya District—and it was just as horrific as Peter implied it would be. We were interrogated collectively and individually, some of us beaten up a little to make a point, but as there was nothing said or recorded within my lab to implicate anyone, the KGB moved on after two weeks of hell.

I stayed tense and ready, however. Prepared to turn myself in at the first hint that anyone else was arrested. But no one was. Peter has been kind to me—he sent monthly notes to dead drops with updates. Gossip circulating between the labs confirmed no arrests as well. Although I never received word about the cyanide pill, those dead-drop messages also informed me that Peter transferred back to the States and I had been assigned a new handler.

Today a green wax mark brings me to Safe House #9 at eleven o'clock. I'm to come in "out of the cold," but come in for what?

A tall man with dark hair, slightly wavy and perfectly managed, opens the door. He doesn't say a word until the door is firmly shut behind me. He's only a few years older than I am, maybe twenty-nine or thirty, thirty-one at the oldest, and he has an incredible Americanness about him. I can't put my finger on what it is—his eyes, the set of his jaw, the slant of his head, the dismissive way he waves me into the room? I want to call it arrogance, but it's more than that. It's brashness: a uniquely American quality.

Once inside, I turn and face him. By the tart expression on his face, I sense he's not impressed by what he sees. Still not speaking, he walks past me to the apartment's center table and pulls out a chair. We both sit and he reaches his hand across the table.

"Skip Duncan. Good to finally meet you. I've read your file ad nauseam, and I've studied every mission, meeting, dead drop, and brush pass. Pete Crenshaw brought me up to speed on every detail of your work, and I can't imagine we'll miss a beat."

"I'm to get back to work?"

"Things have cooled down and you're still strategically placed. Might as well use you." Skip reaches into a briefcase that sits by his chair and pulls out several sheets of copy paper and a pen. "Let's start by you telling me what you've been working on these past months."

He slides the paper my direction, then reaches back into the bag and pulls out a tape recorder. He taps its red button.

I reach across and tap the black Off button next to it. "Please don't. Peter never recorded our meetings."

"Yes, well, things need to change. We can't make the same mistakes. Recording allows me to canvass our discussions and get the details right. Miss something small and it means death around here."

"So does recording my voice." My hands shake and I clasp them in my lap. "With all the agents, double agents, intrigue, and eyes in Moscow, there are ears too. Anyone getting their hands on that tape will recognize me. My accent reveals where I'm from, down to the district here in Moscow, the schools I attended, maybe even the clubs I joined, as we all had certain ways of saying things. Then there are notes of Washington, DC, and a little of Georgia I don't even hear in myself anymore. One KGB linguist gets ahold of this and I'm dead. He doesn't even have to be a good one." I slide the machine a few inches toward Skip. "You can't promise me the CIA doesn't have double agents. You can't promise that tape will be secure."

"No service can guarantee such a thing, but we are careful."

"My father has a good friend who comes for dinner sometimes. Perhaps you've heard of him? Kim Philby?"

Skip's eyebrows disappear into his bangs.

It's not a name I drop often, but it's occasionally useful. The funny thing is, I had no idea who Comrade Philby was for years. He was just the fuddy-duddy friend of my father's who came over to smoke cigars with him. Most of the time he was drunk. Mother never liked him much, so I never paid him much attention either. It was Dmitri who finally told me, after he took one of Philby's courses at MGIMO.

*"Your dad's friend is famous. Really famous,"* Dmitri told me one evening. *"He was part of an NKVD spy ring in Britain called the 'Cambridge Four.' There were four of them recruited out of university. Spied for us against the British for over thirty years . . . Can you believe that? No spy lasts that long. Now he's teaching our class a course on Western spy craft."*

I've always wondered if my father knows all that about his friend. My bet is he doesn't. As I said, no one talks about work.

"Fine." Skip's huff draws me back to the present. "No recordings." He picks up the machine and sets it on the kitchen counter behind him. I watch to make sure he doesn't hit Record. He doesn't. That said, he could have another recording device hidden in the room. Comrade Philby would if he really wanted one.

Skip takes a deep breath to reset the moment and starts over, launching into his résumé and predicting all the good we'll accomplish. It sounds like a script he's been practicing for weeks. Yale undergrad. I was right; his graduation date puts him at thirty, three years older than I am. Langley right after graduation. Skilled in five languages—I concede his Russian is impeccable. He has run operatives in Poland, Hungary, and Morocco. With impressive results, if he does say so himself. By the end I'm believing his hype too. Either we are going to make the best duo in the history of covert intelligence, and I'll save the American defense industry billions of dollars, or he's going to get me killed. I doubt there is any halfway for Skip.

Then he reaches into his bag of tricks again and hands me a Topel camera.

"I can't." I set it on the table. "We're patted down every night and have been for the past year. There's no way to get that in or the film out any longer."

"Put it in sanitary packages." Skip smirks like his answer is brilliant and obvious.

"I can't." I feel something awaken in me. I've been alone so long with my thoughts, my contrition, and my fear that I haven't been living. Now pushed into these dangerous places, I realize I want to stay alive—desperately.

"Skip, I understand you have something to prove here. So do I. I mean, I screwed up and the consequences of that are—"

"Two agents."

"What?"

"In the last fourteen months, two agents have been arrested. Peter's notes said he told you this at your last meeting. PET lost one, as did Mossad . . . It's the business we're in."

I blanch at the casual mention of their lives and loss. Then I get back to the issue at hand. The Topel and sanitary napkins. "I can't take this. We're interviewed every month now, and we watch each other because we have to report something new in those interviews. It's like the KGB under Operation RYAN, when they got perks for making up threats. We get rewarded for tattling on our coworkers. I can't have my period at weird times. Other women will notice and rat me out."

Most of the time people report light stuff that won't hurt someone—too long a break, arrived late to work, packed up their desk early. But with a few rubles on the line or a promotion on offer, people sometimes stretch beyond the innocent stuff and make up infractions too.

"Make photocopies then. We can't have you trying to memorize anymore. It takes too long and it isn't reliable. We can't risk getting details wrong."

"I can't do that either."

He glares at me as if to say, *"What's your excuse this time?"*

"As I said, security has tightened. If I need to photocopy something, I now have to hand over my security badge, list the files, and submit a request to our facility's security office. If they give me permission, I then have to record the exact number of copies I make and of which pages—and that's for unclassified documents. For classified documents, I have to—"

Skip holds up his hand. "Fine. No copies."

So it's back to memorization. Only I'm on my own to create the drawings. I'm to work nightly, *"storing them wherever you stored those copy sheets in October of '83."* Once fully created, I am to pass them along to Skip in a dead drop. No safe-house meetings. No foot-timed drops. No brush passes. Only dead drops.

Bottom line, I'm not out of the cold; I'm still deep in it.

❦

It takes me only three months to break Skip's rule and signal a meeting. A yellow check mark informs me my request is denied. I reply with an escalated red mark. A brown tick left the next day concedes to my demand and tells me when and where we'll meet.

There's no polite chitchat when I enter the safe house. "Is it true? The KGB arrested Adolph Tolkachev last week?"

"Where did you hear that?" Skip blanches.

"He worked in the lab next to mine. It's all anyone can whisper about. They say he was a spy. One of yours. United States."

"He was arrested," Skip confirms.

"What will happen to him?"

"What always happens. The KGB will get everything they can from him, if they haven't already. They won't let another Ogorodnik happen."

"Who's Ogorodnik? What happened to him?" I drop into a chair, a little surprised Skip is talking so freely.

"He cracked a cyanide capsule right under their noses back in '77. He was one of ours too. That's what put us on stand-down."

"Is that why I never got the cyanide pill I requested?"

He scoffs. "You expected a bunch of dads, because that's what these men are, Anya, old family men, to give a suicide pill to a young woman? That was *never* going to happen."

"What do I do?" I feel like I'm right back to a year and a half ago, waiting for someone to knock on my door, take me away, torture me, and kill me. "Does Tolkachev know about me?"

"This all just happened, Anya. I have a secure call with Director Ames tomorrow morning and I'll know more then."

"Is he CIA director now?"

"No. That's still Bill Casey, but Aldrich Ames was just

promoted to chief of Soviet counterintelligence." Skip holds up both hands palms out, metaphorically pushing me away. "Until I talk with him, I don't have any answers. You need to go. This meeting is fruitless and dangerous."

"But you haven't told me anything. Is Tolkachev LUMEN?" My mind is never far from the master spy, even in my dreams. I both fear him and revere him. This shadow, like Kim Philby and his thirty years in an impossible position, makes me nervous.

"I doubt it. It's a business with few secrets. If LUMEN is CIA, it would've gotten leaked internally sometime over the decades." He shakes his head. "I get that you're scared, but I've got nothing for you. The embassy is surrounded. It'll be a diplomatic dustup and a slew of us will get PNG'd and shipped back." He runs his hands through his hair, dark curls ruffling and standing straight. "You wouldn't believe what I had to do to get here. An identity transfer."

He tries to hide the gleam in his eyes, but I can tell he wants to share the details. As it'll keep him from kicking me out, I oblige. "What's that?"

"We used the wiretaps in our office to convince the KGB we had an office party tonight. Everyone is still inside, including a few carefully timed and taped comments from me. I switched identities with the security guard on rounds and left out the back door. Then went off duty when he was supposed to. I'll switch back with the next guard change in three hours."

"How will you get word to me?"

"About what?"

I close my eyes, trying to keep my temper and fear in check. "Tolkachev."

Skip steps back and leans against the kitchen counter. Now that he has told his story, he seems calmer. "The better question is, do you know him?" He gestures between us. "Outside from hearing about his arrest. The KGB will find out if you do."

"Yes." My heart drops. "I mean, we met a couple times at symposiums and lectures, but we never worked together."

"Then assume the KGB *will* interview you. They will interrogate anyone connected to Tolkachev in any way."

"What about the drawings I'm working on? I have six sheets in my vent. You haven't assigned a dead drop."

Skip sighs like I'm slow on the uptake. "Burn them."

"They've taken me months to draw."

"And it'll take seconds for the KGB to find them. Then a few questions will be the least of your worries. Burn them, Anya. Immediately."

# TWENTY-FOUR

# Ingrid

INGRID RUSHED INTO THE APARTMENT. SHE COULD HEAR THE phone ringing out into the hallway. So few people called, she feared something was wrong. She cycled through her list of family and friends and could think of no one with immediate concerns. That brought a wry smile to her face as she crossed from the hall to the living room, shedding her coat as she walked. Everyone had immediate concerns.

"Hello?" she exhaled the word in a whisper. There was no breath to give it force. Sixty-two was too old to be racing around, she mused.

"Nicholi?"

"Nyet." Ingrid froze. "You have the wrong number."

"I apologize." The man hung up.

Ingrid felt the blood drain from her face. It left a cool, clammy sensation in its wake. She took in the apartment, only now feeling its stillness. Leo was not home.

Her hand crept up her neck, and with it, warmth climbed into her cheeks. Rather than pale and chilled, she knew her face would appear anxious and flushed. She'd spent years

312

tamping down the telltale signs of stress and anxiety and knew how they looked and felt when they were beyond her control to moderate.

It was a call—no, *the* call—she never expected.

She snatched up her light coat again. It felt hot and sticky against her skin as she retraced her steps and grabbed her handbag from the hall table. Her dry cleaning had to be impeccable this time. No mistakes.

She headed out the door to weave her way to the designated meeting spot.

One hour later she arrived at a small tearoom. George was sitting in the far back corner, facing the door. She noted every person in the room. No one appeared out of the ordinary, nor did anyone pay her any attention as she passed.

"We have a problem." George pushed out of his chair and kissed her cheeks. A custom everyone would expect without realizing they expected it.

"What kind of problem?"

He reached forward and poured her a cup of tea. "A list is out. Twenty-five names of Western agents working either in or against the Soviet Union reached KGB hands this morning. It's a CIA list, we're almost certain, but it holds the names of three of our agents too. That's what's concerning. Your name is out, Ingrid. We didn't think anyone knew about you . . . Bottom line, it's chaos. Everyone is scrambling."

Ingrid nodded. She felt outside herself. While it was something she deemed inevitable, the reality of it sank her into a darker and deeper abyss than she'd anticipated. She thought of all the names on that list. The lives. The families. Of course, she'd never learned their identities, but Reginald, George, and Adam probably had. They had shared some of their exploits over the years. They were losing friends and colleagues. And, as for herself, knowing the others were out there had brought her a feeling of comfort and camaraderie.

OCTON, PIMLICO, SCOUT, TRACER, BRAMPTON, SPHERE . . . Now all were in danger. All would die.

Her thoughts shifted to her daughter and all that would be left unsaid and undone between them. Adam was wrong. Anya would now learn the truth about her, and she would hate her mother for the rest of her life.

A waitress arrived with more tea. She poured Ingrid a fresh cup before offering one to George. Once she left, Ingrid tried to lift the cup from the saucer. Her hand shook. She set it down, holding the saucer with her other hand to keep the set from rattling.

"I'm on this list." It wasn't a question.

"It's real names. Not code names. Kadinova is third from the top. There's no guesswork for the KGB with this one."

She took a deep breath. "It has been our understanding that the CIA would never learn my identity. That no one beyond you, Adam, and Reginald would *ever* know. What changed in all these years?"

She recalled that first day as if it played across a cinema screen before her.

The sun, the sky, the birds pecking at the bread crumbs. Reginald handed her a piece of paper. She had stared at it, surprised to find it blank. Then Reginald leaned close and, pulling a tiny bottle from his pocket, sprayed it, and words magically appeared.

Dearest Ingrid,

You are in good hands with Reginald Bishop. I wish I could be with you, but you are already taking a great risk. I won't selfishly endanger you further.

LUMEN is your code name. It's how I think of you and will always think of you. In Vienna, you were the light of my life. That has never changed.

Remember that. You will need it in this world of shadows. You must become a shadow. But if anyone can find her way, you can. You are stronger than you realize.

To keep you safe, I make you this promise—Reginald and I will keep this between us. This safety net around you will remain as impenetrable as I can make it for you as long as I live.

God keep you, LUMEN.

Adam

*Light.* Ingrid smiled then and she smiled now.

The words vanished, but the light never had. Through that code name, she had never been alone. Adam had always been with her, and she'd always believed and always hoped. It wasn't only Adam. She'd also had Dolores, Reginald, and now George, who sat pondering her question. Not one moment had she been alone; she had been surrounded by care and love and sacrifice all along.

George. This young man she'd come to love like a son would pay a price for his care of her and her work now. She suspected the pressure on him was unbearable. He had to plan extractions for too many agents in too little time, filled with the dark wonder of what went wrong and who was still out there, willing to betray them all.

He sighed, his lips trembling in ill-hidden panic. "Nothing has changed. I can't fathom how they got it. Your intelligence is parsed so fine you could bake a cake with the flour. Something went terribly wrong." He leaned forward and seized her hand. Her cup rattled between them. "We have to act now. We have a moment to get you out, but only a moment."

Ingrid stared into her teacup as if it might hold answers. It held only one.

*Kadinova.*

At first it surprised her, but as she sat with it, chewed on it, and digested it, she chided herself for never seeing it before. A light shone through her fear, and it left behind peace and a firm resolve. She knew her hands would not shake again. "No. I won't put you through that. It's never been done. No one has ever gotten a spy out of Moscow."

"We're ready. We have a plan, and just because it hasn't been done doesn't mean it can't be. Another team is devising a way to get their asset out too. We'll at least get the KGB scrambling so much you might both get through."

Ingrid took a deep breath and exhaled slowly. "I won't defect to England while my daughter is in danger here."

"But you'll live. That's what matters."

His comment shook her. Once she had believed that was all that mattered—she'd told Adam as much long ago on that park bench in Vienna. She'd been so angry with her parents for risking their lives, for dying. She'd been so angry with Martin for doing the same. But now . . .

She took a long breath, willing herself to stay strong. For if she chose not to run with George right now, the road ahead was going to be horrific. The KGB would not kill her right away. They would extract all she knew, all she'd shared, and with whom she'd shared it. They would plumb the depths of her memory and degrade her humanity to the point nothing was off-limits because she would no longer appear human. Then, when nothing more could be gained from her, they would kill her. And she would call it mercy.

Ingrid regretted the role George now had to play. He was still so young, and despite how good he was at his job, he was out of his depth now. He was not seasoned in the end game.

She reached over and tapped the top of his hand. "I'll take it from here," she whispered. His jaw dropped, but she said nothing more. She simply got up and walked out of the tea shop.

Ingrid stopped at the first pay phone she reached. Lifting the receiver, she did not detect a double click. But to make sure, she untwisted the cap to check for a listening device. The phone was clean. She ran her fingers across the ledge wall and seam lines of the booth. Nothing.

She then dialed a number she had never forgotten, despite never planning to use it again.

"Weber," he answered on the first ring.

"Adam. It's me. I need you to clarify something . . ."

She listened and learned, as she had for years. Yes, her code name had not been revealed, only the last name: Kadinova. It was an assumption, an anomaly, and a shadow she planned to use for her benefit. She shared with Adam the plan that was forming just ahead of her words. "I need a meeting with a CIA agent, code name SCOUT."

"He's not on the list. All the CIA names have been correlated with surnames. SCOUT isn't on it."

"Then this shouldn't be a problem."

"It's a delay, Ingrid. Just get out."

"It's not. It's vital and I want the meeting set for tomorrow in Vienna. There's a crypt room in Peterskirche. I'll leave meeting instructions there at the base of the statue of the archangel Michael at three o'clock precisely."

"Impossible . . . They're in free fall. I can't make this happen."

Ingrid hesitated. She trusted Adam with her life, but no one knew who had compromised the CIA and who might be listening in Washington, DC, as Adam made his request. The fewer details revealed the better.

"Adam, I wouldn't ask if it wasn't important. Don't mention SCOUT is not on the list. Say nothing about the list at all.

Pretend it's business as usual, except this meeting *must* happen. No matter where in the world he is right now, if SCOUT boards a plane soon, he can arrive in Vienna by our meeting tomorrow."

Ingrid was absolutely certain she knew exactly who and where this SCOUT was, but she couldn't risk telling anyone, even Adam.

"Move your meeting to London. I can protect you here."

"London's not an option. I can get to Vienna if I move fast enough. Though neutral, it's swarming with KGB. They don't check borders as much because they have officers on the ground. My understanding is the KGB hasn't fully assessed what they've got?"

"It's a slow-moving bureaucracy, but with something like this they'll figure it out within hours. Search teams might start early morning. Definitely by midday tomorrow."

"You must make this happen."

"How is this agent worth your life? Ingrid—"

"Adam . . . Please." She silenced him with a whisper.

"I'll get it done. How can I reach you?"

"I'll call back in thirty minutes." Ingrid wondered where and how she could find another clean phone.

"That's hardly enough time." He balked. "No . . . I'll make it work."

"Thank you."

"Ingrid—"

"No." She cut him off again. She had heard the crack in his voice. The same catch she felt in her own throat that threatened to cut off her air and reduce her to sobs. It terrified her more than what lay ahead. "Don't, Adam. I love you, and we both know we set out on these paths over forty years ago. You said it when my parents were killed—this day was always a possibility."

"I suppose it was."

She hung up the phone and headed straight for the train station. Thirty minutes later, she called Adam again. There were no preliminaries this time.

"They refused a meeting. Everyone's compromised and they aren't sure of anything. They haven't even notified their agents yet. That's confidential, but—"

"Everything is confidential, Adam." She gripped the phone receiver so tight her fingers ached. "Tell them SCOUT can plan the details. His terms. One meet. It must be Vienna tomorrow, but he can leave me the time and location at the dead drop in the crypt. Let him control the variables. I demand this. After what I've given them, how dare they—"

"You're right," Adam interrupted. "Consider it done. If this is that important."

"It is and I'm on my way to Vienna now."

"Ingrid, stay there, please. Or head west. Just promise me after this meeting, you'll get out."

"Oh, Adam . . . I fought you all those years ago when you told me some things are worth dying for. Have you changed your mind?"

"No."

"Good. Because you were right. It just took me longer to understand."

# TWENTY-FIVE

# Anya

VIENNA
*June 15, 1985*

IT'S BEEN A CRAZY TWENTY-FOUR HOURS.

A red slash sends me running to Safe House #7. Forget work. Forget life. Just get there. That's what red means.

There, I am told in no uncertain terms to hop a flight for Vienna and beg forgiveness from work later rather than permission to go now. After all, Petrov has required my presence there many times, and it might not get flagged immediately.

"You only need a few hours," Skip advises.

He gives me instructions to leave meeting details at a dead drop in Vienna. LUMEN wants a sit-down. No details. No whys or what fors. I'm simply to obey the summons.

"No."

"I advise you not to say no. This comes from the top. Director Casey and Ames want you there. It's our best chance of getting eyes on LUMEN."

"It could be a trap."

"The CIA wants his identity badly enough to risk it. And don't worry. We'll have you covered if things go sideways." He slides a piece of paper toward me. "I've written down some good meeting locations and times. Pick one and that's what you'll leave at the dead drop. You'll never be out of reach."

"But my cover will be blown."

"Not necessarily. We'll watch for the KGB, and there's no reason to believe they'd be there. You forget LUMEN is on our side. While unusual, no one views this as a threat. They view it as a strategic move across the chessboard."

I study the list. Demel. The Belvedere Palace. St. Michael's Church. The State Opera House. All public and popular. I tap Demel. 4:00 p.m.

Skip picks up the paper and steps to the sink. He lights a match and burns it. "Good choice. You'll drop the details at 3:00 p.m. and meet an hour later. It's good to keep the window tight enough to rattle him."

I leave the safe house at 8:00 a.m. and find the nearest pay phone to call into work sick. I then walk toward my apartment, but I don't enter the building. Instead I make sure to get in the frame of the nearest CCTV camera before I turn and head to the pharmacy a few blocks away. I duck behind the building and spend the next hour winding my way via bus to the airport.

I'm hoping that if I'm questioned later, they won't have even learned about the airport, and I can claim to have simply dropped out of view at the pharmacy by walking a different way home. If I'm lucky, none of this will get sent up the KGB flagpole.

While my papers get stamped at the airport, I don't attract any special attention and my name isn't recorded in the security guard's daily log. It takes only a few well-placed questions to accomplish that last one.

"How late is your shift today?" I add a lilt to my voice. It's just enough to throw the guard off, then make him rush to hide it. He waves me on with a wink.

My mind races the entire three-hour flight. Nothing feels

right. I think about running. But where would I go? I live in the heart of Moscow, where everything and everyone are tracked. I have little money on me and few ration cards.

What does LUMEN possibly want? I stood down. I obeyed. I've only given information from my own lab in the last two months, and only what I can memorize. It's been basically nothing and I burned the last drawings. I'm hardly a spy anymore. I'm hardly a human. I don't see my friends. I don't date. I don't live.

The only thing I settle on is the fact that this man must play chess. Like Skip said, this is a calculated move. And LUMEN must be a master. He's outmaneuvered agencies for years, and now I see he's fully capable of moving players about the board—in and outside of Moscow. I'm his latest pawn.

I make my way to the dead drop and quickly scrawl the Demel details on a scrap of paper. Just as I'm about to tuck it into the seam line between the statue of the archangel Michael and his marble base, I pull back.

I cross out *Demel* and write the Hotel Imperial. Unlike Demel, which has only the front windows and opens dark and deep into a long, narrow space, the hotel's café is airy, open, and fully glass. I'm not going to make trapping me easy. I want light. I want witnesses.

I also change the time from 4:00 p.m. to 5:00 p.m. Skip may have been right about keeping LUMEN off his game, which I suspect isn't possible anyway, but I want to be on mine. I need to be clean too. Very clean. Vienna is full of KGB, and I don't want anyone to spot me and make my life harder at work tomorrow. I also don't want the CIA at our meeting. Skip could easily put me in jeopardy because he wants line-of-sight to the board's king, and I suspect he values me less than he would a pawn. I'm an acceptable loss if he learns LUMEN's identity.

After my best game of Cat and Mouse, I pause outside the

Hotel Imperial. There's too much glass. The café faces right onto the street. What was I thinking? Two agents out in the open? It's unheard of. LUMEN will never agree to this and I have no way to reset the meeting.

As it's too late to change anything, I dart around the corner and cross to the next street. I'm fifteen minutes early, and I'm so tense I feel that if I don't keep moving, I'll never move again. Fear will paralyze me.

I duck into a pastry shop. I scan the tables as I work my way to the back service entrance. It's a happy jumble of tinkling silver on china, languages, and laughter. I want to stay. I want life to be this easy. I'm out the service door within a minute and on the street again. The sharp tang of dark chocolate and pastry dough vanishes with the quick *snap* of the heavy door behind me.

The day is beautiful. Blue. Soft. Warm. The streets are crowded with tourists and families, and it makes me miss my own.

I duck into a dress shop. I circle the mannequins, noting one in a bright yellow dress, then leave out another door. It makes me miss Scott, and I see us tucked in that tiny booth at Martin's Tavern. I wonder where he is and what he's doing and if I was wrong not to answer his letters after our Vienna meeting. If I had one last chance, I'd only need three words. *I love you.*

I stride into another corner store just to change directions again. There is so much to regret.

Striding down an alley, I don an American baseball hat and sunglasses to change my nationality. I turn one last corner and step onto the red-carpeted entrance to the Hotel Imperial.

In the ladies' room, I remove both the hat and the sunglasses and take a long last look in the mirror. I'm saying goodbye. Part of me wants to laugh it off, but my own eyes tell me nothing is funny.

This is goodbye. And it's time.

## TWENTY-SIX

# Ingrid

VIENNA
*June 15, 1985*
*5:00 p.m.*

INGRID STARED AT THE DOORWAY. SHE KNEW SHE SHOULDN'T. IT violated the most basic tenets of tradecraft. Focused attention created electricity. Yet she couldn't pull her gaze away.

With effort Ingrid shifted her attention to her tea, lifting the cup to her lips. Her hand's slight shake sloshed the hot liquid onto her bottom lip. She felt resolved in her purpose, but not in her lies. So many lies. So much betrayal.

The sharp pain focused her. She tucked her lip between her teeth as she set the cup into the saucer once more.

*Stay the course.* The plans had changed, but it could still work. SCOUT had left a note with details to meet at the one place she'd never have picked. The Hotel Imperial. It brought back memories of childhood teas, the Anschluss, Hitler, her family, Adam, and Leo. But she had to concede, it was a good strategic choice. The hotel's café featured glass windows both into the lobby and onto the street. One could see from all angles and people came and went at such a rate as to make anyone stopping and lingering easy to spot.

Yes, SCOUT had chosen well.

SCOUT stepped into the doorway.

Ingrid let her daughter's countenance and code name sweep through her. How could she not have guessed this? How could this reality have eluded her for so long? But yesterday, George's simple comment, *"It's real names. Not code names. Kadinova is third from the top,"* brought the truth to her in a startling flash of clarity. Especially when she considered that book she'd taken from under Anya's mattress five years ago and hidden under her own. She couldn't remember the title, but she remembered the story. She'd read it in secret over and over. How she had loved that young girl, Scout, and her devotion to Boo Radley.

And even if that wasn't enough, Ingrid had only and always used Bauer as her last name, unwilling to take the female derivation of Leo's Kadinov for her own. It was a detail few would remember. Even George and Adam had not caught that discrepancy or its significance—and that led her to hope that, with the right incentive, the KGB might not either.

Anya's brief hesitation in the doorway provided her that heartbeat necessary to sweep the room. Though young, Anya knew what she was doing. Ingrid shook her head. *Young.* She hadn't been much older when she began with MI6, and much younger when she was smuggling information out of the Nazis' economic office for Adam and Martin.

How quickly war matured one—any war. Hot or cold.

Ingrid watched as, in that moment, no longer than the length of a breath, Anya canvassed the room, assessed its occupants, and found her target. Her eyes swept over Ingrid in a cursory fashion before whipping back and settling. Only the minute drop of her lower lip betrayed her shock. Anya stared at her and the connection arced with tension.

Ingrid faltered first and dropped her gaze. She allowed one

deep breath to still her nerves before she faced her daughter again.

After all, she requested this meeting—this one dangerous moment in time—and what she needed to propose would either save Anya's life or get them both killed.

# Anya

It's only a few steps from the ladies' room to the entrance of the café. I cycle through what he might look like: age, weight, coloring, demeanor. Is he KGB like I've long suspected? How else has he stayed safe for over thirty years? Will I be able to tell if it's a trap? My head is spinning so fast it's using more oxygen than I can draw in.

I stand at the doorway and take a beat to scan the room.

*Oh God.* The prayer comes unbidden, foreign to my lips, but only he can save me now. I stop breathing and the world blues in my periphery as everything I've ever believed clicks out of place and drops anew. An ever-turning kaleidoscope stills and my crystalline reality comes into view. A million little pieces weave into a finished tapestry I can only now see.

It takes ten steps and a lifetime to reach her table.

"Mama?"

# Ingrid

The little girl she loved stood before her. The towering woman too.

The question—her name—echoed between them as shame

bloomed within Ingrid. Her cheeks warmed and heat prickled her every extremity.

*How can I make her trust me? Where do I begin?* Ingrid gestured to the chair across from her. Her daughter dropped into it.

"I'm sorry . . . I'm so sorry, my darling. This is all my fault." Ingrid lowered her hands into her lap. They were shaking and she feared drawing attention to them, drawing attention to Anya. That's what people noticed, the incongruences. The older woman crying. The young woman yelling. Anything out of the ordinary in an otherwise dull day.

Anya's eyes widened. "Your English carries no accent. No . . . It's . . . British?"

Ingrid dabbed at her eyes. She hadn't realized she apologized in English. But she was exposed and that was what people did when exposed—they went to their most basic level, their roots.

"Your grandmother was British. She met your grandfather after the Great War on holiday here in Vienna. I grew up here." She dropped her focus to the white linen tablecloth. "It was a strategically good place to meet, but I never would have chosen it. I came here for teas often as a child, then Hitler favored this hotel. He destroyed everything good in Vienna."

"I didn't know."

"How could you?" Ingrid's head shot up. "It's my fault . . . There's so much I couldn't share, but we have no time now."

"You're LUMEN."

It wasn't a question, but Ingrid knew her daughter needed confirmation. She nodded.

"Have you known I'm SCOUT all this time?"

"I learned yesterday." Ingrid leaned forward. "There's been a leak. A list, possibly twenty-five names long, was handed to the

KGB. MI6 thinks it's a CIA breach, but no one is sure. You need to get out."

Anya blinked and exhaled. "And you? Are you leaving? What about Father?"

Ingrid raised her hand. Not to cut her daughter off but to slow her down.

"I will leave later." Ingrid paused, only realizing at that moment who would probably lead the search for them. The head of the Seventh Directorate—Leo, if her guess was right. "That's why Vienna. It's your way out. The KGB is only steps behind us." Ingrid reached across the table and grabbed Anya's hand.

Tears filled her daughter's eyes. "All these years . . . There's so much . . ." Anya swiped at her tears with her free hand, letting the other rest within her mother's grasp.

"Don't think, my darling; just run."

Anya shook her head and Ingrid was reminded of her daughter at four years old, resisting her bedtime. "Why? Why'd you do it? Any of it?"

Ingrid widened her eyes. She wanted to push her daughter to move, to run, but also conceded this might be their last moment. Anya deserved some answers. Bedtime could wait.

"You. I wanted the world to be a better place for you. I needed to make it better . . . During the war my parents worked for British Foreign Services. They were spies. I grew up in the life without ever really understanding that's what was happening. Then when I finally digested where I lived and what it all meant, I missed the freedoms I wanted for you. I reached out to MI6 within a month of your birth . . . And you?"

"The same . . . Hope. After Dmitri . . . You sent me to America."

Ingrid smiled at Anya's huff. It was her daughter's way of saying, "*What did you think would happen?*"

But it was exactly what Ingrid hoped would happen, long ago when she first suggested the idea of a Foreign Studies Initiative for the Washington Summit in 1973. It was what she hoped would happen when, during a party in her own living room, she dropped an oblique suggestion in 1976 to the chairman of the Ministry of Culture that Leo's daughter was a perfect candidate. It was what she hoped would happen when she stole into Anya's bedroom one night a month later and shared with her all the wonderful art she hoped her daughter might someday see.

"I wanted you to understand freedom." Ingrid squeezed Anya's hand. "If it ever comes to us in Moscow, it'll be counterfeit. It won't be true freedom. We'll be tricked into believing freedom lies in full grocery shelves and jeans and all that banging music you and Dmitri listened to. But true choice, sacrificial choice, and the ability to think and determine what to do with those choices, will not come easy to the Soviet psyche. True choice is hard-won. It resides in faith and must be cultivated over time. We don't think along those lines. We've been trained not to."

"All along, I thought you were one of them. Part of the 'Soviet psyche.' I never saw it." Anya swiped again at her eyes with her free hand. "All those ways you formed us. Such original thinkers we were and what a conformist you were . . . Dmitri knew, didn't he?"

Ingrid shook her head.

Anya rubbed at her nose. "Not about LUMEN but about you. He saw you more clearly than I did. He saw into your heart in a way I never did. That's why he always turned to you and trusted you, even more than me sometimes."

"You saw me as your mother."

Anya quit trying to stop the tears. They silently fell down her cheeks, her chin, some splashing onto her blue cotton shirt. "What am I to do now?"

Ingrid reached across the small table and swept away her daughter's tears. She trailed her fingers into Anya's dark hair and tucked a strand behind her ear. "Forgive me?"

One word escaped. The one that started their conversation. A simple "Mama," and Ingrid's heart broke again.

# Anya

I tilt my head into her touch. If I could, I would curl into a ball and let her stroke my hair forever.

I want to go back, start again, and see more clearly. What was real? What was imagined? I can't tell and the world tips sideways with the weight of all that's eluded me. My actions feel slow, like I'm moving through water, as I reach for my tea. My stomach has shut down, and none of the teatime delicacies laid before us look appetizing. But I recognize this is a moment outside time and, once it ends, life will never be the same again—not that I have any true concept of what it's been thus far.

My mother wipes away tears I don't realize are falling. She then sits back and tells me stories.

Stories of a young woman I never met. Stories of someone small, insignificant, and quiet—I laugh at that because she's describing the lie she created, the lie I believed. She gives others all the attributes that she, as LUMEN, possesses: bravery, boldness, purpose, and determination.

She tells of her life in Vienna, an Austrian father who forged papers, and a beautiful British mother who hid her accent and heritage as effectively as she hid Jewish families in their attic, and hosted parties, and listened, and conveyed secrets to the British. She tells me of their horrible deaths. She tells me of men named

Adam and Martin, of a bomb, and how she survived a half-life in a torn city, and how my father brought color to her world again.

"The KGB will interrogate him, Mother. They may kill him."

She sighs, and worlds exist within it. "Oh, Anya . . ." She says my name with such tenderness my tears fall faster. "I couldn't tell your father about my family at first because I was holding the pain too tight. Then when I wanted to tell him, it was too late." Her eyes move to the middle distance and her gaze stretches back years. "The KGB will demand loyalty and payment over an easy death. If I'm right, he's very highly placed within their ranks and he'll be demoted, censured, and possibly fired, but not killed."

My jaw drops and the kaleidoscope turns again. All the times my father scanned the house for bugs. All the times my mother marched me out the door when I railed about encroachments and injustices. All the times she changed the subject at dinner when I veered a little outside Party lines. All the times in our own home, at our own table, her eyes widened in fear.

I can't speak. She senses I am overwhelmed. I see it in her eyes. She shares a few more stories before bringing us back to the present, and I note how the light has changed. Afternoon pinks are darkening to purples.

"I wish we had more time." She lifts a shopping bag from the floor. "I would take you in my arms and beg your forgiveness for all that has happened and somehow make you feel my love."

I bite my lip. I don't know what to think. I'm too over-whelmed to feel angry, betrayed, sad, or even shocked. It's almost like nothing. I feel nothing. Other than the fact that I love her and I do, if it is necessary, forgive her. After all, I made all the same decisions—for lesser reasons—and I executed them more poorly.

"I don't think you need it, Mother, but you have it. I forgive you."

She inhales so sharply through her nose that her nostrils collapse with the effort. I've seen her do that gesture a thousand times, always suspecting she was annoyed with me or with something else, but now I understand. It's a self-defense mechanism. She is drawing back from a line beyond which she can't control her emotions or the variables. The cost of exposure was always too high for her—even in the privacy of our little family of three—to risk true vulnerability.

She checks her watch and taps the table between us. She's all business now. I recognize this pragmatic mother.

"This is for you." She stretches the bag to me. "You must change your clothes. Every article. Even your underwear. The KGB sprays closets regularly with radioactive dust."

At my expression she clucks her tongue. "Not enough to harm anyone, just enough to track them. Your job and relationship to Petrov make you a prime candidate. They could have entered your apartment at any time, especially after you caught their attention in the failed brush pass at the Hotel Metropol."

"You heard about that?"

"I've heard a great deal about the impetuous SCOUT." She quirks a half smile and I'm embarrassed my own mother knows how much I've messed up over the years. I'm humiliated that LUMEN—a living legend—knows how much I've messed up over the years.

I take the clothes.

She continues. "There is little time. A car will pull into the alley exactly five minutes after I walk out the hotel's front door. When we stand to leave, go to the powder room and change. Leave your current clothes in the bag in a stall, along with your handbag. Someone else will collect and dispose of them. Take absolutely nothing with you that is not in that bag. I will head straight through the lobby and out. It will take me thirty seconds and then the five-minute timer starts. There is a side door at the end of the hallway. It is unlocked. Walk through it with only fifteen seconds to spare. You mustn't be seen lingering in the alley."

"You arranged this? With the CIA?"

She lifts a single finger to gain my attention. "Other than one agent, the CIA is cut out of this. Whatever has happened, it's in their backyard and there is no one you can trust. Remember that. I called in a favor from an old, dear friend and your security will be flawless."

"And you?"

She touches my cheek. "'Soon . . . There's still work to do.'"

Her voice takes on a strange, soft quality of remembrance. I reach for her and end up clutching the tablecloth between us. "What work? You're in as much danger as I am."

"Don't fret. I have a plan to keep us both safe." She holds my gaze for a long moment. "Someday you may need to forgive your father too, Anya. He loved us the best he could, and this"—she waves her hand between us—"will be incredibly painful for him."

In a flash I skip past my father's pedantic lectures and remember the significant events of my childhood—his pride as I hit each milestone within the Party's youth organizations; his manic love for marching music, parades, and patriotic festivals; his loyalty; and his fear.

That last is a new revelation. In a flash I see and feel it now—my father has been afraid of something his entire life. Maybe the very ideology he built up and I worked to break down. The ideology my mother never embraced. Nevertheless, I love him. And as complex as their relationship must be, I sense she does too. Maybe love isn't so complicated after all.

I remember I once argued with a few kids at school over Party ideals—they were spouting nonsense. But when I relayed the incident to my mother, she said, *"If you've only seen the color red, how could anyone expect you to recognize blue?"* It took me years to understand she wasn't talking about crayons, and only now do I suspect she was talking about my father as well.

She's about to stand when I ask one last question. "Do you enjoy music?"

It feels like a random question, but it's important. I love music. Always have. I truly believe it captures the best essence of a culture. It helps you grasp massive ideas in a compressed time frame. Music seeps into your soul and molds you. But my mother always hated Soviet marching records and the music that blares from street speakers. Her eyes tighten and her jaw gets so square I think she'd crack a tooth. Until I was a teenager, I thought it was just Party music, but then she hated all Dmitri's heavy Soviet rock too. Now I wonder if it was never the music at all.

Her eyes fill with tears. She doesn't try to stop them. One falls with her small single nod.

My heart shatters. How little I know her. How small I've loved her. I pick up my still-full teacup, amazed at how the world can tip on its axis and yet not a drop has spilled. I'm still sitting upright and only the drop of moisture falling from her cheek to her chin, and the soft hum of nothingness surrounding us, tells me life marches on.

"We must go." My mother stands.

"But?" I set down the cup. It's too fast. Too final.

"No buts." She reaches for my hand again. "No looking back. The people picking you up will take care of you. They'll get you to a plane in Paris. I will take care of you, my beloved." She smiles. "It's my job, my life's mission, and my pleasure."

I turn my hand underneath hers to grip it tight for a heartbeat. I then feel her slight pull within our grasp.

It's time.

With no more words, she smooths her cardigan sweater over

her shoulders, picks up her handbag, and, leaving a kiss on my cheek, makes a silent goodbye. Then, with her back straight and regal, she walks out the café's glass door.

I watch her turn and proceed through the Hotel Imperial's decadent lobby. After The Talks here, I read about this hotel—how Hitler seized it immediately as a sign of power and probably as payback for once having to shovel snow from its front walk. It had been an interesting story for me. It was life for my mother—things she experienced and understood at a far deeper level than I ever will.

She steps through the hotel's outer door and onto the red carpet running to the curb. I glance at my watch. Five minutes. I pick up my napkin from where it has fallen onto the floor and fold it. I open the leather billfold lying on the table as if to confirm we've paid the bill, which Mother did in the middle of our tea. I stand, straighten my skirt, pick up my handbag and the shopping bag, and walk with slow, leisurely steps out the cafe's door.

Rather than turn right and circle back into the lobby, I turn left into the ladies' room. It's empty. I stop at the mirror. How can I look no different than an hour earlier? I wonder what's ahead for me. I wonder what I'll tell Skip. He'll demand LUMEN's identity. They all will. I almost laugh at the irony. The spy I feared only slightly less than the KGB turned out to be not only the one who saves me, again, but my own mother.

I change and fold my clothes into the shopping bag. I leave the toilet stall and check my watch again. Forty-five seconds left. Upon entering I'd noticed the exit sign at the end of the short hallway. I'd also noticed the red alarm panel with wires attached to the door. She said it was unlocked.

With a deep breath I roll my shoulders back and walk out the door. This time I am not alone. A group of ladies stand chatting in the hallway, directly between me and my exit. There's no way I'm getting past them without calling attention to myself.

I count down the seconds as I slowly make my way toward them. With three meters to go, one points down a side hall and her four friends follow her away. My approach is clear and I pick up my pace. I suspect I'm about five seconds late now.

I brace my hands against the door's metal bar to push it open and whisper a quick prayer, "Do not be afraid." I'm instantly back with Dmitri on his last night and with Tracy at Georgetown for every Sunday service she dragged me to, and I feel their faith has now become my own. As the door gives way, I realize my time at church with Tracy is another memory, commonality, and understanding I withheld from Dmitri. So much lost. So much wasted.

I close my eyes. No alarm sounds and I step, eyes still shut, into the alley. Opening them, I watch as a black Mercedes sedan rolls toward me from the alley's north entrance. It stops and the trunk pops open as a man, close to my mom's age, emerges from the driver's seat.

"Quick. When you're safe inside take off your sweater and stockings. You'll be too hot otherwise. There's a water bottle in the corner and another empty one if you need to reliev—"

I hold up my hand to stop him, feeling too vulnerable and too human. "I'll be fine."

He gestures *hurry* with his free hand. The other is holding the lid of the trunk, ready to shut it.

Movement catches my eye—nothing more than a shadow. My mother rounds the corner at the alley's entrance. Our eyes catch and I lift my hand in a small wave of goodbye. She presses her fingers to her lips in a silent kiss.

I climb into the car's trunk, then glance back as the lid closes over me. I need to see her one more time.

She is gone.

# TWENTY-SEVEN

# Ingrid

VIENNA
*June 15, 1985*
*6:05 p.m.*

"Soon . . . There's still work to do."

Ingrid had never forgotten Martin's last words. She had purposely used them in answer to Anya's question about her own plans. They created a link to her parents, to Martin, to Adam, to all those she believed in and to all she was now willing to sacrifice for. They played through her mind as she walked from the hotel toward the University of Vienna. For forty-one years they had plagued her. Every time they entered her dreams, she had resisted. Now she understood and had made them her own.

She took a wide circle, passing by the address where she had lived with Adam and Martin. A new building stood there. It held no memories. She walked on. She walked to her childhood home. It stood unchanged and still had the power to drop her to her knees. She gripped a nearby light post as waves of memories assaulted her. Her mother, father, all those families; the smell of cooking; laughter; love; literature; the night she met Adam; that last afternoon; seeing her parents broken and bleeding, pushed, pulled, and beaten as they were thrown from their home. She could feel Adam's strong hand clamped over her mouth and his other arm locked around her waist, dragging her away.

She closed her eyes and said goodbye to all of it. She then walked toward Universitätsring to catch a cab to the airport. She had only a few minutes before the evening's last flight to Moscow. And she needed a plane—traveling again by train, delaying her arrival further, and getting arrested at the station could ruin everything.

She inhaled long and slow, willing the scent of her daughter, which she'd captured in that last kiss on her cheek, to remain with her—that unique scent each human carried. Anya's permeated her hair, her clothes, her very essence, and was only discernible if you knew and loved her well. Ingrid tried to press the memory of it deep into her being.

"You were right," she whispered to her parents, to Martin, and even to Adam. "You did know what you were doing. And now so do I."

She stopped at a pay phone on the corner of Rathausplatz and Universitätsring. She dialed the British embassy in Moscow. "Please connect me to Ambassador Campbell."

One night, deep into drink, Comrade Bartsov had remarked how they had finally secured a listening device within the British embassy. Ingrid had warned Reginald and they'd worked around it, but they had purposely left the device in the ambassador's office active and always manned. It had come in handy over the years and would do just what she needed it to do now.

"Ambassador Campbell's office. How may I help you?" a young voice asked.

"Please tell him that Inga Kadinova—" She stopped and swallowed. She had to make it so simple, so basic, so obvious, that it didn't fail. "Code name LUMEN, wishes to come in."

"I—" The young woman stalled.

Ingrid hung up, trusting the KGB had heard enough.

# TWENTY-EIGHT

# Anya

EN ROUTE TO PARIS
*June 15, 1985*
*Sometime around 11:00 p.m.*

THE MAN WAS RIGHT.

Even after I remove my sweater and my pantyhose, the trunk is stiflingly hot. He was right about the extra bottle too—I can't hold my bladder. How long is this drive?

At first I thought I would hyperventilate. Fear and panic set my heart and breath racing. I had to keep telling myself for that first dark time—I have no idea if it was one hour or three—to breathe slow and easy, to believe I would be fine, and to trust my mother would be as well.

I thought they would pull me from the car once we left Vienna. After all, Austria is a neutral nation. But the car drives on. We stop for petrol several times, but I don't dare move.

The car grows smelly too. One gets used to smells, I've noticed over the years. I could walk into Dmitri's home and be repulsed by the scent of cabbage or onions for the first five minutes, then forget all about it within ten. This scent is my own, however, and I do not grow used to it. It smells of the lily perfume my father gave me for my twenty-first birthday; it smells of my mother's jasmine perfume that caught in my hair while we talked; it smells of wool, warm pantyhose, sweat, fear, and finally urine. That's what catches me.

In its totality, it's the stench of desperation.

Through all I've done—last year's brush pass fiasco when I came close to getting captured and even when I photographed the nuclear missile—I've never experienced this. And I've certainly never smelled it.

The car drives on and time slips away and I am a child again. With my mama. That's what I called her then, and that's how I think of her now. I remember her chastisements and gentle lectures. I always thought she was the model Soviet woman, dedicated to the Party, the Politburo, the ideals. How little I understood. Her greatest cover was in her compliance, but even that wasn't complete. My mind plays through memories I've never allowed myself to dwell upon. They almost feel like dreams, but they are not. There are cracks in her facade, if only I'd looked hard enough.

I recall she was the one who told Dmitri and me to stop teasing the kids with the bast shoes, telling us it wasn't their fault they wore those ugly bark shoes and that their parents weren't Party members, leaving them excluded from coupons, clubs, and approved school trips.

I also remember the moment Dmitri mentioned at the bar before he died. The one I'd forgotten, or perhaps put away on purpose. She'd sat us both down, trembling with fury or fear—I couldn't tell which—and told us what really happened during the 1956 Hungarian Revolution—Hungarian Uprising as I'd been raised to call it. We'd been so proud, parroting our teacher's propaganda. But Mama told a different, and chilling, story. She told us how the students were murdered, how Soviet troops rolled into their country, how two hundred thousand Hungarians fled. And only now do I remember how she finished that lesson. *"You two need the truth, but we will never speak of this again and you must never repeat it, not to either of your fathers nor to anyone."*

I did ask about it again, though. I remember that too. She put me off, saying, *"I was upset about work yesterday. I was just telling tales. Don't think on it again. I never should have spoken like that."* I remember feeling confused, like reality and fantasy merged. I suspect that was her point.

She was also the one who fought for the Moscow Engineering and Physics Institute and must have been the one who wrangled the invite to the Foreign Studies Initiative program. She was certainly the one who enticed me to accept by suggesting all the art and culture I could absorb. *"A glimpse into a world so few are able to see."* And she was the one who held Dmitri's hand all those years and connected with him, took him to church, and tried to guide him in ways I couldn't see he needed.

I even wonder what would have happened if I'd come to her after Dmitri died. Or if—before or after I dropped that Pepsi can into the car—I'd confided in her, gone for a long walk in the park, and poured out my heart. Would she have steered me back to center as she had so many times before when I was searching? Would she have made something up that placated my fears and frustrations? Or would she have respected that I was an adult and opened up? Would she have let me in?

Soon questions about my mother become eclipsed by facts about LUMEN.

He is highly placed.

He is the greatest intelligence service secret in the history of any organization, with information parsed so fine and so thoroughly scrubbed, no one has ever pinned down the source. He probably drives Philby crazy.

He advised nations on the Cuban Missile Crisis, the Prague Spring, the Summits, the Treaties, Reagan's softening after ABLEARCHER in '83, Thatcher's words and behavior at Andropov's funeral, and the recent and immensely successful Thatcher/Gorbachev meeting.

His instincts are impeccable. His intelligence high-grade. He is a legend, a shadow, a mystery, a spymaster, a demigod.

She is my mother.

# TWENTY-NINE

# Ingrid

MOSCOW
*June 16, 1985*
*Midnight*

THE PLANE TOUCHED DOWN AS INGRID'S WATCH STRUCK MID-night. Tired and worn, she made her way home—in full view of every camera, purposefully stepping into every light.

At the corner closest to her apartment, she stopped to gather her thoughts and her courage. She entered the building and chose to take the stairs rather than the elevator. Though exhausted, she wanted to feel each step, take each by the choice of her own free will, and recognize their cost. She did not want to be whisked to her destination.

She was there soon enough regardless. She unlocked the front door and was not surprised to find the apartment lit and Leo awake. They heard her message to Ambassador Campbell, and—even with bureaucracy and security protocols—the KGB would already be tasked to hunt down all twenty-five names on the list.

Leo sat fully dressed in the living room, swirling a glass of vodka in one hand. A single ice cube clinked the side of the crystal, which meant he was sipping, pondering, assessing. He'd also pulled out his best, the Mamont.

What did surprise her, however, was that he was alone.

Her heart softened at the sight of him. It had been years since what they shared could be called love, yet love it still was, of a sort. She knew his vulnerabilities, his fears, his demons, and his triumphs. She knew he gave his best to both his country and his family. To Leo, there was black and white, right and wrong, and, above all, loyalty to the Soviet State—blind and misguided as it seemed to her. It was the lodestar of his life and she, oddly, had always respected that, even envied his surety in many ways.

Ingrid kept her coat on, her handbag tucked close. She surveyed the room and wondered where they'd placed the bugs, because by now they certainly had, and most likely with Leo's permission.

She was thankful for that. It would make this next step easier. It could be done quickly with a few sentences and her confession would be recorded. What came next, she didn't want to fathom.

"I'm sorry . . . It was—it *is*—me. I betrayed you and Anya, and all you believe. You and she are innocent of this, Leo. I hope someday you can forgive me."

Leo took a long drink. His eyes darted to the chandelier hanging above them. It was fleeting and involuntary, but revealing. *Ah* . . . She thought and stepped forward to position herself directly beneath it.

"Where have you been all night and all day? You've been gone for over thirty hours."

"I needed time to think, to pray. There was no point in running."

"All along . . . it was you." Leo's expression clouded, as if his assessment of the spy could not be reconciled with the reality of his wife. "Was this your plan when we met, Inga?"

"Let's be honest now, Leo. My name is Ingrid. And you pursued me." She took a breath and, with the exhale, felt her facade melt away. Who and what she appeared integrated into a whole. She almost smiled. Almost.

"When Anya was born, you said you wanted to make the world a better place for her. So did I. Our ideas of what that world should be differed. They still do."

Leo nodded, accepting her tipping point. After all, it had been his. Everything he did had been in service to the State for the glory of its future, his *liybimaya*'s future.

"I asked to escort you in for an interview. Alone. Is that acceptable?"

She knew what he was asking. Was she going to go willingly, or did he need to employ force? She appreciated being given the dignity of choice. She had not expected it.

Ingrid crossed the room to pour herself a drink. Her hand hovered between two bottles—their finest vodka and the one bottle of scotch they kept, simply because it was in vogue to do so. No one they knew touched the stuff.

She selected the scotch. *Why play games any longer?* She had never enjoyed vodka. She poured a small glass of scotch, watching as the brown liquid took on the red and gold tones of the room.

She took a sip and turned to him. "I am happy to come with you. Now?"

Leo tossed back the last of his drink and stood. "I think it would be best. I can't imagine you or I will sleep tonight."

She did the same, letting the burn in her throat subside before answering. "No, I suppose we won't."

# THIRTY

# Anya

THE CAR'S ENGINE AND THE HEAT MAKE FOR A SLEEPY TIME. WE stop at another petrol station and I wake. I feel movement at the back of the car, and I suspect the driver is leaning against the trunk while he fills the tank. He is chatting in German.

After a few minutes, we drive on and I sleep again.

The car finally stops and the trunk pops open. I close my eyes, expecting the brightness of the day to hurt them, but it's dark.

"Are you okay?" A woman's voice greets me.

"I am." I push myself up.

A strong arm reaches in to help me out of the car. I try to get my bearings. We stand in a parking lot surrounded by buildings. I assume I'm somewhere in Paris. My legs feel wobbly and weak. I take two steps, crumple, and throw up on the pavement.

Someone gathers up my hair and holds it away from my face. I swipe my arm across my mouth. Everything is dry now that I'm empty. I shift to sit on the cool pavement.

The man holding my hair drops next to me.

"Scott?" I push away and stand, unsure what to feel or think.

"Your mother thought you might need a friendly face."

"My mother?" Tears fill my eyes. "Then you *are* CIA."

"What? . . . Not at all." He shakes his head and chuckles softly. "I'm still a market analyst, but for the State Department now. I switched jobs, but it wasn't something I could put in a letter, could I? I'm not a spy—or is it operative? Not like you . . . I had no idea."

I hear the warmth in his voice as I tip into him. I believe him. Tucked within his embrace, I speak to the woman watching us. "Did she get out? Is she okay?"

Rather than answer me, she hands me a bag of clothes. "We need to keep moving. I'm sorry we had to risk driving you through Germany in the trunk, but we wanted the most direct route. We need to get to Paris and get you out of Europe as soon as possible."

While I could remain in Scott's arms right here forever, that isn't the plan. Not caring that three people are watching me, I slide out of my skirt and pull-on jeans and sneakers. My blouse is stuck to my skin. I replace it with a soft cotton T-shirt. So American.

"Did you suspect Peter? Is that why you changed the Vienna Demel meeting?" the woman asks.

"Peter?" My brain isn't firing.

"He was the KGB's man, Anya. They recruited him as he was promoted back to DC. We caught him right before your meeting. We thought you were lost."

I thought back to how I was "stood down" for all those months and wondered if my impetuous mistake might have saved me—along with LUMEN's caution. "What about Skip? I don't trust him."

"You should. He's the one who caught on to Peter and asked a colleague to set a tail on him. But he'd already passed your Demel location to the KGB. If you hadn't changed it . . . They had

Demel surrounded. Think about that win for Moscow—you and
LUMEN in a single day."

The woman whistles. "Then MI6 here"—she gestures to the
man who met me in the alley—"handpicks me for this and Director
Casey himself flies him in." She points to Scott. "Honestly, this is
the craziest operation ever. But it worked."

"What about LUMEN? Is my mother okay?"

Now the woman looks like *her* brain isn't firing. I get the
impression that she has no clue how "crazy" this operation truly
is, and what's just happened.

She glances to the older man, who answers me. "We first
learned your mother is LUMEN a few hours ago. No one knew.
Not the CIA, not most at MI6. Only three people in the world,
outside Ingrid herself, ever did, I gather. But the KGB had your
last name. And she had a solution."

"What solution?"

"Kadinova was the name on the list. The KGB needed a
Kadinova . . . It was always her plan to offer herself. She gave
them easy bait in hopes they'd stop fishing for you."

"But her last name is Bauer. She's never been called Kadinova."
I scrub my eyes, trying to clear away exhaustion, confusion, and
dehydration.

"It was a risk, yes, but the list came from the West so she
hoped the KGB would simply overlook that incongruence, and it
seems they did. She made a call from Vienna to tell the KGB she
was the Kadinova they wanted."

The horror becomes clear and my knees buckle.

Scott pulls me into his arms. "I'm sorry, Anya."

"They only had me?" I twist to face the woman again. "No
one knew about LUMEN at all?"

She doesn't want to answer me, but her eyes finally meet
mine. "No. She wasn't compromised."

"But Peter will name me. He will tell them they have the wrong Kadinova."

"We've got Peter contained, and we don't think he's *the* leak. He didn't have access to all those agents. Another traitor is still out there, Anya, but our hope is that by getting you out of Europe, you'll be safe. Beyond KGB hands. It's the most we can do right now."

"I don't care about my safety. What about my mother? They'll kill her." I push out of Scott's arms. I step toward the man who stands on the far side of the car. "You have to save her. You have to call somebody, somebody in charge, and tell them she's the wrong Kadinova. Give them me. I'll go. Don't you see? They'll break her, torture her, kill her." The image of Dmitri at the morgue rises before me. I feel his ring circling my finger. "I've seen it . . . You have to get her out."

As I say the words, I realize how vapid and silly they sound. *Give the KGB the bumbling fool and surely they'll release the greatest espionage asset in history.*

With tenderness the man walks to me, takes me by the arm, and leads me to the back seat of the car rather than the trunk. He opens the door, gently places me within the car, and crouches to bring our eyes level.

"Your father walked your mother into the Center at Lubyanka just after midnight Moscow time. He exited twenty minutes later, at which time she was escorted alone downstairs to the prison. We have not learned anything more, and we cannot get her out." He shakes his head, eyes never leaving mine. "No one can, Anya . . . But please remember, this was her choice."

# THIRTY-ONE

# Anya

WASHINGTON, DC
*September 10, 1985*

UPON LANDING IN WASHINGTON, I UNDERWENT DAYS OF
debriefing until the CIA said I should rest. But after a few days
of "rest," I needed back in. The silence within my own brain was
terrifying. I needed to be busy. And as I still had tremendous
insights into the Soviet Union, I was assigned to the Soviet / East
European Division at Langley under the watchful eye of Director
Aldrich Ames.

They still hadn't discovered who leaked the twenty-five
names, so they put a protection detail on me for several weeks.
Every day, I was safe as a new death was reported or an agent
simply vanished from somewhere in the world. It was horrible.

While work filled my days, I spent my evenings quietly with
Scott, mostly watching movies from a Blockbuster Video that
opened down the street. I'm sure I stifled his social life, but he
never said a word. I sensed he understood I wasn't yet ready to
engage with the world. Guilt, remorse, and sorrow draped over
me like a heavy coat.

Shame too. Because I finally understood what my mother
meant all along. When faced with the final reality of danger, after
I photographed the nuclear missile, I resisted it. I asked for a

cyanide pill. Put in far more certain danger, my mother did the opposite. She consented to all that faced her and she turned herself in. It didn't change the external horror of what came next, but it changed her internal landscape. She chose it. She chose it to save me.

One night, thinking about her, I picked up *The Man Who Knew Too Much* on my way home from work. It was one of my favorite movies in college. Scott and I had watched it on his apartment's new Betamax, and I had reveled in the perceived glory and glamour of being a spy. Knowing my mother would love hearing about it, especially as she had devised all those spy games for me and my friends growing up, I had made one of my only calls to my parents the next morning.

Her excitement was intoxicating. She sounded so free and eager, wanting to hear every detail and my every impression. My delight fueled hers. Those tiny fissures into my mother's heart were rare, and in them I glimpsed the secret dreams and desires she hid there.

I thought viewing the movie might draw me back to good memories, but I was wrong. Scott pushed Play and I was in tears within minutes. I never even got to Doris Day's "Que Sera, Sera" song.

I sobbed into his shoulder. "Her cover hadn't been blown . . . It was me."

The tears didn't faze Scott. I'd been blubbering for weeks and was beginning to wonder how he could stand me. I didn't dare ask in case he realized he couldn't.

That night, he pulled me close. "Give her some credit. She was *that* good, after all."

He was right. He is right.

It's taken me months to accept, but the more I learn about her at Langley, the more I understand the legend she truly was.

It is also true some answers are not mine to grasp and are never going to be.

How she did it, for one. There are endless stories of spies falling apart and either drinking themselves to death or committing suicide. No one seems to escape the game unscathed. Even the great Kim Philby was a drunken mess at my parents' home most evenings. But my mother was at peace. Yes, she was a good actor, but I sense there was more to it than that. Dmitri's ketman didn't apply to her because, unlike the rest of them, she was never divided. Like she told me, she gave conscious agreement to her circumstances and thereby transformed them. She was free amid the most extraordinary constraints, all while doing her best to destroy them. She laid down her pride and truly became the shadow she needed to become.

Other answers, I don't have to wonder about.

A few days after the movie failure, Director Ames called me into his office to meet with a visitor from MI6.

Former chief Adam Weber.

At first I was surprised to be left alone with such a high-ranking officer—until he started talking. Within sentences I realized this man knew my mother best, possibly better than anyone in the world. Better than me. Better than my father. He also knew what happened to her. Mr. Weber told me she was transferred and survived in a basement cell of Lefortovo Prison for six days, and according to one of MI6's deep-cover informants, she never cracked.

"Everyone breaks. Everyone talks." I pushed back.

"Not Ingrid. She never revealed a name. She never gave up an operation. She never even complained. It's unheard of, but that's who she was." He smiled, small and intimate, and I got the impression it was for my mother rather than for me. "The only words that left her mouth at the beginning of every 'session' were *duc in altum*."

At my blank stare he explained, "It's Latin for 'push into the deep.'"

I knew what it meant. I just couldn't believe she had said it. It was her code phrase for me when I was young and doing the right thing was going to be hard and it was going to hurt. And it was a message now. It was her way of telling me I can survive and rise above the pain—that "right" has its own rewards, especially when I choose it myself.

Although I wasn't sure I wanted the details, Mr. Weber paid me the respect of giving me the whole story. In the end, he recounted that my mother was killed by a single gunshot to the head at 6:00 a.m. on June 22. My father was not present and, by last report, was under house arrest at a new apartment in the Tverskoy District. But he was still alive and he was still my father. So, with Ames's permission, I started a calling campaign from Langley.

My father picked up his telephone occasionally but, upon hearing my voice, hung up each time.

Last week, he stayed on the line. "You should stop calling me, Anya."

*Anya.* My father, never once in my entire life, has called me by my name. I am no longer Liybimaya, his "little darling." It had to be, but it was still hard to hear. I have truly lost both my parents.

"I need to talk to you. Explain. Say I'm sorry. Something," I pleaded. The line clicked and I knew it was bugged, but I didn't care. There were no secrets to share.

My father sighed. "She made her own choices and so did you. Is that why you left? Were you ashamed, or did she make you go to avoid this?" He paused, then added, "This humiliation?"

My jaw dropped. He still didn't know about me. My mother, of course, hadn't told him. And if the KGB now knew the full truth, they wouldn't tell him because he was disgraced and on the outside. Their paranoia, once again, had turned on one of their own. They didn't trust him.

I leaned back in my office chair, marveling at what my mother had accomplished. She had claimed my last name, my very identity, and everything that came with it.

"She told me to leave. She didn't tell me what she was doing." I told my father the barest of truths. To tell him all of it was unnecessary and beyond cruel.

"She's gone now, Anya. It's over. Will you come home?"

I paused. I couldn't say more. What if the KGB had truly not discovered me? I couldn't put my father in further danger. It wasn't just myself I was protecting. To a degree, I could perhaps still protect him. "I'm sorry. I returned to Washington, DC. I will not come home again."

"I see."

I was sure he didn't, but I couldn't explain. Or maybe he did. My father is not an unintelligent man. Following that call, I stopped crying.

*Duc in altum.*

I "put out into the deep" of this life I created, the life my mother died to ensure for me—I am not going to waste a minute of it.

Well, I haven't stopped crying completely. I cried when Scott asked me to marry him tonight.

# EPILOGUE

# Ingrid O'Neill

WASHINGTON, DC
*June 13, 2023*

I FIDGET OUTSIDE THE DOOR. HER ASSISTANT JUST SAID, "YOU may go in," but I can't step forward. No first-level, first-day field agent gets called into the director's office.

*What have I done wrong? What unwritten rule have I already violated in my first hours, and how I am going to tell the Big Five I failed before I launched?*

Director Weston's assistant waves his hand at the door again. "Go . . . Go . . . She's waiting."

I gulp and turn the knob.

"Please come in, Agent O'Neill."

"Thank you, Director, ma'am, I mean, yes, thank you."

The director gestures to a set of plush leather armchairs in the room's corner. "Director Weston is fine. Please sit. I simply want to say it's good to have you here."

I perch on the chair's edge and wait as the director sits across from me.

She continues. "I knew your mother, Anya, back in the day. I was one of the agents who brought her out of Vienna. It was quite a day. And then when she worked here on the Soviet Desk

355

for Aldrich Ames. To think that traitor was under our noses all that time."

"Ames? My mom knew *the* Aldrich Ames? The Soviet spy?"

Director Weston narrows her eyes. "You sound surprised."

"It's just . . . I've read about him. And you, too, of course. You were a field agent, one of the last behind the Iron Curtain when it fell, and you were in Cuba . . . My mom said she was here at Langley for a couple years, but I never heard about Ames. Didn't she file papers? I figured if you knew anyone it would be my dad, Scott O'Neill. He worked economics and diplomacy at the State Department for over twenty years. But Mom, she—" I clamp my mouth shut. I've just blabbed all over the director.

She tilts her head as if my verbal diarrhea was expected. "My children are the same. I expect no child truly understands her mother outside that vital role. There's a certain myopia. Perhaps it's our survival instinct. How is Anya?"

"She's good. There are six of us kids . . . I'm the youngest by several years. When I started school, Mom got her master's degree. She teaches literature and philosophy now." I draw a breath and press my lips shut again. I seriously blab when I get nervous. It's the main reason my five older siblings, the Big Five, say I'll fail at working for the CIA. *"One simple challenge and you'll crumble like a day-old biscuit."* I can't remember which one said that, but they all agreed.

Not Mom. She stuck up for me. I remember that too.

Director Weston smiles. It's soft and full of memory. I get the impression she knows things about my own family I do not. I expect it's probably true on myriad levels. "You are named after your maternal grandmother?"

"Yes." I feel my spine lengthen, and more nervous now, I start twisting the heavy gold ring my mom gave me when I passed my final requirements last week. She said it was her childhood friend Dmitri's ring, a hero's ring, and that it would serve me well. That's how she phrased it.

"How did you know?" I ask.

Director Weston sinks back into the leather armchair. "I met your grandmother several times in Moscow. She accompanied your grandfather to embassy events. Of course, I didn't understand who she was until much later . . . Thinking back, it was like being near light, or a legend. The two are similar in many respects, I suppose."

"My grandfather, Leonid Igorevich Kadinov, lived with us for some time before he died, but he never talked about her. I suppose Mom didn't, too, out of respect for him."

"Your grandfather moved here? To the States? I'm not sure I knew that." Director Weston's voice arcs with curiosity.

"After the Soviet Union dissolved, Mom worked hard to get him out. That was about the time she quit working here. I guess she thought my former KGB officer *dedushka* wouldn't approve." I use the Russian name for "grandfather," trying to add a lightness to the story. I've always felt a little strange my grandfather was once part of the KGB. After all, I've heard the stories.

"I didn't realize . . . I was in Hungary at that time. That must have been wonderful for her."

"It was, I think. She doted on him and took really good care of him. Both my parents did. He didn't speak English, so it was a crash course in Russian for my older siblings. But Russian was, perhaps, my first language. He'd been living with us for several years before I was born."

Director Weston smiles again, but it's not warm this time. It's thoughtful. "And you fell in love with the culture? I heard you asked to work on the Russia Desk."

"No. I mean, yes, I requested the assignment, but I didn't fall in love. He shared the bad too. In fact, that's what he wanted to talk about the most. He and Mom spent hours talking. Oftentimes, she wouldn't let any of us even listen. She said he needed to get it all out, all the things he was never allowed to speak or even think over there. The propaganda. The brainwashing. Some of his stories I was allowed to hear were pretty horrible. And after what Putin did? . . . I speak Russian fluently and I think I can be most useful in that division."

"I see." Director Weston raises a brow and I wonder what she's thinking. She doesn't tell me. She simply adds, "I wanted to personally welcome you."

"Yes, ma'am." I stand and turn toward the door, certain I'm being dismissed.

"O'Neill?"

I twist back and watch as she straightens in her chair. Even sitting, she is formidable, and I feel my anxiety rise.

"I have an assignment for you. You need to understand your family better. Please ask your mother to tell you about the Kadinovas, code names LUMEN and SCOUT. They were a remarkable mother-daughter pair of agents, though they never knew it while operational. One worked for MI6 for over thirty years, right in the heart of Moscow, at the highest levels of security, and is still considered the greatest intelligence asset in the history of any service. The younger, the daughter, specialized in military intelligence at a highly classified laboratory in Moscow from 1982 to 1985. They are a legendary pair and there will never be anyone like them again."

My eyes feel like saucers, and I can't think of anything to say. Though I've never been told, her statement illuminates all the shadows dancing around my mom, and her mom. My brain turns fuzzy as stories and details click like puzzle pieces into place faster than I can process.

"And remind Anya that her files and your grandmother's

have been declassified. They can be accessed by anyone at any time. Even by her daughter."

Director Weston stands. Now she's genuinely smiling again, probably at my gaping jaw. "Furthermore, tell her that her story and her mother's story are too important to forget. Can you do all that?"

The air takes on a strange, heavy thrum around me. "Yes. I can," I hear myself reply. "I'll talk to her."

"Good." The director laughs. "I think you'll find it very enlightening. And please give her my best."

I turn to leave.

"Oh . . . Agent O'Neill?"

I turn back again, still speechless.

"Welcome to the CIA."

# *Author's Note*

WHILE CREATING *A SHADOW IN MOSCOW*, I TURNED MY ATTEN-
tion from *The London House*'s courageous and resourceful
women spies within Britain's SOE during World War II, to women
working within the Cold War era. I was, again, astonished by
the conviction, determination, and dedication displayed while, at
the same time, shocked by how often these women were under-
estimated and mischaracterized by the male-dominated world
around them.

Early in my research I found this quote from the early 1940s:

> When interviewed by American officials,
> one European intelligence officer said:
> "An agent should be calm, unostentatious
> and reticent. Women are emotional, vain,
> loquacious. They fall in love easily and
> without discrimination. They are impatient
> with the strict requirements of secu-
> rity measures. They withstand hardships
> poorly."[1]

---

1. A. J. Baime, "The History of Female Spies in the CIA," History.com, last modified
   August 31, 2018, https://www.history.com/news/cia-women-spy-leaders.

This outlandish statement provided a little inspiration for Ingrid Bauer. While she does not become the "loquacious," flighty woman assumed here, she does adopt the persona everyone expects—quiet, subdued, obedient, and a consummate hostess. It is within these shadows and misconceptions that she operates and quickly becomes MI6's most prized intelligence asset.

That said, much more than a single quote formed Ingrid and Anya. Real spies and their real stories provide much of my starting material—Stephanie Rader, Jeanne Vertefeuille, Angeline Nanni, Oleg Gordievsky, Adolf Tolkachev, Pyotr Popov, and Oleg Penkovsky to name a few.

In fact, the code name PIMLICO, mentioned in the story, was not a code name at all but the operational name for MI6's extraction of Oleg Gordievsky from Moscow after, it is thought, Aldrich Ames gave his name to the KGB. MI6 drove Gordievsky, whose code names included NOCTON and SUNBEAM, from Moscow through Leningrad north into Finland. It was an extraordinary feat, involving a checkpoint, a guard dog, and the inventive deployment of a dirty diaper. All this and more is relayed brilliantly in Ben MacIntyre's *The Spy and the Traitor*. Furthermore, Anya's approach to the CIA with the Pepsi can honors Adolf Tolkachev's use of a similar can to convey his interest to the CIA, as described in David Hoffman's *The Billion Dollar Spy*.

As you can imagine, I had tremendous fun writing this story. Anya and Ingrid came to life quickly for me, as did their voices, struggles, strictures, and world, and—in many ways—they took me on this adventure.

While I like to write stories set where I've lived, as I think that is the only way one truly understands a culture, I have broken that rule here. I was able to visit the Soviet Union in 1985, the year this novel ends, but I have never lived there. That's one reason Ingrid is born outside its borders and why Anya spends a good deal of time in America. That said, my memories and notes from that visit played a vital role to create both tone and texture within this story. But, of course, the details come from research. So much research! I have listed a few of my favorite books on my website under the Book Clubs tab. It's not a comprehensive list but a good, solid one I hope you will enjoy.

There's one more thing I want to say about research—when it's involved, there will always be mistakes. And those mistakes are all mine. Some inconsistencies are not mistakes, however, but a bit of fictional license. While I do like populating my stories with real people and real events, this is first and foremost a work of fiction.

For instance, while Yuri Andropov was the first KGB chairman to lead the USSR, no one named Nikolai Ivanovich Petrov ever served as the minister of defense. I needed Petrov to play a larger role in the story, and I wanted to move him and Anya between Moscow and Vienna. I did not feel comfortable taking such liberties with the real minister of defense and marshal of the Soviet Union, Dmitry Ustinov, so I didn't include him within the narrative.

I also took a few liberties with my maps in both Vienna and Moscow so that Ingrid's childhood home could be within the American quarter post–World War II and she could visit a park within walking distance anytime she needed one.

I also had fun with food—fun most Soviets did not have with food during the 1980s. It was a time of scarcity and economic stagnation. Yet Anya ate fairly well, as the elite were able to do. Most of my dishes came from a wonderful cookbook written by Darra Goldstein, *Beyond the North Wind: Russia in Recipes and Lore*. She does a fabulous job of providing not only recipes but the stories and significance behind the dishes. I learned a lot from her about the Soviet culture, especially outside the cities, where life was much more challenging.

Other things to note: Operations RYAN and ABLEARCHER '83 are both real, as are so many of the events recounted in this story. The horrors that occurred in Poland's Katyn Forest are also true. Twenty-two thousand Polish military officers and civilian men were massacred in April and May 1940, and the Soviet Union denied responsibility until 1990. Additionally, while we think of Kim Philby as being a member of the famed "Cambridge Five," he was actually part of the "Cambridge Four" until 1990 when John Cairncross was added to the roster and we changed the group's moniker. Philby did defect to Moscow, train KGB spies, and drink a lot. He died in Moscow in 1988 and was given a hero's funeral and more Soviet medals than I want to list here.

And, finally, yes, Aldrich Ames is real and, starting in 1985, began to systematically betray the US for lots and lots of money until he was arrested in 1994. Peter Crenshaw, within this story, does take on a bit of the role Edward Lee Howard played in the real Ames drama. Howard, too, was selling secrets to the Soviets, but he could not have known all the names Ames gave the KGB, as Ames had far greater access, serving as the CIA's chief of Soviet counterintelligence. So while Howard was a traitor and was captured, he was not *the* traitor the CIA frantically sought— and continued to seek until 1994 when a CIA team led by Jeanne Vertefeuille followed the money and arrested "their man."

While the number of names on that fateful "first" list varies and the amount of money Ames received from the KGB also varies, the result of his treachery does not. He was responsible for the imprisonment and deaths of three dozen agents in the Soviet Union and for betraying hundreds more working for the US throughout the world. The death toll is staggering.

There is so much more to share of the rich history and brave men and women of the first and second Cold War eras, and I do hope you'll enjoy learning more. I'll continue to add thoughts to my website at katherinereay.com and, again, that's where you'll find a list of books. I truly do recommend each and every one of them, as I also recommend studying history. Only in truly understanding our pasts will we be able to navigate—with empathy, humanity, and wisdom—our presents well.

All the best to you,

*Katherine*

# Acknowledgments

As always, I didn't travel this road alone . . .

Thank you to Claudia, my agent and friend. Thanks to my publishing family at Harper Muse—Amanda, Becky, Julee, Jodi, Kerri, Margaret, Nekasha, Halie, Mallory, Jere, Patrick, Savannah, Colleen, and the entire sales team—for your dedication to this story! Thank you to Kathie for answering my query and for believing in me. A special thanks also goes to E Katernia Reznichenko for being generous with her time and memories of growing up in Moscow during the 1980s.

I also need to thank family and friends. Elizabeth—my first and best reader—your navigation is vital! Kristy and Sarah—you two are lifelines! Rachel and Marie—you are both inspirations and safe havens. Team Reay—always my anchor! And thank you to all my writer friends who support one another and lift up one another every day. I can't imagine this writing life without you.

Thanks to all the bookstores and libraries that have generously opened their doors to me. I have so much fun sharing my love of books with you! And thank you, dear readers, for trusting me with your time and your hearts once more! I hope we meet within the pages of a book again soon.

Happy reading!

Katherine

# Discussion Questions

1. Anya says in the intro that the "best stories are love stories." Do you agree, and how would you define a "love story"?

2. Do you think the secrets Ingrid's parents kept from her were justifiable?

3. How dangerous was it for Anya to admit to Scott or to herself that "there's a lot to love about America"?

4. What do you think of Anya's assessment, based on Thomas More's philosophy, that we have an "end point," a point past which our consciences won't allow us to venture?

5. What do you think of Anya's surprise at how easily she feels Americans share their thoughts? She comments how rare transparency is at home, even stating about her close friends, "I trust them with my life and, more importantly, with my true thoughts."

6. Dmitri states, "Do you think if I got that assignment and learned about rocks, earthquakes, and tsunamis, all this would feel okay? On some level I could study a thing and know what it was." Do you feel it is hard or easy to discern what something is? Does Dmitri's question make sense?

7. What do you think Anya meant when she said, "The *why* matters most—maybe both in living and in spying." Do you agree?

8. Hope is alluded to throughout the novel. What does *hope* mean, and why is or isn't it important?

9. Ingrid tries to share with her daughter an idea of freedom within strictures, even using her own mother's phrase, *duc in altum* ("into the deep"), to impress upon Anya the freedom in being able to choose even while living within constraints. Why was this so important to Ingrid to convey? Is it relevant for people today?

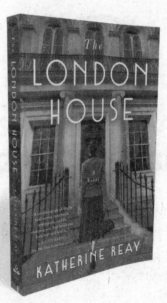

# *About the Author*

Corinne Stagen Photography

KATHERINE REAY IS A NATIONAL BESTSELLING and award-winning author who has enjoyed a lifelong affair with books. She publishes both fiction and nonfiction, holds a BA and MS from Northwestern University, and currently lives outside Chicago, Illinois, with her husband.

KatherineReay.com
Instagram: @katherinereay
Facebook: @katherinereaybooks
Twitter: @Katherine_Reay